Perion's jaw dropped. The ship—wooden, twin-masted, driving on under the push of the wind—was a ship such as Perion had never seen on Earth. There was a figure at the rail, looking at him intently. He waved and got a wave in return. He sank back into the pod and switched off the thrusters. Saved! But beneath him something large and gray rose in the transparent water. And suddenly the sea-beast crossed him at right angles, underneath, and lashed him across the chest. A sharp thorn, jagged and bony, protruded through the fabric over his ribs. He tried to pluck it out, felt his fingers burning, then saw a thin, steady thread of blood.

The sun danced above the horizon as someone leaped into the water beside him to tow him back to ship. Murmuring something even he could not have interpreted, Perion reached out to his rescuer, but his hand and mind fell away before he could touch her. . . .

TO STAND
BENEATH THE SUN

TO STAND BENEATH THE SUN

Brad Strickland

A SIGNET BOOK

NEW AMERICAN LIBRARY

NAL BOOKS ARE AVAILABLE AT QUANTITY DISCOUNTS
WHEN USED TO PROMOTE PRODUCTS OR SERVICES.
FOR INFORMATION PLEASE WRITE TO PREMIUM MARKETING DIVISION,
NEW AMERICAN LIBRARY, 1633 BROADWAY,
NEW YORK, NEW YORK 10019.

SIGNET TRADEMARK REG. U.S. PAT. OFF. AND FOREIGN COUNTRIES
REGISTERED TRADEMARK—MARCA REGISTRADA
HECHO EN CHICAGO, U.S.A.

SIGNET, SIGNET CLASSIC, MENTOR, PLUME, MERIDIAN and NAL BOOKS
are published by New American Library,
1633 Broadway, New York, New York 10019

First Printing, April, 1986

1   2   3   4   5   6   7   8   9

PRINTED IN THE UNITED STATES OF AMERICA

This book is dedicated with love
to Barbara,
who made the writing of it possible,
and to Amy and Jonathan,
who made it necessary.

Chapter 1

From troubled dreams of falling, Tomas Perion tumbled into nightmare. He reached convulsively for something solid, found only the armrests of his stasis pod couch, and cried out in fear.

Above his stifled shout Perion heard the quick hiss of attitude jets, and the capsule stabilized. The instruments chattered at, or across, him. The brilliant light of a nearby star flashed momentarily through the viewport; then all once more was dark.

Dry. His mouth was dry, his tongue thick and swollen, feeling like an unsanded chunk of wood. Ignoring the yatter of the instruments, Perion moved, unshackled his arms from the restraining rests, unplugged the life-support feeds from the valves set in the soft flesh inside his elbows, and raised himself to take his first real look outside, at space, a dazzling sun, a new world.

It was all wrong.

A curving horizon already nearly filled the viewport. The planet's bulk was stippled with white cloud, spread with ocher land, smeared with green growth, and swirled with deep blue, nearly black, sea. But Perion, along with every other colonist aboard the *Galileo*, knew intimately the contours of New Terra, the target planet, had studied its every fold and bulge with the same attention a desperately ill man gives his symptoms. This was not the target. It was some other world.

A twittering noise from the data readout insisted on his attention. The screen urgently twinkled a status report, ending with "POD 22,871 IMPACT ESTIMATE . . ." and a stream of meaningless numbers.

The capsule bucked. The atmosphere accepted it, but like a playful cat, cuffed the craft. A dull orange glow, streaked bright yellow here and there, filled the port. Perion's datascreen dissolved into static patterns as the air outside ionized, cutting him off from direct contact with the ship.

The ship. Something there had gone badly wrong; otherwise, Perion would not be riding his stasis capsule to the surface, bobsledding over the invisible and immaterial slopes of air. Jettisoning was an emergency procedure. He was falling from space, falling onto the wrong world. He would land wherever chance and trajectory took him.

When the datascreen regained coherence, the world outside had vanished in an enveloping mist as the capsule, more stable now in its descent, plummeted through thick layers of cloud. Perion keyed the capsule systems for ship-to-ship communication. The screen gave him the curt notice "GALILEO O/O/R."

Out of range. And even that was bad: the ship should have been in a high polar orbit, not one so low as to carry it beyond standard communicator range this quickly.

A slewing shock blurred Perion's vision. The chutes had deployed. The gray nothing outside the viewport thinned and brightened to pearl, then slipped away like a thin veil. Perion, hanging almost vertical in his restraints, looked out the port and saw only sky, the ragged underside of a canopy of cloud, broken here and there by deep blue, almost violet, rifts.

He could do something about the view. He used a manual control to rotate the capsule, and a horizon, flat by this time, slanted into his field of vision. But it was a dark blue and featureless horizon.

"Damn." The word scratched itself out over his dehydrated tongue. He was falling into an ocean. He keyed in a homing signal and an automatic distress call. If any of the others were already down, if someone had brought down a lander, perhaps he would be picked up as soon as he arrived. If not—well, the capsule would float indefinitely. He had rations for a month, six weeks at a pinch. Surely in that amount of time . . .

Frowning, Perion bent closer to the port, shading his eyes. He was at about ten thousand meters, and the sea below looked frozen, its undulant surface arrested by distance. But there, not halfway to the horizon, a thin white arrowhead was etched on the impermanent face of the water. It pointed his way. The wake of a ship?

Perion added other signals, *I-am-here* cries pleading for notice. He dropped a red flare and ignited a slow-burning smoke marker. He was rewarded by a drift of bright orange fume past the port. Then he turned back to his instruments, only to find the communicator dead except for the crackling voice of the strange sun.

The ocean neared. Perion reached for a portable dataset, waiting beside his left elbow, and activated it, accumulating in its memory whatever the capsule systems had picked up about the ship and the planet.

Touchdown was a slow backward fall. A muted explosion told him that the chute rigs had been jettisoned. The capsule bobbed, then righted itself. Perion was almost standing now, and the port showed alternate glimpses of a horizon roughly one meter away and the upper centimeters of an effervescent sea, clear green water dancing with bubbles and wriggling with little somethings, flat translucent segmented ribbons as long as Perion's little finger, dark eyespots at the leading end.

Perion checked the radio again. Nothing except the sun's muttering complaint. He activated another smoke marker and fished a ration case from its cache behind his knees. He took a long, long drink of water. Only then, almost idly, did he check the life-support-system readout.

What he found made him check it twice more. The system had been exhausted of all nutrient for more than two days, subjective. Under the glacial creep of stasis temporality, that translated to—he used the databoard as a calculator—four hundred and ninety-one years.

Perion drew a deep and unsteady breath. The target planet, the new settlement, was distant from Earth, but even at *Galileo*'s sublight speed, the one-way colonization flight would have taken little more than seven hundred years. And if the nutrients had been completely exhausted, including the generous emergency reserve . . .

Perion calculated again.

The *Galileo* had been en route to—this, here, wherever—for something like five thousand years.

A buzzer warned that the last of the smoke was belching from the flare. Perion reached to set off another, and the capsule rocked gently at the motion. He checked the environmental readout.

To his astonishment, things looked all right. The ocean

was, well, ocean—good old H_2O with various minerals in solution, salt predominating. The air was tolerable, with less oxygen than Earth's, but at a slightly higher pressure. Bacterial life forms, no way of telling if benign or harmful. A water temperature of thirty-six, an air temperature of thirty-eight—tropical, but bearable.

"I might even live," Perion said aloud.

If the ship came in time. Had its crew seen his signals? He couldn't be sure, and with the viewport practically underwater, he had no way of visually locating the vessel.

Perion checked to make sure the antenna was fully extended and began a monotonous round of signaling, up and down the wavelengths. The communicator whispered back to him in papery isolation for what seemed hours. He set off more flares at intervals, wondering just how far away the ship had been and how fast it could get to him; but he had no way of knowing, of course. It might even have been one of the little ten-person exploration craft instead of a large vessel, in which case it might be very slow indeed.

Idly Perion opened the ration kit again, drank more water, munched a tasteless wafer. It occurred to him that one way Earth Deep Space Administration made death on an uncharted planet less threatening was to furnish such food. Better a quick death than slow starvation on EDSA rations!

He washed down the wafer with another gulp of water, then lay deep in thought. What had happened? The ship was automated for the centuries-long journey, loaded with backup systems and all the touches a sophisticated Terran technology could supply. What, then, had happened to the ship out there, in the space between the stars?

At length the communicator called him back to attention. "GALILEO I/R," it told him now. He keyed in a question, asking the one intelligence that might be able to answer it, the ship's onboard computer.

But this, too, failed. As soon as he transmitted the query, the screen displayed, "E/M INTERFERENCE. REENTER DATA."

He was midway through his sixth try when the screen told him the ship was once more out of range. Perion grunted. The ship was in low orbit, much too low.

He was low himself, on the ocean's surface. If the capsule

in for recreation and balance, a collection the size of a small municipal library back on Earth. The portable dataset. A hand-held communicator. Rations? No. His rescuers would bring food. Cheerfully, he chucked the open package of wafers through the open hatch. Weapons? The pod offered none, really, but there was a combination cutting tool—

Lurch!

The pod tipped crazily, and for a split second Perion could see the approaching ship. Water splashed in, stinging his eyes, but the pod bobbed back to the vertical. From outside came a thrashing and a spray of water. Something large had collided with the pod.

And did it again! This time the sea washed cleanly into the hatch, and the pod was sinking. Perion drew a deep breath, just as the training manuals advised, and waited until the pod was full of water. Then, not fighting the incoming rush, he easily slipped through the hatch and rose to the surface. His suit was buoyant enough to hold his head above water.

It tastes like seawater, he thought. He coughed and spat, his vision sharply cut by the chopping waves around him. Where the hell was the ship?

Something chunked him hard under the chin, bringing a white explosion of light. He splashed back, startled, then saw it was an aluminum case, one of the ration kits. Others floated to the surface, along with smaller debris. Beneath him something large and gray rose in the transparent water.

Perion gasped sharply, coughing on a few stray drops of ocean. Whatever it was looked alive and immense. He backstroked frantically. Something torpedo-shaped, mottled gray and green, broke the surface five meters from him. It looked more whalelike than sharklike; then it dived and looked more eellike than whalelike. It rose again—yes, it puffed vapor through a blowhole—and opened its mouth. It seemed to be *all* mouth, and the mouth, three-lobed and gaping, seemed all teeth. The mouth closed like the fingers of a hand on one floating aluminum case (*ping*, it said forlornly), and the creature sounded.

Perion trod water and opened the knife blade of the multitool. The blade was only twenty centimeters long, and the eel thing seemed to be in the neighborhood of fifteen meters, but still— Where was it? Perion worked himself in a circle and caught sight of the ship, quite near now. A figure in brown peered over the bows, searching the water. "Here!" Perion screamed, choking on brine.

Something roughly nudged his legs. Reflexively he pulled them in, plunging his head under the water. Passing him was the creature, huge pectoral fins flapping like sea wings, bulging eyes regarding him coldly, tapering tail whipping. Perion scrambled back to the surface.

The figure aboard the ship yelled something he could not catch in a high, piping voice. He needed no encouragement; he swam for the ship. The sea beast crossed him at right angles, underneath, and suddenly lashed its tail, striking him hard across the chest, a walloping blow out of all proportion to the tiny end of the tail.

Fighting to keep his head up and his grip on the knife tight, Perion felt his side with his left hand. Something jagged and bony protruded through the fabric over his ribs. He tried to pluck it out, felt his fingers burning, saw a thready flow of blood. But he worked the thing loose, and it spun away, a thornlike spur half as long as his thumb.

The sun danced above the horizon, split into three, a green one, an orange one, and a white one. Perion held his hand up. He had gashed thumb and forefinger deeply. Behind him came a snuffling sound. Ahead loomed the wall of the ship.

And leaning over the rail, pointing a weapon at his face, was the figure in brown, human, long dark hair bleached at the edges by the sun. "No!" Perion gasped as the weapon sang. He ducked and something whizzed over his head.

A huge body thrust him harshly aside, and he caught a glimpse of the eel thing, three-lobed jaws agape, charging past him, biting at the ship itself. Again the figure on the boat loosed a bolt, and this one struck the creature just behind its bulging eyes. It writhed, striking the ship with its tail, and rolled to its back.

Perion's arm had become dreadfully heavy, a weight trying to drag his whole body under. And his vision seemed impaired: he looked down a long, ill-defined tunnel, darkness surrounding a blurry circle of light that jolted smaller with each pulsebeat. He splashed ineffectually, managing only to spin himself around. Now he faced away from the ship.

A splash sent water over his head. He brandished the knife in his right hand, trying to turn. Something grappled with him from behind. He lacked the strength to strike—

But the body pressing against his back was clearly mammalian. And he felt strong legs scissoring against his. Someone had leaped into the sea to help him, was trying to tow him back to the ship. But there, rising from the sea, only an arm's length from his trailing feet, was the triple-jawed horror. It snuffled past on his right, and with more will than he thought he possessed Perion slashed at the near lobe of the open mouth, sank the blade in the flesh of the jaw, felt a gash scoring, felt the thing sheer away. "Ha!" grunted his rescuer behind him.

He blacked out. Came to himself as a rope under his arms hoisted him free of the ocean. Saw, as at the bottom of a deep, deep well, the eel thing writhing at the surface, framed between his dangling, dripping feet.

Then he was on his back, staring up. Such a tiny blue circle of sky, so far away: proportions distorted as through a fisheye lens, a towering mast, a ribbed sail squashed to ludicrous dimensions, vague moving figures stooping over him, pulling away his garments, water dripping in his face. He closed his eyes.

At the sound of a soft voice he opened them again. The only thing he could see was a distant object like an inverted cathedral dome, brown and pink and dripping bombs of water from its absurdly small spire. Murmuring something even he could not have interpreted, Perion reached for the female breast, but his hand and mind fell away before he could touch it, and he slipped into the oblivion of complete unconsciousness.

Chapter 2

Perion floated, sometimes asleep, sometimes in a state bordering wakefulness. He opened his eyes to darkness, then to blurred day; closed them a moment and opened them again in the dark. He had visions: a doe-eyed, dark-skinned girl of sixteen metamorphosed into a crone of sixty. He heard the constant creak of wood and rope, the hiss of water, occasionally the kettledrums of distant thunder. And all the time he floated.

When he washed across the final barrier and came to full consciousness, it was with disconcerting suddenness. The girl was there, real, with a cool hand at the back of his neck, urging him to sit up. In the red light of a hanging oil lamp he saw that he lay in a sort of bunk with side rails of wood. The girl pressed a beaker against his lips. Perion opened his mouth, and something astringent and biting flowed in, bitter and harsh. He swallowed.

Then he was awake again, with no memory of having dozed; but he was alone, with just the aftertaste of the liquid to tell him that it had ever existed at all. Perion raised his head. It was dark now, but there, away to the left, a hairline of light outlined the door. It was not far.

He rolled to his left side, found it tingling and sluggish. A rough blanket of some kind covered him. He pushed it away, found that he was naked underneath, except for a coarse bandage around his chest. He lifted his legs over the side-board of the bunk and slipped to the deck. His leg crumpled beneath him.

He crept on hands and knees toward the door, cursing once as a long splinter pierced the soft pad at the base of his right thumb. He held hand to mouth, found the butt of the splinter with his teeth, and pulled it out, tasting the rusted iron of blood.

After a moment which might have been an hour he crawled again, reached the door. It was shut fast, bolted from the outside by the feel of it.

The ship rolled and pitched. Perion edged back, found a wooden chest against a bulkhead, then found the bunk again. He dragged himself back into it as the ship plunged down an endless wave. Nausea rammed a finger down his throat, and dizziness spun his head. He gagged and heaved until he lay exhausted, panting.

It was day—light streamed through a square port at the foot of his bunk—and the old woman chanted beside him. She seemed ancient as an idol, almost toothless, her face a relief map of hard years, her hair and brows gray going white. She rocked rhythmically as she chanted, kneeling beside his bunk.

"Who are you?" Perion asked.

The old woman froze in midchant. Her obsidian irises glittered terribly bright in the pale daylight of the cabin. She leaned closer, looming in his vision. "Wassayu?" she barked. "Yuspik haispik?"

Perion shook his head. "What? What did you say?"

The woman grunted, straightened her back, and in a throaty singsong asked, "Do you speak the High Speech?"

"High Speech? Angloss, lady, like you. What—where are you going?"

The old woman had pushed away, had tottered to her feet; she backed toward the door.

"Wait!" Clutching the rough white blanket, Perion rolled to his side, got his feet on the deck, managed to stand. "I want to talk to—"

Quicker than seemed possible, the old woman skipped back to the door. Perion lunged after her, got one hand on her arm while the other perilously protected his modesty. "Now, wait, lady. I—"

She did something intricate and tricky with her arms and legs, and Perion found himself flat on his back, the deck hard under him. She spun, opening the door. He grabbed a bony ankle and jerked. She whirled, extricated herself from his grasp, and kicked him over his wounded ribs.

"Damn!" Perion grunted. He rolled, got his back against the door, and slammed it to. She waited warily, shifting her weight from foot to foot. The blanket was a tangle around his hips and legs. Sitting there, Perion said, "Please. I don't want to fight."

The trouble was that she did. He caught the hard edge of her foot on his shoulder; it had been aimed at his chin. He threw up his hands, palms out. "Wait, wait," he puffed. "If you can understand what I'm saying—"

"Blasphemer," she said coldly. "Unbeliever from the Under Islands."

"No. Really, no. I'm Tom Perion, from—"

"Infidel!"

"Please. I know who I am. I'm not from the Under Islands, wherever they are, and I'm not an unbeliever."

The woman's brows contracted. The wrinkles in her face looked like a tree in winter, branches spread across her forehead, trunk descending on either side of her nose, roots lost in the folds of chin and throat. Her gray eyes were hooded, alert. "What are the three orders of belief?" she chanted.

Perion got wearily to his feet, leaning on the door against the roll of the ship. He clutched the blanket against him. "Listen," he said carefully. "I am a stranger here. I expected human life, but not you, not—not this. I don't know your religion, but—"

"Your sex," the woman barked.

"Male," Perion said automatically.

"No—show it."

"*Show?*"

The old woman crouched again and raised her hands.

"Jesus, lady!"

"Show—now!"

"Show." Perion took a deep breath. "All right. Take a peek." He dropped the blanket and stood bare.

The old woman gasped, a sharp, whistling sound. Then she closed her eyes as though mortally insulted.

"Now, wait," Perion said, fumbling the blanket up again. "You told me to do it."

The old woman opened her eyes and inclined her head in a formal bow. "You do not bear the mark of the Under Islands," she said. "Your pardon, O lord of Mara. But how comes it that you speak the High Speech, my lord?"

"What High Speech? We're speaking Angloss, the only tongue I'm fluent in. Why do you call it the High Speech?"

The old eyes were puzzled "It is the speech of the gods," she said. "You cannot speak our common tongue?"

Perion shook his head. "No, I cannot."

"Is it perhaps your memory? Sometimes an eater's poison can affect one's recollection. Do you remember how you are called, lord?"

"Yes. I told you once, I'm Tom Perion, apprentice geologist."

The woman cupped her left palm in her right, extended her open hands in a gesture. "Welcome to the ship of Captain Theslo of Home, O Tomperion. Now move back to the bed, lest I emasculate you."

"Hold on," Perion said, though in truth he raised and turned his left knee protectively. "Wait, please. Look, I'm trying to be honest with you. All I want is to talk. Will you please just sit down and talk to me?"

The woman's eyes were cold, but she sank onto the chest near the bunk. Perion pushed from the door and staggered to the bunk. He half fell into it, conscious of the sweat pouring from his body, of the soupy air he gasped into his lungs. He was weaker than he had thought. The woman leaned close, fingered and adjusted the bandage on his chest. Close to, she had a musty, leathery smell, like an antique bookstore Perion had once visited.

"Thank you," Perion said.

She grunted and leaned back. "You have questions?"

"Where am I now?"

"You are aboard the *Windbird,* a private ship from Homereaches. We are high, far to the north of Twin Islands, near the trade routes of the Aladian Islanders."

Perion felt cobwebs against his face and reached to brush them away. "I don't understand," he said. "How did you get here?"

"I am Teyo, priestess of the Eighth Ascension. My care is the spiritual guidance of the crew, and the propitiation of the spirits of the seas."

"Teyo," Perion said. "No, I didn't mean that, not exactly. Here, this planet, this world—what is the name of the world?"

"Kalea," the old woman said softly.

"Kalea. And are there others on Kalea like me?"

"Men? Of course there are, many tens of tens in every island."

"Not men. Not just men. People from the sky, I mean. From the air. Are there more?"

"We are all from the sky," Teyo said. "Long, long ago, Kalea herself planted us here on this world. We fell in seeds from the sky, and the seeds took root on the islands of the world. The daughters of Kalea sprang from those seeds, and we from the daughters." Teyo leaned very close again. "Lord Tomperion? You shiver. Is it from the cold?"

"Not the cold," Perion croaked. "It can't be. Seeds. Landing pods. It can't—"

"Teyo, answer this. People have, ah, been here, on the planet, for how long?"

"The planet?"

"The world, Kalea. How long have people been here?"

"For many generations, Lord Tomperion." Teyo's old voice rose half an octave as she began to intone, "Hear! These are the generations of the people of Kalea, of the seas and the lands. The first were the Swimmers, who came to land; and their clans were called—"

"Please, can you tell me the number of generations?" Perion asked.

Teyo clamped her wrinkled mouth shut and looked at him with disdain.

"I need to know. The number of generations. Please, Teyo."

The old gray eyes held deep affront. She inhaled, then muttered in a much lower voice, "The generations of all the daughters of Kalea have been nine and sixty."

Perion grew dizzy, not from the rocking of the ship this time but from the dance of years in his head. Sixty-nine generations of humans at—what? Estimate the average as, say, twenty-five years. That would be about—

"My God," Perion groaned. "Seventeen hundred years."

Teyo had risen, stood staring down at him. "Your words are most strange. I cannot believe you are a lord of Mara at all. Even your coloring is odd. Who are you?"

Perion blinked, his eyes burning. "They're all dead," he said. He laughed hollowly. "All of them dead."

"Who is dead? Your family? Your fellows? You can remember them?"

Perion covered his eyes. "Please leave me. I need to be alone."

"I think perhaps you do." At the door, Teyo turned. In her lilting singsong, she said, "I have not spoken the High Speech since I was a novice in the House of Teachers. Not for conversation, anyway. I use it in the rituals, of course. I find it—pleasant. If you wish, I will return with food for you, later."

"Yes," Perion agreed without enthusiasm. She inclined her head in stiff farewell and went outside.

Perion swung his feet back to the deck, ran a hand through his short-cropped hair. He looked at the cabin—*really* looked, for the first time. It was less than three meters on a side, furnished sparsely with the oblong wooden chest, the bunk, and in the corner opposite the head of the bunk a simple table and backless bench. The square port at the foot of the bunk provided illumination in the day; toward the center of the cabin, a single hanging earthenware lamp swayed to the motions of the ship.

All was of the same dark, close-fibered wood, rough with long usage but clean and spare. Sitting on the bunk, he was aware of a congress of odors: the stink of stale fish, the clovery smell from the rustling mattress pad under him, the rank odor of his own sweat. He scraped a hand against a stiff bristle of beard.

"Dead," he said aloud, to no echo.

The *Galileo* had carried a complement the size of a respectable Earth town, twenty-three thousand people between the ages of eighteen and thirty-five. They had been winnowed from a prospective population on L-5 of more than a hundred thousand—most of them had, indeed, been chosen from before their birth, from the moment of conception, for this mission. He had been. And he had never questioned his destiny, to carry humanity to the far stars, away from the dissension and impending dissolution of Terrasystem civilization. It was what he was made to do.

But a hundred thousand people is a great many, and twenty-three thousand still too many to know individually. Still, he had a circle of life-friends, and a few lovers, and a still wider acquaintance, teachers, mentors, rivals. No family, of course. Few on the ship had family. But his life had touched, oh, a hundred, two hundred other lives more or less deeply. And now all were gone.

Perion shook his head. He could not realize the fact of their deaths; he could recognize it, but could not make it real, could not feel it. He felt instead a great numbness at the center of his being, a numbness akin to the feeling he had experienced years ago, on his first untethered spacewalk, with only the pinprick stars and the velvet black for company, with all space dark around him and himself dwindled to insignificance at the center of it all.

But now he floated in time, not space.

Perion forced his legs to lift him. He took three unsteady steps to the door, found it barred as he had expected. He made his way to the chest, raised its lid. There was his silvery exosuit, neatly folded; beneath it, undergarments and boots.

To his surprise, the clothing was not crusted with salt but was fresh and soft. The tear three inches below the left armpit had been stitched with coarse thread. The thigh pockets were empty.

Perion cursed, but pulled on the undergarments and the exosuit with the elaborate slowness of an invalid. Sweat ran into his eyes and dripped from his nose and chin to form gear-toothed dark blotches on the deck as he stooped to get his legs into the suit. He tugged the suit up, got his arms in, and ran a thumb over the seamseals.

The battery pack at the waist was intact, and the controls on the left thigh, behind the pocket, worked. He set the suit for maximum cooling—in this climate, that would last for maybe one week, he thought glumly—and, exhausted by his efforts, he stretched out again on the bunk.

The coolness and the ship's motion lulled him. He drifted into odd dreams for a time, then abruptly woke again. "My number," he murmured into the soft light of evening. Twenty-three thousand pods, and he had been pod number 22,871.

He pushed up from the bunk, tottered to its foot, grasped the edge of the port. It was high, its lower edge level with his nose. He looked out and up, at a purpling sky, then dropped his gaze to a slate-gray, foam-flecked sea and an empty, far horizon.

The sky drew back his attention. Right now it was free of stars, though soon they would appear. Up there, somewhere, among the stars, was the *Galileo*, tirelessly orbiting. And aboard it, if what he thought had happened actually *had* happened . . .

Maybe, maybe, he thought, willing it to be so. Maybe they're still aboard, still alive, still asleep. One hundred and twenty-nine of them. My people.

My friends.

Chapter 3

The door behind him clacked, and Perion turned from the port. Teyo was back, and with her the doe-eyed girl, perhaps fifteen or sixteen, very dark, the white of her garment seeming to illuminate the small cabin. She held a wooden tray on which rested a platter and an earthenware mug.

"You are dressed," Teyo said. "You should have called. We would have done the task for you, my lord."

"I—didn't know how to call."

Teyo wordlessly balled her fist, struck the closed door twice. "We will hear and come." She turned to the girl and rattled off something Perion could not understand. To Perion, Teyo said, "Will you eat at the table, my lord, or shall I have this one feed you as you recline?"

"I'll sit," Perion said. "I've had enough time in the bunk for a while."

"As you will." Teyo fired instructions to the girl, who went to the table and began to unload the tray, darting shy sideways glances at Perion. Her eyes were deep and brown, under black, curving brows. She had the coloring of an Indian, with a faint peach blush in her cheeks. Teyo grunted as she kindled a light and applied it to the hanging lamp. "That one's name is Kayla. She is a relative of the captain's and is cabingirl."

"Kayla," Perion said, and the girl giggled.

"Sit yourself," Teyo said. "Eat."

Perion followed her orders. Beside the platter were two wooden prongs, sharpened at one end; these evidently were his utensils. The platter itself held a grayish flesh, some brownish-green oblongs something like beans, and a flat, round biscuit, cooked to gold. It was the only thing that looked faintly edible.

"What is this?" Perion asked, prodding at the meat.

24

"Eater," Teyo said. "The one that tried to eat you."

Perion thought of the triple-jawed sea beast and fought down his rising gorge.

The girl, Kayla, laughed. "Itta trideetu," she said. "Nu yeeta itta nuh?"

Perion turned a puzzled face toward Teyo. "The girl makes a small joke," Teyo said. "The eater would have eaten you, but now you eat the eater instead."

"Funny," Perion said, but his laugh was not enthusiastic.

"It is good flesh, my lord," Teyo said quietly. "And if you do not eat it, you will offend those who wish only to serve you."

"I was about to start," Perion said.

The flesh fell apart under the wooden skewers, and he speared a bite. It was salty, chewy—not unlike lobster-flavored chewing gum, he thought—but at least palatable. Kayla giggled again as he chased one of the bean things around with the point of a skewer, showed him how to use the two sticks chopstick-fashion. He smiled his thanks. The beany seeds had a crunchy texture and a faintly nutty taste. The bread was crackly and savored of coffee. But the mug—

Ah. The mug held a fruity, full-bodied wine, with a sharp tang and a delightful capacity for providing inner warmth. The mug made the rest of the meal worthwhile.

When Perion had finished, Kayla efficiently restacked the tray with the empty dishes and made her way out, smiling back at Perion from the door.

"You will feel better now," Teyo said.

"I do, a little," Perion admitted. "Uh, Teyo—there's one other thing—"

"It is under the bed," Teyo said dryly.

"Oh. I see—the earthenware jar. Well—later."

"Make yourself comfortable if you wish," Teyo said.

"Uh—no, really. I—our people do such things in private."

"How do you suppose you did them in your illness? I was here then."

"That's a little different," Perion said.

"You are very strange, Tomperion," Teyo told him. "If I went outside for a few moments?"

"Ah," Perion said. "I'll tap when I'm ready."

"Tap?"

"Knock." Perion demonstrated with a double rap on the table.

"I shall wait."

"Thank you."

Later, when Teyo had returned, Perion had her sit on the backless chair while he took the edge of the bunk. "I want to ask you something," he said. "Many things, in fact."

"I shall try to answer, my lord Tomperion."

"Tom," he said absently. "Perion is my family name."

"It is a strange one."

"To you. But just call me Tom, please. Teyo, do you—have you ever heard of the *Galileo*?"

"Kalea."

"No, the—oh, I see. The language has changed. Kalea. Do you know what Kalea is?"

"Kalea is the Mother of all, the Goddess whose light brightens the sky. She gave her name to the world, and her daughters to the islands to rule the world for her."

"The *Galileo* is a ship, Teyo."

"The scriptures tell of the ship of Kalea, that sailed the ocean of stars."

"Yes!" Perion cried. "That's right. It did. It still does. And I came from the ship."

The flickering, smoky lamp reddened the cabin. It cast deep shadows into the folds and wrinkles of Teyo's face, making it seem both ageless and ancient. Teyo said in a very quiet voice, "You would be put to death for saying such a thing among the people."

"But it's true—you saw my pod fall from the sky!"

"We saw a narn-colored cloud in the midst of the sky. No one could recall having seen or heard of such a thing. And we saw it come to the sea, and when we came toward the place where it had come, we found you."

"Where do you think I came from, then?"

Teyo tilted her chin back. "Different ones say different things. Most believe you were in a small boat sunk by the eater. We are not far from the trade routes. If you are the survivor of a shipwreck, your memory stolen by the sun and the water, that would explain much."

Perion shook his head. "You must have stories, records, of the *Galileo*. Don't you have any stories about—the beginning of things?"

"Many. They are written and passed from generation to

generation by those of the Tenth Ascension, by the Teachers of Teachers.''

"Could I see them?''

"You—read, my lord?''

"Yes. I read.''

Teyo studied him impassively. "That, too, would cost your life—in some quarters. We of Homereaches are not as easily disturbed as some others. In the Under Islands, a man who professed reading would be put to death as an insane one.''

Perion said, "Where I come from, things are much different. Could I see your records?''

"I dare not show you the scriptures, Lord Tom. But I have my copybooks, from when I was a novice. They contain tales and sayings. I will give you some of them—if you truly read.''

"Another thing, Teyo. My dataset.''

"I do not understand.''

"It's a portable unit—I mean, it—well, it's flat, and about this big, and was in my pocket, here—''

"Ah. We thought it to be a strange talisman.''

"A talisman. Yes, it is, in a way. That and my other things. Where are they?''

"The Captain has them. Such is the law.''

"I would like them back.''

Teyo rose. "I will ask the Captain. You sleep now. You are still very weak, and I am still very uncertain about you. I have inside me a fear or a hope—I cannot yet see its face. You are most strange, Tom Perion. I have not seen your like before.''

"Teyo, you have been kind to me.''

"Such is the will of Kalea.''

She left him to the darkness of the cabin. Teyo climbed a companionway to the open deck, found herself under the early stars and amid the soft sound of twilight songs. The sheets were taut, the sails full of wind, the sea flat and calm.

Teyo made her way to the tiller. The Captain was there, beside the helm, feet comfortably apart, sharply chiseled profile back-tilted against the evening sky. Teyo made the palm-cupping gesture of greeting.

"Fair winds and happy voyage to you, my Captain.''

"And to you, Teacher." The Captain's voice was low and rich. "A shade more to windward, helm. There, he feels it, he feels it. Ready now! Haul away!"

The sheets creaked as the sail swung, seeking the best angle. The ship eased toward the wind, then found new life and leaped ahead like a living thing. Teyo felt the suddenly increased tension in the deck beneath her feet, the eager forward strain.

The Captain laughed softly. "That is how you know a really fine sailing ship, Teacher, the way he pulls ahead even so close to the wind."

From the darkness a voice, one of the sailors, said, "That is because the *Windbird* is the last of the Southfaring runners. The last one built at the yards owned by the Makew clans. None other on Home like him now."

The sailor at the helm grunted. "No, not so. The Tasho family of Westhaven own the *Cloud* and the *Firefall*. And the Halven Islanders sail, oh, many, all made to the same pattern."

"Made to the same pattern, but not by the Makews," the Captain said. "The *Cloud* and the *Firefall* are Makew ships, I grant. But look at how the damn Westhaveners keep them up! You can call them brothers of the *Windbird* if you want; but if you said the *Windbird* is a faster vessel than either, or a better, I wouldn't say no."

The figure at the helm spat disdainfully. "Cleaner, too. That old *Firefall*, now—Captain Halo loads him with felat root and janje and such trash, and the ship a runner! I tell you, you *smell* that vessel long before you see it. That's how the Westhaveners know Halo is returning. They stick their long noses in the air and say, 'Whoo! The old *Firefall* due in harbor in' "—two elaborate sniffs—" 'three days, exactly!' "

Two sailors who had been coiling line close by laughed in the dark, and the Captain's laugh echoed theirs. Teyo stood silent.

"You are very solemn tonight, Teacher," the Captain said. "You are bothered by something?"

"By the man."

"Mm. He continues to be—odd?"

"Yes. He is eating now. His body will heal soon. But his mind—I don't know. I have strange feelings about this one."

"I thought Teachers were celibate."

Teyo ignored the good-natured taunt. "He wishes his property returned, Captain."

"The shiny boxes? Why?"

Teyo paused before answering. "I think they have religious meaning for him. They are his talismans."

"A man the keeper of talismans?"

Teyo did the shrugging lift of her chin. "He is unlike men in other ways, too. He knows the High Speech, Captain. He reads."

For a few moments all was silence, save for the hiss of the prow cutting the water and the song of the wind in the sheets. "Perhaps we had better put him overboard," said the one at the helm.

"No." The Captain's refusal permitted no dream of opposition. "He is certain, the prizes from the Asland routes doubtful. Better the small fish on your line than the big one in the sea."

"I think you should return the talismans," Teyo said simply.

"They are pretty toys," the Captain said. "They would bring a fine price in Headwater or Easthaven."

"The price, to you, might be high, Captain."

"You think a man has such influence with the spirits, then?"

"This man is unlike any I have seen. He is not from the Under Islands, yet he is not a lord of Mara."

"There are other islands. The Outlaws. Maybe he is a barbarian."

"The barbarian Teachers do not know the High Speech, let alone their men. He is—different. He tells a tale of falling from the sky."

The Captain grunted in half-amused wonder. "And you saw the signs and portents, didn't you? The strange cloud, the garments he wore."

Teyo chanted something in the High Speech. "There are scriptures," she said. "When Kalea is satisfied that our guilt has been purged away, she will send to us a new birth and a new people."

"A man's loins do not bring forth babes."

"The ways of the Goddess cannot be counted those of the people."

"Ease the helm, there!" barked the Captain. "Can't you feel the shift in the winds! Dolt!"

The ship adjusted course, hugging the slightly changed ways of the wind. Teyo said, "He has asked for my copybooks. I will let him have one. I wish to see for myself whether or not he can read.''

"Reading. What a useless attainment, for a man.''

"This one may change our ideas of what is and is not useful.''

"You are a strange old bird yourself, Teyo.'' The Captain moved forward. "Come, then. You may take the talismans to your prodigy, if you wish. Giving them up goes against the law and against my will, but you have been a good friend to me all of my days. I will not say no, but for your sake—not for his.''

"The morning is time enough, I think," said Teyo. "He is still very weak. He will sleep deeply after the wine.''

"No, come with me now. I have other things I want to speak to you about.''

The two descended the companionway. Outside the barred cabin door, the Captain hesitated. "Kayla said that his skin began to come off four days after we took him.''

"His face and hands were burned by the sun.''

"It is not a disease?''

"No. His skin was like that of a young child—and it is very white still. Another strange thing in all the strangeness. I have never seen such a man.''

"I still think he may be a barbarian.''

The two made their way aft to the Captain's cabin. It was somewhat larger than the one assigned Perion, but scarcely more luxurious. Two hanging lanterns gave it a smoky red illumination, and against the walls standing cabinets provided storage space. A desk and chart locker were built into the left wall, at the foot of the bunk, but otherwise the furnishings were much the same as in the other cabin.

The Captain rummaged in one cabinet and produced a bundle wrapped in thinskin and tied with twine. "Here are the talismans. He wants the shiny box too?''

"I do not know.''

"Better take it.'' The Captain hefted the aluminum case from the lowest shelf of the cabinet. "Pity. The metal would make wonderful barter material. Though I do not know what the things inside are.''

"Thank you.''

"Sit, Teyo. I wanted to ask you about the man, out of the hearing of the crew.''

"Yes."

"He speaks only the High Speech?"

"Yes, Captain. No Common at all."

"This you think is the result of a sickness of memory?"

"I do not know," Teyo confessed. "It may be so. But I have never heard of such a sickness taking one's tongue with it."

"No." The Captain paced, two steps this way, two back. "Teyo, I have no fear of the Teachers. My family has always paid its tithes and is pious enough. Yet they could cause trouble for us over this man, you know. Trouble I cannot now afford, when I am on the brink of claiming haremhood."

"Truly, the higher Ascensions would wonder at a man who seems privy to so many of their mysteries."

"Yes. You can teach him the Common Speech?"

"He is not stupid, Captain."

"I did not call him so."

"I think, if he knows the reason, he will agree to learn."

"More, Teyo. He cannot rave of falls from the sky. He must appear to be one of us—a barbarian, if he is not one in actuality. His ways and speaking would never qualify him to pass as a lord of Mara."

"The honor of capturing a barbarian is not a high one."

"I know that. But it is something—it would justify the expense of the voyage, if not of greater things. It would persuade my family to let me try again, even if this voyage is otherwise unproductive. You will persuade the man to pose as a barbarian?"

Teyo looked at the Captain without expression. "Kalea knows our natures. We cannot easily change them. I think this man is no barbarian, Captain; he is like a spark thrown out by Akala. Cover it how you will with leaves, it will burn through at last. You cannot for long hide his strangeness from the Council."

"Perhaps I will not need to do so for long. But surely the man himself would feel easier among us if he could speak with us, understand what we say. He cannot expect to have a Teacher as translator always."

"I will try to instruct him, Captain."

"Good." The Captain stretched and yawned. "You may go now, and take those things with you. I am ready for bed. Tomorrow we stand early watch. The season is getting away from us, and unless we sight sails in the next few days, we must turn back. Thank you, Teyo. Please find Kayla and send her here."

"I will, Captain."

"Captain, Captain!" the other snorted. "You would think you had never known me before I took the ship. In my cabin, Teyo, call me by name. It is as much a part of our family home as the halls of my mothers were."

Teyo's thin lips twitched in a half-smile. She regarded the Captain, a woman well grown, finely muscled, with dark coloring, black eyes, black hair.

"Very well," Teyo said. "I give you good night, Atina Theslo, Flyer of the *Windbird*."

OF THE BEGINNING OF THINGS

(From the Copybook of Teyo da-Theslo, Teacher)

In the beginning there were no people and no worlds, only the endless dark seas of night skies. No stars shone in them, for there were no stars to shine; and no winds sighed, for the winds were not yet born.

There was only night and First-Mother. But with the turning of thought, she became lonely, and conceived and brought forth the First-Daughters, the Goddesses.

They were a vain group, the Goddesses. To see their own beauty, they kindled lights, and placed them in the darkness; and these were the stars. They built themselves a home, and called it Ertha, and there they lived. But they forgot First-Mother, and came to believe themselves responsible for all that is, and for their own existence as well; all but Kalea.

Now, it fell out that the Goddesses had a disagreement among themselves; some said that the Ertha that they had created did not move, and that all things in the skies circled about it; for they believed themselves very powerful.

But Kalea laughed, and said, "First-Mother brought us forth, and we are but creations ourselves; and Ertha a creation of creations. How, then, should it not move?"

And the others grew very angry with Kalea, and shut her away in a high tower, for they would not be convinced that Ertha itself moved like a sailing raft on the ocean of the dark.

But the Goddesses had themselves conceived and had brought forth children: some had given birth to spirits, and some to demons, and some to elementals. But Kalea had given birth to the daughters of Kalea, and they were people.

Now, when they became aware that Kalea was gone from the world, they fell into great sorrow and cried aloud for her.

And high in her prison tower Kalea heard their voices, and her heart was moved. She sang a song of finding, and the scattered daughters of Kalea began to hear, and to creep toward it, fearful of the other Goddesses in the dark, for they did not favor the offspring of Kalea.

Now, guarding the door to the tower was stupid Hilta, dim of sight and of wit. So when the daughters of Kalea at last came in sight of the tower, they feared Hilta and would not approach. Hidden in the night, they called out, "O Kalea! We hear thy song, but we cannot come to thee, for a Goddess bars the way!"

And stupid Hilta, who had been half asleep, cried, "What voices are these?"

From the top of the tower, Kalea said, "It is the wind, Hilta. Only the wind in the night."

And Kalea sang a song of wind, so that the air began to move, and the sound hid the sounds of the daughters as they approached nearer and nearer the tower.

And when the daughters of Kalea clustered about the foot of the tower, still they feared. But Kalea sang a song of sleep, and stupid Hilta heard it and her head nodded on her breast, and the daughters made their way in, and climbed the stair.

Great was the rejoicing when the daughters of Kalea met their mother; but she was troubled, and said to them, "The Goddesses of Ertha have grown too powerful and proud. Destruction will take them! We must leave, and find our way across the dark sea."

And Kalea sang a wondrous song of flight, and the tower itself lifted from Ertha, and rose in the sky. And

the Goddesses who remained there heard the song from
on high, and grew angry, and hurled curses and weapons at the source of the sound; and some sent their own
daughters in pursuit.

But Kalea's song was strong and true, and the tower
became as a brightly shining ship, and it cleaved the
waves of darkness, with the light of stars and in the
foam at its prow.

For a long time the ship sailed the night, farther and
farther away; and Kalea's voice grew weak from singing, but still she sang.

At last Kalea wept from exhaustion. And her tears
fell under the ship, and formed themselves into the
Mara, the seas. And the daughters of Kalea looked
down in fear and cried, "Is this our new home? Where
are we to live in all this waste of water?"

"I will take care of my children," said Kalea, and
she sang a song of land.

But weary as she was, the notes of the song fell
scattered into the seas; and where each note fell, a
burning mountain appeared, bursting through the waters; and these became the islands of the seas.

"Here, my daughters," said Kalea. "This is your
world."

And so the tears of Kalea are the seas; and the seas
can be bitter and harsh, and cause lamentation. And the
islands can be rough, for they are the products of
weariness, and the toil we must undertake to live on
them makes us in turn weary.

But the song of Kalea is here, too, in the air, and in
the land, and in the sea. Her light is in the sky, for still
the Ship of Light travels overhead; and from it Kalea
watches her daughters.

And in the song of Kalea is joy as well as fear, ease
as well as toil, pleasure as well as pain; for she is all
and the source of all.

And this is the story of the beginning of all things,
and of the Song of Kalea, which is the world.

Chapter 4

"I," Perion said to his datakit, "am on a planet dominated by women."

Having said that, he ran short of inspiration and switched off the recorder. With a sigh he tugged absently at his beard, now half an inch long. The best-laid plans of mice and men, he mused. A month, almost, had passed (or rather more than a month, judging from the passages of Kalea's small moon), and except for acquiring a tan and a beard and the beginnings of language, his plans were quite agley.

Perion shook his head and switched the recorder on again. "I have not yet been able to speak with the Captain," he said. "Teyo seems fairly satisfied with my progress in Common—and after all, Common is only a time-altered dialect of Angloss—but she hasn't yet agreed to let me speak to Atina Theslo or to any member of the crew. Some sort of taboo is working, I expect. . . .

"It's odd that the people have so little memory of the *Galileo* expedition. From Teyo's copybooks I get the impression that the first years after landing were especially harsh, with many deaths. And only a few generations later was the Great Death, which seems to have been a plague that carried off the majority of the elders. That, and a combination of other things, might explain why the era of the expedition has become distorted into legend and superstition.

"One other thing is clear: the colonists who survived the initial descent to Kalea were never able to reestablish communication with the ship. That is very disturbing; it means that a hundred stasis-locked command pods somehow went wrong. There's no telling how many colonists died when their pods malfunctioned—or starved when they landed at sea, too far from an island to gain land.

"At any rate, the failure to communicate with the ship

definitely accounts for the female-male ratio. The concept is somewhat too complex for Teyo—or maybe the society does not concern itself with counting its members—but I estimate it must still be in the neighborhood of the target ratio: eight to one.''

Perion turned the device off again. He had not confided to it his darker thoughts, his frustration at Teyo's stubborn opposition to his wishes, his growing conviction that something had to be done. He rested his back against the mainmast and idly began to daydream. If only he could get to the *Galileo*, bring back the technology . . . the weaponry . . .

In his mind Perion saw himself as a true lord of Kalea, commanding respect and obedience from an awed populace. Lord, he thought contemptuously. They called him a lord of Mara, a hollow title. But if he only had a chance, he could show them a few things. . . .

"Time to eat," Teyo said. She had been standing a respectful distance away while he communed with his talisman; now she stepped forward with determination in her posture.

Perion pressed a control and looked at the screen of his datakit. Days on Kalea, as far as he could time them from sunrise to sunrise, were nineteen hours, fifty-seven minutes long. He had arbitrarily made that twenty hours, shaving a fraction off each second of the day to make the timer function acceptably. Sunrise came at one; noon at five; sunset at ten; midnight at fifteen. Now it was 9:20, with a westering sun in a high, hard blue sky.

With a grunt, Perion rose. He was almost accustomed to the heat and humidity now—at least the air didn't seem like thin soup to his lungs anymore, and a midday high of forty was bearable, if he kept his activity down. Still, he had little energy. Part of that, he suspected, was the lingering effect of the eater's poison; part was his old ingrained twenty-four-hour biological clock, rebelling against the rhythms of this new world.

He looked up at the sails, fan-folded and ribbed like the sails of those ancient Oriental ships—junks, were they?—and saw high overhead a blond woman busily rigging line and replacing worn blocks. Her name he knew: Lito. She was about his age and had a quick laugh, a delicate bone structure, and eyes the blue-violet color of the sky. She sang as she worked, and Perion picked up a few words of Common from her song: "lonely sea," "rain in the clouds," "sun and wind." The ancient immemorial concerns of every sailor, he thought.

"Time to go," Teyo insisted again, and with a sigh Perion preceded her down the companionway.

The fare was uninspiring. When the flesh of the eater had given out, the ship had gone back to regular rations, dried flesh, the eternal beans, and bread. The flesh, as Teyo had explained, came from a "bird." From her description, Perion gathered that the creature stood half as high as a man, had a sinuous neck, membranous scaled wings, and a nasty temper. Its flesh tasted like smoked rubber.

"Now," Teyo said in Common when he had finished the meal and had drunk the last of his mug of wine, "we talk again. You question me today."

Slowly, turning his tongue to the shapes of the new words, Perion said, "I will soon be able to speak to the Captain?"

"We will see. She is very busy now. Next question."

"The . . . temperature, the word I do not know, the heat, yes—the heat is growing. We are going north?"

"We have not sighted Aslandian ships. Captain Theslo now goes farther northward, toward the Edgelands. Sometimes the Aslandians take this path if their cargo is valuable."

"Captain Theslo hopes to . . . take Aslandian lords?"

"She does. The crew support her; otherwise, under another Captain, they would have returned to Homereaches days ago. Most of the crew are young; many have never had a man. The lords we may capture must be assigned homes and harems by the Council; but until we return home, the crew may share them. Such is the law."

"But I may not be shared?" Perion said with a grin.

Teyo's face did not lose its solemnity. "You are not a common man. You are a special problem for the Council. Until they have decided, you must be treated differently."

"Now I would speak," Perion said.

"Speak, Lord Perion."

Perion struggled for a moment, then said, "I still have much trouble with the—words for yesterday, the—"

"Past tenses?"

"Say that again."

"Past tenses of words to describe past events?"

"Past tenses," Perion said, the words strange in his mouth.
"Yes."

"Listen to me."

This is insane, Perion thought. But for half an hour he sat,
head bowed in concentration, datakit surreptitiously record-
ing, while Teyo declined various common verbs with him.
Then, the lesson over, Perion said, "Thank you. Now, let me
try again. The old ones—your ancestors. My people. We
were have—no, we *were*—selected and altered on the basis
of—how do you say *genetics*?"

But Teyo couldn't puzzle his meaning out. Finally, he tried
to simplify: "All of your ancestor women gave birth to more
women than men. Eight women to every one man. That was
the intent. They were to populate the planet. After a few
generations had established a base—a foundation—the male
birthrate was to rise. There were to be more men born."

"The birth of a man is a fair sky and a calm sea," Teyo
said. "How is this miracle to come about?"

How, indeed. How could he tell her about stasis-preserved
semen and artificial insemination, about embryos already conceived and just waiting to be implanted, about a carefully
selected battery of scientific and genetic remedies intended
to work with a population of at least five hundred thousand?
He couldn't, he found after some time of struggling in a
linguistic thicket; at last he gave up and said, "The old ones
had ways we know not."

Teyo raised her right hand automatically, in a religious
gesture answering the platitude he had just spouted. "And
you are an old one," she said, with an ambiguous inflection
that could have made it a statement or a question. "Lord
Perion, you will shortly begin to speak with the crew. You
must not speak of such things to them. It would mean trouble
for you, and perhaps for them as well. When the time comes,
you may tell your tale to the Council. I will stand by your
side and help you speak then."

"And I may tell my story to the Captain?"

Teyo hesitated, the gray eyes losing expression for a moment. At last, without enthusiasm, she said, "Captain Theslo
is my family-sister and my leader. You may speak to her all
things you speak to me."

"When?"

Teyo's face gave every sign of reluctance. "She will have

you dine with her tomorrow,'' she said slowly. "I will be with you then, too."

"You want me not to speak of—strange things?"

Teyo pushed up from her seat and reached for the tray. "You are the lord, not I," she said flatly.

That night passed quickly—too quickly, as all the abbreviated nights on Kalea seemed to do. Teyo came back in the morning to drill Perion on etiquette and language. She stressed to him the imperative and intricate niceties of communicating with so august a personage as Atina Theslo of Shelda Bay, made sure he understood the things he must remember to mention and those he must not mention.

Later in the afternoon a group of three women, Kayla the cabingirl, Zerba the mender of sails, and one other whom Perion did not know, came to his cabin. Laughing and nodding, they had him undress; then they brought in a wooden basin of steaming water and aromatic soap like translucent purple jelly, and they scrubbed him.

Perion stared straight ahead through the process, but more than once he blushed as he caught a rapid-fire, sly comment on his physique and appearance. This invariably launched the women into short flights of laughter. Still, as custom dictated, he did not speak to his dressers.

The clothing they brought had been especially tailored for him: white breeches, loose in the calves and tight in the thighs, overworked with fantastic swirls and loops of flat, buttonlike "pearls," not pearl-colored but a lustrous pale blue; a blue tunic, worked with golden thread and embroidered with otherworldly flowers of pink, yellow, and pale gray; a dark blue sash tied in a precise knot over his left hipbone; and blue slippers of a soft, pliable leather.

They dressed his hair, too, arranging it and holding it in place with a kind of tiara of small shells strung together on more gold thread. And when they had finished, they had him turn this way and that, commented critically on their own handiwork, and stepped forward now and again to tug the sash into a better position or to tuck a stray lock of dark hair back under the tiara. At last, with murmurs of approval, they all nodded their farewells to him and left him alone.

Teyo joined him in a few minutes. "You now truly look like a lord of Mara," she said, with a wry smile.

"I feel like a doll," he said in Angloss. "I am used to dressing myself, Teyo."

"Only Common, please," Teyo said in that tongue. "Our ways are not as yours, Lord Perion. You must learn to change yourself, since you cannot change our ways."

We'll see about that, Perion thought grimly. But to Teyo he said, "I am now worthy of meeting the Captain?"

"I will take you to her," Teyo said.

Atina Theslo sat in state in her cabin. Teyo ushered Perion in, saw him through the requisite greetings, and then retired to a corner, where she hovered like a looming stormcloud, a frown stitched permanently on her wrinkled face.

"Sit, Lord Perion," the Captain said. "I have heard much of you."

"Your kindness is as wide as the sea," Perion said. The Captain, he noted, was dressed much more simply than he, wearing the standard bleached white blouse and trousers of all the crew. Her dark face was devoid of makeup, her black hair loose and lustrous on her shoulders. She returned his gaze frankly, with a hint of humor in her black eyes.

"You are very pretty," she told him. "My dressers have done a good job with your raiment. It pleases you?"

"You are kind to provide them," Perion said. "You are pretty yourself."

The Captain straightened, her eyes wide; for a moment, anger and amusement struggled in her face. Then, with a laugh, she turned to Teyo. "Truly you spoke when you said this one has strange ways, Teacher. I have never been so insulted, ashore or aboard!"

Perion said stiffly, "I have used the wrong word?"

Before Teyo could speak, the Captain said, "An unusual word, Lord Perion. But let it pass. Teyo has spoken of your strange ways and of your—illness. You must really stop giving her such bad ideas."

"What ideas?"

"Ideas about men," she said firmly. "And ideas about what the old ones could do."

"The old ones had ways—" Teyo mumbled from her corner.

"Yes, yes, Teyo," the Captain said. Her dark eyes flashed merrily at Perion. "Teyo is very old and believes the old tales of ships in the sky," she said mischievously.

"They are true," Teyo said evenly.

"We will speak of them tonight," the Captain said. "And while you are on my ship, Lord Perion, please call me by my person-name. I am Atina, if you will."

"And I Tom," Perion said, remembering Teyo's drill in the formulae of greeting.

"We will speak of many things, Tom," the Captain told him. "But first we will have our meal." She clapped her hands, and Kayla brought in the meal. Perion sat in silence while she dished into his plate a small mound of ribbon things, little crustacean creatures which looked, remotely, like moldy spaghetti. As Kayla left, Perion used his food sticks to try a bite. They crunched, but the flavor was pleasant, despite their nauseating appearance.

"Here," Atina said, lifting an earthenware decanter. "Wine?"

"Please." He held out his mug.

"I pour well," Atina said, and it was true: though the ship rolled in a moderate sea, she spilled not a drop and expertly cut off the red flow of wine. "I shall make a fine harema for some lord."

"Teyo has spoken of harems. I don't understand why you cannot simply join one," Perion said.

Atina smiled as she poured her own wine. "You are indeed very odd, Tom. I almost could believe your tale of falling from the clouds."

"You saw my stasis pod!"

"We saw smoke and a man swimming from an eater."

Perion sipped his wine. "You tell me about your problems in joining a harem, and I will tell you about the things of legend."

Atina put on a resigned expression. "We are ranked by the number of clan-sisters we have. Those with only three or four mother-sisters and one mother-brother are placed in schools at a young age. They become the powerful ones; the Council haremas come from their ranks, and the handmaidens. Those with five to seven sisters must work from their seventh to their fourteenth year before becoming eligible for marriage. These are the practical haremas, the ones who earn a living and increase the family's wealth. And finally, those with seven or more sisters must wait until they are eighteen before joining a harem. By then they are well into their child-bearing years, and can produce only one or two children before becoming too old." She shrugged. "My mother had nine children, all girls. I must take the alternate way: if I bring males to my home Council at Shelda Bay, they will be counted as brothers, and I may qualify immediately as a harema. I wish to have children, you see." Atina smiled in Teyo's direction. "Fortunately, my sisters are influential, and they have been able to secure this command for me. I have trained; now, if I succeed, I may marry before my tenth year."

Perion watched her sip her wine. "How old are you now?"

"Nine and three-quarters. The best child-bearing age. Look at my hips!"

"They are good," Perion murmured. He did a quick mental calculation; judging from Atina's apparent age, a year on this planet would be the equivalent of about 2.1 or 2.2 Earth years. "I think I understand," he said. "The system is meant to keep women whose mothers have borne many daughters from themselves bearing more daughters." To himself, he thought that the problem was with the fathers, not the mothers; but he decided not to volunteer the news that males, not females, determine the sex of the unborn. "How many wives are in a harem?" he asked.

"I do not understand," Atina said.

Perion recast his syntax and inflection: "A harem has how many haremas in it?"

"Ah. That varies. In some cases, as few as eight or ten. In others, twelve or even more. The Council decides how many are needed on each estate. But of late years many harems have become crowded; there is much ocean and few islands."

Perion savored again the tangy bite of his wine. "You will join what lord's harem?" he asked.

She shrugged by raising her chin. "I have little say in the matter. I have the right to refuse, once; then I must agree to the harem assigned me by the Council, or remain unmarried. I have no great ambitions. I wish only that my husband be lordly and remote, one who can make just decisions and lead a great family." Her black eyes twinkled. "I could never join *yours*, Tom. You chatter like a narnbird."

He smiled. "We all have our faults."

"Now tell me of the fables," she said.

Perion tried. He spoke, as well as he could, of the *Galileo*, of the suffering, overpopulated Earth of 2167, of the rising excitement felt there when the data from the first unmanned Procyon probe returned, bearing news of a marvelous Earth-like planet.

New Terra, the planet was quickly dubbed: a world the fourth from its sun, with seas, continents, icecaps, abundant plant and animal life, and, most important of all, *room*. Luna was crowded, Mars a rapidly filling frontier, and the orbital colonies regimented and unappealing to all but fanatics. New Terra promised to be a haven for humanity.

The hope drove humans for thirty years. Much happened in those decades—the wars, the Die-Off—that made immediate pressure less severe. But the goal was there, and the desire, and so lives were shaped and planned with the expedition in mind; and finally, in 2199 the *Galileo* mission, the first of the Earth Deep Space colonies, was launched from Jupiter orbit. The trip would take many lifetimes of humans; and so the crew was placed in stasis, to sleep until the end of the journey.

"But the journey did not end," Perion finished. "At least, not in Procyon System. Something happened to the ship. It passed far beyond New Terra—from the constellations I have seen at night, I guess at least three hundred light-years—"

"Pardon," Atina said. "A *liteer* is what?"

"It is—a long way," Perion said. "A great distance. Anyway, the ship found this sun and this world and made it a secondary target. And that is where the old ones came from: the *Galileo*. They were my friends and my crewmates."

Smiling, Atina poured another cup of wine for Perion. "A charming story. But I cannot believe it. If the old ones ever existed at all, they have been dust and bone for many, many turnings of the world."

Perion tried to explain stasis and rammed head-on into the language barrier. And when Atina teasingly asked him specifics about the old ones—"Did they truly settle first in Homereaches, as our Teachers say, or did they rather come first to the Under Islands, as the heretics claim?"—Perion had to admit defeat.

"There is much I have no way of knowing," he admitted ruefully.

Atina laughed, sipped her wine. "Take care, Tom, when

you speak to others. You are worth something to me alive; put to death as a heretic, you would be wasted.''

Perion's irritated retort was cut off by an insistent knock. "Come," Atina ordered, rising.

The door opened. Kayla was there, excitement dancing in her eyes. "The lookout has spotted a cooking fire, Captain," she said. "The ship is still far off; we have the wind of him. He could only be an Aslandian craft, this far north.''

"At last," the Captain said. She turned to Perion with a tight smile. "Your stories have amused me, Tom. I hope they cause you no trouble later. Now you will go back to your cabin. When the dawn comes, we shall have much work to do.''

And from the wall she took an odd, curved black sword. It was made of wood, not metal, and it was short; but for all of that, it looked as if it could very efficiently deal death to a foe.

Chapter 5

As always, the night seemed too short. Perion seemed hardly to have dozed when a clatter and uproar of activity roused him. He hastily drew on a plain white pair of trousers and shirt (sailcloth donated and sewn by the sailmaster) and climbed to a deck awash in dawnlight activity. Nearly the whole ship's company of twenty-eight seemed there, scrambling amid the sheets or distributing weapons.

The crossbow-like sprinbo that had dispatched the eater showed up in several hands, and swords like Atina's, curiously made of some black, heavy-seeming wood, appeared from a locker at the foot of the mainmast. Atina had her own strapped to her waist. She stood on the poop near the helm, her dark hair whipping in the dawn wind, her dark eyes darting everywhere. Perion hurried across to her.

"What's going—"

She cut him off. "Stay below, Lord Perion. We're in pursuit of an Aslandian vessel. There will be fighting."

Perion whirled and peered forward. Yes, there, far ahead, was the white oblong of a sail against the sun-glittered water. "Pirates," Perion said to himself more than to Atina. "I did not believe you until now."

"Common, Tom, if you wish to speak to me," Atina said. Then she whipped out a louder command: "More sail! Helm, bring us more to port."

"But you don't have to fight," Perion said weakly. "You have me."

"You'll do me no good. Homereachers want sound husbands, not doubtful ones who babble stories about the stars. You're a curiosity, Tom, not a prize. You'll have to go below when we get near enough for action. Stay on deck until then, if you want, but stay out of our way."

For an hour they closed steadily on the other ship. Perion

could see that it was a three-master, larger by a third than the *Windbird*, but heavier, too, and slower to take the wind.

Atina seemed everywhere at once, shouting orders and laughing encouragement. Now she paused beside Perion and seemed to read his mind. "They will fight hard," she told him. "That is an embassy ship, probably separated from a convoy—remember the storm last week? A fortunate chance for us. Better to take him here, alone, than to try to break a company of fighting ships to get at him."

"What will happen?" Perion asked her.

"You ask questions oddly," Atina complained. "We will challenge the ship. If the crew surrenders, they will turn their lords over to us, and we will depart, having first dismasted the ship. If they refuse, then we will fight until one crew or the other gives in." She smiled—a grim smile. "A man will not wish to see what will happen."

In his heart, Perion agreed with her. Fighting had never been one of his primary diversions, and he was unlikely to be good at it—especially against female foes. He turned to the Captain. "Atina, I tell you that I can bring your people great knowledge, knowledge worth tens of tens of lords. Turn back."

They were near enough to see armed figures standing at the rail of the enemy ship. Atina's eyes were on them as she said, "I cannot make such a bargain. You know I desire children—"

"Then get me a sword," Perion said.

Atina looked at him in round-eyed astonishment; then, to Perion's discomfiture, the Captain broke into laughter. "You are joking, or insane. A man fight! Men were not made for fighting."

"I have no choice," he said. "I must get back to your homeland and tell my story. That is the only way I can hope to find a means of getting back to my ship in the sky. My friends may still be there, still alive. That is worth fighting for."

"You are not trained."

"I have had survival training. I think I could help."

She shook her head, amusement still twinkling in her eyes. "I almost believe your story of dropping from the stars. A man fight! As if a man could do a woman's work! No, Tom, this is not allowed. But I will do this: take a sword and remain aboveboard to tend our wounded. You will not need the sword, but it might supply another's need. Now, to the deck. We are almost in range. Down, Tom! From sprinbo range our enemies may not be able to tell that you are a man.''

Tom made his way to the arms chest and hefted a sword. It was almost like a child's toy scimitar, curved, light, crafted of the strange black wood, very hard and—he ran a thumb over the edge and drew blood—sharp. He thrust the sword under his sash. Lito, the blond woman he had noticed before, crouched behind a forward gunwale. Perion joined her there.

He met her startled violet glance with a gruff explanation: ''I'm supposed to tend the wounded. But I'll fight if I have to.''

The other members of the crew crouched behind protection, or stood with sprinbos ready. At a shouted order from Atina, every other bowwoman fired—and Perion heard a voice, not very distant, yell out in sudden pain.

Something whizzed inches over his head, and there were several loud *chunks* as bolts struck wood. Perion blinked at one embedded in the mainmast, a half-meter quarrel crafted of wood and bone, still quivering angrily.

''Second group fire!'' cried Atina as the first women reloaded their weapons. This time more shouts came across the water, but the bowwoman nearest Perion and Lito dropped to the deck swearing. A bloody bolt hung from her upper left arm. Perion crawled to her side. ''What do I do?''

But the woman had already broken off the head and—Perion thought for a second he would pass out—had raspingly drawn the shaft through her arm. ''It missed bone,'' she grunted. ''Tie it for me.''

Perion improvised a bandage from a strip torn off his sash. The bowwoman, her left arm bound and dangling, sprang to her feet and fired her own weapon. She dropped back down grinning. ''Hang on, Lord Tom Perion!''

The *Windbird* ground against something, and suddenly women were running, leaping over him. Perion got warily to his feet and saw that they had closed with the other ship. He could cross the deck, step on the rail, leap across a meter-and-a-half gap, and be on the other vessel, where the decks already glistened here and there with blood and the air was filled with swinging blades and curses.

He heard a loud, desperate cry: the Captain's voice. Without planning, Perion made the leap to the deck of the enemy ship. He stepped into whirling chaos. Women struggled everywhere, hand-to-hand—and there was Atina, cornered against the rail by two of the enemy. Perion pushed forward, brandishing his cutlass. With the flat of it he struck the nearest enemy a resounding blow across the buttocks.

She spun, slashed wildly at him with a blow he just managed to parry. She drew back for a whistling sweep of blade.

Perion threw his own blade up to meet the attack—and when the other broke her swing, let it come apart in sections, halting the sword, Perion's momentum carried his blade against her side. He felt the black wood grind against the bones of her rib cage.

The woman dropped her sword, stared at him, her mouth open, her left side bloodied. She said something in a dialect Perion did not understand, then staggered back. A lurch of the deck caught her by surprise, and before Perion could react, she fell over the rail. The two ships rolled together a moment later, and from between them came a stomach-wrenching crunch.

Cries split the air. Perion whirled, bringing his sword up, only to find that the fight was over. Everywhere Atina's crew and the enemy stopped, some frozen in attitudes of combat, as the shouts continued. As Perion watched, first one, then another of the enemy threw swords to the deck.

"Aft," a harsh voice said in his ear. It was Atina. She spoke to her crew, not to him.

"What happened?" he asked her.

"Back to the ship," she said. "You do not know what you have done."

"It was—"

"Back to the ship—or I'll throw you over myself," Atina growled, and her fierce look left no doubt that she would try. Perion retreated.

From the rail he watched as the *Windbird* crew herded the sullen enemy amidships. A blonde—Lito, he saw, her thigh bound and bloodstained—limped around the deck, gathering fallen weapons and casting them overboard.

At the after part of the ship, a crew of three had opened a hatch. From it stepped five men, tall, slender, dressed in gaudy blues and reds. They were all brown-haired and tanned.

Atina, her own dark skin strangely yellowish, supervised their descent into the *Windbird*. They gave him curious looks as they were taken down the companionway.

Back on the other vessel a small gang chipped away at the ship's masts, using spade-shaped axes of the dark wood, the blades edged with metal. Perion went to the rail and helped the wounded crewwomen back aboard. They gave him grim looks and no greeting.

The masts of the Aslandian vessel fell; the work crew released the grapples and scrambled back aboard the *Windbird*. As they left the other ship behind, they sent up a shrill, spiritless cheer.

A body floated face down in the widening space between the two ships. Perion, looking back, saw a woman from the Aslandian vessel dive overboard and swim toward the body. A rope snaked into the water. The enemy were reclaiming their own.

Perion felt a gentle touch on his shoulder and looked up into the seamed face of Teyo. "You can no more call back the dead," she said in a kindly voice, "than stand beneath the sun."

Perion nodded, feeling numb. The body, roped beneath its arms, dangled against the side of the enemy ship, then disappeared over the rail.

He turned away and walked stiff-legged to the companionway.

He found Atina in her cabin, with Kayla, the cabingirl, tending her leg wound. She called him inside, making no move to cover herself or to reach for clothing. "We have a run ahead of us," she said. "The other Aslandian ships will seek us out. We'll find them on our tails if we tarry. But it will be hard, beating back against the winds into friendly waters. Still, the crew know they can enjoy the captives when we feel safe again. That should spur them on."

Perion averted his eyes. Atina's long legs were lovely, despite the poultice bandaged to the tender inside of her right thing, but . . .

"I didn't intend what happened," he said.

Atina sighed. "I know. They fought very hard. I think they were fortunate to lose only one."

Kayla rose, bowed, and passed Perion on the way out. Her face was a tight fist of anger. When she had gone, Perion asked, "What's wrong with her?"

"Please. Your questions are so hard to understand when you phrase them that way—"

"Something is wrong with Kayla?"

"Ah. She takes the death to heart. The responsibility is mine, you see."

"No, I don't. I distracted the woman; I hit her. She fell because of me."

"But it is my expedition; I command. Therefore, the responsibility is mine. The Aslandians will not take a death lightly. There may well be war."

"Over a single death?"

"Of course." Atina gingerly drew on her trousers, stood shifting her weight from foot to foot. "It hurts, but it should heal well. By the time we arrive at Home, I should be able to walk without a limp."

"Wait—explain to me about the death."

Atina turned her dark eyes to him. "There is not much to explain. She will be buried at sea tonight, and their Teachers will sing hymns to the Sailing Star to take away her spirit. Her harem-sisters will consider the manner of her death, and whether they should demand restitution. If they decide so, they will send a deputation to Home to demand that I be turned over to their justice."

"This means—what?"

"Nothing. For the dead one, less than nothing. They believe her spirit will rise to the Sailing Star tonight. I believe that dead is dead. She cares no longer for vengeance. As for me, if they come for me, I will not go."

"And that ends it?"

Atina's smile was one-sided. "You have much to learn, Lord Perion. Don't concern yourself. It is nothing for a man to worry about."

"So now we go back to your island."

"We try. Freebooters rarely come this far. We have hostile water to travel before we can call ourselves safe."

"And what will happen to me when we arrive?"

"You wish to know your fate. That is hard to say. I will turn you over to the Council. They will listen to your story— though I warn you, half of them are Teachers, Ninth Ascension and higher, and they are unlikely to believe a word you say. Most probably you will be assigned to an estate on one of the outlying islands and will be allowed to build your harem. Though I doubt you will ever attract the choicest of wives, since there will be a suspicion of madness about you. You will probably have to settle for the sisters of seven sisters, like me.''

Perion laughed. At Atina's quizzical look, he said, "You undervalue yourself, Atina. Even one wife like you would be—most delightful. But I don't intend to be put out to stud. I will fight, if I must, for my freedom.''

Amusement quirked Atina's lips. "Talk like that, and they will truly think you mad. You could not defeat a six-year-old in a fair fight.''

Nettled, Perion said, "I did well enough today.''

"Because of your beard. The Aslandians have never seen a man try to fight. Their instincts are to protect men, not to attack them. You looked so weak and helpless flailing that cutlass around that they drew away from you. They couldn't bring themselves to strike you down, even when you cut at them.''

Perion stared at her, appalled. "What?''

"It's true, Lord Perion. When you came to try to help me, you surely saw that for yourself.''

"Do you—you mean I wounded her only because she would not fight back?''

"Tom, Tom. You did what you thought was right. If you had not come to help me, I would have been taken, and that would have been the end of the *Windbird* and the expedition. My crew would have been imprisoned, you would have been placed in an Aslandian harem. Do not worry about the dead. She is gone; and your fate will be the same in any case.''

"But to wound, to kill, a woman—''

"Don't tell Teyo I said this, but I believe you performed a service. We have too many women as it is, and far too many Aslandians. And you did save me from captivity.''

"But—you would not have killed any of them?''

"No. We raid the Aslandians for lords, and they do the same to us. But blood spilled is rarely lifeblood, and when one dies, trouble will come like carrion bugs to the corpse. But that is my concern, not yours. Now, back to your cabin, Tom. I need to see to my crew.''

Perion stepped aside and let her pass. In the corridor he

watched her climb the companionway, favoring her injured leg. Then, alone, he asked himself in the High Speech, "What am I getting into?"

He found no answer in either tongue.

Chapter 6

The run to the southeast took days. On the morning of the ninth day after the ship was taken—a Fridi in the Kalean's abbreviated six-day week, and the fortieth day of the season they called nearsun—Perion awoke to sounds of celebration. He dressed hurriedly and went above. Selridir, a black-haired woman who served as Atina's first mate, was in charge. "It is something?" he called to her.

"We have seen sails of Homereach ships," she said. "And there—look there."

He followed her pointing finger into the sky. White some-things, obviously far away, wheeled and whirled against the mottled blue background of cloud and sky. Shading his eyes, he said, "They are alive?"

"Windbirds," Selridir replied. "For which the ship was named. They are large, their wings as long as the boom of our sail. They nest on our islands. This time of the year, they go flying. When the days grow cooler, they leave us and fly north, high, so high they can be seen only as specks. And they say they always return to the island where they were born."

Tatal, taking her turn at the helm despite her wounded arm—she was the bowwoman who had been hit in the attack, and she still carried the arm in a sling—said, "That is true. Very mysterious birds, the windbirds. No one knows how far they go, or where they spend the farsun time. Once a clan-aunt of mine, Italka the Merchant, was becalmed so far to the north that she saw the edge of the world. Her whole crew was starving. A windbird came down to fish in the shallows, and one of her crew tried to harpoon it—"

"Bad luck to harpoon a windbird," Selridir muttered. "Italka wouldn't be becalmed if she didn't do foolish things like that."

53

Tatal gave her a look of contempt. "She was *already* becalmed. That's what I tell you. Bird came *after* the wind died."

"Still."

Perion said, "And tell the rest of the story?"

Tatal made the slow upward nod that Perion now accepted as a shrug. "Nothing to tell. Harpooner hit the bird in the thigh—the bird flew away. But when Italka got back to Tobria—"

"Tobrians are liars," Selridir said flatly.

"*These* Tobrians are clan-kin of mine and do not lie to me. They said the bird was in the harbor there three days after Italka's harpooner hit it. They knew it by the harpoon in its leg—it had the clan mark carved in the haft. So they expected Italka back anytime. But it was sixty and four days before she got back."

"That bird flew fast," Selridir said.

"Very mysterious birds, the windbirds," Tatal repeated.

"I am thinking of the lottery, not of birds," Selridir said.

Perion raised his eyebrows. "A lottery will be held?"

"For the lords," she replied. Selridir was muscular and chunky, with a loud, braying laugh and biceps a weightlifter might be proud of. She gave Perion a playful, stinging poke in the ribs. "See if you can talk old Teyo into putting your name in as one of the prizes. I wouldn't mind sharing your cabin with you for a night."

Perion did not reply, but as he turned and walked away he heard Selridir's brassy laughter rattling after him. And he blushed.

Damn it, ever since the five lords had come aboard, the women had been treating him like a—well, like a sex object. He had learned from Teyo that the crew would insist on a lottery when they felt safe, and that he alone would be excluded from participation. He had asked her to be allowed to speak to the five men from Aslandia, but she had resolutely vetoed the request. "They must live in peace among our people," she had said. "I cannot allow you to speak to them of what they would think heretical ideas."

And so he had been confined to his cabin when they were above decks, released to much greater freedom than before when they were sequestered. But now, in friendly waters, perhaps security would be relaxed, and maybe . . .

He paused in the corridor outside his cabin, made up his mind, walked to the end, and tapped at Atina's cabin door.

"Come in." Atina's voice sounded thick with sleep, though it was already midmorning and she was normally an early riser.

Perion opened the door and stood rooted to the spot. Atina reclined naked on her bunk, and equally naked and caressing her lay Kayla, the cabingirl. Both looked curiously in his direction.

"I'll come back," Perion choked.

He spent more than an hour in his cabin. Later, on deck, he found Atina alone at the bows, gazing ahead. She saw him approach and smiled at him. "You ran away earlier. Why?"

Perion closed his hand on the rail, felt the tough, splintery wood. He, too, looked ahead, not directly at Atina. "I thought you wanted privacy."

"For that?"

"My people believe in privacy for sex," Perion said, feeling at once bigoted and correct. The crew of the *Galileo*, colony ship that she was, had been carefully screened for heterosexual preference.

Atina's voice was indulgent. "That was only recreation, Tom. For the first time in many days I feel safe from Aslandian pursuit. It is time to relax a little."

"The—enjoyment—of the same sex is common in Home-reaches?"

"I do not understand."

"Sex between two women. Or two men."

His head exploded in red light. He found himself on his knees, his ear ringing. The whole side of his head throbbed. He staggered back to his feet, became aware that the crew had stopped in midaction and was staring with wide eyes at him. He looked at Atina's furious face, blinked. "You hit me. Why?"

Atina's dark eyes were cold. "You filthy krana. Never mention that idea again."

"Which?" Perion was genuinely bewildered. He rubbed his jaw.

"The one about—about lords," Atina said, her voice a low, harsh rush. She colored and looked away. The crew, fearing her gaze, fell busily to work again.

Tom nodded. "I think I see. There are few men, and they

are essential to reproduction. A—uh, a deviant preference among them is not permitted. But among women it's acceptable?"

Athina avoided his eyes, staring stonily ahead. "Recreation among women is common. Everyone does it in the harems. The other"—she shuddered, and he realized that the thought made her physically ill—"we will not speak of."

Tom retired below. He had collided head-on, and painfully, with an ingrained taboo, and he needed time to recover. He took up the copybook that Teyo had given him, marveling again at the paper. It was thin and tan, with faint horizontal ribbing that varied in density. He realized that it was organic, the leaf or bark of some plant, carefully dried and flattened; but that was no longer surprising. Even the things he had thought to be iron nails were organic, the spiky thorns of the blackwood tree, the same tree that furnished wood for the swords. Teyo had explained how these were heated until they shrank, then driven into the wood like nails. Within a few hours they reabsorbed water from the atmosphere and swelled, making a tight join.

Perion sighed and read. The ancient crabbed script, the half-elided letters, the idiosyncratic spelling, made his progress slow. But there were things to be learned from Teyo's books.

At midday a commotion pulled his attention away. From above, Selridir's metallic laugh rang out triumphantly and clear. Perion smiled, the gesture hurting. Selridir, it seemed, was a lucky winner in the lottery. Perion wished the unknown Aslandian prize well.

As the next days passed the weather moderated. The *Windbird* slipped farther and farther south, and before long the sun, now lower in the sky at noon, was less of an inferno, and daily temperatures dropped accordingly. Sixteen days after the battle, Perion's datakit recorded the maximum temperature belowdecks as a relatively chilly thirty-two. Just as well, Perion thought; his exosuit cooling system had long since gone dead, the batteries exhausted.

They passed through several storms, more or less severe ones; and in the intervals between, Perion took time to contemplate the heavens. The small, cold, distant moon seemed only about a third the size of Terra's and gave a dismal bluish light. In contrast, the brilliant Sailing Star, far brighter than

Venus in the skies of Earth, dazzled the eyes. It pursued a stately course, north to south. Perion tried several times to contact it with his personal communicator, to no avail. The failure did not surprise him—the small radios had little range— but it did frustrate him. The Sailing Star, the Ship of Souls, was indeed a ship of a kind: he recognized the *Galileo*, could almost imagine he could make out her lopsided dumbbell shape as she traveled in her perilously low polar orbit.

Four or five times they sighted friendly sails, and occasionally they neared a ship and hailed it. Atina, still uneasy with him, ordered him below when this happened, but even from his cabin he could hear the excited voices and shouted compliments when another vessel learned of the cargo of five Aslandian lords carried by the *Windbird*.

And still Atina refused to allow Perion to speak to the other males. He glimpsed them from time to time, slim, slow-moving creatures, somehow elegant in their economical languor of movement. They carried an air of remove, as disinterested and placid and self-contained as so many oysters.

A frustrated Perion concentrated on Teyo's religious instruction, on learning the language, and on reading legends. He pieced together in this way a rough history of the first two generations of the old ones.

There was, he learned, a leader named Jansmeet. This leader he privately identified as James Smith, a Eurafrican engineer famous among the colonists for his quick tongue and temper. Jansmeet and the others apparently landed, by accident or design, near the Homereaches archipelago. There had been perhaps hundreds, perhaps thousands ("tens of tens," the legend said), of survivors. Years of Crusoe-like building, planting, and planning had ensued. Children were born, grew to young adulthood, and themselves began to produce children.

At length the grizzled Jansmeet (Perion found it hard to picture Smith, whom he had known as a thirty-year-old, as a graybeard leader) managed to construct sailing vessels large enough to carry an expedition northward, to the edge of the world.

Something went wrong. Perion still could not quite tell what the problem was—Teyo would only repeat that it was impossible to stand beneath the sun when he asked why ships did not go farther north—but disaster somehow took the expedition. Out of many who left, only three returned. They

spoke of rugged lands, of an enormous desert beyond high
mountains, of seeking an apparently nonexistent sea passage,
of disease, heat, and beasts, and of some unfathomable
calamity.

A second leader, whose name was given by Teyo as Tritrita,
and whom Perion could not identify, raised another expedition, but at some point before it set out a revolt occurred.

The lives of a hundred young people, it seemed, were too
high a price to pay for the struggling colony. Tritrita led,
finally, an unspecified group away from Homereaches. These
people became the Aslandians, occupying a hot, northern
land, and the hereditary foes of the Homereachers. Evidently
they, too, failed to penetrate to the northern hemisphere of
Kalea. At any rate, they remained isolated by distance and
preference from the Homereachers for many years, until a
growing population forced the latter into exploration and
emigration, roughly two centuries back. The Aslandians, apparently, suffered similar problems, and any encounter between the two peoples nowadays seemed foredoomed to be an
episode of piracy or pillage.

Not that the two populations were radically different, really. Both spoke dialects of the same common language, both
had developed similar social systems—numerically dominant
females preeminent in politics, commerce, and administration, males pampered and idealized—and both faced short-
ages in land and resources, with metals especially at a premium.

As to the men, Perion received conflicting impressions.
Teyo spoke of them reverently as ''lords of wisdom'' who
made every important decision, who directed the society,
who were the true receptacles and preservers of ancient knowledge, the actual leaders of nations.

Privately, judging from the crew's chatter about himself
and about the five Aslandians, Perion wryly concluded that
the lords were like the husband in the old joke who made all
the important decisions in his family. While his wife decided
how many children to have, where the family would live, and
what profession her husband would pursue, *he* decided such
really important issues as what to do should the sun go nova.

When not reading Teyo's books or talking to her, Perion
scandalized the crew by working as one of them. His beard
became thick and heavy, and he tied his hair piratically with a
scarf. His skin acquired a saddle-leather tan, and his stomach

grew lean and hard. Once, weeks after the taking of the Aslandians, Perion caught sight of himself in a polished obsidian mirror, one of Atina's most prized possessions, and was astonished to see the bearded, glowering face of a barbarian staring back at him.

He was disturbed at the time. Lords of Mara, to judge from Teyo's talk and from the five Aslandians, were expected to be tall, slender, fair of skin, and delicate of manner. He wondered if he would be more likely to win the cooperation and sympathy of the ruling Council or to frighten them. When he mentioned the problem to Atina, he only amused her.

"Men are such showbirds—all alike, only concerned about your appearance."

"But I want to get the Council on my side, Atina. Your advice?"

From her old accustomed corner Teyo snorted. "Remain as you are. You look like the beast-men Kalea sent to punish the wrongdoing of the old ones. That will surely impress the Council."

Atina looked as though she were holding back laughter, but her voice sounded serious. "Teyo may be right, Tom. The Council sometimes favors men who are out of the ordinary. And you certainly look—different. Your muscles are almost as hard as a woman's now. In a way that is very provocative."

Perion held his tongue for a few moments; but when he spoke, anger bubbled below the surface of his words. "Atina, on Earth this same problem occurred many times. Finally there people decided that a person's sex was of less importance than the person's worth as an individual. I've tried to prove that to you."

"You prove it by doing woman's work?"

The fury in him boiled over. "Why should sailing a ship be woman's work, any more than making a decision should be a man's? Atina, *you* make decisions every day. You led the crew in the fight with the Aslandians. You are less of a woman for that?"

Atina made a sideways sweep of her hand, a gesture of negation. "My voyage was planned by the Council, who are under the direction of three of our island's men. I am instrument, not originator."

Perion struck the bulkhead with his fist. "In ancient history

on Earth, Atina, men did all the things that women do now.
They considered women too frail and weak to—"

Both Teyo and Atina cut him off with uproarious laughter.

"I'm sorry, Tom," Atina gasped at last. "You are a sly
joker."

"I do not see the joke," Perion muttered.

"To say that men could ever consider women weak!"

Teyo nodded. "Yes, that is the foolishness that makes us
laugh. Just look at men: their bodies are vulnerable, soft.
They carry their most tender parts exposed! They are clearly
constructed by nature for their roles as fathers and planners.
Their bodies are weak, their minds strong. Women are given
more muscle than men, more endurance than men—"

"Because of the work you do! You know your bodies grow
stronger with exercise. The same is true of men. Look at me!
Am I the same weakling you fished from the sea weeks ago?
I've grown stronger, tougher—"

Atina looked significantly at Teyo. Teyo, bent old Teyo,
wordlessly rose to her feet, pushed aside a short bench, and
approached Perion. She stopped an arm's length away and
held out her right hand, balled into a fist. She was offering a
form of arm-wrestling that Perion had seen the crew members
occasionally play at. The object was to put the opponent off
balance, to force her to take a step forward or back.

"You're an old woman," Perion objected.

"And a strong young man should be able to best her. By
your reasoning, Lord Tom Perion," Atina said.

Perion clamped his lips and set his jaw in a determined
way. If this was what it took to be listened to . . .

He extended his own arm and grasped Teyo's fingers with
his own hooked fingers. He began to pull. The sinews in
Teyo's arms corded beneath the flesh. She leaned against his
pull. Craftily, he suddenly pushed forward, but she rode with
him, stopped his motion, countered. Perion pulled again,
grinding his teeth. It was like trying to uproot a tree, but he
felt a yielding.

He squinted into Teyo's eyes, blank and depthless. Sweat
trickled down his face, stinging in the corners of his own
eyes. "Sorry, Teyo," he said between clenched teeth, and
put his back into a final herculean heave.

He might as well have tried to topple a mountain by

spitting on it. To his astonishment, he felt the leverage shift, felt his *own* arm being drawn forward, until—

With a lurch, he took a stumbling step forward. Teyo dropped his hand, backed away. Atina laughed, not derisively but delightedly, as though he had staged the whole charade for her private amusement.

Perion palmed the sweat from his forehead and stalked out of the cabin. He could already foresee the difficulties he would face with the Council. He hoped that he could think of some way of convincing *them* of his value as a person; or at least that he could keep from being thrown to the floor by them.

In his own cabin, Perion flung himself into his bunk. Teyo's copybook lay beneath his mattress pad, a flat splinter marking his place. He opened the book, jammed the splinter between his teeth, and chewed it as he began again to read.

DISOBEDIENCE, PUNISHMENT, AND WOE

(From the Copybook of Teyo da-Theslo, Teacher)

Now, after Kalea had brought her daughters to the new world she had shaped from song, they grew impatient to possess it; and they begged Kalea to allow them to walk on its islands, and to swim in its waters.

So Kalea caused a deep sleep to come upon her daughters, and placed their sleeping spirits in seeds; and these seeds she scattered over the face of the waters, and the ones that fell nearest the islands came to rest upon land. From these sprang the Homereach peoples, the first to awaken on the shores of the new world.

But the daughters of the enemies of Kalea had followed when she lifted the tower into the air and changed it to a Sailing Star. Some of these evil ones had clung to the ship as it made its way across the ocean of darkness; and now they, too, fell to the sea and to the islands; and they bore no love for Kalea or for her kindred.

At first the daughters of Kalea found delight in their new home. Then the trees bore abundance of fruit without cultivation, the sun did not flee for part of the year, leaving the world cold and rainy, and the animals of the land and the water lived in harmony with each other. All was delight and happiness.

But the daughters of Kalea watched the animals live their simple lives, and wondered. For they saw that the beasts had not one kind, as did they, but three. For each beast there was a seed-father and an egg-mother and a body-mother; and only when the three came together was it possible for young to be born. And the daughters of Kalea wondered at this, and they spoke to Kalea (for she sometimes in those days visited her kindred), saying, "Mother, why are we not made as the animals? Why are we all daughters, with no sons or body-mothers to share our burdens and our joys?"

And Kalea laughed her golden laugh, and said, "The animals are not whole. Each is alive, but each is only one part of a larger life. You, my daughters, are whole; and you have souls that are whole. You are perfect in yourselves, and need no partners; as for your burdens, what are they? The shadows of clouds that flit across the sea, to make you love the more the sparkling sunlight. No, my daughters, you are whole; you need no completion."

But the spirits that had come unbidden into the world heard, and watched, and waited their chance. And when one of Kalea's daughters, a woman named Avi, went one evening to watch the sun set on the waters, Satha came to her. Satha was a demon-spirit, one of the daughters of Ertha, and very cunning; and she hid her shape, so that she seemed a ribbonfish, and came in that guise.

"Kalea deceives you," the ribbonfish said to Avi.

"How can she deceive us?" Avi asked. "For she is our mother, and we are of her."

"Still."

"In what way are we deceived?"

"The animals have pleasure you know nothing of. In

their matings, they find joy. This joy Kalea has known—for have you ever seen a body-mother bring forth any young, unless she has received the egg from the egg-mother and the seed from the seed-father? So Kalea must have joyed, long ago. But the pleasure is keen, and worthy, she thinks, of Goddesses only; and so she keeps you ignorant.''

Now, Avi was curious, and said, "What is this pleasure like?''

And Satha the cunning replied, ''It is like starlight on the waves. It is like the breath of the flaming mountain. It is like the heat of the sun, and the chill of the ocean. It is the smell of growing things and the laughter of happiness. How should one describe a sunrise to the blind?''

And Avi lingered long, until the moon had climbed into the sky, and whispered to Satha of these and other things; and at last Satha said, "There is one other reason that Kalea hides the truth from you.''

"What is the reason?" asked Avi, for now she half believed the deceiving Satha.

"Look to the sky,'' said Satha. "Do you see there the Sailing Star?''

"Yes, O Satha. One can often see it at night.''

"Can you return to the Sailing Star?''

"No, O Satha. We cannot fly through the air, as Kalea can.''

"You see what she has done. She has put you here, that she may abandon you when she wishes. You are toys to her; nothing but playthings. And when she tires, she will leave you.''

And Avi sprang to her feet. "How can we stop this?''

"You must learn the ways of the animals. For when you, too, know the pleasure and the joy, you will bring forth young; and they will be many. So many will they be that you may when you wish overpower Kalea; and when she is forced to give you all of her secrets, then you will be as Goddesses yourself.''

So spoke Satha, and so believed Avi. Now, when Avi came back among the daughters, she crept here and there, and found some that believed the tale of Satha; and these were the eighth part of the people.

These daughters met in secret, under the shadows of the trees. They tried to emulate the animals, with one playing the part of seed-father, and one of egg-mother, and one of body-mother; and indeed they found pleasure and sport, but all was baseless and vain, for they were not made as animals, but as humans.

And as the sun rose, they became aware of one in their presence, and that one was Kalea. They shrank away from the Goddess, for they were conscious of having done wrong; not from their play, but from their having wished to become as she was, and more powerful than she.

"My daughters," she said with sorrow mingled together with her wrath, "what do you wish?"

And Avi, thrust forward by the others, stood first on one foot, then on the other, and said, "Mother, we wish to have children."

"Then your souls must be splintered," Kalea said.

"If that is what it takes," Avi said.

Kalea raised her voice in a bitter song. "Go to the shore," she told the daughters. "There you will find the seeds of sleep. From them will grow men—but they will always be a care to you, and a problem for you, and a desire for you. Much pleasure they will bring you, but the pleasure will be paid for with much pain. I will give you one boon, because you are my daughters: and this it shall be. You will not be like the animals. You will need only two kinds to bring forth young, a father and a body-mother. Thus your souls are sundered only, and not shattered; but even sundered, they can never return to the Sailing Star while your bodies still hold them."

And Kalea was vanished from their midst. Timidly, by ones and twos, the erring daughters crept to the seashore; and there they found the seeds, and from the seeds grew men, one for each erring daughter.

But when the other daughters of Kalea discovered what had happened, they grew jealous of those who had sinned, wrongly thinking that they had gained a blessing; and they insisted that the men be shared among them. So they all tasted of pleasure, and so they all became worthy of Kalea's anger.

Now, when the fullness of time had come, and the daughters began to labor to give birth, they felt pain for the first time in their lives; and they cried out in fear and agony.

But the Sailing Star sailed on unheeding, for this was the price they had to pay. And since that day, men have been among us, always too few and always a trouble to us; and in men we see a part of our own souls, and we yearn to repossess it; but Kalea will not permit this, until the world is overturned and the order of things is changed.

And so men came into the world, an imagined reward, but an actual punishment; and we must suffer them until Kalea wills otherwise.

Chapter 7

Nights of wind, rain, and lightning; days of plunging drops down sheer-sided waves, water washing down the companionways, cold food, weariness.

Perion astounded the crew by taking his own turn at the sheets, at the helm, relieving those so exhausted by the storm that they had to stagger below for a few minutes of sleep. Captain Theslo refused to allow him aloft, but she tolerated his eccentricity in other matters, for she was anxious to return to Home before the Aslandian ship could send a delegation looking for her. At times Perion thought of the Aslandian lords—such as when a suddenly tautening rope raised blisters on his palms, while a breaking sea stung his eyes and all but drowned him. Oh, yes, he thought of the lords then, and of the two snug cabins they occupied amidships; but he kept his opinions to himself.

At last the winds died to fitful gusts, then to a steady, fresh breeze that swept away the rack of cloud. Atina called Perion to her cabin one morning to thank him for his help and to ask him now, seeing that they were nearing their home port, to *please* try to act more like a man.

Perion smiled and agreed; but as he turned to leave, a chart on Atina's table caught his eye. He gestured at it. "I might have a look?"

"If you wish. It is a good chart. The former owner of the *Windbird* commissioned a full set."

Atina explained the mechanics of the projection, insofar as she understood them. Perion looked at the whole set, pieced them together, frowning, and at last looked up at Atina. "There is much land to the north," he said.

"Yes. The Edge. And Aslandia, of course, with the Aladian Islands to the south."

"If the maps are correct, the land is everywhere—it goes right around the world."

"It is the Edge of things." Atina laughed. "What else should it do?"

What else. Except for the Aslandian peninsula, Atina explained, the Edgelands were poorly charted, for they were the abode of beasts and barbarians and were seldom visited. Still, from studying the sketched outlines, Perion thought he could see that the globe-girdling continent was more likely at least three separate continents, driven together by tectonic forces. If the plates were subtending in a generally southerly direction, that would build mountains along the southern rim of land. The mountains would wring moisture from the sea winds, and beyond them would be—

"Desert," Perion said. "Where it's impossible to stand beneath the sun. Oh, my God."

"What?" asked Atina.

"Nothing. I just—a thought, that's all. Tell me, if you keep sailing south, do you come to a place of great cold?"

"If you sail very far. Sometimes, it is said, you sail so far to the south that you leave the sun behind. But that is a far journey, and few make it. The cold is oppressive, and strange sea creatures grow there, dangerous beasts."

Tom began to replace the charts. This hemisphere, then, had a cold sink to generate weather, though his observations told him that the planet's axial tilt was small, between four and five degrees as opposed to Earth's twenty-three and a half degrees. The Arctic and Antarctic Circles would be tiny; but the tropics would be very close to the equator, and that implied many things.

Perion mentally sketched in this picture of Kalea, and found it after all not so alien: at one time in Earth's geologic past all the landmasses had been jammed together in one hemisphere. If the *Galileo* had happened onto Kalea a hundred million years in the past or future, it probably would have found a world comfortably "normal" by human standards. But it hadn't. . . .

Atina stroked his beard, snapping him out of his reverie. "Sorry," she said as he started.

"It's all right. I guess I'm just not used to being touched so much."

"Then stay out of the marketplaces in Shelda Bay," Atina

laughed. "You will be surrounded by women on every side—and touched in more, ah, *interesting* ways, when no Teacher is looking."

"I'll try to protect my virtue," Perion said dryly.

"When you get your harem, bearers will carry you in a closed litter if you wish. Most men travel that way to avoid being bothered by hands or comments. Until then—well, if the Council will permit, I will guide you through your first few weeks with us."

"Thank you."

"You will try, won't you?" Atina said earnestly.

"I will try to do what?"

"To behave normally. At least until the Council have determined your status. It means a great deal to me, Tom."

Perion tried to evade: "I have my own problems, Atina." He looked at her dark eyes, her determined expression. "You believe me, don't you?"

She tilted her head. "I don't know what to believe. It seems plain that you are no ordinary man. And yet to accept the ancient stories as fact, to see the Sailing Star as an actual ship—well, I *cannot* accept that. But I am interested in you, Tom. And I like that foolish growth on your face." She tugged his beard painfully. "You know, I've thought of asking the Council to give you to me. They have done that before, allowing a Captain to take one of her captures to another island, eventually, for prestige and for political advantage. But that's still in the future." She reached to caress his face, and Perion felt her hard palm, curiously cool and gentle, on his cheek. He leaned toward her. She parted her lips.

And Kayla chose that moment to bang open the cabin door. Both Atina and Perion snapped upright; but Kayla, excited, had taken no note of them. "Land!" she shouted. "Land ahead!"

"Thank the Goddess," Atina said. Perion followed her out and up to the deck.

The land was not much—a remote sharp-pointed dot on the horizon ahead and to port. The bow was crowded with the crew, chattering excitedly. "Is that it?" Perion yelled at Atina's ear.

"That is Westpeak," she said. "It is an outpost of

Homereaches. We will be in port in five days now, with a good wind and fair sailing.''

"Will we put in there?"

"No," Atina replied. "We have neither need nor authorization. Besides, the women of Westpeak are on the fringes of Council authority. With such prizes as ours on board, we could arouse greed on their part and danger on ours. I didn't take lords from the Aslandians to give to the Westrons."

"You don't seem to have a high regard for your fellow Homereachers."

Lito, on the edges of the group, looked in his direction. "The Westrons have a poor land," she explained. "They scratch the soil, till the sea, and live miserably huddled along the one waterway the island gives them. They have almost no timber, a tiny fleet. Who would want to be exiled to Westpeak?"

"Lito speaks truly," Atina said. "Take my advice, Tom. If the Council decide to send you to a remote island, beg them not to send you to Westpeak."

Perion grunted. Several times that day he was on deck, watching the island swell green and peaked in the sunlight. They passed it to the south, and from a distance of perhaps ten kilometers Perion admired the green-flocked living sides of the mountain, the exposed outcroppings of black bare rock, and in one wonderful deep glen the silvery ribbon of a waterfall. Teyo joined him at the rail, silent and remote as usual, and he gave her a glance. "The island is volcanic," he said.

"I do not know the word."

"It is—a burning mountain," he said.

"Yes. Most islands are," Teyo said, her voice arching in faint surprise.

"Home?"

"Home has two of these burning mountains in the far north. The Sisters, they are called: Kala and Akala. There are other peaks on the island, five other large ones, and these look as if once long ago they too burned. But they slumber now."

"I look forward to seeing the island," Perion said.

Teyo stood at his side until finally he pushed away and went down to his cabin.

*   *   *

After a few moments, Teyo made her way back to the tiller, where Atina herself stood a tour, guiding the ship easily around the shallows on this side of Westpeak. Atina gave her a grim smile. "You think it will work?" she asked.

"I do not know," Teyo confessed. "If Perion will agree to act the part of a barbarian, and if the Council do not question him too closely, it might. But sooner or later, he *will* tell his tale."

"By that time, I shall be far away, and a harema. It will be no matter then."

"I am troubled, Atina, clan-sister."

"I am not happy myself," Atina said wryly. "But you and I know that the Aslandians will not suffer the death he caused lightly. They will come for me. The Council will protect me and will forbid the hunt if I am a harema; if I am not, then none of my crew will be safe. I, too, hate to cast Tom Perion away, but I do not know what else to do. We must convince him that his best hope is in gaining acceptance from the Council; then his failure or success is in his own hands."

"He trusts you."

"So do my crew. If it were I alone, I would stand by Tom, with all his foolishness and his wild tales. But I have others to think of, Teyo."

From the watchtree, high up the mainmast, Lito's clear voice called their notice to a sail astern. Both Teyo and Atina shaded their eyes against the hot glare of the westering sun and sought the sail. They had it at last, to port and far behind.

"Only a fishing vessel," Atina said. "But one day it will be an Aslandian runner, seeking my blood."

"If it comes to that, I will stand with you, clan-sister."

"I thank you for offering what was not asked." Atina sighed. "Things were so simple when I set out on this journey," she said. "I would find some men, bring them to the Council, and gain permission to marry. It was straightforward. But Tom Perion is a complication, a worry. He makes me see the world as if I stood on my head; he turns the old truths inside out, like a hastily stripped garment."

"He makes me think," Teyo said. "And I am not sure that all the thoughts are wrong ones. There are prophecies—"

"Spare me."

"You will believe," Teyo said. "One day you will believe." She turned and shuffled off, a tired old woman on a hot day, her bare feet making a small swishing sound, like a rock serpent gliding through leaves. Atina watched her go.

And when she was alone, Atina said to herself, "Goddess help me, I fear that one day I *may* believe."

Below, Perion had taken to his bunk at about the time Teyo left Atina. He, too, was looking ahead—to the Council, to their power over him, to the best ways to let them know that he was what he said. He did not want to finish his days on Kalea by being given to an Atina or—he shuddered—to a Selridir as a house pet. But he still lacked perspective, information, leverage. He had read widely in Teyo's copybook, and almost as widely in the microvolumes his dataset offered on anthropology; but they were scant help.

He puzzled through the problem until Kayla brought his dinner; and as he ate the meal, he spoke with her. She had the easy assurance and unfailing cheer of a girl well on the way to becoming a woman, and she loved to chatter. He put her on the subject of the five Aslandian males, and as she talked, he began to formulate a plan. He thanked her as she took his tray; and then he lay back on the bunk, waiting for darkness.

When it came, he went up again, and stepped onto a deck washed in the cold light of the stars and the minuscule moon, halfway to zenith and nearly full. Ahead, in the shadows of the bow, a face, moon-pale, glimmered at him. A soft, throaty voice challenged: "Who?"

"Tom Perion. Is that Jana?"

In the dark he felt rather than saw her relax; but he sensed, too, that even in her relaxation there was a curious bowstring tension. "Jana, yes."

Perion drew near enough to smell the clovery scent of the woman. She was a younger member of the crew, hardly out of her teens by Earth standards. "You have a quiet watch?" Perion asked.

She sighed. "Too quiet, too dull." She lowered her voice to a querulous near-whisper. "What does Captain Theslo expect in home waters, anyway? Sela is up there"—the moonlit chin jerked to a figure high overhead, in the watchtree—"to spot shoals or other ships. I have nothing to watch for."

Perion made a sympathetic noise. Jana quartered a guest in her cabin tonight, one of the captured Aslandians, and she had waited long for the opportunity. "Who else is entertaining?" he asked.

"No one." Jana's voice was peevish. "They've all had their turns. The cabingirl is too young, and the Captain will not participate. I'm the last one on rotation. Four of the lords are still in their cabin; and mine might as well be with them."

Perion waited for a moment. Jana had confirmed the information Kayla had thoughtlessly given him, and he was glad to see that his estimation of Jana's frustrated sense of injured privilege was near the mark. Casually, he said at last, "Well, at least you have a choice—being last, I mean. Which?"

"There is no other choice for me," Jana said. "Dilbosk, the tall one. What children he could give a mate!"

"You come from a family of many sisters?"

"Seven of them," Jana said. "And I the youngest. But four of us have become haremas in the last five years. And now, with the men we bring back, the Council will allow me to marry, too."

"But you will not be able to choose which harem?"

A note of resigned regret crept into Jana's voice: "No. The Captain may gain that right, and perhaps two or three others she may name to the Council. But as for me, the Council will decide, and I'm sure they'll put me on some out-of-the-way rock with a wheezing, infertile old stump of a husband."

"It isn't right," Perion said.

"No. But that is how sisters of many sisters are treated."

Perion let their conversation float on the soft air for a few moments. Then he said, "Well, I can certainly understand your choosing Dilbosk. A fine figure of a man, from all I hear."

Jana's eyes almost sparkled in the night. "He is! He is! Oh, wouldn't it be wonderul if he gave me a child on our first night together!"

"Wonderful," Perion agreed. "But he will hardly have time. Your watch ends, when—moonhigh? —and by then both you and Dilbosk will be tired. Too bad you can't go to him now, when both of you would enjoy it so much."

"Don't speak of it."

The wind slackened, then freshened again. The ropes creaked, the canvas made a plopping sound, and Perion thought he could smell a spicy fragrance, the heady scent of land. He stretched elaborately and yawned. "I wish you luck when your watch ends. If Captain Theslo wishes to make all headway for Home tomorrow, your time with Dilbosk may be cut very short indeed."

Jana groaned.

As if the idea had just then come to him from the warm, tree-scented night, Perion asked, "You could, could you not, exchange your duties for those of a friend?"

"If I had a friend kind enough," Jana said. "But you know how they are when you're close to home, and when you're eager for a favor. They like to tease."

"Wait. *I* could take watch for you."

The silence went on so long that Perion feared she had tumbled to his trickery. But she spoke at last, uncertainly: "I don't know. Captain Theslo—"

"Oh, really," Perion chuckled. "You worry about Atina? Why, she and I are friends. You know that in the storm she let me do every other job on board. But if you fear, she need never know about this little favor. You could go below now, enjoy your time with Dilbosk, and just before moonhigh come above again to meet your relief."

Silence again. Sensing Jana's hesitation, Perion added smoothly, "They say that the full moon is a good time to try to conceive male children."

"I have never heard that."

"We all believe it where I come from."

Jana's face tilted as she looked at the moon. "I would have a quarter of the night. That is a good, comfortable time. You would not mind this?"

"I am sleepless tonight. Go. Dilbosk will be grateful if you do."

Jana gave Perion a comradely pat on the bottom. "You are almost like a woman, Lord Perion. I thank you. Anytime I can help you—"

"Don't be silly. Along with you now, and quietly."

"I will be in the cabin Selridir and I share. It is the port cabin amidships."

"Go quietly, then, and make your way back quietly. And be silent with Dilbosk, too—as silent as possible. We don't want the Captain to hear your joy."

Jana giggled—it struck Perion that a woman's giggle was something he had not heard for a long, long time—and ghosted away in the darkness. Perion took up his post in the

bow and turned his gaze seaward. Empty ocean stretched to
the horizon, touched with the silver glimmer and sparkle of
moonstruck waves. The ship rocked along, creaking content-
edly on a light sea, with the sails easily filling from the mild
following wind. It was a fine night with good visibility and a
clear sky. A silver-blue meteor etched its way across the
ship's path, from right to left: a good omen, according to
some members of the crew.

Perion had stood there for perhaps twenty minutes when a
voice from the watchtree came: "The Sailing Star!"

Perion pitched his voice high, made it breathy: "Ah!" He
hoped the lookout wouldn't demand a more drawn-out
conversation.

She did not, and he watched the stately, brilliant progress
of the *Galileo*, a moonlet just three hundred kilometers above
where he stood, but to him almost totally inaccessible. His
communicator could establish only the most fitful connection,
inevitably just good enough to produce an in-range signal but
not enough to convey information. If the pod had not sunk,
he could, under especially good conditions, have established
communication with the shipboard computer; but the pod and
its equipment were gone, and Perion glumly watched the spark
gutter as it descended the southern curve of the sky and sank
beyond the rim of the world.

Then, judging that Dilbosk and Jana were by now suffi-
ciently occupied, Perion made his way to the forward hatch—
guarding that hatch was also one of the lookout's duties—and
descended the companionway.

He passed the galley, heard snores from the crew quarters,
and made his way back to the cabins occupied by the
Aslandians. He listened at the starboard door and heard nothing but the creaking of the ship's timbers; but when he
pressed his ear against the port door, he heard, unmistakably,
the low mutter of masculine conversation. Quickly he un-
bolted the door and stepped inside, gesturing for silence.

The Aslandians, sitting knee to knee around a game board
painted with green, orange, and yellow triangles, threw him a
look of astonishment, then passed a similar look around
among themselves. One of them—he was winning the game,
to judge from the pile of copper coins beside his elbow—
said, "The barbarian. We wondered how long it would take
you to make your way here."

The language was Common, the intonation rolling, with open vowels, half-trilled r's, and a delicate flutter of pitch at the end of phrases. Perion stood with his back against the door, for this cabin, like all he had seen, was small, crowded with three bunks and the central table. The hanging lamps swung gently back and forth. "You expected me?" Perion asked.

The man who had spoken—pale, like the others, with long, sensitive fingers, a lean, long-nosed face, and a sweep of jet hair above two sea-blue eyes—raked another three coins to his side of the board. "Of course," he said. "These women have talked of nothing but you the whole voyage in. They find you a most excellent curiosity."

One of the other three lords, an indolent-looking man who wore a layer of fat with a kind of self-satisfied air of accomplishment, drawled softly, "Where did you find your clothing? I have never seen material like that."

Perion had worn his uniform. He made a gesture of negation. "It is not important. And it is a long story. But you'll understand when—"

The second man turned to the dark-haired one and said, "Trennon, I don't suppose you would drop out of the game? Our barbarian here might like to play. I'd like to play him, for a chance of winning that outfit."

Trennon smiled and made a slow flipping movement with his right hand. It was a slightly rude refinement of the "no" gesture he had given earlier. Trennon looked back at Perion. "I suppose I should introduce us all. I am Trennon Fane, formerly destined to be lord of Siddhia. My companions are Yannow Tully"—this was the indolent man, auburn-haired and double-chinned—"Varr Sask, and Marzon Kant." Perion made mental notes: Sask was short, dour-looking, with shoulder-length brown hair done in elaborate crisscrossing ribbons, Kant a muscular figure with close-set eyes and reddish-brown hair that fell in short curls over his forehead.

"Our fifth member"—Trennon smiled—"is Dilbosk Otho, but he is elsewhere. And your name is Tom Perion?"

"Yes," Perion said. "I suppose you have heard of how I came to be on the ship?"

"Only that you were picked up at sea—with no one to fight for you, evidently." Tully, Sask, and Kant chuckled at

Trennon's jape, and Trennon himself smiled broadly. "But outside of that, your origin seems a mystery to the crew."

"It is," Perion said. Of the whole crew, only Atina and Teyo had heard in full his tale of having dropped from the stars, and they were not the two to spread rumors. "Let me give you the whole story."

Quickly he filled them in, leaving out nothing important. The four men—Sask and Kant had hitched their stools around so they could look at him too—listened with widening eyes and occasionally exchanged knowing glances. "The ship, the *Galileo*, is still there," Perion finished. "It's what you call the Sailing Star. And also aboard are my friends. With them and the *Galileo*'s equipment, any man could become the lord of all Kalea."

The four men burst into laughter. Trennon flipped one of the small coppers at Perion; he snatched it from the air inches from his face. "Payment for the story," Trennon explained. "Did Atina Theslo send you here tonight to entertain us, fearing we would be bored at the end of rotation?"

Perion felt his face growing hot. "It's true."

Yannow Tully leaned closer to Fane. "Look at him. I think he believes it," he murmured.

Trennon lifted an eyebrow. "You *do* believe it?"

"Because it is true," Perion insisted. "You can see the Sailing Star with your own eyes. You know the stories about it, the legends."

Kant waved a stubby-fingered hand, dispelling the smoke of myth. "But the legends are just that—legends, pure and simple. We Aslandians recognize that; at least the educated ones do. It's the benighted Homereachers who persist in that outworn theology."

"You believe the Sailing Star is not a ship?" Perion challenged.

Kant looked at Trennon, tugged at a lock of his reddish hair, and said, "We know it as a natural satellite of this world. Our astronomers have determined that it shines by reflected sunlight, like Lun, the moon. It happens to be smaller and closer than Lun. And it is getting closer still as the years pass."

"What?"

Kant looked at Trennon again, as though seeking aid.

"Fane, do you know any of the details of this? I was never much good with natural philosophy. Boring subject."

Trennon rested his blue-eyed gaze on Perion. "I know a little about the subject, yes. Our observers have noted that the Sailing Star's passage has grown faster over about a century. The theory is that eventually it will plunge into the ocean, when it gains enough speed to overcome the lift of the atmosphere—"

"What?"

Trennon blinked. "It is upheld by air, just as birds and clouds are. Oh, look, you didn't come here to lecture us on science, or to be lectured by us. You will join our game?"

Perion closed his eyes, deliberately and slowly. "No, thank you." When he opened his eyes again, the four were still there. "I came to offer you all a chance of escape," he said.

Trennon coughed, Kant spluttered, and the sour, slight Sask said in a thin voice, "Escape from what, you madman?"

"You're captives. Would you not like to return to your own lands?"

"Why?" demanded Trennon.

"To be with your families," Perion said. "Your harems."

Trennon flipped his hand. "We have none. We have been trained in the arts of lordship, but have not yet practiced them. In fact, we were on our way to our assigned domains when your Captain took us. You know nothing of these affairs? You have perhaps lost your memory?"

"Lost his member, more likely," said Tully. "Look at him. He's brown as a bride."

Perion leaned against the door, felt its splintered surface hard and real at his back. "Tell me if I'm wrong. I thought the Homereachers were at war with the Aslandians."

"They are. Have been for ages."

"Then you've been captured by your enemies?"

"Oh, really, this is too much," growled Kant. "We are men, even as you are. This war, all war, has nothing to do with us."

"Marzon is right," said Trennon. "Men are above politics, Tom; surely you know that. We take our wisdom and serve where we are needed. Nature has given our sex a purpose that transcends territorial disputes and squabbles."

"So you will now become lords of Homereaches?"

"Of course we will. Their need for us is shown by our

presence on this ship. And once there, we will serve to the best of our abilities—correct, men?" A round of lusty chuckles seconded Trenon.

Perion's head began to ache. "And if in the future by chance the Aslandians should recapture you—"

"We would follow our destinies. We would return to our own people and do the work we were created for. You see, our Teachers reason that men are selected by nature. This occasional redirecting of geography is part of a mechanism to improve the species." Trennon launched forth into a sort of garbled Darwinism.

Perion broke in. "Wait, wait. You despise the Homereachers for superstition and theology. You have your own beliefs, your own sort of fatalism. Surely in its way it is just as bad?"

Kant growled deep in his throat, but Trennon lifted a silencing finger. "We count among our ancestors Jansmeet and his followers. They had one goal: to pursue the path of knowledge, of science, of gathering wisdom about the world and all in it. We have kept their dream alive in Aslandia. The Homereachers have allowed it to falter. Perion, I do not know what ails you, but be warned: we do not look kindly on one who derides our pursuit of knowledge."

Perion clenched his teeth. "All right. I'm sorry. I apologize. But tell me this. In your history, you have stories of how Jansmeet explored the northern lands?"

"He and his followers did try that on two occasions," Trennon acknowledged. "Jansmeet perished on the first try, the one that first circumnavigated the globe. The second was a generation later, and it proved that the northern lands are uninhabitable. There one cannot stand beneath the sun. The world, you see, is like a ball floating in the ocean of space. The sun hovers high in the air over the center of that ball. As you come closer and closer to the center, you approach the sun more nearly, until finally life itself becomes impossible."

Perion shook his head. "This is your science? I suppose you men would not be interested in seizing a ship and returning to your homeland?"

They laughed again, as though Perion had been leading up the whole time to this excellent joke. "No, Tom," Trennon said firmly. "We could never find the women to sail the ship, for one thing—"

"We could sail it ourselves."

Kant stood up, deliberately and slowly, his hands clenched. "You may be a bearded woman," he said, danger rumbling in his voice, "but you will not spread your perversions to us. Get out of here, or I'll call a woman to deal with you."

Perion went back on deck feeling drained. In the bows he held onto a line and stared at the sea and the sky. Lun was very nearly at zenith when Jana came quietly up behind him. Standing close to her, Perion could feel the radiated warmth of her skin, could sense the loose contentment of muscle and flesh in her, like that of a cat resting before a fire.

"It was wonderful," she whispered to him. "Thank you, Tom. Dilbosk thanks you, too. He is eager for my return." Her laughter ran lightly in the soft air of the night. "I judged correctly. He is well trained and skilled. With any luck, I may present my own lord with one of Dilbosk's children. Think what favor that would bring."

"Oh, yes," Perion said. "There's no more manly blood anywhere than in those Aslandians."

Jana reached to ruffle his hair. "You have the soul of a woman, Lord Tom Perion."

Perion smiled in the darkness. "This must be my night for compliments. This is the second time I've heard that one."

"It is not an empty compliment," Jana protested. "I really mean it."

"Thank you."

On the way aft, Perion realized that he still held in his hand the small copper coin Trennon had thrown to him. Viciously he hurled it over the rail, into the quartering wind. The wind caught and boomeranged it, and Perion heard its sharp *click* as it hit the deck somewhere behind him. Just my luck, he thought grimly to himself. Everything is going to be back-asswards from now on.

Chapter 8

They raised Home Island early in the forenoon of the fifth day after Perion's interview with the Aslandians. Perion, restless enough to be adventurous and rebellious, climbed to the watchtree for a look. The island was not large by Earth standards—he was reminded of the Hawaiians—but it was the most land he had seen since coming to the surface of Kalea.

Atina planned to pass the island on its northern side, and by doing so she gave Perion a good view of Akala and Kala, the Sisters, two domed volcanoes. A plume of steam drifted from Akala, the southeasternly peak. Her larger northern sister slumbered peacefully. The island was mountainous, with each volcanic peak falling away to ridges and valleys, the valleys deep-shaded in the morning light, the ridges rich and green. Far to the south, the valleys were terraced, with brighter green patches—estate farms, Teyo explained—shining like jewels.

As the *Windbird* rounded the tip of the island, a stretch of open water heavily dotted with other vessels came into view. The craft seemed endless in both number and variety: Perion saw everything from two-person canoes to three-masted merchant ships plying the waters, and every vessel seemed to be crewed exclusively by women. Perion moved to starboard as the *Windbird* nosed southward, and leaning on the rail he watched a good stretch of forest slide by.

"Preserves of the Council," Teyo informed him. "Trees are farmed there. They furnish the lumber and the blackwood for our ships."

They drew even nearer, and now Perion could see the houses that sprinkled the island, gleaming white for the most part, and all capped with red tile roofs. They clung to the ridges and overlooked the cultivated, terraced fields in between. Seen from this distance, the island had an intricate geometric beauty, as though it had been put together from a jigsaw kit of greens, yellows, browns, reds, and other hues.

Ahead the island split: a waterway led southwestward, defined by black volcanic cliffs tens of meters high and crowned with apparently wild vegetation. This was the Larapé, a central rift that nearly split the island in two and provided the catch basin for six of the island's largest rivers. Their goal lay around the projecting eastward point that marked the lower lip of the Larapé, in a sheltered bay that opened directly to the sea.

"Headwater is there," Teyo said, nodding down the narrow stretch of the Larapé. "It is the principal city of the island, and the Grand Council meets there. The Island Council, though, will meet in Shelda Bay."

They passed farther south and saw Easthaven, a city clustered at the knees of a low, dead volcano; then they cleared another point, and Atina ordered the sails adjusted as they prepared to tack into port almost against the prevailing wind.

Perion was charmed. The waters of Shelda Bay gleamed brilliantly in the early sun. The bay itself was shaped, he saw, like a key with a rounded head. The shaft of the key lay northeastward, and jammed into the open sea as a key would fit a lock; the broad head was the bay itself, ringed with buildings and bristling, at the edges, with stone piers.

The bay was alive with shipping. Teyo touched his shoulder as the *Windbird* eased past an outbound merchant vessel. "Lord Perion, it is time for you to return to your cabin, as you agreed."

With a last look at the island, Perion pushed away from the rail and followed the priestess. Teyo waited for him at the aft companionway. "I will prepare the way for transporting you to the Council," she said. "They will meet at the end of the month, not long from now. Until then you and the lords will be quartered in a place of rest that belongs to Atina's family. You will find it pleasant."

Perion went below, but he pulled his stool over and stood on it, staring out his port as the ship neared the dock. The waterfront was a cluster of buildings, some white, some dark volcanic stone, a few frame buildings painted a variety of pastel colors. They all stood practically on the water, and from them stone piers and wooden wharves thrust into the harbor like the fingers of a giant.

Ships were berthed at many, and all along the waterfront bustled throngs of women, loading or unloading vessels, inspecting stacks of piled cargo, or perhaps just loitering. Here and there squatted a beggar, and once Perion saw a sudden commotion as though some local excitement—a pickpocket, perhaps—had momentarily disturbed the flow of the crowd, creating an eddy.

The *Windbird* glided into a dock, lines hissed overhead, and Perion found himself looking at the stone pilings of a pier.

Perion sat at the table, drummed his fingers, looked at the small wooden chest that held all his goods—the exosuit and boots, the clothing the sailmaster had fashioned for him (he wore, now, the formal outfit he had worn to his first meal with Atina), the datakit and communicator, Teyo's book. From overhead came the rumble and clatter of unloading, the buzz of feminine chatter, and once an outburst of delighted yelps and shrieks and laughter—the women on the wharf had, he surmised, just found out the Aslandian triumph.

Perion paced the cabin. At last he lay on the bunk, hands locked behind his head. The heat finally lulled him into a light drowse. He lingered for some time in the delightful state in which he could, to some extent, direct his dreams. He saw himself entering the city, explaining to the Council, winning their support, reestablishing the link to *Galileo*, and being hailed as the savior of the colony.

A hand roughly shook him out of his imagination. "Come, Tom," Atina said. "Time to move."

He got up, reached for the chest containing his possessions, and found that a grinning Kayla already carried it. He followed Atina to the deck.

The four Aslandian lords he had met, plus a broad-shouldered, wavy-haired brunet he presumed to be Dilbosk Otho, waited in a loose group. They nodded formally to him as he joined them.

"Lord Perion has been told that he will not speak overmuch to you," Atina said without prelude. "He has agreed. You will help him by not questioning him."

"Agreed," drawled the plump Yannow Tully. "A barbarian has no conversation worth listening to, anyway." The others snickered at the sally, and Perion calmly resolved to hit Tully hard when the chance best presented itself.

"My crew have cleared the wharf. A carriage will take you to the House of Waiting, where handmaidens will see to your needs and make you presentable. Teyo has sent a request to the Council to deliberate about your cases when they next meet, in seven days' time. I must file my voyage log with the harbormaster. Tomorrow, or at the latest the next day, I shall see you."

Kayla had taken Perion's chest to the carriage; now she returned with the news that all was ready.

Perion turned to follow the others to the carriage, but Atina stopped him with a hand on his arm. "A word, Tom." She brushed back a strand of her black hair. "You will be lodged separately, as on the ship; but in the House of Waiting you will not need to sneak to the Aslandians' rooms to speak with them. But whatever you say to them, to the women in the house say nothing of your origin. Until the Council hearing, we are leaving it as a case of exposure and loss of memory. As far as anyone knows, you are a barbarian who was inexplicably swept to sea. Not a word, remember; you could put everything in danger if you speak too soon."

"I will keep quiet," Perion said, "if you will stand by me at the hearing and confirm as much of my story as you can."

"There is no bargain," she said, laughing. "for I would do as much in any case. Go now, Tom, and enjoy your stay in my family's House of Waiting. The handmaidens are professionals who have certain, ah, dispensations that we poor sailors lack. I envy them."

He looked into her dark, dark eyes. "You don't need to. You are far more beautiful than they could be. To me you are."

Spots of angry color appeared on her cheeks. "Don't behave that way! The last thing we want is for a handmaiden to appear in court to testify that you are—deviant. At least *try* to behave like a normal man for the next seven days!"

Perion sighed. "Very well."

"Go along now."

Perion found that a screen had been set up at the end of the wharf to cut him and the Aslandians off from the direct view of the women; but some peeked over and around, and he heard them assessing his appearance as he walked the wharf.

An elongated box of a coach, with six spoked wood wheels, waited for him. It was hitched to a chest-high four-legged

creature with the same kind of three-lobed mouth he had seen
on the eater. Perion stared at the beast, which wore wrinkled
gray-green skin and a dull expression on its short-snouted
face. The lines were not quite reptilian, not quite mammalian.

Kayla clucked at him. She held the coach door open and
gestured toward it. He hurried inside.

The windows had been glazed with what seemed to be
obsidian, and he had a distorted, creosote-colored view of the
crowded wharf, the narrow streets, and the swarming marketplaces. Four of the Aslandian lords sat on the forward-facing
seat, though they were cramped; Tully shared Perion's seat,
and he had moved as far from Perion as the tight confines of
the carriage would allow.

The carriage clattered slowly over rough-cobbled streets.
Smells of cooking, sweat, and strange foods filtered into the
carriage, and the afternoon sun stewed the mixture to nauseating ripeness. Still the six men rode in silence. Perion had the
impression that the route the carriage took, though winding,
trended upward. Gradually they left the sounds and smells of
the city. At length the carriage stopped, and a moment later
Kayla opened it.

Without ceremony, the five lords rose, stooping under the
low roof, and stepped over Perion's feet to descend. Perion
contrived with seeming innocence to move as though to make
the passage easier just as Tully stepped down. He caught the
Aslandian's ankle with his toe, and Tully tumbled forward,
landing sprawled in the dust.

Perion hopped lightly down from the coach and gave Tully
a hand up. "Bad luck!" he said, slapping the dust from the
Aslandian's clothes with energetic whaps. "You haven't got
your land legs back, old fellow."

Kayla gave him an angry "Shh!" and Tully added a
murderous glare. Then three slender young women came to
escort the lords inside a sprawling one-story plaster structure
with an elaborate red tile roof. Kayla said to Perion, "I will
stay until they come for you."

Perion nodded and looked around. He was in a square
enclosure, fifteen meters on a side, with the house forming
the rear of the square and three-meter-high walls the other
three sides. The carriage had passed through an arched opening in the wall opposite the house, an opening now closed by
a wooden gate shaped to fit it. Perion walked around the

carriage, his feet crunching in coarse black sand, and stopped near the beast that had drawn the vehicle. "What kind of animal is this?" he asked, running his gaze over the creature.

"We call them noxes," Kayla said. "They are bred for transport. They are stupid, but strong."

The nox placidly munched at tussocks of a ferny, low-growing plant, uprooting one now and again. It shook its head, scattering grains of sand, then with evident relish sucked the plant into its mouth. The three lobes ground busily together before each swallow. Perion asked, "I may touch it?"

"It is safe to touch. They eat only plants."

Perion patted the flank. The nox moved its neck to peer back at him with vacant interest, then returned to its grazing. The animal felt like a rubber bag full of pliant dough. "Seems cold-blooded," he said. "It has, ah, it does—" He broke off, groping for the Common phrase meaning "lay eggs," and discovered that he did not know it. "Its young are born in what way?"

"I do not understand."

"Are they—it bears its young like children?"

"Oh. Yes, they bear live young. But this one is an egg-mother. It would have to be mated with a male and a body-mother to breed, and this one is too old for that now."

A viviparous, trisexed, semireptilian creature with skin like a bald elephant's and no scales in evidence. But not reptilian at all, really. Another world's answer, ecologically, to the wild cattle of Earth.

Kayla said, "They wait. They are ready for you now."

Perion took a last look around the little enclosed yard. It was small enough to give him a mild feeling of claustrophobia. "Say farewell to Atina for me," he said.

"You will see her again," Kayla told him, and she hefted his luggage.

He found a handmaiden waiting for him at the door of the House of Waiting, a tall woman with a smile on her lips. Her name, it seemed, was Mela, and she was eight and a half years old (eighteen, Perion approximated mentally, taking appreciative note of the way her hips swayed as she walked ahead of him). She led him through a large open room thick with plants growing from cubical pottery containers into a corridor lined on either side with doors. They went to the

very end of the corridor, to the last door on the left, and
entered his quarters.

He was to have a large room (five meters by three, approx-
imately, but large in comparison to the cramped quarters of
the *Windbird*) as sleeping quarters, with an adjoining smaller
room for dining, a closet, and a small toilet with—surprise!
—running water, thanks to an ingenious arrangement of what
looked like fired-clay pipes.

From his bedroom a window, glazed with obsidian scales
set in an arched, leaded frame, looked out into another walled-in
space perhaps three times the size of the front yard, this one a
lush garden rich with flowering plants. Most were thick-
stemmed with greenish-purple leaves the size of his hand,
bearing orange starburst flowers, but there were lower shrubs
and a few trees, one spotted with tiny blue-and-white blooms
the size of his thumbnail. With the window swiveled open,
the garden scent drifted in, a sweet, slightly spicy odor that
was nearly cloying in its intensity. Birds—if you could call
black-and-green pseudoreptiles whose forelimbs had evolved
into functional wings *birds*—clattered and creaked and fluttered and snapped at pseudoinsects with their flexible three-
lobed beaks.

"It's very nice," Perion said. "A wonderful room. Thank
you, Mela."

The woman looked pleased. "You are kind, Lord Tom
Perion." She sat on the low bed, smoothing its indigo-
colored quilted coverlet. "We will be comfortable here. Shall
I undress for you?"

"Ah—maybe later, Mela. You are, I'm sure, very professional"—Mela beamed—"but I'm sure you understand how
tired one becomes on a long and weary sea-journey."

Mela leaped to her feet. "How remiss of me! You will
want a bath and a good sleep. Then tomorrow—"

"Yes," Perion said. "Tomorrow."

"I will have hot water brought to you," Mela said. "I will
be back soon."

Alone, Perion unpacked his few belongings—they filled
only one small drawer in the low chest at the foot of the
bed—and stretched out, still clothed, on the bed itself. It was
comfortable, all right, with a real mattress, not just a pad.

"The water is coming. This way." Mela had materialized

silently beside the bed. She took his hand, raised him, led him into the bathroom.

The tub was a rectangular box crafted of a dark brown wood, caulked and varnished to a high shine. Mela stoppered the drain, swung an ever-flowing ceramic pipe from its position over the sink to the tub, and solicitously tested the temperature of the water on her wrist. Nodding her satisfaction, she reached for a box on a shelf, took a handful of orange granules from it, and scattered them in the water. A light perfume, faintly cinnamon, steamed into the air. "I will be back soon," Mela said again, and left Perion alone.

The tub was more than half full when she returned with a rough-textured light brown towel and a pair of leather-and-wood slippers. She gave him an arched look of surprise. "The water is not warm enough for you?"

"Uh—I'm sure it's fine," Perion said.

She frowned. She had an elfin face, with a splash of darker freckles across a tanned snub nose, and the frown was most enticing. "You wish me to help you undress?"

"Oh. No. That won't be necessary. Thank you anyway, Mela." She stood watching him, expectation evident in her posture. "You are going to bathe me," he said.

"Of course."

"I should have guessed." Perion sighed and untied the sash at his waist. Mela took his tunic and trousers, and he stood in his skivvies.

"I'll fold these," she said. As soon as she was out of the bathroom, Perion shucked off his shorts and climbed into the tub.

Mela was back in a moment, holding his uniform jacket. "You must indeed be a great lord," she said, looking at him with wide brown eyes. "I have never seen such fabric." She ran her palm lovingly over the silvery sleeve. "It looks like metal, but it is so soft."

Perion felt the water hot on his legs. The cinnamon perfume drifted up, giddy in its pleasantness. "Yes, well, making the fabric is an ancient art form among my people," Perion told her. "The elder men take the fibers created by the jubjub bird at night—jubjub birds never make fibers in the day, you know—and weave them together with bandersnatch fur. The fabric then must be dyed in the blood of a freshly killed Jabberwock—" He broke off. Mela was hanging on his

words, her face intense and solemn. "It—it is a very long
and complicated process," he finished lamely.

"It must be. Here." Mela swung the ceramic pipe back up
and over the sink again, not spilling a drop in the process.
Perion allowed himself to slip lower in the tub, luxuriating as
the hot water crept over chest and up to chin. He gave Mela a
blissful smile.

"Good," she said, returning it. "I am glad the bath meets
your approval." She tilted her head. "I have never seen a
man with such a beard. May I . . ."

Perion tilted his head back. "Be my guest."

She ran her fingers through it. "It's so soft," she said.
"Some of the South Islanders wear beards, I'm told, but I
have never seen one. I like yours."

"Thank you."

"Now your bath." Mela cupped her palm and scooped
water over his head, then gave him an expert shampoo with
coarse but not unpleasant soap. She swung the pipe back for a
rinse. When she had finished and Perion could open his eyes,
he discovered that she had removed her pale blue shirt—to
avoid wetting it, he supposed, self-consciously shifting his
position in the tub—and was industriously soaping a spongelike
cube. "Your back," she said, leaning close enough for him
to feel the warmth of her breath on his cheek.

Perion sighed. The rough sponging invigorated him, no
question, and he realized just how dirty he must have been.
He had bathed only once, ritually, aboard the *Windbird*, and
had had an occasional dip in the ocean on other occasions. He
recalled now how the ship had smelled to him on his first
evenings aboard. His nose had long become accustomed to
the aroma, and no doubt he had been adding to it himself.

Mela's soft hand caressed his shoulder, slippery with suds.
"You are so brown," she said. "I think it a shame that so
many lords stay out of the sun for the sake of their beauty. I
think a pale lord looks ill. I prefer men to appear healthy."

She eased him back. He opened his eyes. Mela was leaning
very close over him. She, too, was healthy-looking, and
brown—his gaze wandered—all over. The sponge insinuated
its way across his chest. "Just lean back," Mela told him.

"I think I should catalogue igneous rock," Perion murmured to himself.

"That sounded almost like High Speech," laughed Mela.

"Basalt and basaltic derivatives," he muttered.

The sponge was underwater now, down to his stomach.

"Please do not be so tense," Mela said. "If you are truly so tired, a nice hot bath is the very best thing to put you in the mood for a good night's—oh, Goddess!"

Perion determined that evening on the bathroom floor that Mela, at least, would have no cause at all to offer negative testimony before the Council when it met again in seven days' time.

Chapter 9

When Perion awoke the next morning, he was nestled tight against the delectable curve of Mela's back, his arm thrown over her and his hand warmly full. He drew in a deep breath. Mela gave a little contented murmur and snuggled more closely against him.

Perion smiled to himself. He had missed that. He felt more human than he had for weeks. Then his mind drifted to Celia Bowen, one of the colonists he had trained with. Mela reminded him of Celia. Celia was shorter, paler, but they had the same mischievous facial structure, the same color of curly brownish-blond hair.

And Perion, thinking of Celia, found a cold place in the pit of his stomach. Celia had been a medical apprentice, and her crew number was 4008. She had died somewhere on the surface of Kalea something like seventeen hundred years ago.

His ardor disappeared. Perion disengaged his arm and slipped quietly out of bed. He padded to the bathroom, spent some time there, and returned to dress. Mela had awakened and was just stepping into her own clothing. She tossed him a sunny smile. "Will my lord have a full breakfast or a light one?"

"Full, please," Perion said. "I could eat a nox."

She gave him a wondering look as she tugged on her shirt. "They are used for food where you come from?"

"No. Just a way of speaking. How do you feel this morning? You are happy?"

"Very happy. And you?"

"I—approve of everything. You are very good at what you do."

"Thank you."

Mela brought the breakfast—a refreshing array of fruits, one green-fleshed and faintly reminiscent of banana, two tart orange pear-shaped things, reddish berrylike globules with a sweet, faintly alcoholic tang, and a beverage that tasted a bit like coconut. There was also a stack of flat breads, not quite pancakes, and a syrup that reminded him of orange marmalade. He ate everything.

After breakfast they strolled in the enclosed garden. Perion noted for the first time that the wall here was higher, four meters or better, and looked more as though it has been built to keep inmates inside than to keep others out. But the garden itself was pleasant. A path paved with crushed shells wandered through tall growths of different plants, from a spiky bamboolike flowering grass to a purple plant like heaped and quivering suds that trembled in the faint stir of their passing. The sun was warm and relatively low in the sky at midmorning.

"You have changes of season here?" Perion asked the handmaiden.

"Yes. We're now in the season of nearsun. In a few weeks we will be in waning, then sunfall, and next farsun. That is the cold time. But today is very mild. Sometimes when a storm is approaching it brings these cool days ahead of it."

The air felt mild to Perion, too, although he judged the temperature to be in the low thirties. He had become accustomed to forty-plus heat in the higher latitudes. A day like this would be a scorcher in old New York, but with Perion's degree of acclimatization, it was hardly more than a balmy spring day. "How does the—let me see, how do I ask it? Tell me how farsun differs from nearsun."

"It is the time of year when the sun grows smaller. The Teachers say it sails away to take the souls of all those who have gone to the Sailing Star. It takes them to their final harbor, and makes the voyage once each year."

"It grows smaller. Does it change its position? No, let me say that again. At noon during farsun, is it in a very different place in the sky than it is at noon during nearsun?"

"A little more to the north, but not much."

Perion nodded. His world-picture agreed with this: Kalea had a minimal axial tilt, meaning that the equator received a year-round bombardment of nearly vertical heat and light. And with the tropics nearly coinciding with the equator, he could better understand how a globe-circling desert—or at least a hot belt—could come into existence. Still, there were many questions. . . .

"It is time to return to the house," Mela said. "We will rest a little before the midday meal."

They returned to the room, but Perion got little rest. In the afternoon, while the five Aslandian lords enjoyed string music and rather plaintive singing in a great room of the House of Waiting, Mela took Perion out into yet another closed-in courtyard for exercise. They both stripped to the waist and perspired heavily as they fought a mock battle with light, padded "swords." Mela was dexterous and wily, feinting time and again to fake Perion out of position before delivering a stinging slap on thigh or buttock. Perion finally gave up trying to mount any kind of offensive and desperately tried just to parry her attacks. Now he realized how fortunate he had been during the attack on the Aslandian ship: he would have stood no chance at all had the enemy not been paralyzed by his masculinity.

"Ha!" shouted Mela triumphantly as she swatted Perion for the sixth consecutive time.

Perion laughed, tossed aside his weapon, and ducked inside Mela's circle. He enfolded her, pinning her arms to her side. She wriggled, opening her mouth to protest, but he pressed his own mouth on hers first. He heard her sword clatter to the earth, and she returned his embrace, slippery and soft against his chest.

She pushed away and grinned. "You are like no other lord I have served," she said. "I have a feeling you are very different—or very wicked. A bath now, and then bed again?"

"No," laughed Perion. "The bath will be fine. But the other—you're about to bed me to death!"

But he accepted the bath, and a backrub from Mela, and late in the afternoon they lay together in bed listening to the cackle and gabble of the pseudobirds in the garden. Mela stretched in the lazy afternoon heat and said, "The sea must be good for men. I wish there were more lords who would follow the example of you barbarians."

Perion had noticed for the first time that the white plaster ceiling had an intricate pattern of bas-relief whorls and lines. Looking up at it, he murmured, "You were told I'm a barbarian?"

Mela turned on her side and arranged her pillow more comfortably. "I know a little of your story. But I don't care about your past. You seem to be a very good man."

"You are an excellent woman."

"You really think so? I am pleased. Being a handmaiden is a privilege, you know. Not many qualify."

"Let me guess. Handmaidens must come from a family in which there are several brothers."

"Yes. And I have three brothers, full brothers, the same mother and father. One is the lord of Garda, far to the southwest in this island. Another is on Blue Island, and another started his harem just last year on Tobria. You see, only a woman from a male-heavy family can ever apply to be a handmaiden. We have wonderful chances, you know. We entertain the young lords from the time their training is complete until they are assigned a harem by the Council. It is almost as though we have our own harem of men. A really good handmaiden may have, oh, many children, by many fathers!"

"My people would call your profession degrading," Perion said.

"I do not understand."

"You are used by men—you exist only to give them pleasure."

Mela laughed. "We look at it differently," she said. "We see ourselves as using men for our own purposes."

"Then one of us is being used."

"I suppose," she said with a smile. "I wonder which one."

"I don't think it matters. Mela, you would like to choose your own husband? One man, shared with no other woman?"

"No," she said. "That seems—distasteful."

Perion did not reply immediately. His gaze wandered through the patterns of the ceiling, his mind through the patterns of the expedition. For the first time he contemplated the plans made in Terrasystem for the colony. They had decided, there, that the first generations would be heavily female. And they had decided that when the time came, the women who were still unborn when plans were being made would welcome the chance to bear the children of dead men. To put things right. To make things the way they were on Earth. On dying Earth.

He wondered whose semen the ship carried. Geniuses, men of note, men of talent, the crew had been assured. And enough work had been done with those little swimmers before they were bottled and frozen into sleep to make sure that the proud, dead daddies would produce offspring in a ratio of six males to four females. Just to put things right.

Someone, Perion thought, was being used.

"Your thoughts are far away," Mela said.

He stirred. "Sorry, Mela. What were you saying?"

"I spoke of my child."

"Oh. Only one?"

"Yes, a daughter," Mela said. "She is a pretty little thing. Almost a whole year old now. She lives with my sisters in Shelda Bay. I see her every few days."

"Mothers do not raise their own children?"

Mela shrugged. "Most do. Handmaidens, though, must devote much attention to their lords. We cannot give much time to raising a family. But I am paid well for my work, and my daughter receives very good care from my sisters."

"I'm sure." The setting sun glowed in the obsidian panes of the window. It threw onto the ceiling intricate patterns of shadow woven with others of golden light, abstract and labyrinthine. Perion said, "Tell me about the Council, Mela. I must face them soon. I would like to know what to expect."

"Each island has its own Council," Mela said. "One from every clan on the island. There are about three hundred on Home's Council. And there is the Great Council, too, with one representative from each island; but it is not concerned with matters like lordships. Cases like yours are heard by panels, chosen by lot, from the general Council. They will include about twenty members. I have heard that old Ruisa will serve on the panel hearing your case and those of the Aslandians. She is very powerful. For the past two years she has been the Headwoman of the Island Council, and our representative to the Great Council. She is many times a grandmother and said to be very wise."

"What will the meeting be like?"

"Oh, they will call you into a room in Council Hall. You will stand in the center of a circle—the panel. Old Ruisa will lead the others in questioning you, determining your fitness, your aptitudes. They may call me in—they will certainly call Atina Theslo, and perhaps Teyo da-Theslo, too. Then they will confer together and decide which course of action to take with you, doing what will be best for you and for Homereaches. That is all."

"What if I disagree with the decision of the Council?"

Mela laughed. "A man disagreeing with the Council? I have never heard of that happening. I *think* they might then move your case to the Great Council, which will meet again before next nearsun. In the meantime, I suppose you would stay here. I would like that, though you understand that I could not be the handmaiden for one man for so long a time. That would be a little—perverse."

"What if—if I go before the Great Council, hear their decision, and still I disagree?"

"You will not. Perion, you must realize that the Councils have much wisdom. The members are guided by the interests of their lords in reaching a just decision. If you listen well and patiently and give their solution a chance, you will find it is really the best one."

"But suppose . . ." Perion lifted himself on one elbow, looked down into Mela's face, dim in the growing twilight. "Suppose that some man did disagree, and continued to disagree. What would the Council do with such a man?"

Mela pressed a soft hand against his mouth. "Hush. Do not speak of such things. You would not wish to know."

Perion took her hand in his, kissed her palm, looked into her eyes. "But I do."

Mela sat up, looked away from him. "There is a small island, a rock, really, in Eastbay. If men or women are evildoers and are incorrigible, at last they are placed on the island at sunturn, either on Farsun Day or Nearsun Day, and they are publicly burned." She swung her legs off the bed and turned her back on him. "I was ready for a very pleasant night, and now I'm upset."

Perion touched her shoulder and felt a faint trembling. "I'm sorry. I had to know."

"You may never have seen a person burned. I did once, when I was a girl. I have never forgotten the smoke, the screams. It is too hideous."

"And people still allow it to continue?"

"We are told we must remove the heretics from among us, that their deaths alone will show how strongly we abhor their blasphemy. We would risk losing the favor of Kalea by refusing. The Council are wisest among us, and their voice is our voice. They have only the best interests of Homereaches in their hearts."

"As they see them. But if an outsider had a different viewpoint . . ."

Mela stood and stepped silently to the window. Perion saw her profile faintly lit by the waning dusklight filtering in from the garden. "We have made a good way of life in Homereaches," she said. "Things are ordered. We have many people, and yet no one starves; we have poor people, and yet no one is homeless. To challenge this, to speak about the Council as lacking in wisdom, is unthinkable. We might as well surrender to the Aslandians or the Aladian Islanders as try to change the settled paths, the ancient ways. Our way of life has been proved." She took a deep breath. "When you go before the Council, tell them you are a barbarian. Tell them our ways are strange to you, but you will learn them. Tell them you are from a family of many brothers. Do this for me, for Homereaches."

Perion got out of bed, came up behind Mela. "These are not your words," he said. "Atina told you to say this to me?"

She turned toward him. "I have spoken to many people."

"They told you to convince me? To persuade me to act as you say?"

She put her arms around him, laid her head on his shoulder. He felt her warmth, the solid thudding of her heart. "No. Not like that. I fear for you. I wish to save you from folly. I have come to like you. You are a good man—"

"You know nothing of me," he said. "You have not fallen in love with me since yesterday. We have *made* love, but that was a union of bodies, not of spirits. You don't know me, my spirit, my mind, at all."

She said into his shoulder, "I know well enough that you will make a foolish mistake if you argue with the Council. I wish to see no man exiled to a barren island, or put to death because of his foolishness. Nothing you can do will prevent one or the other from happening if you argue with the Council."

"If I agree to do as you say?"

"Atina and Teyo will speak with the Council. I will add my voice, if they will hear. We will try to convince them that you are in truth a barbarian, in need of training. We will try to secure their permission to keep you here, in the House of Waiting on the Theslo clan, for the coming year. I will be your first instructor, and your personal handmaiden, and there will be others, as many as you wish. We will instruct you in the necessary arts of pleasing women, of being a just and good and wise lord; and at the end of that time, with our favorable testimony for you, you may choose the island on which you wish your harem. An estate will be found for you, and you may then become as wealthy and powerful as your ambition will take you. Then, Perion, when you have gained strength and a following of good fighting women, and a fleet of ships, *then* you may plan what you will, question the Council if you dare." She guided his hands to her softness. "Is it such a bad plan? To remain here, for a year? To spend a year with me?"

Perion held her. A year—more than two of his own years—training, then how many more of establishing a harem and an estate? Say ten Earth years? He would be in his mid-thirties, then, still young, still capable of finding a way to the *Galileo*. And allies would help. . . .

He said, "If I asked you to be a member of my harem?"

She stiffened momentarily beneath his touch, then said, "Being a handmaiden is a high and envied honor. But I do not know. After a year with you—we would see. I have never had the training of a lord entirely in my own hands before."

They loved each other, or their bodies did. Later Perion lay wakeful, letting his mind play with fantasies: he saw himself as Lord Perion the Conqueror, leader and commander of an Amazonian army, bringing a planet to its knees to save it, to lead it from its medievalism into a new era. He could open half the world to them, could show these people a vast new territory, could take them away from the tiny specks of islands that Kalea, the stingy Goddess, had given them. And in after years, he would become the stuff of legend and myth himself, a Moses who had led his people through to a new promised land. His children's children would walk like kings. . . .

Drugged with idle visions, he dozed into a night of pleasant dreams, broken only once by a nightmare in which he was a tiny driven creature, harried and pursued this way and that by beings half shadow, half substance, driven at last to a treacherous path of escape that led, finally, into a cage.

Dawn wakened him. He was alone in the bed. He slipped from under the quilted coverlet and called for Mela; but she was nowhere in the apartment. He dressed in the new clothing Mela had given him, richly woven blue-and-gold trousers and a tunic of blue pointed with decorative stones of yellow and red, and he slipped his feet into woven-reed sandals. The pseudobirds chittered and yawked in the garden. A look through the window told him he had awakened early indeed, for the sun was hardly high enough to touch the tallest of the trees.

Wondering where Mela had gone, Perion tried the door. It was barred from the outside. Cursing under his breath, Perion pressed his face against the frame to peep through the crack. Yes, there it was, a black wooden bar at waist level. Perion left the door and roamed the apartment rooms, looking for something flat. He found it in the closet, a carved wooden hanger. He returned with it to the door. The hanger was barely thin enough to slip through the crack. It wanted to stick, but he worked it up under the bar, felt its weight, and clumsily raised it a few centimeters. Then the hanger lost its purchase and the bar clacked solidly back into place.

Perion grunted and tried again. Once more the bar slipped down. The next try brought the same result. Perion considered. Then he braced his shoulder against the door, and as the bar lifted, he pressed against the door. The friction caught the bar before it could fall, and he was able to move the hanger up to renew his efforts. Another centimeter, and another— and the bar clacked to the floor outside. The door swung open.

Perion went into the corridor, retrieved the bar, and replaced it in its hasps. He walked quietly down the corridor. None of the other doors, he noticed, were barred. Two doors down from his room, he opened a door out of curiosity. This apartment was identical to his, but the bed had not been made, and the bare mattress looked a little forlorn. He missed something else, too, after a moment realizing it was the trickle of water. This apartment's bathroom was dry, evidently, awaiting its next guest. Perion went into the room and looked through the distorting panes of the window into the walled garden. Then he turned and went back into the corridor.

The corridor disgorged into the leafy common room. Other corridors branched off at angles, and he realized now that the building was laid out in spokes radiating from a central hub: he stood in a pentagon, which meant four different wings, plus the main entrance.

At a venture he explored the left-hand corridor. He heard sounds here, and cautiously cracked open the first door.

The room was—occupied. A man lay on his arched back in the bed, and mounted on him like a rider on a horse was a young woman, head thrown back, bare skin glistening with exertion. Neither the man nor the woman noticed Perion. He quietly reclosed the door.

The last two doorways here were open, and from them he heard a bustle of activity and caught a whiff of food. He had found the kitchen. He silently retraced his steps to the central common room.

The large main door was closed but unbarred. He opened it and looked into the enclosed yard where the carriage had stopped. There, sitting on a bench with their backs to him, were Mela and Atina. They did not look around. Standing in the doorway, he could just hear their words. Atina was saying, ". . . stand a good chance with the Council if he does. And it's really in his best interest. They say a fishing vessel saw an Aslandian cutter under truce flag coming this way. Our best hope is that they don't arrive before the Council meets.''

"He knows of this?" Mela asked.

Atina's reply was so low that Perion could not make it out.

Mela sighed. "I have tried to make him understand what he must do," she said. "It is difficult." She said something low to Atina, something that ended on the rising note of inquiry.

Atina laughed. "I wanted to, but Teyo put me under interdict, damn her. I never even got to touch the Aslandians. Trust an old Teacher to make the Captain walk the narrowest line of all." She gave Mela a sideways glance, and Perion sank back into the shadowed doorway. "How is he?" Atina asked.

Mela's soft laughter rustled. "Like a little boy. So eager. Very inept, though. He seems to be telling the truth about one thing: he's had no training at all. That almost makes me believe the story you tell; training is a thing a man cannot forget.''

Atina nodded. "I almost envy you. I *do* envy you. I've never had a man." She sighed. "Well, if anyone can keep him happy, you surely can.''

Mela laid a hand on Atina's arm. "Envy me some other

lord," she said. "Be sure you select a man who has the training and knowledge one needs to walk the paths of love. One like this one—he can give you only little and fleeting pleasure."

"I don't want pleasure," Atina said. "I want children."

Mela gave her a sisterly kiss on the cheek. "I know, dear. And one day you will find a wonderful adventurous fellow and have all sorts of little brown boys at your knees." Mela laughed again. "Even I have had an offer. Perion wishes me to join his harem."

Atina's glance was speculative and unamused. "Oh?"

"Not that I would, of course. But I think that it was sweet of him to ask. He's so innocent and guileless. Do you know what he did the first time we were alone together?" The two heads bent close to each other for a session of whispering that ended with Atina's burst of laughter.

Perion saw her toss her dark hair back, her face merry in the dawn light. "A blushing virgin?"

Perion softly closed the door and drifted down the corridor to his rooms. The bar was a problem in engineering, but with careful balancing and two patient tries, he managed to close the door and hear the satisfying clack of the lock falling into place. He was now, as far as anyone could see, locked in exactly as before. He undressed and returned to bed, where he lay awake wondering about this world, its people, and the treachery of strangers.

Chapter 10

Atina and Mela came in with breakfast. Perion sat in bed and ate with them, listening to Atina's news with an occasional nod or understanding grunt. She had seen her family; the Council was ready to hear the cases of the Aslandian lords on its first day of meeting, and in the afternoon of the same day they would sit on the question of Perion. Atina's advice paralleled (not surprisingly, Perion thought) Mela's: he was to confess to being a barbarian, ask for hospitality, request the favor of a year's training before assignment.

Atina carefully sketched in the approach she believed best for him. He was an outlander who had been weakened by long exposure in a small open boat. He had suffered loss of memory and could recall nothing of his origin or training. He would ask for retraining; Mela would volunteer for the task. Atina would sponsor him. Then, if things went well, the Council would agree to the suggestion and grant Atina status as harema, and the whole episode would be resolved.

"And my future would be assured?" Perion asked.

Atina shrugged. "For the time being. You would receive training here, in my family's House of Waiting. You would not think it a bad place? I think you like Mela"—and right on cue, Mela reached to take one of Perion's hands in hers— "and you should be comfortable here. You will have time, then, to think of your other plans and desires."

"And should I want to take lordship immediately instead?" Perion asked. "I think I would have more freedom to pursue these other plans if I could act as a lord."

Worry stitched a furrow between Atina's eyebrows. "I would not ask that, Tom. The Council would examine you closely, might even detail a group of women to stay with you for several nights. You could not pretend to training you do not have. They would discover the lie immediately. But you would want to do such a thing?"

Perion smiled. "Well, it is a possibility. There is the freedom of action, as I said. Then, too, you will be gaining status if the Council grants your request to become a harema. I take it the Council would allow you to join a harem immediately?"

"Perhaps. I will probably have the responsibility, as Captain of the *Windbird*, of transporting the Aslandians to their new estates, if they are sent off-island. After that has been accomplished, then yes, I may become a harema."

"Wonderful," said Perion. "I congratulate you. I want you to join my harem."

Atina and Mela exchanged a complex glance. Atina faltered, "But I—that is, I—"

Mela tried to rescue her by teasing, "But I thought you wanted *me*, Tom!"

"Why, sure!" With a sudden grab, Perion embraced both women. Taken unawares, they fell with him onto the soft bed. He pulled them close, one on either side, both wriggling and pushing. "It will be wonderful!" he crowed. "You are both wonderful woman and together we will be a great team."

Both women laughed, and Atina pushed away from him, her face suffusing with blood. "Really, Perion—"

"I'm sorry," Perion said. "The two of you would not like to be in my harem? But I thought you were close friends."

"We are friends, and clan-sisters," Mela said. "But that doesn't mean that we—"

"Of course, we'll need a good estate," Perion said. "I know some tricks and secrets that your society doesn't know. If you and my other wives are hard workers, we'll make the land rich with crops, we'll dip riches from the sea like water in cupped hands. We'll have to have a large house—I want many wives. And we'll need a big bed, five times the size of this one."

Atina punched Perion in the ribs, hard enough to *whuff* the air from his lungs. "You stop it," she said.

He released the women and gingerly rubbed his side. "Something is wrong? You have persuaded me that it would be best to take on your way of life. I thought you would be happy."

"You're pretending," Atina accused. "It is obvious that

you mean nothing you say. And if you mouth such prattle before the Council—it is strange to you. You don't even sound like yourself.''

"But I'm trying to do all the things you say I should do,'' Perion countered. ''I thought a good lord should be ambitious and lusty. Mela, do you see anything wrong with my behavior?''

The handmaiden's face clouded, and she turned away. ''I have no right to speak of such things.''

''*I* have,'' Atina persisted. ''You can't fool the Council by putting on such an outrageous pretense. You must make them believe you, you must be yourself.''

Perion sat up. ''Ah. The whole point. I must be myself. But I cannot. I am just what I claim to be: an Earthman, a member of the colony expedition that first began the human race on Kalea. If I am true to my real self, and to my own culture, your Council will believe me insane. And if I don't take that course, if I do as you say and fool the Council into believing me a Kalean male who somehow has lost his memory, I will be chained to your way of life for years. I cannot afford the time.''

''Time, time,'' Atina scoffed. ''What is time to a lord?''

''More than you know,'' Perion said. ''There is the matter of the ship, the *Galileo*. From certain things I've heard and seen, I fear that the ship may be about to fall.''

''I don't understand.''

Perion shook his head. ''I cannot explain well about orbits without using the High Speech. But there is a real danger that soon, perhaps within only a year or two, the Sailing Star will fall to Kalea, burning as it comes. It is so huge that a large portion of it will not burn up but will crash to the surface. But it can bring nothing living with it. If I want to save my friends, I cannot spend years as a lord of a harem.''

Mela looked at Atina. ''You believe this? That there are living people aboard the Sailing Star?''

''No,'' Atina snapped. Then she gave an exasperated shrug. ''I do not know what to believe. Tell her all the rest, Lord Perion.''

Perion tried to explain that the ship could rectify the population imbalance, could create more man-children. Although Mela grew visibly excited at the notion that one day there might be one man for every woman on Kalea, soon she frowned and shook her head. "But even if that is so, it would happen a generation or more from now," she said. "And what harm would it do to the harem system?"

"I don't know," Perion confessed. "But without the change, your people cannot go on. Soon all the islands will be filled with people. That will bring misery for all."

Mela stood and walked to the window. "Some say that in the Under Islands, mothers kill their first girl-children," she said.

"There's more. The north part of Kalea has land, and I'm almost sure it is habitable. You could expand there, find new estates, have a new world to conquer."

Mela turned to face them, and Atina skeptically asked, "Well, clan-sister? You believe his story, now that you have heard it all?"

Mela paced. "It sounds insane," she said. "Yet I know men, Atina. I have been handmaiden to many of them. Somehow I cannot think that Lord Perion lies."

"Not consciously lying, perhaps," Atina said. "But if he has truly lost his memory and has become confused . . ."

"I have never heard of madness this circumstantial," Mela said, hugging herself. "Anyway, don't speak of madness. You know what happens to those who are incurable."

Atina nodded, her face grim. Perion looked from woman to woman. "What happens?" he asked. When neither of the two replied, he guessed; "Public burning?"

Atina gave one sharp, wordless nod. Mela said, "It sounds harsh, Lord Perion, but the Council shows mercy to the ill. Those who have committed no crime are made unconscious before the fire is lighted—"

"Very humane," Perion said dryly.

"We don't want it to happen to you," Atina said. "So let's go over what you will say to the Council next week."

The two women decided that Perion would remain as silent as possible, answering only direct questions and claiming loss of memory if he ran into ones for which he had no ready answer. They drilled him for a time, asking him questions about his body-mother, his harem-mothers, his father, his clan, his island. Perion quickly grew tired of claiming lapse of memory for everything.

So did Mela. "This is no good," she said at last. "The

Council will consider him crazed if he has so little recollection of his own history.''

Atina reluctantly conceded. "I'm afraid you are right.'' She looked appraisingly at Perion. "On Kalea, men are said to be liars by birth and deceivers by preference. You are not so different from them. You think you could act a part?''

"I don't know," Perion said. "Tell me what kind of part you wish me to act first.''

"Something like this. When the Council ask where you came from, tell them that your home was on Creusa. That is an isolated northern outpost of the Under Islands, many months' sail from here. Not much is known about it. What was your mother's name, your real mother?''

"Diane Randolph Perion.''

"Call her Dian of Ran. That sounds enough like a Kalean name to pass. Your father is Lord Ran of Creusa. Make him a minor lord, on a small estate growing—let's see—vern fiber.''

"He would have to have a reason for being in Aladian waters," Mela said, getting into the spirit of the game.

"Good," Atina said. "Here it is. Your father is trying for an alliance with Aslandia. He wishes you to marry a woman from there as your first harema. She comes from Teron. Say it. Teron is the island from which our Aslandian lords departed shortly before we captured them. Your ship foundered while on the way to Teron. Say that your wife's family were the Larads—''

"No, no," interrupted Mela. "Say the Zhonz.''

Atina smiled. "Good, good. The Zhonz clan is so large that members of it can never puzzle out their exact relationship anyway. Say your wife's family were the Zhonz, Teron branch of the family, and that her harem-mother had asked that the solemnities be performed in the family hall. You were on your way there; a sudden storm came up, your ship capsized, and you awakened in a lifeboat to find yourself quite alone. You can recall nothing else.''

Perion looked at her deadpan. "*Men* are liars?" he asked.

"Improve it if you wish!" Atina snapped. "Now tell the story back to me.''

Perion rehearsed the lie several times, until he had the names and the places firm in his memory. Mela shook her head in dissatisfaction. "He doesn't *sound* like a Kalean,'' she complained. "His accent is not of Aslandia, and not of Homereaches."

"He will practice," Atina said. "After all, who knows what a Creusan male sounds like? But you will instruct him in ways to sound less strange. And if you can think of anything else—"

"I can," Perion said.

The two looked at him with startled expressions, as though he were a piece of furniture that had begun to talk. He said, "If I go through with this, I'll want some favors from you in return."

"What are they?" Atina asked.

"I want to see Teyo again."

Atina nodded. "You will tomorrow or the next day. She is in the Hall of Teachers in Headwater, making the usual purification rituals. She will be back soon."

"I want out."

"Out of what?"

"Out of the House of Waiting. I want to see something of this island. You lock me in here."

Mela blushed. "I am sorry," she said.

"Other lords are not locked in."

"Other lords," Atina said briskly, "are not in danger of becoming a public bonfire. But if the Council accept your story and set you down for training, you will then have the usual male freedoms."

"Fine. But I want to get out a little now."

"No," Atina said. "You would be taking too great a chance. The wrong word to the wrong person—"

"Wait," Mela interrupted. "Lord Perion has a point. If he could see more of the island, he would be more convincing to the Council."

"I don't have to go alone," Perion said. "You could send a guard."

They argued for several minutes, and Atina finally and grudgingly agreed to leave the question to Teyo: if the old Teacher agreed to accompany him, and if Perion would agree to certain stipulations, then he could venture outside the House of Waiting.

"I will shave you," Mela said.

Perion grimaced. "I've never worn a beard before," he said. "I'm rather fond of it now."

"But you would look strange," Atina said. "Your hair is short, as it is—but you may wear a hood to conceal that. Some lords are interested in the abstractions of religion. You may be taken for a young acolyte, if Teyo is with you in her ecclesiastical robes. That would make people hesitant to speak directly to you, and would help to protect you from any mischief-makers."

"Very well," Perion said. "And there is one other thing as well: I want to be free to speak to the other males here in the house."

"I don't think that a wise idea," Mela said. "Most men here are young ones, training for lordship; they are our clan-cousins from other parts of the island. Then there are the Aslandians, of course. And in one wing we keep rooms for travelers, relatives or friends of the clan, who need a place to stay."

"You do not wish me to corrupt the children?" Perion asked, amused.

"They are not children. Those in training are between their seventh and tenth years. But they will be curious—you know how men are, how they jabber and gossip. You will find it difficult to remain silent among them."

"Then it would be good practice for the Council session," Perion countered. "I have already spoken to the Aslandians. I will not corrupt them—they disbelieve my story. I will not mention my true origin to any of the others. I give my word."

Atina asked, "You have many lords-in-training here now?"

"The Great Council meeting at nearsun assigned harems to many of them," Mela told her. "We have only sixteen at present, not counting your captives. More will be coming in during the next months, of course."

Atina shrugged. "Then let us allow Perion his freedom in the house. I, too, dislike the feeling of being penned. I think he will be able to keep his secrets."

"Thank you," Perion said. "All right. In return, I will agree to do as you think I should, to petition for a year of training; but I must be allowed to work on my own problems, to try to devise a way to communicate with the *Galileo*. If I can have that degree of freedom, then I'll do anything else you ask."

With the agreement reached, the two women relaxed visibly. Perion, speaking with them, discovered that the House of Waiting had a library of sorts, a book room. "Little used by men," Mela said. "Visiting women, especially Teachers, often like to read or to copy a book; but men may use the materials there, if they desire. Some lords have a bookish bent."

She showed him the room, and while Atina and Mela made arrangements and plans of their own, Perion dipped into the two hundred or so volumes shelved in the little library. The books were almost all the same size, about thirty centimeters square, and all were bound in thin wooden boards. Their paper was the same kind of substance that he had seen in Teyo's copybook, thin, yellow, and organic. The ink had a tendency to bleed a little on its fine-ribbed surface, and the blurred letters had acquired strange shapes over the years, but he could read them with some facility now.

One book in particular interested him. The neatly lettered cover title was *The Island of Home*, and according to the first page it had been compiled in the Year of Council of Home Seven Hundred and Forty-one, whenever that was. The book was perhaps three hundred pages long and seemed to combine geography, economics, politics, and genealogy.

He leafed through it, pausing over a map of the island. It was, he saw, roughly triangular, tailing off to the south in a group of smaller islands, each probably the summit of a dead volcano. The map had been rendered in meticulous detail; looking at it, Perion easily confirmed an earlier guess. Shelda Bay was the collapsed caldera of an immense volcanic shield, one side eroded. It nestled in the island's southeast side, below the long notch of the Larapé and the Water. Perion was about to turn the page when a small mark near the town of Headwater caught his attention. In minuscule, blurry script near the mark was the notation "Here the Teachers have enshrined the relics of Kalea in the House of Beginnings."

His interest piqued, Perion scanned the book looking for further information; but the text did not seem to refer directly to the map. He took the book and wandered in search of Mela and Atina. He found only the former, who said that the Captain had gone back to her family. But Mela knew nothing of the relics of Kalea. "The Teachers keep some things a great secret," she said. "The House of Beginnings I know. It is a training hall for Teachers, and it is in the oldest part of

Headwater. It is very old itself—they say it consists of houses within houses, and a maze of passages. But what it holds, what these relics are, I do not know.''

"Teyo may know,'' Perion said.

"She may.''

"Then I shall ask her.''

Mela wanted to know if Perion would mingle with the other lords that day. To her visible relief, he said he would wait a day or so, trying to improve his accent and practicing enough of his story to put off any overly inquisitive male. They spent a pleasant day together in the garden. Perion made Mela laugh more than once, and he was diligent in practicing the sounds she corrected. But he was bothered by what he had heard that morning. Mela saw him with a double vision: he was a lord, or a potential lord, and thus deserving of the respect and honor any such exalted male would expect; but he was also a man, and could be laughed at, gossiped about, belittled.

But together they could be friends. That evening, Mela told him, the Sailing Star would be visible. He asked permission to remain in the garden, alone, while it passed over; and Mela, after having dropped a discreet question about his religious beliefs, agreed.

He waited under a tall pseudopalm, a "tree" whose trunk was a bundle of thick fibers and whose crown was a single huge sawtoothed leaf, bent and bowed like the top petal of a Jack-in-the-pulpit. He had his communicator with him—still his "talisman," in Mela's view—and when he saw the bright spark moving from pole to pole, he activated it on the ground-to-ship band.

Teasingly, the ship acknowledged that it was in range, but complained of electromagnetic interference after every entry. Perion grunted as the *Galileo* dropped out of sight over the roof of the House of Waiting. He suspected that a slight amplification would be sufficient to break the barrier—or perhaps just an auxiliary antenna.

But on this metal-poor ocean world, he saw no way he could fabricate either.

Mela waited in the room. "I watched you," she said.

"I don't mind."

"The talisman—it has lights."

He smiled and showed her the miniature screen. "Nothing showing on it now," he said. "But letters appear there."

"A magical device."

"No. Just a tool. Useless, right now."

He took the datakit out and amused her for a while by running datachip pages across its screen. He had the complete works of Shakespeare, the Novels in English series of old Oxford, others; they were all strange to her, and indecipherable, in letter shape and language. Haltingly, for her amusement, he translated for her, reading the first meeting of Romeo and Juliet, the opening of *Pride and Prejudice*—"True," she said, "every lord wants good wives"—this and that. Then, devilishly, he punched up a curiosity, an illustrated sex manual from the twentieth century. Mela laughed in delight over this.

Translation proved an enjoyable chore.

SOME QUESTIONS OF LAW

Excerpted from the Book of *The Island of Home*

The islands are the property of all, for Kalea gave them to all.

The land is in the care of the Councils. The Councils may give the use of the land to lords and their harems. Unless a family is idle and lazy, they have the use of the land until the death of the lord.

Such wealth as the land produces is the property of the lord and his family. If he has a wife who raises borrits, their meat and fur is hers to dispose of; and any profit she gains from her work is hers. She cannot be compelled to give her money to her lord or to her family.

If a family buys a ship for a woman, and she sails it for a profit, then she is entitled to one-half of the profit. The family must receive the other half, for they deserve the reward for their first investment.

If a woman chooses to enrich a family's coffers by contributing part or all of her profits, a strict account must be kept; and whenever such a woman wishes to receive goods or money from the family, she may do so in the amount of her contribution.

A lord's children may not inherit from him his estate.

If a lord dies, his sons must be placed in the families of his wives, and raised there; his sons may not return to the estate.

His wives and daughters, if they wish, may petition the Council for a new lord.

If the estate has been well run and well kept, the Council shall agree to provide a new lord, that it may continue to support the wives and daughters of the estate. But the new lord must be no closer in blood relation than the fourth degree to the old lord.

If an estate is broken on the death of the lord, a new lord and a new harem may take the estate. The wives of the estate must return to their own families; or if they wish, they may enter a House of Sisterhood, to work for the Teachers. Once a harema has entered a House of Sisterhood, she may no longer marry.

Each estate should be kept carefully and should be used to best profit the family. Estates in river basins should produce water-loving crops: venn, traff, melons, thresil, tree fruits (narans, affles, drupes), and other foodstuff. Estates in hilly regions should plant grains and fiber plants. Estates on mountain terraces should produce oil-berries, spice plants, and other plants that love cool breezes and dry soil.

Estate animals should be carefully raised and cared for. The estate should use no more than one-third of all edible animals in one year, lest numbers suffer and prices rise. They should sell no more than one-third. One-third at least they should keep as breeding stock.

The Council may set tax rates for estates. Estates that have suffered from drought or storm may upon application be declared exempt from taxation; but poor management is not a reason for remission of taxes.

Of the revenues collected, one-tenth shall go to the Teachers, who are to maintain schools, hospitals, and places of worship. They may also charge fees for their services as instructors and healers; but they shall not profit from their services, beyond the needs of their bodies.

Some of the taxes must support the Council ships. In time of need, the Council may further require any shipowner to sail and to fight in defense of the island.

Murder is a private affair.

If a person dies at the hands of another, the dead one's clan may meet and decide on the proper course of action. If the murderer is one of their own, they shall punish the murderer as the codes of Kalea stipulate.

If the murderer is a member of another clan, the aggrieved clan may demand that she be given to them for justice. If the second clan will not agree, the aggrieved clan may petition the Council for hearing. There the circumstances must be described to the satisfaction of the Council.

The Council may then fine the murderer's clan, if the case is proved; or the accusing clan, if they fail to prove their case.

But if murder is proved, the aggrieved clan may ask that the murderer be declared outlaw for a year and a day.

In that time, if the aggrieved clan members are able, they may kill the murderer and any who help her without fear of punishment. . . .

Chapter 11

The next day Perion found himself the star and subject of a drama: the Transformation of Tomas Perion. Teyo was there early, and Atina. They watched as he sat in a steaming tub and permitted Mela to scrape away at his beard with a razor of volcanic glass, a crescent of dark obsidian with a wickedly sharp edge. Though he winced, Perion was not cut even once; and his beard came off by soggy handfuls. Mela put the finishing touches on her work, rinsed the suds from his chin, and backed away to eye him critically; then she and the others broke into laughter.

"There is a joke?" Perion asked.

"Wait," Mela said. She brought a small polished copper mirror to Perion, held the light close. He inspected his face. The image staring back at him was leaner than he remembered, all null-g flab burned off by heat and activity, but the dark blue eyes were the same, under their heavy brows, and the sharp nose, and— "Oh," Perion said. His jaw and chin were as white as a fish's belly, in strong contrast to his tanned forehead and cheeks.

But that was no great hurdle. Women on Kalea seldom used cosmetics, but many lords did, and one young fellow in the east wing in particular had a splendidly equipped chest of ointments, colorings, and scents. With great deliberation, the women borrowed the kit and mixed colors. Perion suffered his face to be used as an experiment several times, and finally they were satisfied. Mela deftly applied the color, blended, touched his cheeks with red ("Many men do, and it goes nicely with your face," she said), and finally pronounced herself satisfied with the effect.

Then came the matter of clothing. Teyo produced a monkish robe that swallowed him. The cloth was thin and light, but opaque, and the accompanying hood was made of thicker stuff, so that it peaked over his forehead and gave his eyes and cheeks shade. When he had gotten into the apparel, the women marched him around, making changes—a dark brown sash around the waist, a copper pin at the breast, the hood tilted, the hood straight—until finally no one could think of any more objections.

"Well," Teyo said at last, "if you do not chatter in an unseemly fashion, we may move about fairly freely. Though I do not know why you wish to leave the House of Waiting, for it has all that any lord should want."

"I will hold my tongue," Perion said. "As for my reasons, you yourself know I am no ordinary lord."

"And where do you wish to go, now that we have made you ready?" Atina asked, tugging at his robe to bring the hem a fraction lower.

"It is permitted to visit Headwater?" Perion asked.

"Yes, if you wish," Teyo said. "There is something you wish to see there?"

"I think the Teachers have a House in Headwater?"

"Our order keeps the House of Beginnings there, yes. I see your course, Tom Perion. You wish to examine the records there, to find confirmation of your story."

"Yes, Teyo."

Atina looked at the Teacher. "It is permitted?"

Teyo sighed. "It is not *forbidden*," she said. "But I have never heard of a man entering the house's sanctums. Still, he may stay there in the Rooms of Waiting, and we shall see what happens then."

Atina looked critically at Perion. "Well, I did say he would have freedom. Perion, I may accompany you?"

"If you wish."

"Good. Most lords would travel with at least one guard, even with a Teacher as companion. Come, then, and as soon as I equip myself we will set forth."

A lighter carriage, a sort of open buggy, awaited them in the yard. Perion gave Mela a quick farewell embrace and accepted Atina's aid in stepping up to the vehicle. "The rear seat," Atina said. This was partially protected by a half-roof of leather stretched over a wood frame, and Perion slipped into it. Teyo climbed onto the front seat, and Atina herself took the reins of the nox. She whistled to the creature, shook the reins, and the gray-green behemoth bestirred itself to a fast walk, pulling its spraddling legs beneath its baggy body. Mela had opened the gate; they passed through now and turned right, following a winding unpaved road. Perion saw now that they were on the side of a mountain, and turning to look back, he saw the white House of Waiting nestled comfortably on a broad ledge cut from the flank of a dormant volcano. Teyo noticed his gaze.

"The mountain is Shelda," she told him. "Its fires are out, but still it has springs of hot water. In the rainy months there is a steaming lake in its cup."

"Ah."

The road curved first south, then west. The trees to the left occasionally parted enough to give him a glimpse of the sea, far away and misty this morning, and once when the road climbed a short ridge he had a grand view of the open circle of Shelda Bay itself, a sparkling blue harbor set in the multicolored mosaic of the city, perhaps five kilometers away and a thousand meters below them.

"This is preserve land," Atina explained. "All part of my father Theslo's estate. The farms are there, to the left—see the terraces down through the trees? The workers are weeding the food crops today." Sure enough, rows of tiny women worked their way in lines through the nearest field, stooping, tugging, rising, and moving on again.

"Hired workers?" Perion asked.

"Some. Most are daughters," Atina said. "I have pulled many a weed in those very fields."

They passed a singing group of five women, walking along the road with farm tools, spades and hoes, cast over their shoulders. The five gave Atina a merry greeting, one girl of fifteen or sixteen hailing her as "clan-sister." When they had passed, Perion said, "They seem happy enough, to be doing such hard work."

"They are happy. Each has her own plot of land to till, and each produces wealth for the family. We are female-heavy, and have been for the past two generations, but never have we lost the estate. When Teyo's father died, my father, then a young man, was given the landholding and the name; and so well has he served that when he dies, he will be replaced by another lord who will take the name Theslo. Not many estates have been held in the same name for as much as three generations."

The land on either side of the road leveled a bit as the road curved downward, and the surroundings began to take on the appearance of tamed land instead of wilderness. A stream fell from the mountain at one point into an artificial pond, and the road passed over the small dam that retained it. "Irrigation water," Atina explained. "And my father has it stocked with freshwater fish, too, considered a delicacy by many."

Then they passed a group of women who were busily building a stone wall. Carts drawn by pairs of noxes—*noxen*? wondered Perion—had brought slabs of flat rock that on Earth he would have named sandstone, and perhaps twenty women were dry-laying it into a chest-high barrier. "One of my clan-mothers is planning to raise hovas," Atina explained. "They are useful for flesh and fur, but they are creatures of colder islands and must be carefully penned and watched to do well here. But if any woman can make them breed, Sesto can. And there is the house."

The center of the Theslo estate was a rambling one-story house, plastered and painted a light tan, roofed with red tile. It seemed to throw parts of itself in all different directions, and almost all of it was enclosed by an arched and colonnaded veranda. An extension of this served as a porte-cochere, and Atina stopped the carriage there. Instantly a young girl had taken the rein of the nox—which, freed from the urging of Atina, showed absolutely no inclination to go a step farther anyway—and another had come bearing a wooden platform which Atina, then Teyo, and finally Perion stepped on in debarking from the carriage.

"Come with me," Atina said. "Speak to no one." She tugged his hood forward, and he followed obediently into the house. The floors here were tiled, in intricate designs of white, blue, green, and gold, and the walls were hung with woven tapestries of abstract color. "We are going where?" Perion hissed.

"To my father," Atina said. "It is custom. But you need say little to him. You will wait with him while I change for the journey to Headwater."

Atina checked in at three different stops before she found her father. He was in the back, sitting in a wooden chair with plush cushions under and behind him, his feet tipped up on a small table, a mug of wine in his hands. He stared at a small pond, lined with rock and measuring perhaps ten meters in diameter, behind the house. Stork-legged pseudobirds waded there and occasionally clacked up a struggling silver fish from the water. When they did, the old man breathed "Ha!" and took a contented sip of wine.

Old, Perion thought with shock. The man looked as old as Teyo, sixty-five or seventy in Earth terms, but he had a softness not seen in her. He was not absolutely fat, but wore extra flesh that did not become him, and his white hair, long in back, was sparse on top. He turned toward them as they approached along the colonnade, and he smiled a wide greeting to Atina. "So, Sea-Daughter! Back again, so soon! You spoil me in my dotage."

Atina touched his face with quick affection. "You are my father and the Lord Theslo," she said. "When I am on Home, your estate is my only home."

The old man looked pleased, then raised his eyes—and now Perion saw where Atina got her almost black pupils—to Perion. "A pilgrim?"

"Lord Tom Perion," Atina said. "One of the prizes."

"Ah." Theslo nodded to Perion. "You have suffered a glad fate, my friend. My daughter is a famous Captain."

"The honor of captivity is mine," Perion improvised. Atina rolled her eyes, but Theslo looked happy.

"I will leave him here with you for a moment, Father," she said. "Then he, I, and Teyo are going on a two-day journey."

Theslo nodded and turned his gaze again to the pond. Atina left them there. For a few seconds Perion, too, watched the wading creatures fish for their meals.

"Her life is in danger," Theslo said quietly.

"Atina's?" Perion asked, surprised.

"Yes. I am not supposed to know. Men are kept from these things. You know how it is. But I hear, I understand." Old Theslo turned in his seat and squinted up at Perion. "My legs are going. I cannot rise, forgive me. You are the one they call the stranger?"

"I am."

Theslo nodded. "You caused the death, then, of the Aslandian."

"Without meaning to."

"I thought as much." The old man sighed. "The Aslandians will demand justice," he said.

Perion thought of the laws he had read. "You mean they will want to take Atina's life?"

"They will want our Council to give it them," Theslo said. "I have some influence left, though, and that will not happen. But I fear she will be put outside the law, and that may mean a great deal of trouble."

"How?"

"War," the old man said bleakly.

"But I understand that Aslandia and Homereaches are already at war."

Theslo shook his head, gulped his wine. "Not a real war. Not fighting and killing. Raids, yes, but never killing. At least not in my life. But they say that years ago, one generation, two, there were island raids, burnings of estates, death, death, death."

Perion was silent. In the pond a pseudobird stole a fish from another, took off, flapped high into the air, with the injured party flying a raucous ten meters behind. Theslo barked once with laughter. "The rascal," he said. "She does it every time, every time, and the other never learns. Or else he permits it to happen." He looked again at Perion. "I hear you are very strange. You would entertain a strange request from a dying old man?"

The automatic reassuring platitude dropped unsaid from Perion's lips when he saw the seriousness of the old face. "Yes," he said simply.

"Do not let the Aslandians kill my daughter," the old man said. "They think men can do nothing. We know better, eh? Keep her out of the way, get her back to sea. You can hide the world in the ocean, they say. Keep her safe, if she is outlawed. I do not want my family to perish in flame and blood."

"I will try," Perion said.

"I thank you."

Atina came a few minutes later, walking into Theslo's garrulous account of how he had requested permission to expand cultivation into one of the preserve meadows and how he was waiting to hear the decision of the Great Council. Atina bade him farewell with a hands-open gesture and a slight bow, and Perion followed her back to the carriage. Atina had changed into dark blue trousers and white tunic, and she wore a short sword at her side. Teyo materialized a moment after they reached the carriage and climbed back to her spot.

"You were saying a farewell?" Atina guessed.

"To my mother," Teyo said.

"Your *mother*?" Perion asked, incredulous.

"She has forty and one years now," Teyo said. "I was her firstborn, when she was but eight. She is old and nearly blind now, but she lives in honor. Six strong daughters she bore, three of us Teachers. A good life, Lord Perion."

"Indeed," Perion said. After a moment, he added, "I am sorry if I sounded rude. I honor your mother."

"Thank you, Lord Perion."

The sun was climbing. They followed a road south, then turned to the west, passing on either side fields worked by families that Atina casually identified for him and that he as casually forgot. They crossed one wide river, over a substantial stone bridge, sturdy and arched. Perion saw beauty everywhere: in the domed, deep green mountains, in the rolling hills leading to them, in the spill of black-and-white water rushing beneath the bridge, in the symmetry and order of tilled fields. The air here was fresh, clear, spiced with a thousand hauntingly familiar yet alien fragrances, and overhead the violet-blue sky was dappled with glowing white clouds. They passed farmhouses, none of them as large as Atina's (and occasionally she snobbishly dismissed one or another as "new estate," with the clear implication that its holder would not hold it for long), but all of them clean and bright in the sunshine.

They stopped in a glade near a river for the midday meal, packed beneath the front seat in a basket. Perion discovered something new: flying midges, absolutely invisible to the eye, but stingingly real to the skin when they landed and drilled. He slapped and cursed, much to the amusement of old Teyo, who seemed immune—or maybe, with her leathery skin, just distasteful to the creatures.

"Smallflies," she said. "They are bad this time of year around the water." Teyo got up, stretched, wandered away into the brush. A little later she was back, holding in her hand a sprig of plant with bubbly purplish-green leaves. "Here," she said, giving it to him.

He took the spray of leaves and looked at it. "I do what with this?"

Teyo rubbed her hands together illustratively. "Crush the leaves, then rub the juice around your eyes and on your throat. Be careful not to smear your coloring, though."

Atina said, "Go ahead. It will keep the smallflies away. We do this for children with tender skin."

Perion did as he was told. The juice that the leaves produced smelled minty and had the cool feel of alcohol, but it helped. He heard the whining drone of the smallflies several times after he applied the juice, but felt no more bites.

The road led westward, and they followed it toward a setting sun. Behind them their shadows stretched long and longer. The houses became more frequent, and at last they topped a rise and looked down on a city. "Headwater," Teyo said. "We will be there by dusk."

The sun left them as they clattered along the first cobbled street, the object of half-curious glances. Perion saw that here most houses were two-storied, and frequently the lower floor was given over to shops of various kinds. "Who owns these?" he asked.

"Women of different estates," Atina said. "Sometimes their children run the shops, sometimes hired help. I have a sailcloth shop in Shelda Bay, and my youngest body-sister keeps it for me."

"Then you own the land?"

"The Council owns the land. They grant it to the estate that has proved it can make use of it."

A few stars glittered overhead, amid heavier clouds. Atina seemed to know where she was going; she guided the nox past markets, keeping the beast's obvious predilection for market goods under control, alongside the broad, still waterway that was the Larapé, across a graceful, high-arched bridge, and through a wandering labyrinth of streets until finally she guided the carriage through a high gate and into the courtyard of a looming dark building. Lights glimmered here and there in windows on the second and topmost stories, and a woman in the plain white robe of a novice Teacher came to unhitch the nox and lead it to a stall and to food. Teyo leaped lightly down, spoke in hushed tones to the novice as she worked at the nox's traces, and beckoned Atina and Perion.

"The house is in retirement for the night," she said. "We may have a cold meal in the kitchens, and then we will retire, too. This is a time for meditation for high Teachers, before the holy days of Council time. We will be quiet, so as not to disturb their prayers; and they will be too preoccupied to pay any attention to us."

The provender was simple but good, with plenty of the mild spicy wine and a delicious honey-flavored bread, and when they finished eating, Teyo led them to an upper story and along a meandering path of hallways. "I am told that we can choose any of the rooms on the left side here," she said. "We shall take the first."

It was really three rooms, a small study with desk and curious thin tapers in stone holders occupying the wall opposite a tall, narrow window, and a private room with eathenware vessels—no running water here, Perion noted—and the bedroom, with four beds comfortably spaced one against each wall, around a central round table. Their chest of clothes had already been sent up, and by the red light of a single lamp they unfolded and hung the garments in the private room.

"I am not sleepy," Atina announced as they finished.

"Nor I," Perion said.

"The old sleep long enough at last," Teyo said wryly. "What shall we do?"

"I'd like to know about this place," Perion said. "It seems very old."

"It is," Atina said. "The core of the building goes back five hundred years or more. The legend says that this was the first home of the daughters of Kalea, after they came to the island. I have heard that somewhere in the house are cellars dating back to the most ancient of days."

"Yes," Teyo agreed.

Atina turned to the old Teacher. "You tell the tale, Teyo. You know it better than I, anyway."

"Let us go to bed first," Teyo said. "It can be told as easily in the dark."

Perion undressed—he was rapidly going native, he thought ruefully—in the dark and climbed into the bed under one of the high open windows. A night breeze came lightly through them, and he actually felt cool. He drew a rough-woven but soft sheet over him and listened to rustles and creaks as Atina and Teyo turned in. When all was silence, Teyo began to speak in the soft singsong she reserved for discussing sacred matters.

"The daughters of Kalea came to this island first of all the lands of Kalea," she said. "And they called it Home.

"When women and men first made a life here, the land was pleasant, though existence was sometimes harsh. In those days fruits grew without cultivation on all the trees, and the beasts of the land and of the water were not yet killed for their meat.

"But the people were fearful of their new home, all the same. They did not know which animals were harmful, which wholesome. And so they sought a place of safety. They searched for a long time. The Two Sisters in the north were full of fire then, and the island often shook with the fury of their eruptions. The humans fled away from the anger of Kala and Akala, searching the coast for a haven.

"They came to the mouth of the Larapé, and saw that it was a waterway lined with steep cliffs. Fearfully they followed the cliffs inland, and saw that they gradually sank, until the waterway opened on either side to rich land, drained with many streams.

"And at last they came to Headwater, where the streams spilled into Larapé. Here were great stones the size of houses, and hills that gave a good view all around, and meadows beyond the stones, with no dense forests in which animals might hide.

"And so they built their home at Headwater. The first to rise was a part of this house, a structure of stone for the safety of the people. And in it they put their dearest belongings, and to it they returned each night.

"Now, the land welcomed them, but their numbers grew. They added more houses of stone, and began to cultivate the soil and to tame or kill the animals of the island, for their need grew with their numbers.

"Kalea, they say, grew angry with the heedless way that the people overspread her islands. They were thoughtless. They cut the trees and left the bare soil to wash away when the rains came; they killed the animals that fed on their own food, such as the galexes that preyed on borrits, and the smaller animals, like the borrits, became numerous and destructive. The people grew with no plan or sense, spreading across the face of the island like a disease.

"And that at last is how Kalea dealt with them. She sent a

terrible sickness, and many died; at first the elders, and later even the younger adults, until only the young ones were left.

"These, too, had suffered from the plague, but not to death. And once they had recovered, they were safe from the sickness. But one by one they had seen their parents die; and at last there were but few alive in the whole island, and they were of the age of ten or younger.

"And then one of them, a woman named Adala, saw in a fever-vision Kalea herself. Kalea told Adala to care for the world, to nourish it and be nourished by it, and not to despoil it. When she recovered, she went among the others and began to teach them; and she was the first Teacher.

"Adala had the old House of Safety renamed the House of Teachers; and since her time we have passed knowledge of the world and of Kalea from generation unto generation. And now the Council guides our lives, by Kalea's will; and the Goddess is happy, and holds back the arrows of illness."

Silence fell in the room as thick as the darkness. Perion asked, "And the things they had brought to the house? Their dearest belongings?"

"Are in the oldest part of the building even today," Teyo said. "Teachers of the highest Ascension care for them and keep them. I have never seen them myself; it is long and long since any of the relics was on public display."

Perion felt his heart beating a little faster than usual. Beneath his pillow his dataset and communicator waited. Somewhere in the bowels of this house something else waited— the "dearest belongings" of the old ones, brought here for protection centuries ago. And no one knew what they were— not Atina, not Teyo, and certainly not Tom Perion of Earth. He least of all.

But, he thought to himself before he dropped into sleep, before I leave this place, I'm damn sure going to find out.

Chapter 12

Out of the east and the sunrise came a fan of cloud, gray and heavy, presaging rain. Perion had risen early, had walked out with Atina as his guard—Teyo chose to remain inside and join the Teachers in certain rituals—and rambled in and out of the alleyways and courtyards of the House of Beginnings, admiring its architecture and style as Atina grumbled and kept a wary eye on the clouds.

The house was in fact practically a small village in itself. Gardens grew in unsuspected nooks; barns and stables were tucked far in the heart of the structure, approachable only by narrow, crooked ways and tunneled and arched passages; in places, windows looked onto bare stone wall only five meters away. Clearly the house had grown with little reason or plan.

But at last, in a passage on the northwest side of the structure, Perion saw something interesting. A low building, with battlements, had once stood there. The growing house had engulfed it, had incorporated it, so that in a sense the old building no longer existed; yet there it was, its outline clear in darker, time-pitted stone much rougher than the gray stone that began at the battlements and rose for two more stories over the original modest structure. "That part of the wall looks very old," Perion said.

Atina gave it a cursory glance. "The house is very old," she said. "That may be part of the old ones' fortress."

"I hope it is," Perion replied. "Let's find out."

But there was no direct way into the wing from the passage where they stood, and winding their way through false corridors and misleading hallways took more than an hour. Finally Atina, at the end of patience, asked a novice for direction. She came back to Perion with a look of finality on her face. "We are near it now, but we cannot go there," she told Perion.

"Why not?"

"It is forbidden, that's why not. Only Teachers of Twelfth Ascension or better may enter. It is a sacred place. Let's go back now—I want breakfast, even if you do not."

"Wait. How do we get to this place?"

Atina shook her head. "We do not," she said. Then, with a sigh: "Back to the cross hall, left, to the next hall to the left, to the end, down the flight of steps at the end, and there is the only entrance to the cellar."

"I want to try."

"No. There are Teachers all about, for one thing. For another, I dare not. I have trouble of my own that you know nothing about. I cannot risk gaining the enmity of the Teachers at this time."

Perion finally allowed himself to be persuaded, though he grumbled, and they went back to the guest rooms. Teyo had food there, fruit mainly, and they ate. Then Teyo, replying to Perion's questions, said that the time fewest Teachers would be about was likely to be in early afternoon, meditation time, when most would be congregated in the various halls.

Atina gave him a hard look. "I hope you do not plan to go back," she said.

Perion was all innocence. "How could I? You think I could recall all the twists and turns of the hallways we followed, the route to the old hall you discovered? The corridors here all look alike to me."

True enough, as far as it went. But Perion did not mention the dakakit under his tunic. Its electronic memory for detail was dependable.

The storm broke at noon, an explosion of rain and thunder, vibrating in the very stones of the walls. Perion asked Teyo to accompany him to an open library, and he sat there for some time while the wind howled somewhere beyond the wall at his back. When Teyo began to appear restless, Perion said, "You wish to join the meditation? Go. I will remain here. Call for me when it is over."

The hooded gray eyes looked at him for a long moment. "I go, Lord Perion," she said at last.

Perion gave her half an hour before he left the library. He carried a book—Teyo's copybook, in fact—which he seemed to study. Actually, he was following a lightly glowing map etched on the screen of his datakit, now left, now right, now through a door, now past one. The storm had thrown the hallways in gloom, and water puddled beneath some of the east-facing windows; but red light flickered in lantern holders at intervals along the hall, and the display screen, turned low, provided its own dim illumination.

He found the correct hallway, moved along it until he came to the stone stair. It led down into darkness. Perion retraced his route back to the last lantern, caught it off its holder, and with it he descended the stair. It gave only a shivery, dim circle of light, but it was enough to show him his surroundings.

The stair was deeper than he had thought. Down here the storm was muted, faraway, and even the thunder sounded no louder than a remote drumming, heard across a great distance. At the foot of the stair was a small anteroom, walls and floor of rough stone; and opposite the foot of the stair, a doorway opened into even deeper darkness, a doorway made on the lintel principle, not arched. It looked very old. Perion saw projecting stone blocks, hollowed, that once had held ponderous hinges, but the door was long gone now. Through the doorway, Perion found himself once again in an empty stone room, but now he faced a closed wooden door twice his height and at least three meters wide. He held the lantern aloft. It did not bring light to the corners to his left and right, but he could see the stone ceiling, dripping with moisture here and there, and he could tell that the stone floor had been worn in a pathway from the outer door to the inner by the passing of generations of feet.

The doorway was barred, the latch at eye level, and above it was a smoothed stone incised with warnings against opening the door. He ignored these, lifted the latch, and leaned hard and fruitlessly against the massive gate before realizing that it was designed to swing outward.

Feeling foolish, he tugged, and the door swung easily outward, though the wooden hinges growled in protest. He stepped inside and pulled the door almost shut behind him.

A circular basin in the floor here held a bubbling spring, which drained through a channel cut into the floor and passed finally through a low, dark arch to the outside. The sight gave Perion heart: the earliest settlers would have wanted a fresh-water supply, and the spring would have been an ideal one. He prowled the room, found short passages leading left and right from it, and took the right one first. This led to a small warren of rooms, empty save for dust and for small scuttling creatures that he never quite caught in the light. Back to the spring room, across, and into the left passage. More rooms. In the first was loose stone, apparently left over from the long-ago time when the old structure was incorporated into the new. The next room—eureka!

The light grew more uncertain. Perion realized his hand was shaking, and with it the lantern. He set the lantern down on a waist-high stone shelf that ran around three walls of the room, trimmed the wick, and looked again at the landing pod.

For that occupied the center of the room. It was standard: five meters long, just large enough to hold one person, identical in every respect to Perion's. Every respect but one.

It was *old*.

Perion walked over to it, ran his hand over its surface, dulled now with the oxides the ages had brought out of the metal. The hatch was gone. He brought the lantern over, ducked, looked inside. The capsule had been gutted. It was all shell now, its few remaining plastic fixtures pitted and ruined. He touched a panel with his left hand, felt it yield, then, brittle, dissolve into a cloudy star. He remembered it as a plastic plaque with instructions on operating the air cycler. Any message it had held was long since gone, flaked away by time.

More relics waited, ranged with careful art on the stone shelf. He found a skeletonized revolver, made entirely of rust and looking as if a breath would destroy it. Strange tubes and circles of clear glass puzzled him for a moment, until he thought of the women aboard the *Galileo*. Despite himself, he smiled. One of them had smuggled a cosmetic kit into her capsule.

A skull—whose?—missing all teeth, looking absurdly shrunken and forlorn. The eyeholes gazed up at Perion with a sort of imploring resignation. Not our fault, old boy. We didn't mean to leave you up there for nearly two millennia. We had troubles of our own, you know.

Not one but two communicators, their solar packs long gone, their circuits eroded away. And did you, too, try to call the *Galileo*, crewmates? Did you curse, weep, when the ship taunted you with electromagnetic interference before sailing out of range?

A special wooden box, of recent make, created to hold a few flakes of silver. Perion recognized them. Someone's uniform, so age-ridden now that he could thrust his finger through a fabric that was bulletproof when new. Perion shivered, feeling something brushing his spine; but it was nothing material, and he continued his circuit of the room.

Another wooden box, smaller. Inside a lump of something, dark brown, the size of his hand, roughly rectangular, its edges laminations of some kind—oh. A book. What book? he wondered. It had to be a souvenir. All serious reading material was recorded in the datakit, or on the datacards that provided additional external memory. This was a diary. Or a Bible, a Koran, the Vedas. Or pornography. Or the words of Earth, unknowable but hallowed now by the turning years.

And then the cards.

Perion set the lantern down and sorted through the small stack. Five, six, eight, ten datacards, thirty-five millimeters on a side, each as thin as a sheet of paper but infinitely tough, flexible. He slipped his datakit out of the tunic, set it to play, and inserted one of the cards.

It was a technical journal of practical farm methods, with observations on nutritional standards, conversation, and the best organic fertilizers to use for optimum crop yield. Perion scanned through the card for five minutes, touching down here and there but stopping nowhere. At last he was sure it was only a textbook and nothing more, and he popped it out of the datakit. He reached for a second one.

Baby and child care. The psychology of the infant. Learning disabilities. Sex education. Out with it, in with the next.

Structures for shelter. The use of native materials. The suitability of different types of plant and inorganic materials as insulation. Out, in.

Log of the *Galileo* expedition, Engineer James Smith, Acting Commander.

"My God," Perion said, and his voice was loud in the closed-in space. Sweat dripped from his face and stung his eyes. He swabbed them with a sleeve and scanned:

"—the ship cannot be raised unless we locate a command pod. We can account for only four out of one hundred, and those four are all out of commission. The recorder in Pod 1000 indicates landing sites for . . .

"—some six thousand pods close to the islands. We do not know if any to the north or south were close enough to land for the passengers to survive. Our situation is bleak, but not hopeless. . . .

"—war on Earth? We expected it long ago. But would they have somehow disabled our ship, even if they had some means of doing it? We cannot make that decision. . . .

"—ship is finished. We must try to reach the one command pod that we know to be intact. It is stasis-sealed and should remain so indefinitely. The settlers are divided, for this means taking nearly half of the strongest men away, perhaps on a dangerous mission. But without the attempt we have no hope of reaching the ship again, no means of establishing the kind of colony. . . .

"End of record. This is a COPY of the original datacard."

Tom's datakit held, in a small compartment, twenty-five blank datacards. He thumbed one out, placed it on the stone ledge in place of the one he was taking. He reached for the next untried datacard on the shelf, then froze as he heard voices, not too far away.

For a moment he stood irresolute; but the voices were getting louder. Perion hastily scooped up the six remaining datacards, thumbed out six blank ones to replace them, and hurried out. The wooden door groaned again, and light spilled from the opening into the spring room.

Three robed women, all old, came in. Two held torches. In the light all three looked at him without apparent surprise, but with a baleful glower that promised no mirth. Under his tunic he held his datakit tight against his ribs.

They stood that way, a tableau, for a long moment. Then the eldest woman turned and said through the open door, "He is indeed here, Teacher Teyo."

Teyo pushed through, came to him. "Why?" she mouthed, scowling, her back to the three Teachers.

"Uhh—" grunted Perion.

"He is—mute?" asked the eldest Teacher, a head taller than Teyo and looking even more ancient.

Teyo took a deep breath. "Your grace, some believe that springs such as this one, springs in holy places, have healing properties."

"A superstition not to be tolerated, let alone encouraged."

Teyo turned, and Perion realized that she was wholly given

to the deception she wove. "True, your grace, but a man whose brother has a fine estate, and who himself is kept from lordship by an accident of nature—such a man feels desperate enough to try any remedy."

"You will examine the reliquary," the old Teacher said to one of her acolytes, a thin woman with steel-gray hair and features that might have been filed to sharpness. She left silently, remained away for a minute or more, and then returned.

"All seems in place, Teacher," she reported.

"Take this man to the small meditation room on this wing," the elder said. "We must examine him."

Teyo looked at Perion. He unobtrusively gestured, "No."

To the Teacher, Teyo said, "I will take responsibility for this man's actions, your grace. Does not Kalea smile on those whose faith is very strong? And his coming here surely shows his strong faith, though it may be misplaced."

The old woman stared at Teyo for so long that Perion had already begun to tense his muscles for a spring that would carry him past the elder, out the doorway, into the house. But at last, in a soft, rusty voice, she said, "Your family is an old and honored one, Teyo. You realize the greatness of the favor you ask of me?"

"I do, your grace. My obligation to you and to the house would be very great indeed."

"We need the land across Water Street for a dormitory. The shopkeepers there refuse to relinquish."

Teyo nodded. "I think my family can add to your purchase price. You should be able to persuade the Council that you offer the shopkeepers a fair price for their buildings. I am sure that if the price is high enough, the Council will grant you the use of the land."

Another long pause. Finally the elder said, "For the sake of your family, then, Teyo, and that of our friendship, I will exact no punishment for this transgression. But it brings you no credit. You realize I must report this to the House Council?"

"Yes, your grace. We will leave within one taper."

"A taper I can give you. No more." To Perion she added, "Be gone, and be grateful for the rest of your life to the graciousness of Teyo da-Theslo."

He passed under her stern gaze, shrinking within himself;

then Teyo was beside him, and they quick-marched through the corridors. "You have some explanation, no doubt?" hissed Teyo when they were away from the reliquary wing altogether.

"Mm."

"Save it. We are in great haste. Atina is already waiting in the outer court with the carriage. We have all of your things in the traveling chest. There is no need to return to the room."

The rain dashed in sheets across the stone-paved courtyard, and overhead the sky was a purplish-gray chaos occasionally sketched silver by a bolt of lightning. The nox hitched to the carriage shifted its weight forlornly, looking distinctly unhappy at its lot this afternoon. Perion and Teyo dashed the ten paces between the portico of the House of Beginnings and the carriage, but when he climbed into the carriage, Perion was as wet as he had been when he floundered in the ocean.

Atina wordlessly urged their beast into action, and with a resentful lumbering gait the nox pulled the carriage forward, rattling the wheels over the uneven cobbles. The rain had driven everyone indoors, and they clattered through the deserted twisting streets of Headwater without so much as seeing another vehicle. The half-open carriage lurched in the wind, seemed to invite drenching gusts of rain, but it kept moving. When they had crossed the arched bridge, Teyo turned. "I hope your trip was worthwhile," she said.

Perion spat the six datacards into his hand. "I think it was." He grinned. "Don't worry; I took these, but gave them new ones that will serve just as well as relics. But now I have a voice from my people at last. I think these may be the key to my problem."

Atina cursed as they splashed through a low flooded place, the nox floundering and beginning to bleat like a goat. Teyo looked at her clan-sister, then turned again to Perion. "I am sorry," she said. "We were interrupted in meditation—a thing that hardly ever happens—and I learned we had to leave, quickly. I came to look for you, and found you missing. The novices had noticed the way you went, and Grisla, the old Teacher, took up the search."

"No harm done," Perion said.

"None except to my family," Teyo replied. Her eyes flashed. "The Teachers have a hand in our purse now! Do you know what that means? No, of course not. Our family may be crippled for years by the pledge I made. If it is too severe a drain, when our present lord dies, the estate may even be broken. But you would never think of that."

"Enough," said Atina. "We have other worries."

"I think I can make it up to you," Perion said. "If I understood what I saw, there may be a way to communicate with the Sailing Star. There is a command capsule, still under stasis if all has gone well, in the north. If we travel there, I can release the stasis with my datakit; then we can communicate with the ship, can have it wake the sleepers, can have them send a craft down for me. Teyo, they have crops aboard that you've never dreamed of! They have animals, tools, that would make your family wealthy beyond the dreams of the Teachers of the House of Beginnings. They—"

"Be quiet," Teyo said. "The scriptures say that Kalea will one day send down a greater Teacher than any we have known, that the Teacher will lead the people through a time of great trouble to a golden time. I heard your story and thought you were the promised one. A man. The last thing I would expect. I don't know. I don't know. To this time you have brought so much trouble—"

"It was not of his making, Teyo," Atina said. "Quiet, now. It's hard enough to guide this beast without your quarreling."

Teyo turned around, and Perion dropped back into the carriage, cowering against the rear to avoid the worst touch of the clammy rain. The carriage jolted on, and Perion slipped his datakit out of his tunic. He reactivated it, scanned again through the information placed there so long ago by James Smith. He passed something he had not noticed before, backed to it, and ran it through several degrees of enlargement and scanning.

He saw a colored map of Kalea.

Not all of Kalea; only a tiny part, a shape like a teardrop suspended from a cobweb, slanted. It was pocked and speckled with points of light, differently colored. It stretched, in its thin portion, across part of the northern continent, leaving it and leaping to sea in a coastline of deep fjords and inlets. Then it began to broaden, becoming at last a fat oval, five hundred kilometers or more on its widest diameter; and that diameter was centered over a stretch of islands, the largest of them familiar to him in shape. It was Home.

The text told him that the map recorded the landing sites of something like twenty thousand jettisoned lifepods. The yellow pinpricks marked the locations of command pods. But of all the yellow marks, nearly a hundred in all, the survivors, the handful who counted themselves as about six thousand, could account for only four with certainty. One had been wrestled to shore, but lost to a raging storm; two had sunk at sea, one carrying its occupant with it; one had been seen to drop into a lava lake in the crater of an active volcano.

The others, ninety-two others, had gone down in the sea and had never made it to land. All but one.

On the north continent, at the extreme edge of the mapped portion, a yellow light glimmered. The command pod had landed there, on dry land, and the last communication from the ship indicated that it had landed with stasis generator intact and functioning.

And so it still might wait, for if it truly was locked in stasis, no living force could move it. It might be buried under a landslide, or covered by floodwaters, or even hidden in the depths of the sea; but with the stasis generator operating, it was cocooned in Time, intact, whole, just waiting for someone to find it, release it, and use it.

If it could be reached. "I've got to go to the north continent," Perion said, and when he spoke he saw for the first time that the rain had abated to a steady spattering shower.

"We won't talk of that now," Atina said.

"We have to!"

With a snarl, Atina turned on him and lashed out with the end of the reins. Perion fell back, dazed from her action as much as from the blinding gash of pain across his cheek and nose. He held his hand to his face, and it came away wet and sticky. "Why?" he asked.

"Damn you, shut up!" Atina redoubled her efforts to make the nox move through the deepening twilight.

Teyo turned. "A messenger from Shelda Bay came just after noon," she said. "An Aslandian ship, under the banners of truce, came into harbor there before dawn. Their Captain is a hunter named Halindo; she came aboard the ship, the *Windbird*, seeking for Atina."

"The Aslandians seek revenge for the woman's death?" Perion asked.

"They have it, damn them," cried Atina in a voice too raging for tears. "Kayla was there, little Kayla."

Perion felt the heart within him fall. "Did she—Kayla is—what—?"

"Hush," said Teyo. "Kayla is dead."

Chapter 13

Either because the handmaidens of the House of Waiting had been told to allow him his freedom or because the death of Kayla had sent a shock through the whole estate, Perion's door was not barred the next day; nor was Mela with him. A second handmaiden brought his dinner, and did not stay to converse. After the meal, Perion, restless, went into the corridor and then to the central room.

The House of Waiting was empty, it seemed; or at least no one was about. Perion paced among the potted plants, ill at ease. After a few minutes, he dimly became aware that soft music, plaintive and melancholy, had begun: someone was playing a stringed instrument. Perion followed the sound down a corridor to the third door. He knocked.

"Yes, enter," said a familiar voice.

Perion opened the door. The musician was Trennon Fane, his instrument a small harplike affair with a round reverberation chamber. Fane gave him a lopsided smile. "The barbarian," he murmured. "More muscular than ever."

"I heard the music," Perion said.

"I was only amusing myself."

"Play," Perion said.

"Surely. Have a seat, my barbarian friend."

Perion sat, and watched as Trennon's long, nervous fingers played over the strings. The melody was thin, but it lingered in the mind. Perion was reminded of Oriental music, somehow, though the composition had something of an austere north European bleakness in it, too. Trennon's face knitted in concentration over the instrument, the muscles of his mouth and cheek occasionally twitching as he reached for a handful of music and turned it loose in the room. The melody died away, failing in echoes and memories. Perion took a deep breath. "Very good," he said.

"Ah. So barbarians appreciate the finer things?" Trennon smiled. He laid the instrument aside carefully. "My skill is not as it once was. Still, I find the luta a relaxation."

"The house needs relaxation," Perion said.

"So I understand. Pity that the woman was killed."

"Kayla was only a girl, not even a woman," Perion said bitterly.

Trennon blinked. "Kayla? No, I meant the woman on our ship. I do not even know her name. Yes, it is a pity about the Homereach girl, too, but the death of the Aslandian began all this. I have heard of Halindo the Hunter."

"She is here for revenge?"

"Yes. And she's begun with Kayla, I see."

Perion got up, paced again. "Teyo began to explain to me, but she was tired and broke off. I don't understand. Halindo can come to Home and kill any member of Atina's crew?"

"Not just like that. As I understand it, Halindo boarded the *Windbird*. Kayla was there, watching the ship. Halindo insisted that Kayla surrender the Captain of the ship to her justice; Kayla challenged her. They fought. No one from Home is going to defeat Halindo in a fair fight. The girl died."

"And now the Theslo family can demand revenge against Halindo?"

"Not that simple. The Aslandians are the injured party; and Kayla did issue challenge. Since one death has already taken place, that of the Aslandian woman, any more deaths that result from challenge—such as Kayla's—cannot be legally avenged. Though I understand that Homereachers are not above a little illegal vengeance."

"This is complex. I thought the Council would meet on the question."

"So they will, and probably on the first day as well. Look to have our hearings delayed. But their question is whether to declare Atina outlaw. I would guess they will."

"But why?"

"To avoid more deaths," Trennon said. "You see, if the Aslandians have hired Halindo, a professional hunter, to gain vengeance, then she will not stop. She can be turned away from harbor, but nothing is to prevent her from preying on Homereach ships. Eventually she would kill so many that the life of one, Atina, would be held small price to pay for sending her away. Of course, by that time many Home families would have blood scores to settle with Aslandia, and so the deaths would continue. It would grow into a killing war.''

Perion shook his head. "So useless."

"I think so," Trennon said dryly. "But then I saw no reason for Captain Theslo to take our ship."

"You know the reason for that. Men are in short supply."

"Yes. The same is true in my country as well." Trennon stood, produced a beaker and two mugs. "Wine?"

"Thank you." Perion accepted the mug, sipped from it. "Your training goes well?"

Trennon shrugged. "It goes. Actually, I do not have to be trained; but my handmaiden, Dominice, has told me that an old lord of Easthaven is very ill. He cannot expect to live out the next half-year. If I have to have just the right *amount* of training, I shall be on hand for his estate when the old fellow goes to the Sailing Star." Trennon winked. "It's a second-generation estate, I understand. Choice haremas, good properties. It's so nice to be placed on an established estate, don't you think? Then one hasn't any worry about the tedious business of accumulating enough wealth to be comfortable."

Perion drained his cup. "Trennon, what would you say if I told you I could change the world?"

Trennon's rolling accent hinted hidden laughter. "I would say that the wine is far more potent than I believed."

"No, really. I told you about myself, back on the ship. It's all true. More, now I have a means of proving it. But I must travel to the north to do it; I must cross to—a special place there.''

"You could no more do that, my barbarian, than you could stand beneath the sun," Trennon said. "To do it you *would* have to stand beneath the sun. And that is impossible."

"You mean it has never been done."

"And never will be."

Perion looked at the floor. Then he turned his gaze back to Trennon. "You would like to see proof of what I say? You will come to my room?"

"If I may bring the wine."

"By all means."

Perion's window was open—he gave silent thanks that the ecology of Kalea seemed to get along quite well without the equivalent of a mosquito—and the evening breeze was drifting in. Perion rummaged in the chest, brought out Teyo's copybook, a few sheets of loose paper, and a stick of charcoal. "I've done most of these just today," Perion said. "Some are copied from books here in the House of Waiting, others from—another place."

Trennon leafed through the papers as Perion extended them. "Maps and charts."

"Yes."

"You copied these? You can read?"

"I've learned to read your script, yes."

Trennon's eyes widened in astonishment. "My dear Tom, whatever for? Reading is hardly a masculine accomplishment. Why, I'd no sooner learn to read than I'd—I'd—"

"Learn to handle a sword," Perion suggested, sipping the acidic, warming wine. "Yes, well, I plan to learn that, too."

"You have reasons of your own, no doubt."

"Yes. But let me show you this." Perion shuffled through the charts, singled one out, smoothed it across his knee, and pointed to a sketched coastline, ragged triangular peninsula, thicker at the base than at the point where it joined a mainland. "This is Aslandia," Perion said. His finger swept southward. "There," he said, indicating a semicircle of dots leading to the southwest, "are islands, the Aladians. I make them out to be thirty-four islands in five separate groups, with three groups forming a cluster. There are smaller ones, too, that are not shown here."

Trennon nodded. "Yes, from what I've heard those would be the Aladians. I've never visited any but my home island, though."

"Which is it?"

"Varn."

"Yes." Perion tapped the paper. "Here."

"Is that it? I wouldn't have thought it would be so small. And of course the surrounding space is all ocean."

"That's right. A great deal of ocean for such a small speck of land, wouldn't you say?"

Trennon made a face and poured another cup of wine. "Varn is as good as any other island, I suppose. But there is a large burning mountain in the center of it, which is a luxury mercifully omitted here. It is disturbing to be awakened in the middle of the night by shaking earth and falling stones."

Perion leaped like a cat. "Shaking what? What word did you use?"

Trennon frowned and repeated the Common word: "*Yrth.*"

"*Yrth.* Earth. Trennon, don't you see? Don't you realize that says something? You use the same word for 'ground' that I use for my home planet. Remember my story?"

Trennon waved his winecup. "It's an old word. The trembling of an island is called an earthquake, and I suppose it derives from there. Earthquake—a shaking sent by the gods, I suppose it means."

"That, Trennon, is what linguists of my world called a false etymology. It means you're casting about for a complex explanation of a very simple term. As I told you, I come from a world called Earth, and there when the ground shakes we very properly call it an earthquake. Your use of the term is a carryover, don't you see? The myths you've heard about the old ones are true, or have a germ of truth in them."

"My word," Trennon said. "You are becoming a true believer, aren't you? Are you sure you haven't something hidden from me?"

"I have," Perion admitted. "Like you with your ailing lord of Easthaven, I want something, and I am plotting to get it."

"And the barbarian desires—?"

"Power."

Trennon's checkle was indulgent. "And you have a means of getting it?"

Perion rummaged again in the stack of charts and finally produced one of a deeply indented coastline, a range of mountains, and a diminishing swath of land slanting to the northeast. "Here," he said. "I'll find power by looking here, in the north continent."

"You'll find heat there," Trennon amended. "Heat enough to fry your brain. Though that seems no great loss."

"No. I'll find a way through," Perion insisted. "The northern continent is larger than you dream, and it offers more than you know. You are scheming to be lord of a minor estate. Man, you could be ruler of an estate five times the size of this island—bigger! The land lies there for the taking!"

"But science tells us—"

"Damn science! I *am* a scientist! I can tell you why there are burning mountains, what types of rock are found on your island, what the sea bed is like. I know these things; I've studied them all my life. And all the science I know convinces me that the zone of heat is finite. If we can cross it going north, we can certainly recross it going south. We can lead people there, establish our own domain, come back for whatever we need.''

"But why?''

"Why? You are happy with the way society is? Have you never thought you could create a better world than the one you live in? Have you, a man, never wanted to be equal to a woman?''

"We are superior!'' Trennon objected.

Perion snorted. "Show me the man who sits on Council. Show me a man who is a Teacher, who commands a ship, who owns a house—*really* owns it. My people believed that all possibilities should be open to all.''

Trennon tipped the wine container, found it empty, and looked up at Perion. "But even if I said yes, how would you get there? The women would never let us go, and we're certainly no match for them.''

"I will find a way. Will you consider my words?''

Trennon tipped his empty cup. "The wine assures that much, anyway. But I make no promises.''

"I ask for none but this: you will not speak to any of the women about what I say.''

"Done. They would believe me insane, anyway.''

Perion reached for a fresh paper and the charcoal stick. Like a lecturer at a blackboard, he sketched in a globe and a rayed representation of the sun, and defined the equator on the planet. Quickly he explained the physics of insolation, the geology of tectonics. Trennon watched with growing interest.

"I see,'' he said excitedly at one point. "As this plate slips, the melted rock from below seeks another path to the surface, and forms another burning mountain, an island, as the old one is carried away. That is why islands come in chains!''

"Right!'' Perion said. "And I believe that right now most of this equatorial continent is trying to move southward. That would build up a rim of mountains around here, and behind the mountains would be the desert.''

"Yes. My people have gone beyond the mountains in the north of Aslandia, but briefly, for nothing lives there.''

"Yes. The problem is crossing the desert. Here," Perion said, shading the flat stretch behind the mountains, "will be the worst part. This is the land where they say one cannot stand beneath the sun. This is the part that must be crossed quickly."

"How?"

"By traveling only at night and resting in the day."

Trennon got up, paced. "But to rest would be to die. The heat is enough to boil one's blood, they say."

"*If* one remains in the open."

"Where else can one go?"

"Into shelters, tents, even underground," Perion said. "There are ways. If I choose the terrain well, we should be able to march for seven hours, set up camp for two, and have an hour of twilight either way as a safety factor. With good luck, we might cover as much as forty kilometers in a march."

"I do not know this measure. How wide would be the desert?"

"That is a guess. I think, if I choose a good route, we should be able to cross the worst stretch in twelve days, maybe fourteen—given luck."

"There is no water. You would try to carry enough?"

"We could do it, I think. The weight would grow less as we continued. And if by the eighth day I saw no signs that we were nearing the limits of the desert, I would turn back. By rationing ourselves, we could reach bearable climates again."

Trennon puffed out his cheeks. "They say that eons ago, Jansmeet tried to cross that desert and found only death there."

"Jansmeet was a man who believed in technology, in the works of hands. I knew him. He would try for a direct assault, a simple cross-country march, relying on reflective suits and persistence. I'm no hero, Trennon, If anything, I guess I'm a bit of a coward. I take the route that promises survival."

Trennon rubbed his chin. "I don't know. You have a reason for wishing me to go?"

"Yes. You are a man. You can help me recruit other men. Trennon, if this works, if we succeed, we change Kalea forever. Men will have new rights, new responsibilities. We must have both men and women as leaders in the new world."

Trennon watched, doubt flickering in his eyes. He stirred.

"You advise me to surrender a perfectly reliable future here for these uncertain prospects?"

Perion sat on the foot of his bed. "Something must be done. Your prospects here are certain? I have been outside, Trennon. I have seen how closely farmed is the land, how crowded the cities. Homereaches is strangling. There are too many people for the land. And things are the same in Aslandia?"

Trennon made a sour face. "Much the same," he admitted in a grudging voice. "I was being sent from Varn, which after all is a rather pleasant place, to Georn, famous for heat and aridity. It has poor soil, little water. Yet even Georn is becoming crowded."

Perion spread his hands. "There you are. The harem system does it. When every man must father eight women to be sure of producing one male, the population will grow denser and denser. And every woman seems to desire a man-child, so each woman has several children. Sooner or later, they will overrun all of the islands here to the south. But there in the north is a secret, a way of calling down the power of the Sailing Star—don't scoff; I am speaking of science, truly, not of religion—and of changing the number of male children born, of making them equal in numbers to the females."

"That sounds bad to me. Men have a special place—"

"They will not have it for long, if the population continues to grow. Whatever you may think, Trennon, I do not hate Kalea or her people. They are my people, too, and I want them to live, to have a chance to learn about their world and the universe. They cannot do that cramped as they are, closed in by a sea of water and a sea of people."

Trennon stood. "My head is thick. You have not convinced me, but you have given me much to consider. I will think on it. Thank you, Perion. We shall talk further on this."

"Not a word to any of the women."

"No, of course not. Good night, Perion."

But in the doorway the Aslandian hesitated. With a half-smile on his face, he turned back to Perion. "One thing more: you have not approached my countrymen about this matter?"

"Only you."

"There is a reason?"

"Yes. You are lively, curious, quick. I thought of all the Aslandians you would be the animal who wished to see the other side of the hill."

Trennon laughed. "May the holy Goddess keep you safe, O Tom Perion," he said. "And may she keep others safe from you!"

Perion folded the maps, stacked them, put them away. He blew out the lamps and stood for a time at the window, looking out into the night garden, faint in the silver light of Lun. If he was wrong . . .

He grunted, turned away from the window and the possibility. He risked a great deal in speaking to Trennon Fane; certainly his plan, and very likely his life. But he thought he could read the man's character. Perion turned in, tossed in the bed, sought for sleep.

But it rode away from him, riding the waves northward, toward the unknown continent. Seeing its rugged borders in his mind, feeling its sandy wastes under his feet in his imagination, Perion finally closed his fist on sleep and sank deep with it into a night of fitful dreams.

At about the time Perion finally fell asleep, a carriage stopped in the yard of the House of Waitihg. A figure, bent with age, rose from the bench in the yard and hobbled toward the carriage. Atina stepped down from it, saluted Teyo.

"You have spoken with the Aslandians?" Teyo asked.

Atina's voice was flat, weary. "I have spoken with them."

"Yes?"

"I rejected the challenge, of course. I would have no hope against Halindo the Hunter. You have heard of her prowess. They have agreed to petition the Council for my outlawing. Now we shall see."

Teyo shook her head. "No. No. Even the Theslo clan cannot persuade the Council to vote against outlawing. That would mean war for everyone."

"I know."

"What, then?"

"They will give me a week's grace, I think. I will take the *Windbird* to sea and run. They say Halindo has the eyes of a fish-spear bird, and that she can follow a trail even across the ocean; but at sea I would stand some sort of chance. If I can move and keep moving for a year and a day, I may satisfy the Council.''

"I will go."

"Thank you, clan-sister. I will not ask that of you. It is a dark voyage, into who knows what perils. I think ten or twelve of my crew will go, some for the chance to avenge Kayla. That will be enough."

"There are not enough islands. You will run out of places to hide."

"Then I will seek new places." Atina staggered a little.

"You are tired. Come inside and rest."

"Yes, I will. Soon. I dare not stay in the house of my father; here at least the law of hospitality will keep the Aslandians out."

"Come in now."

"Not yet. There is one more thing. Kayla?"

"Mela and five others have taken her up the mountain. At dawn the fire will be lighted."

"Then I will stay here."

"If you wish to sleep, I will wake you in time."

"No. I will see the smoke before I sleep."

Teyo nodded, led Atina to the bench. "I will keep vigil with you."

"Thank you, Teyo."

Much later, as the sky paled with the coming of the sun, Teyo said, "You could tell them that the death was the fault of the barbarian. That he did not understand the ways."

"He is a man, Teyo. He deserves protection."

"Ah," Teyo said, and began to chant a song of passage. From the summit of Shelda, the old extinct volcano, the thinnest trickle of white smoke appeared, silvered in the earliest rays of the sun.

Atina watched it through undimmed eyes. When it drifted away at last, she rose and followed Teyo into the House of Waiting. She did not speak to Teyo again that day.

Chapter 14

The day should have been Sundi, but it was not. It was, instead, Reaping-Month Council Day One, Perion learned, and a holiday. Three more would follow; and after that, Sundi would come, Sundi the first day of Ramm, the last month of the season of nearsun. It was all very regular, very sensible, and very confusing.

The carriage took them to a square in Shelda Bay, and there it stopped. The five Aslandian lords and Perion got down and found themselves near a fountain, surrounded by the curious citizens of Shelda Bay, all of them women. An approving "Ahh!" ran through the crowd as they began to walk behind Teyo and Atina, toward the Council Hall. "I hope it isn't too far," Yannow Tully drawled. Tully had, if anything, gained weight during his imprisonment. He rolled it along now complacently, nodding his double chins to the women who thronged either side of the roadway. Now and again he was the subject of a high-pitched lascivious remark. He winked at those who called out.

Perion managed to fall in beside Trennon Fane. "Have you thought it over?" he asked quietly.

Trennon did not look directly at him, but rather continued to beam at the appreciative audience all around them. "I'm still thinking," he said.

"Oh?"

"Much depends on how well or ill a certain old lord in Easthaven is," Trennon said frankly.

"I see."

They walked down what seemed to be the main street of Easthaven, a street lined with shops and warehouses, groceries, woodcarvers' shops, ropemakers', carters', lantern and candle shops, leather workers' establishments, restaurants, more.

"Many ill people," Trennon said at one point.

They had passed eyeless beggars, cripples with withered limbs, wretches who seemed to lack intellect. "Not illness," grunted Perion. "Inbreeding."

The street ended perhaps two and a half kilometers from the place where they began their march. A circular building was at the end of it, rather like a stadium, two-storied, red-roofed, crafted of dark stone. Teyo and Atina halted at the foot of a broad stairway leading up to the second floor. "Here," Teyo said to them. "This is the Council Hall. I will take you up."

They climbed the steps; at the summit, Teyo turned and gestured for them to do the same. While they stood there, looking down over the street, now packed with women who had followed them the whole way, a cheer went up, like the sound of surf on stone; and then Teyo led them inside the building.

They found themselves in a curving hall. Teyo led them down the hall to a room furnished with a table, ten or twelve chairs, and a pitcher of wine. "You will wait here," Teyo said. "The Council will first practice the rites of purification; then you will come into the Great Council Room, and your cases, and Atina's, will be considered. I will be back."

Kant went straight for the pitcher, and in a moment was smacking his lips over a cup of wine. Perion wandered to the curving wall, pulled aside a tapestry, and looked down on a street corner of Shelda Bay. The crowd was dispersing now, clusters of three or four or five women drifting along, deep in conversation and laughter. A half-dozen little girls, eight or ten years old, were playing with a rope threaded through brightly colored wooden blocks. Perion smiled to himself as two of the girls began to turn the rope and a third to skip it as the blocks set up a clacking rhythm on the ground. The girls began to chant, and Perion leaned partway out of the glassless window opening to catch the rhyme:

"Fisher-boat, fisher-boat, don't catch me;
Catch all the fishes in the sea!
Can you name them? Yes, I can.
One is a flatface in the sand,
Two is a saw-jaw with sharp teeth,
Three is a mud-bore down beneath,

Four is a stinger, sharp of tail,
Five is an eater, gray and pale,
Six is—''

Suppressing a mild *frisson*, Perion let fall the tapestry and turned back to the Aslandians. For a moment things had seemed so—so *Earthlike*.

Trennon sat a little apart from the others, who were deep in discussion, considering their chances for gaining good estates, rehearsing arguments that would most likely gain the favor of the Council. Perion pulled a chair beside Trennon's, sat near him. "They don't understand," Perion said in an undertone.

Trennon raised his eyebrows. "About Atina? They have heard, but they don't regard her problems as their own. You are troubled?''

"Of course I am," Perion said. "Atina has been kind to me, as she understands kindness. I would not like to see her hurt."

"Ah, well, we cannot wish a storm to vanish," Trennon said.

They remained in the room, talking or locked alone in moody thoughts, for perhaps an hour. Then Teyo was back, and they followed her around the hall, through a door to their left, and into a room vast by Kalean standards. They found themselves in a kind of pit, and surrounding them at more than a man's height were the Council. Atina was already there, and they joined her. The Council women, all of them at least as old as Teyo, were conferring with one another, some of them out of their seats; a skylight overhead allowed the sun to throw the pit into harsh illumination, while leaving the Council in gloom. Perion sniffed; the room had a strange perfume, as of incense.

"The Aslandians will be heard first," Atina said to Perion. "Their cases are deemed simple, and they can easily be disposed of. Then they will hear Halindo's appeal against me; and finally they will hear your story, Tom."

Perion nodded. "Is there a chance they will dismiss Halindo's case?"

"A chance. Her murder of my kinswoman does not sit well with the Council. But she will be brought in later." The Council were beginning to return to their seats. Atina nodded at one of them, a very old, hawk-faced woman, who was nearly bald. "That is Ruisa," Atina whispered. "The most powerful member here. Take care you do not offend her."

"I will," Perion whispered back.

Ruisa had craned her head this way and that on a thin, corded neck; now she thumped the floor beside her chair three times with a crooked staff. "The Island Council of Homereaches, Home, Beren, Labalda, Tobria, and Aketo Islands now meets. We sit as Hearers of Appeals," she said in a firm high voice. "The session of Day One, After-Reaping, in the seventh year of the rule of Law-Divider Cathara of Home Island is called to order. What business do we hear today?"

One of the women behind Perion stood and responded: "Honored Ruisa, Atina Theslo of Shelda Bay, sister to eight sisters, approaches the Council with a request for permission to gain the status of harema."

Ruisa looked directly at Atina and asked, "Atina Theslo is here present?"

Atina bowed her head. "Here, honored Ruisa."

The old woman squinted down at her. "Atina Theslo, you now stand before the Hearers of Appeals of the Council of Homereaches. By what right do you approach us to ask that we give you the status of harema?"

"I claim the right of adoption of brothers, honored Ruisa." Atina made a graceful gesture including Perion and the Aslandians. "Ninety-two days ago, these men were adopted as my brothers in a ceremony aboard the *Windbird*, the ship granted me at the after-Hetmo meeting of this Council. These men I now offer to the Council in the place of sons of my mother: six lords, honored Ruisa, each now or soon suitable for taking harems and occupying estates."

Perion noticed that the Aslandian lords had settled to the floor, and he joined them, sitting on half-crossed legs. It looked like a long session. In ritualistic detail, Atina re-counted the entire story of her voyage, including an earlier, unsuccessful attempt to take an Aslandian vessel that he had not heard about. She came to his capture and told of it succinctly, making it seem as though he were the victim of shipwreck and exposure—and, Perion noted, in a strict sense she was entirely truthful, hinting more than she said, leading the Council down the paths she wished them to take. Then she narrated the taking of the Aslandian lords, omitting only the death of the Aslandian crewwoman. She concluded with a repetition of her request: "I have no brothers, honored Ruisa; but I have adopted these, under the guidance of Teacher Teyo da-Theslo. I add these six to the Council's command; surely they justify my request."

She, too, sank down as the Council members leaned close to each other, buzzing comments back and forth. Under his breath, Perion asked, "It is going well?"

"As well as I hoped so far. Now it is time for the Aslandian males to be examined."

The woman behind Perion, who seemed to function as bailiff, called Dilbosk Otho first. The man stood, running a hand carefully over his wavy dark hair, and straightened his broad shoulders. All the men had been decked out that morning in new finery, and Dilbosk was arrayed in an elaborately embroidered blue-and-yellow tunic and white trousers. Perion, who had never really spoken to Otho, watched the man with some interest.

"Your name, lord of Mara, and the place you are from?" Ruisa asked.

"Dilbosk Otho." His voice was a pleasant light baritone. "I am brother to three sisters and one brother"—a murmur arose in the Council—"and I was born on an estate on the island of Harn, near Aslandia."

"Have you completed training for lordship?"

"I have, according to the teachings of the Rulers of Aslandia. As I was taken from our ship, I was on my way to the island of Georn, to take the estate of a lord who died there on the three hundred and first day of farsun, by our accounting. My estate would have included six young haremas."

The Council buzzed and muttered again. "That means something?" Perion whispered.

"He has very high status in his own land. Quiet now."

Ruisa asked Dilbosk more questions, ascertaining that his harem-sisters were women of high repute and well-known attainments in Aslandia. Then she passed the questioning along to the other Council members. One proved to be a Teacher, and she was much concerned with orthodoxy. The first demand Dilbosk got from her was one Perion had himself been drilled in: "Name the three great orders of belief."

With complete assurance, Dilbosk said, "We believe that

the Goddess Kalea crossed the sea of stars in the Sailing Star. We believe that she begot the peoples of Kalea in her own image. We believe that after death we shall be cleansed of our sins and be permitted to sail with Kalea.''

The Teacher nodded her curt satisfaction and asked an involved question about Aslandian heresies. To Perion's surprise, Dilbosk readily admitted that he had been taught error all his life. ''But,'' he added, ''I have received some instruction in orthodoxy now. I am certain that as I live in your domains, wise haremas will be able to train me in your beliefs, guiding my opinions in the correct courses for Homereaches.''

More in a similar vein followed. At last, the Council finished with Dilbosk. They called two witnesses, Jana of the *Windbird* and the handmaiden from the House of Waiting who had served Dilbosk, to testify to the thoroughness of his training, and to his stamina and his virility. Jana in particular waxed enthusiastic, recounting Dilbosk's attributes in vivid, near-clinical detail. Dilbosk modestly lowered his eyes as he attracted the envious stare of the other lords and the speculative ones of the Council members. ''The Council leaves out nothing at all?'' Perion whispered, appalled.

''This is important testimony. Hush.''

Finally the testimony ended. Ruisa asked for last questions or arguments; and when none were forthcoming, she said, ''I wait for requests from the Council.''

There was a rustle as the members of the Council brought out lists on the rough-toothed brown paper used in Homereaches. One stood. ''Honored Ruisa,'' she said, ''a very good harem in my home city of Fairstream is in need of an apprentice lord. The present lord, Palo Gren, grows old. His harem numbers eleven, with four of child-bearing age. The estate is ten sturoks in extent, and produces wood, grain, and fruit. We do not expect the present lord to live out the next full year, and upon his death Lord Dilbosk would succeed to an honorable and rewarding estate.''

Ruisa nodded. ''Another?''

A Teacher stood. ''Honored Ruisa, the estate of Rosk Kaley at Greenhill stands vacant since the lord's death on the fifth day of Storm-Month. The lord had a harem of only five. Two have taken the Orders and are entered as Teachers of First Ascension now; the other three have returned to the worldly paths to seek a new lord. The estate is valuable, producing both wood and copper ore. A new lord could gather about him new haremas, thus giving places to many of the women of our town who are not now married.''

Other estates were put into contention, and the Council fell to an energetic debate about the merits of the various estates. Finally, after a vote, Dilbosk's fate was decided: he was now the apprentice lord of the estate of Palo of Fairstream. Dilbosk smiled broadly, bowed, and thanked the Council. Teyo escorted him out. Perion asked, "Now he goes?"

"He will be sent to his new home as soon as the holidays are over. He is a deserving lord."

The others were disposed of in turn, with two breaks in between. All found immediate homes except for Trennon Fane. The black-haired lord disturbed some of the Teachers with his groping, ignorant answers to some of their more arcane queries about religion, and one of the Council members had noted aloud that his bright blue eyes had seemed to flash mockingly now and again. The Council retired to private chambers for a half-hour's deliberation, and then returned with the compromise that Trennon's case would be carried over to the next meeting, at the first Council session in the season of waning. The intervening month would be spent in training at the House of Waiting, with Trennon specifically admonished to improve his knowledge of details of worship. Trennon accepted the decision with even spirits and good grace. At that point the Council broke, rather late in the day, Perion thought, for the midday meal.

Atina rose, an angry flush on her face, her dark eyes snapping. After the Council filed gravely out, Atina led Trennon and Tom into a small private room where a meal of fruit and uncooked vegetables had been set for them. As soon as she had closed the door, Atina burst out: "Damn you, Trennon Fane! Why did you do that? You enjoy mocking my people's Council?"

Fane's smile was rather aristocratic. "Not at all. But I shall hold to my ignorance for some little time," he said. "My handmaiden tells me that a rich old lord of Easthaven suffers from a wasting disease and cannot live long; but his elder haremas are stubborn and will not hear of an apprentice lord. If I gradually, very gradually, improve my theology until the old fellow passes on to the Sailing Star—well, this island is a nice enough spot, and I should like to call it home.''

Atina gave a warped smile at the pun. ''And no one has more faith than a hard-won convert,'' she said. ''You are a crafty one, Lord Trennon.''

Fane looked pleased. ''I thank you. I begin to believe that the women of Home have more taste and understanding than those of my own country. None of them, I think, would so readily have appreciated the wisdom of my scheme.''

''But I *don't* appreciate it,'' growled Atina. ''I have trouble enough; your antics could ruin whatever chance I may have of resolving my own problems.''

''I hardly think so,'' Trennon said soothingly. ''The old lord should be dead before long, and that will take me away from here. And anyway, you have already delivered four lords to the Council; that alone should win a woman the right to name her harem.''

''It's more than that,'' Perion said. The other two looked at him. ''Atina is worried about Halindo,'' he explained.

Trennon shrugged. ''I regret that. But I have no power to alter Halindo's enmity.''

''Eat,'' Atina commanded.

The fruits were tangy, but dry, the consistency of slightly stale bread. The vegetables tended to be crunchy—like water chestnuts and celery in texture, something like cucumbers and broccoli in taste. ''There are no meats?'' Perion asked.

''Famine day,'' Atina grunted. ''The Council Days are days of uncooked foods and no meat, by tradition. At least in the Council Hall itself; you'll find that others celebrate in different ways.''

''Ah,'' Perion said, still mystified.

They had hardly finished eating when a sharp rap on the door summoned them back to the Council Room. ''Good luck, Atina,'' whispered Perion. She gave no acknowledgment, but stared up at the Council ring as the members retook their seats.

When at last the old women had settled, Ruisa raised her chin and stared around the circle.

''Let the outlander be brought before us,'' she said.

Atina turned, and Perion with her. Behind them, through the same door they had used, a woman came in. She paused on the edge of the circle cast by the skylight, then stepped forward.

Perion saw a woman perhaps thirty-five by Earth standards, strongly built, rather square of face; yet, strangely, looking at her he had no sense of masculinity. Halindo the Hunter, whatever else, was all woman. She stood nearly as tall as Perion—a hundred and eighty centimeters, he estimated—and her red hair was bound by a sweatband of some yellow material. She wore a yellow tunic, cinched at the waist by a broad leather belt; a knife sheath over her left hipbone was empty. Her trousers were white, her boots a rough-textured gray leather. Her eyes were green, direct, and challenging. Once she entered the circle of light, she strode to within a pace or two of Atina, surveyed the other woman, gave Perion a cursory, uninterested glance, and then looked up expectantly at Ruisa.

The old Council woman said, "You are the hunter who has claim against the life of one of our people?"

"I am Halindo Delev, of Prime, on the Aslandian coast," the other said in the same sort of musical, rolling dialect as the five lords had used. "I have a rightful claim to the life of Atina Theslo of Shelda Bay, for in unprovoked battle she killed a woman of Prime, one Fial Joret, of the Aslandian ship *Sunrise*."

"You are a believer in the Goddess Kalea?"

"I am."

"Then swear by your hope of joining the Sailing Star that what you will say before this Council shall be true."

"I so swear."

Ruisa, who apparently was attorney as well as magistrate, leaned forward. "You have a family interest in your demand for vengeance?"

"I represent the family."

"You act out of duty?"

"I am a paid hunter. The family has bought my services."

"Ah. Have you knowledge of the death of Fial Joret of your own mind?"

No, it seemed, she did not; but waiting outside were two women who had been aboard the *Sunrise*, and both came in to testify. Perion thought they had the outlines pretty much as he remembered them; but neither had actually seen Fial Joret's death. They both agreed that when last they noticed, Fial was fighting against Atina, whom they both identified; and when they recovered the body, they found that Fial had been wounded by a weapon such as the Homereachers used.

When they had told their tale, Ruisa turned again to Halindo. "If this Council should judge that you have the right, what do you ask of us?"

"That the killer Atina Theslo be given to me, for our justice; that I be allowed to take her life, as she took the life of one of our people, by the sword; that my ship and my crew then be allowed to depart in peace, with the killing ended for all."

"We will consider. Atina Theslo, you must now speak. You have words to say in your defense?"

"I have, honored Ruisa." Atina stood with bowed head for a few moments before looking up. Softly, she said, "The death of the hunter's countrywoman was not intended. We fought, true; but I did not strike to kill."

Atina turned toward Halindo. "Then there is this," she continued. "This hunter has taken life as well. I had a kinswoman, a youngster not yet of age. This hunter has killed her."

Looking in Atina's eyes, Halindo responded, "The woman I slew, Council. But I slew her in fair fight, when she accepted my challenge. I sought this one, not her; and her blood does no honor to the memory of Fial Joret, killed during an unlawful raid in Aslandian waters."

"But Kayla, my kinswoman, was not of age," insisted Atina. "She had no right to accept or refuse challenge."

"I had no way of knowing," Halindo said.

"Silence," Ruisa commanded.

Another Council member raised a pointing finger. When Ruisa nodded to her, the woman leaned forward and asked, "Halindo, you do not demand the return of the lords?"

"No, honored one. We see the lords as prizes won by the crew of this one, not as plunder taken by her. They are yours."

"But if we returned the lords to you, that would satisfy your patron?"

"No, honored one, it would not. Blood for blood."

The Council member pushed back in her seat with a sigh.

Atina said, "If I took one of our countrywomen as a sailor, and if she died in an accident at sea, the Council would not grant vengeance to her family. Accidents are the will of Kalea, not of humans. And the death was an accident."

"But it resulted from your attack," Halindo insisted.

"Our own waters," said Ruisa, "are no strangers to Aslandian raiders."

"No, honored one," Halindo acknowledged. "Yet it has been long and long since an Aslandian woman has in a raid killed one of your people."

The Council murmured, but no one spoke aloud. Ruisa nodded, then turned to Atina and questioned her about the two deaths, that of Fial Joret and that of Kayla. Perion felt his face burn as he heard her story, for she left him entirely out of the account. According to her recital, she and Fial had fought, the ship had listed suddenly, and Fial had been caught between the vessels when she fell. All true enough, as Perion knew; and yet he had been the agent of her fall, as much as the movement of the ship.

The Council heard Atina out, asked Halindo a further question or two, and retired to consider its decision. As they left, Halindo turned her back to Atina and Perion and walked again to the shadows, away from the circle of light. Perion said, very softly, to Atina, "Now they decide?"

"They vote. No one can abstain; and the side which gains the most votes gains the decision of the Council."

"I should have told them—"

"No," Atina whispered. "We have decided your story already; we will not alter it. No matter what happens to me, you may hope for a good judgment from the Council. Even if they outlaw me, they will give me at least a half-month grace; and if it comes to that, they may well be more indulgent toward you, if they first have dealt harshly with me."

Perion chewed on that. He looked sideways at Halindo, but she had not stirred; she stood, head inclined, arms crossed, absolutely silent and still. Perion said, "If I told the hunter the truth—"

"The truth is what the Council decides," Atina said.

They waited, Perion fidgeting, the two women like statues, for what seemed a long time before the Council returned. When the old women had seated themselves, Ruisa called Atina toward her. "Atina Theslo, you have done well in bringing to the Council your adopted brothers, and we praise you for that. But in taking the life of another, you have erred.

We have no one here who saw the death of Fial Joret; and you, as accused, must be heard with a doubting ear, as you know. We must declare you outlaw for a year and a day, the time to begin on the first day of Otimo, forty-three days from now. You have that time in which to make your arrangements with your family and to decide how you will meet the hunter's challenge, whether you will fight or attempt to flee; but after that time, none on Home may help you, or they shall share your outlawing. The decree of the Council is—"

"Wait," said Perion in a low voice.

Ruisa's eyes were distant as she turned them toward him. "The lord has something to say?"

Atina began, "O honored Ruisa—"

But Perion drowned her out. "I have something to say to the Council. One person saw the death of Fial Joret. He is here. I am the witness."

"Quiet!" Atina cried, whirling on him furiously.

Ruisa's harsh voice cracked, a whip cutting across their quarrel: "The man will speak."

"Thank you, honored Ruisa," Perion said. "I was on the *Windbird* when Captain Theslo took the Aslandian ship."

"Then be sworn, man. You are a believer in the Goddess Kalea?"

"Believe me, honored Ruisa, I wish most devoutly one day to be taken up to the Sailing Star," Perion said carefully. "To that I swear."

"Then speak. How came you to be on the *Windbird*?"

"Captain Theslo had found me at sea days before and had rescued me. I was the victim of shipwreck; my—craft—had sunk. I was fortunate that the *Windbird* passed when it did, or I would have lost my life."

To Atina, Ruisa said, "This is true?"

"Yes, Ruisa. But the man—"

"Silence." To Perion, Ruisa said, "And you were on the deck of the ship during the engagement?"

"Yes, by my own wish. I was grateful to Captain Theslo, and wished no harm to her or to her crew. The Captain agreed to let me remain on deck to care for the wounded."

"Tell what happened."

Perion shook his head. "It was confusing. I was new to their way of fighting, you see. The women of the *Windbird* fought against those of the *Sunrise* with swords. I thought they fought to kill. When I saw Atina in danger, I took a sword and came to her aid. I struck at the woman, whom I now know to be Fial Joret—"

"Honored Ruisa!" cried Halindo. "I beg you, this blasphemy, this mockery, must—"

"We are hearing the man," Ruisa said. "You will continue, witness."

"I came to Fial Joret, and struck at her with the sword. I have no training. I meant to disarm her, but my blow was badly directed. I cut her, here." Perion indicated his left side. "She fell back from me, and the ship rolled then; Fial Joret fell from the ship, and was caught between it and the *Windbird*. So she died, I swear."

Ruisa turned her cold eyes to Atina. "What this man says—there is truth in it?"

Atina could not hold the old woman's gaze and return it. She lowered her eyes. "It is true," she mumbled.

A Council woman said, "You allowed a man to have a sword, to be on deck while your crew was fighting? Have you no sense of decency?"

"Please!" Perion cried. "Captain Atina tried to keep me below. But I insisted. I am not—not like the men of your country. My customs are—"

"You have no further right to speak," Ruisa told him.

Halindo's voice, low and furious, almost quivering, came from behind him and to his right: "If this be true, honored Ruisa, if this woman has allowed an Aslandian to be so foully killed, killed by the hand of a—a man, then the case is not as I thought."

"It would seem not," Ruisa said dryly. "Separate them. We will discuss the case now."

A woman took Perion away, back to the little room where he, Trennon, and Atina had eaten. He moved the tapestry here, but found no window behind it. He paced, started at every sound of a footfall in the corridor outside, but found himself left alone for over an hour. Finally the door opened, and the guard beckoned him. "The Council will have you hear their decision," she said.

The sun was down, the light from the overhead opening now a golden, diffuse glow rather than a hard circle. Torches behind the Council provided additional illumination. On the floor of the Council room, Atina and Halindo stood many paces apart; and the guard placed Perion so that the three of them stood at the apexes of an equilateral triangle.

Ruisa, without preamble, said, "We have never dealt with such a dishonorable action as this. It is without precedent. You, Atina Theslo, have shown a lack of judgment in allowing a man to be present during a battle. You know well that men are fragile and delicate, that they lack the knowledge and skills necessary for fighting. We have heard rumors before that this man you have with you is strange. We believe now we see why: his mind has been unsettled by the horror of his situation.

"Further, in allowing this man to fight, you have acted in a criminal fashion. Though a man cannot hope to match a woman in strength or dexterity, yet the appearance of a man wielding, or trying to wield, a sword would certainly dumbfound an enemy. This is unfair advantage of the worst kind, and a grave offense.

"Therefore, Atina Theslo, the Council considers it has no alternative than to declare you outlaw, effective immediately at the end of the Council days, on the first day of Septimo. You have our protection for three days; after that, you are outlawed for a time of five years. In that time you may not marry; you may not own property; you may not associate with other citizens of Home. If the Aslandian hunters wish to exact vengeance on you during that time, they may do so without fear of our retaliation. When this is finished, let it be finished forever."

Perion started, took a half-step forward, felt his arm tight in the grip of the guard. Ruisa lifted her eyes to him. "You, man. You have shown yourself deranged. Whether your madness is permanent or temporary is beyond our knowing. The task of judging the severity of your disorder we must leave to the next meeting of the Grand Council, at the time of farsun. In the months until then, you will be held a prisoner at the House of Waiting of the Theslo family, at that family's sole expense. You will be confined alone, without a handmaiden during the night hours. You will be allowed no communication with the other males who may from time to time be quartered there. At the time of farsun, the whole Council will decide your case, and at that time we will determine whether you shall live or whether you shall be burned."

Finally, with a grudging air of resentment, Ruisa turned to

Halindo. "Hunter of Aslandia, the Council wish to offer their apology to you. We had no idea the case stood as it has proved to stand. You may pursue full vengeance beginning in three days' time. Until then, you will be lodged at Council expense, if you wish. The Council will further require money from the Theslo clan to pay the expenses of your journey here. We shall order that no citizen of Homereaches may legally come between you and your vengeance."

Ruisa, leaning on her staff, stood.

"No, wait!" Perion cried. "Wait! Don't go, you foolish old—"

The guard easily swept his arm behind him, doubled him over as she pressed higher, finally forced him to his knees, then to the floor. The cold, rough stone pressed against his cheek, and red lights of pain seemed to flash behind his eyes. He heard himself groan, then sob.

From far away, it seemed, Ruisa's old voice drifted down to him: "The Council has determined these cases in good order. Let the Council's judgments stand."

It sounded like a voice beyond any human appeal.

Chapter 15

"What will you do?" Teyo asked.

Atina turned from the window, let fall the curtain. Outside the night was deep and old, Lun a faint waning crescent. Around the House of Waiting the darkness was wrapped like a blanket. Atina shook her head. "The *Windbird* will be watched," she said. "And if it were not, I could ask no crew to share such an exile. Five years! No one has survived such a sentence before."

Someone tapped at the door. Teyo turned and opened it. The newcomer was Mela, wan and tired-looking. "He is locked in," she said. "What possessed him to do such a thing? I could kill him!"

"No," Atina said. "He believed he was helping. Though for what he has done to my family—"

"No anger now," Teyo said. "This is the time for calm thought."

"Yes. You are right."

"Have any of the crew seen you since the hearing?" Teyo asked.

"Jana. Selridir. They say that they are willing to make a run for it. But I cannot ask them to do that."

"You have an alternative?"

"I could accept Halindo's challenge."

"No," Teyo said. "For one thing, she would rescind it; she has only to wait two days, and then she can kill you at any time, from ambush. She has no need to fight you openly."

"For another thing," Mela said, "you might be killed."

"I know," Atina said. She smiled ruefully. "Men—this whole thing began because of men. I wonder if they are really worth the trouble."

Teyo said, "You know I will go with you, wherever you go."

"And I," Mela said.

"Thank you both. But I cannot draw you into the whirlpool with me. And besides—I have no idea of where to go."

"I do," said a voice.

Despite herself, Atina started and gasped. Perion stepped quietly into the room. Atina glanced sharply at Mela. "I thought that you—"

"She did bar the door," Perion said. "I have a way of opening such doors. But now to business."

"Go away, Perion," groaned Atina. "You have caused trouble enough."

"I know," Perion said. "And now I come to help. Accept my help. I can hardly get you in worse trouble."

"You offer anything more than fantasy?"

"Power," Perion said. "I offer you power. So much that the Council will have to listen to you, have to lift their decree."

Teyo looked narrowly at him, her gray eyes deep in shadow. "And the source of this power?"

"The Sailing Star."

Atina laughed. "I'll be finding what it carries soon enough, if what the Teachers tell us is true! What do you propose to do—sprout wings and fly to the Star?"

"No," Perion said. "To go to the northern lands, and there find a thing that can speak to the Star. I know it is there. My talisman can locate it, when we are near enough. Then I shall call the Star, awaken my friends, and bring down such things are you have never seen. There are vessels that fly through the air; there are devices that cast explosions about them, like the burning mountains themselves; there are sprinbos that shoot lightning instead of wooden bolts. You and your crew, Atina, could control all of Homereaches, all of Aslandia, all of the world."

"Talk, talk," Atina scoffed. "To go north is as impossible as to stand beneath the—"

"We can do it," Perion said, and his voice held so much assurance that even Atina faltered. "We'll need your ship. We'll need provisions. We could get food, water, from other islands?"

"Yes," Teyo said. "There are many islands friendly to us in the north and west, and news of Atina's outlawing will not travel as fast as the *Windbird* could sail."

"Wait!" Atina said. "We have no one to sail the ship."

"You have Teyo, you have Jana and Selridir—and I think they will find others. And you have me," Perion countered.

Atina scowled. "You joke," she said. "Men do not sail; they lack the skills to handle a ship. If you were a lord, you might hire a shipowner to take you on a pleasure cruise, but the *Windbird*, with all the sailors I could raise, would be so underwomanned that you would have to work—"

"I did work. I did almost every job on the ship as we returned from the north."

"But only now and again; you would have incessant toil, day in and out. Men are not built for such rigors." Atina looked around at Teyo, saw something strange in the old woman's face, and said, "You can't be agreeing with him?"

"The old scriptures tell of one who will lead our people on a great journey," Teyo said. "Who will reconcile our fallen natures to the goodness of Kalea, who will unite us again with the Goddess. Though I never thought it would be a man."

"Don't talk nonsense!" Atina shouted. "A man could never survive the work of sailing a ship, let alone the journey into the burning lands."

"Men can do more than you think, Atina," Perion said. "We are not as weak and helpless as you believe. And we do have minds of our own. Your society keeps men prisoner—"

"Lords are honored and respected!" Mela protested. "They are held higher than we hold ourselves."

"But they have no freedom," argued Perion.

"They have every freedom," Atina said. "We do not keep lords prisoner—not sane ones, at any rate."

"You say that they have freedom, but they have none," Perion said, exasperated. "Look—if a woman wishes to love a woman, you call that recreation. But what if a man wished to love another man?"

Mela gave him a fascinated, revolted look; Atina made a sound of disgust.

Perion nodded. "That is blasphemy," he said. "Or vulgarity, Atina, for those who are not believers. But women have the freedom that men lack; I expect that you and Mela have—"

Atina swung open-handed at him. Perion was not quick enough to avoid the blow, but he parried it, taking only a stinging smash on his forearm that seemed to echo in the small room. Atina's face was red, her teeth clenched, her dark eyes full of fire. Teyo stepped forward, but Perion waved her off. "Don't do that again," he said to Atina.

Mela took a step toward the door. "Don't," Atina called. When the other woman paused, Atina said, "I will not hurt him badly. But I intend to teach him a lesson."

"Don't try it, Atina," warned Perion, moving to his left as Atina began to circle him. He shoved a small table aside, kicked a stool out of his way.

Atina did not bother to reply. Her eyes narrowed, watching for an opening. Perion feinted, and she came for him, slashing hard with an open palm. Perion took it on his elbow, gave her a mocking pat on the cheek, and danced back. Atina paled with anger. She came forward again, whirled, and suddenly kicked, doubling Perion with a bare foot in the pit of his stomach. He staggered back, gasping, and Atina moved in.

But Perion twisted just out of her reach, dropped back against the wall, pushed away from it, and invited another kick. She faked one, and when he reached for her foot, it was gone; but her fist was there, and it hit him, hard, in the stomach. The pain brought tears to Perion's eyes. He shook his head, gulped air, and ducked away from another blow. He allowed himself to stagger, unfocused his eyes, as though the punch had dazed him. Atina swung again.

This time Perion caught her wrist, pivoted, and pulled her through. She flailed against the door, and Perion gave her rump a hard slap. She turned and was on him again with lightning speed, but this time he was ready, danced back from her kick, caught her leg, and threw her back onto the floor.

She hit, rolled, and was up again, darting in to rain annoying but not really painful slaps on his arms, head, and ribs. Just when he caught her rhythm enough to counter, she shifted and delivered a tooth-rattling blow to his mouth.

He grinned at her through bloody teeth. "You fight just like a man," he said.

Fury blazed in her black eyes. She redoubled the force of her blows, and Perion escaped them more easily—her eagerness betrayed her accuracy. He let himself appear to stumble once, and when she leaped forward, he swept a leg forward,

hooked her feet from under her, and sent her to the floor
again.

This time he leaped. He started a hammerlock, like the one
that had almost stunned him in the Council Hall, but she
broke it, threw him against a wall. She aimed another tremendous blow at his stomach, but he anticipated, raised a knee,
and felt a bone-jarring crunch. Atina grunted and backed
away, nursing a damaged hand; and Perion felt that one of
his legs had gone dead on him.

They stood glaring at each other, panting, dripping sweat.
Mela and Teyo had backed into corners and looked on in
silence. After a long moment, Perion smiled. "Well, Atina?"
he gasped.

Atina's tunic had been torn and flapped away from her
brown left breast. She tugged the fabric back into place, and
it flopped promptly down again. She pulled again—and tore
the whole left side of the tunic loose. She looked at it, then
down at herself, and at last chuckled. "You—you fight like a
woman," she said, her breath short.

Perion laughed too, laughed so hard that at last he had to
sit down on the floor, his back braced against a wall. "For
the sake of the Goddess, Mela," he said at last. "Don't stand
there wringing your hands. At least pour us some water!"

Mela ran to a corner cabinet, produced a pitcher and mugs.
Both Atina and Perion accepted and gulped gratefully. Atina
opened and closed her right hand experimentally, then shucked
the torn and useless tunic. "It was a good fight," she said,
her voice almost sensual. "I needed to let go of some of the
anger."

Perion got to his feet, one of his legs still shot full of
stinging needles. "I would call it a draw," he said, wiping
his mouth.

"Mm. You could not have done that two months ago,"
Atina said.

"Probably not."

"You goaded me deliberately."

"I did?"

"Of course you did. You wanted to teach me a lesson: that
men can be as good as women. Well, I admit it, at least in
certain circumstances, and for certain men. But for the old
ones' sake, don't let any Teachers hear about what happened.
You—you did not mean what you said?"

"What is that?"

"The bit about—men and men."

"Is it important?"

Atina sighed. "Tom, men behaving—in the way you said—that's not only blasphemy, it is a capital offense. In your case, if that were added to what the Council have already heard from you—well, it would be a quick way of starting a bonfire."

Tom wiped his hand across his mouth again. His teeth felt sound to his tongue, but the inside of his lips was puffy, and he had the iron taste of blood in his mouth. "I did not mean it for myself. But think, Atina: it is an example of what I meant. You claim that men have freedom, equality, superiority even, but it is not so. That is a myth, fostered by the culture here. But the culture can change—I don't mean in that way, but in other ways. And one way it must change is in the birth rate, or in finding new lands. You are crowded already; soon there will be wars in earnest, real killing."

"Lord Perion speaks truly," Teyo said from her corner. "We have seen it coming for many years now."

Atina shook her head wearily. "What a day. You think your trip to the north would alleviate our problem?"

"Alleviate it for a time. But sooner or later the culture must change, must adapt to a stable rate of birth, or no solution can last. But that, too, lies in the power of the Sailing Star. It will mean changes far greater than I can tell, but it is possible, with the knowledge carried by the *Galileo*."

Atina closed her eyes. "Tom, I still cannot believe you. But I will say this: any way that can avoid war, that can avoid Kalean slaying Kalean, seems good to me. If the other changes must follow, I suppose that people can learn to live with them. I may not be a good believer, but I do believe this: the most important thing is for the people to survive."

Mela was less certain. "But if what you say could happen, will it all come true? Will there be one man for every woman? Will the other—the thing about men and men—will it happen?"

Tom grunted. "I don't know. But consider this: there must be much good land far in the north, past the burning places, where it is cool again. For generations everyone should have space to do what she wants, if she does not bother anyone else. I wouldn't object to the idea of you and Atina—"

"Stop," Atina said. "I don't know where you got the idea, but Mela and I are not lovers. She is my sister, and she has been trained as a handmaiden."

"Sister? But I thought that you—"

"Clan-sister," Mela said. "The sister of Atina's mother was formerly a harema of the first Theslo, before Atina's mother was old enough herself to marry the new Theslo. I was a child of Atina's mother's sister by—"

"I will take your word for it," Perion said. Kalean relations, he thought, were nearly as complicated as Terran tax laws.

"The night grows old," Teyo said. "And Atina is tired already. We must have an idea of a plan; then Atina must rest. Otherwise, we have no hope at all."

"Right," Perion said briskly. "First: we can take the *Windbird?*"

Atina shook her head. "The Aslandians keep a guard at the head of the pier, and their own craft is anchored nearby. They would surely fight us if we tried to board, Council decision or no."

"Mm. Is anyone actually on board the ship?"

"The Council granted us one to be left there as guard. Zerba, the sailmaster, is there now."

"Good. Do any of you know details of the harbor?"

"We all do," Mela said, surprised.

"I'll need you for an hour or so, then, while Atina tries to get some sleep. Teyo, can you have Jana and Selridir round up a crew, enough to sail the ship without exhausting us all?"

"That would be twelve at least," Teyo said. "I will tell them."

"As I see it," Perion said, "our problem in escaping the harbor is threefold. First, we must board the ship without causing an outcry; second, we must leave the harbor as quickly as possible; and third, we must prevent the Aslandian vessel from stopping us before we reach the open sea. From then on, I have no ready help to give. Our first goal must be an island where we can take on supplies—and perhaps leave Zerba, if she does not wish to go with us. Then I must find a suitable place along the coast of the northern land to go ashore. That I will not be able to do until we are actually there."

Atina looked at him wonderingly. "You are all confidence," she said. "You think we can actually do this thing?"

"I don't know," Perion admitted. "And if you know how I feel inside, you'd say nothing about *confidence*. But for me, it is a matter of slim hope and no hope; if I stay here, sooner or later my chance will be gone forever. If I journey to the north, at least I will have a chance to try for my goal." He turned to Mela. "The Council says I am to be deprived of a handmaiden in the hours of night," he told her. "But I think they had other reasons in mind for the order. Will you go with me to my room, so that we can study the harbor and find a way to board the *Windbird*?"

"Yes, of course. And I'll go with you."

Perion glanced at Atina. She made a surreptitious sign for "no," for his seeing only. He smiled. "I am sorry, Mela, but on a ship you would be of no use. You must remain here."

She looked so stricken that Perion almost relented; but he found it within him to remain firm on one point. The two of them left Atina alone, and in his room Mela supervised as Perion drew in the harbor, carefully placing each pier in its correct relation to the others. Fortunately Mela, though she lacked artistic talent, had an excellent memory for distances and relationships. Before the hour was up, Perion had a large-scale map of the northern curve of Shelda Bay, with the details carefully marked.

He looked at his work. The *Windbird* lay at the foot of Leather Street, the only vessel tied at its particular pier, one owned by the Theslo clan. Six berths to the right, at a rented pier, the Aslandian ship, the *Serpent*, was moored. According to Mela, the guards posted by Halindo remained at the foot of the pier housing the *Windbird*—and, Perion reflected, any guards of Halindo were apt to be well trained and alert indeed. Perion asked Mela a few questions, then studied the map. At this latitude, the prevailing trades were northwesterly for the most part; but he thought he saw a way of taking advantage of the local winds, as well.

At last, feeling the tug of sleep on his eyelids, he rolled up the paper, stretched, and rose from the little table. "I have to sleep now, Mela," he said. "In the morning, we will meet the others. We must be prepared to go tomorrow night—or so late that it will be the morning of the day after tomorrow. For your help, I thank you."

"I may remain with you?" Mela asked.

Perion half smiled. "What of the Council's orders?"

"We are on Theslo land," she said. "I should like to see the Council try to come here and pull me out of my chosen bed."

"All right," he told her. "But I am tired, Mela. Very tired."

"I want to be close to you this night. That is all."

That night Perion's sleep was sweet, untroubled by dreams. He woke to the gabble of the birds out in the garden, and saw from the position of the sun through the window that it was early afternoon. Mela had already arisen. He got out of bed, padded into the bathroom, and began to get ready for the day. But when he took out the obsidian razor and prepared to scrape his face, he paused. "What the hell," he finally said, and lay the razor aside. If one was going to be a barbarian, one might as well avoid the minor discomforts of civilization.

The corridor door was unbarred, and as soon as Perion opened it he saw Mela coming toward him, bearing a tray laden with food. "The others are gathering," she told him. "Teyo got Jana out of bed last night, and she others. Almost everyone they asked has agreed to come. You will have your dozen, I think; or if not, very close to it."

"That is good news," Perion told her, and settled in to the hearty breakfast she had brought. He finished in only a few minutes, and then rose. "Let's go," he said. "I think you'd better be in on the planning, too, Mela. You know the harbor, and if anything we come up with might not work, you'd be the one to point that out."

"I am honored. Only I wish that I, too, could sail."

"I know. But this will be no place for—" He caught himself. He had been about to say, "for a woman," and the thought forced a smile from him. "No place for so valuable a handmaiden as you," he finished. "And one day we shall return, I swear. I want you to wait here for that."

"If I must," Mela said, but she looked unhappy.

They had gathered in a large room on the northern wing, the same wing formerly used to house the Aslandian lords. Perion came in to a babble of excitement, with Atina trying hard to answer forty questions at once. They turned to him when he came in; one or two shouted comradely greetings, which Perion acknowledged with a smile. He came to join Atina, who sat at the head of a long table. "Ready," he said to her.

Atina nodded, then cried, "Be seated, everyone! We have much to do, and little time."

There was a clamor of chairs and a scraping of wood as the crew pulled itself close to the table. Perion took a mental headcount: there were Selridir and Jana, as he expected; then Len, Illa, and Hetha, young and able sailors whose labors Perion remembered as enthusiastic and wholehearted, each of them seemingly strong enough to sail the ship alone. There was taciturn Rodally, older than any of the rest except Teyo, but far keener in knowledge of the sea and in her ability to pilot a ship than even Atina. At the foot of the table, Yania and Varo spoke together in whispers. One of them Perion had once relieved at the tiller; the other he remembered as a singer, whose light voice carried surprisingly through the ship when she struck up a tune of the sea. Ten of them, then; eleven, counting himself, and twelve, if Zerba decided to join them. It was a bare minimum.

Atina sketched in for them the proposition, and to a woman they agreed. In a rare display of volubility, Rodally shrugged. "They'd certainly kill you if you stayed here. I'd rather chance the desert than that Halindo bitch. Get us on the ship, and I'll take him wherever you want."

"Good," Perion said. He turned and, using a peg meant to hang clothing on, hung up his map of the harbor, braced at top and bottom with dowellike sticks of blackwood. "Let me tell you what I think we should do; then you can tell me how we can make it work." He tapped a pointed figure with his finger. "This is the *Windbird*. The guards will be here, on the pier itself. Now, what we have to do—"

Turning, he broke off. The door had opened silently, and there framed in it was a dark-haired, aristocratic figure. The others followed his gaze, but no one interrupted the silence.

Until, with a smile at his dramatic entrance, Trennon Fane stepped into the room. "I've been thinking," he said. "If I were a lord, I'd get fat and lazy and miss all the excitement. Tom Perion, if you still want me, I'm your man."

Chapter 16

The first trip, they all realized, was the most dangerous.
Atina had to make that one.

They emerged from the shadows at the south end of Shelda
Bay and looked at the broad expanse of water, rippled with
starlight reflections here and there. The air had a strong,
damp smell of salt, and the sleeping town was not entirely
asleep. The uneven strains of faint wine-soaked song came to
them now and again, from some celebration of the Council
Days holiday that still was in boozy session. It was as dark as
Perion could have wished, with no moon and only a few
flaring torches near the ship—torches jammed into holders
near the two guards who, more than a kilometer away, stood
watching the ship.

"Here," Atina said, threading past Perion. He followed
her more by sensing her location than by seeing her, for the
darkness on this side of the harbor was almost complete. She
paused ahead of him. "The ladder is here," her voice said,
from low toward the ground. Perion stooped, felt ahead with
his fingers, and located the ladder that led down the embankment to the surface of the water. He carefully began to
descend.

"Coming down," he said.

A hand caught his foot. "This way. Easy. It's a very light
boat."

Perion found unsteady footing. The boat was small and
indeed light, bobbing underfoot like a raft. "You sit in the
stern," Atina said. Then, somewhat louder, she called, "All
right, Selridir."

The woman climbed down; a moment later Varo, much
smaller and lighter, followed her. "Got everything?" Perion
asked.

"Yes, my lor—yes, Tom," said Varo. "Ready."

"Then let's go." Selridir took one set of oars, Varo the other. The blades had been muffled, and they bit the water with hardly a sound. Perion, at the stern, had the tiller. His job was simply to steer toward the distant orange smears that marked the ship. They glided noiselessly through the black water. Once a small fish leaped to their left, and they all started so much that the boat wallowed a bit. Now and again they lost sight of the torches, as other larger vessels or piers came between; but Atina kept them on a correct heading by softly calling back adjustments to Perion.

The trip took long minutes; to Perion they seemed endless. At last Atina took them in very close to the harbor side. They passed a moored vessel, then came about and went under its very nose, under the pier to which it was moored. Here they paused a moment. "All right," Atina said. "Now we have to follow the embankment. No rowing; just use the oars to push us along, quietly. The next pier is ours. We'll go under it here, follow it seaward, and come out astern of the *Windbird*. Varo, are you ready?"

"Yes, Captain."

"If I know Zerba, she will sleep on deck, with more than one weapon at hand. You must be absolutely quiet until I have reached the deck. She will know my voice at once."

"I understand."

"Then let's go."

The muted oars made scraping noises so low that Perion felt their vibration instead of hearing their sound; but they seemed loud indeed to him. They could actually look up and see one of the torches from here, the flames licking the black belly of night; but so close were they to the embankment that the guard herself was not seen.

In moments they had gained the dark shadow of the pier. They glided between its wooden supports, then turned again and moved down the length of the structure. The tide, such as it was, was out, to their advantage, for the cross supports under the pier were so low as to oblige them to stoop almost under the gunwales of the little boat. Then they were out again, in open water, and over them, a darker loom in the darkness, was the ship itself. They came up against the stern, and Varo rose as the others steadied the boat.

How can she do it? thought Perion, looking up at the

indistinct overhang of the ship. It was an impossible climb, offering no handholds or toeholds.

But Varo made it. She found spaces where none, to Perion, seemed to exist; clambered up the overhang like an oversized spider; got a hand on the sill of the large port opening out of Atina's cabin; put her foot where her fingers had been, rose again, a small lighter spot in the general gloom. Then she was over the rail, and for a few moments all was still again, except for the steady plash of wavelets against the wooden hull and the groaning of the hawsers as the ship slowly tested and released them.

Then a hiss, and the rope that Varo had carried coiled around one shoulder thumped into the water just to Perion's right. It might have been another leaping fish. With one hand on the ship's rudder, Perion flailed the other arm, caught the rope, and passed it to Selridir, who gave it to Atina. The captain scrambled up hand over hand, making only the sound of breathing as she did.

Then they waited for what seemed a small eternity. At last a light glimmered overhead, a very dim one: they had lighted a lantern in the corridor outside Atina's cabin, and the stern port caught the pale red glow. From it a moment later another rope hissed down, and this time Selridir began to climb. The moment she had gone, Perion, now alone in the boat, moved into the middle of the little craft, lifted one of the shipped oars, and with it turned the boat. He thumped the hull twice, but not loudly, and at last he pulled himself back under the pier. Then he retraced their first route, and at last began to row, with the same slow, steady, noiseless pull the women had used. He stopped toward the middle of the open bay and looked over his shoulder. The single candle left burning in a window of a shop there was a yellow spark on the face of the night; and he had been heading too far to his left. He adjusted and began to pull again. In a few moments, he thumped against the embankment, found the low ledge that served as a tie-up for little vessels, and made the boat fast. The others waited eagerly onshore.

"Everything is all right so far," he said to them. "The three women are on the ship, and the way is open to climb through the port into Atina's cabin, so Zerba must have been awakened without a sound. Get the other boat and let's go. Jana, Hetha, Rodally, with me; the rest, Tayo, Yania, Illa,

Len, Trennon, take the longboat. They should be ready with the towlines by the time we return.''

Again the voyage in the dark, seemingly without movement or goal, except for the sparks of the torches, growing larger as the noiseless oars dipped, pulled, rose again. This time, only Hetha in his own boat scrambled up the line, and she made more noise than had the others, for she was laden heavily with gear. Then Rodally and Jana pulled away, allowing the boat to hover in the water as they touched its trim up now and again with the oars. So softly did the other boat come up that Perion was unaware of its presence until he saw the dark silhouette of a climber—Yania, that would be, judging from the burdens she bore—against the pale outline of the red lantern-glow. A slower figure followed, half climbing, half pulled into the port. That was Teyo. Now the other boat, like his own, had three in it. They pulled back under the stern and felt with the oars until they located the hanging cable on the starboard side. Selridir had prepared well, as he had thought she would; now Jana took the cable and expertly made it fast to a cleat in the stern of the little boat. She gave the line a tug, and they settled to wait.

Something dragged across wood, and a splash came from their right. ''The hawser's cut,'' Jana breathed.

A voice came from overhead and to the rear. ''They heard,'' Perion said, more to himself than aloud. ''Come on, come on!''

But Jana still held the cable. At last, someone above gave two quick tugs—even Perion could feel them, through the boat—and Jana turned and took up her oars. ''Pull now,'' she whispered.

The cable tautened behind Perion as they pulled away; and at last they seemed to run into a solid wall, halting their progress. But this was illusion. Slowly, ever so slowly, they were pulling the *Windbird* out of the dock. It was just a question of—

A clatter came from above, a quick curse, a yelp of pain, and then the sound of running feet. ''They're onto us!'' Selridir yelled from the deck. ''Pull, now, pull, for all you're worth!''

The muffles slipped off the oars in an instant, and to his right Perion could hear the splashes as the oars of the other boat, too, bit into the water. He felt the strain, the power of muscle attempting to move the absurd weight of the nearly twenty-meter vessel behind; and he knew that they were doing it, that the ship was moving, slowly, slowly.

"Clear of the dock," Selridir called down. "Hoisting sail. Keep it up!"

They pulled and pulled, the women grunting now from exertion, the cable creaking as they put more strain on it. Perion suddenly became aware that he could see the silhouette of the other boat, and he realized that more torches had appeared on the pier behind. He heard a thud or two, puzzling small sounds; then Jana growled, "Sprinbos. Much good it will do them!"

There came a flap and thump as the sails began to catch the wind, sweeping away from shore now, toward the narrow key-shaft opening to the sea. The ship suddenly slackened the tow ropes.

"Change now!" Selridir cried from overhead.

Quick as a squirrel, Jana scrambled back, loosed the cable, and moved it to the bow of the little boat, as Rodally turned them in a circle. Then they were off, no longer rowing, but towed behind the *Windbird* as, like his namesake, the ship caught the wind. Perion turned in the stern and looked back. The figures on the pier were receding, already out of sprinbo range; but there were lights and activity away to his left now, too, as the *Serpent*, the Aslandian vessel, made ready to cast off.

"They're rowing after us," Rodally said suddenly. Perion looked astern again. Yes, there was a small boat, its crew rowing hard, visible against the red-and-yellow reflections of the torches on the water. Something sailed past Perion, and cold salty water dashed in his face. Rodally had dived overboard.

He watched, worried, until the pursuing boat suddenly tipped, producing screams and curses from the women in it. Then he understood. He heard Rodally's gasps without seeing her, but guessed at her location and dived in himself, holding in one hand the end of a line made fast to his boat's stern cleat. He had reached almost the end when his hand hit her on the shoulder. "Perion," he gasped. "Hang on. Got a line."

The *Windbird* was moving now, and they struggled up the line against the pull of the water. Rodally clambered in first, then gave a hand to Perion. Together they hauled the line in.

"That was stupid," gasped Perion.

"I enjoyed it," Rodally returned.

Jana said, "The *Serpent* is trying to cut us off. Look."

They could trace the lower, sleeker Aslandian vessel by his lights; indeed, he was bearing down across their course, trying to come between the *Windbird* and the open passage to sea. "If they're ready," Perion breathed. "If they're only ready—"

A red streak, an arching meteor, appeared, curved downward, and fell short of the *Serpent*. From the deck, Perion heard Atina's barked order: "Not yet! Not yet!"

The *Serpent* closed. Seventy meters, fifty—he heard again the *thunk* of shafts hitting wood. They were firing on the *Windbird*. "Now!" came Atina's voice.

This time three streaks of light arched through the air, and two of them found lodgment in the *Serpent*'s sails. Where they touched, red fingers of flame appeared; and then three more sparks had joined them, and three more. The sails of the Aslandian vessel took flame rapidly, the wind driving the ship also feeding the flames. Perion heard curses and shouts from the Aslandian ship. More fire arrows, their heads thick with the flaming pitch of a low, evil-smelling bush, found their targets; and one evidently hit a living bull's-eye, for there came a shriek, and the spark of fire tumbled from the deck into the water.

"We've done it!" cried Len, across the water in the other small boat. "They're falling off!"

They glided past the *Serpent*, and in the light of the flames they saw the crew scrambling to fight the fire, chopping at lines, clambering up rigging, passing buckets of water.

The *Windbird* was like an animal returning home. He took the passage eastward straight and true, and in minutes the harbor was only a scattering of a few points of light behind them. Perion settled back and closed his eyes. Sleep. He had almost forgotten what it was. . . .

He opened them a moment later and found that several hours had passed. The *Windbird* was hove to, and the small boats were pulling alongside. From the deck above, a grinning Selridir kicked down a rope ladder, and Perion climbed it, feeling aches in his back and arms that he did not remember from the night before. Then Jana came up, and finally

Rodally; and then they hauled the boat on deck and made it fast.

Perion felt a handclap on his shoulder. He turned and looked into the grinning blue eyes of Trennon Fane. "We did it!" he said. "By the Goddess and all her minions, we actually did it!" He held out a hand. "Look at this, will you? Just look at this?"

Perion frowned. "What am I supposed to see?"

"Blisters!" Trennon laughed. "Was there ever a lord of Aslandia who had blisters on his hands before, from his own work?"

Perion shook his head and smiled. "The first of many, I fear."

From the bow of the ship, Atina called to him, and Perion made his way to her. "We did not lose one person to injury or death," she told him. "Though we came close. See these?"

The jib was peppered with short spikes, the butts of sprinbo bolts, at least half a dozen of them. "That foolish Zerba was here, firing back bolt after bolt as fast as she could work the bow. She hit no one, she thinks, but she kept them far enough away so that they did us no damage." She looked ahead. "There," she said.

Perion followed her pointing finger. The rim of the world was ablaze, a glorious red glow; and a moment later, the arc of the sun appeared, glimmered wider as the sunrise came sudden and bright over the water. "We sail in the free light of the sun," Atina said. "Where we shall wind up, Goddess knows; but we are on our way. Whatever happens, Tomas Perion, thank you for your belief in me."

"And you for your strength of mind and purpose," Perion said. "We have a chance now."

"A chance," agreed Atina.

An old voice raised itself behind them, and Perion felt his scalp crawl. The voice was familiar—it was Teyo's—but the words were in the High Speech, in Perion's own native Angloss, and to him at first they seemed alien and strange. Atina and Perion both fell silent, standing in the bow of the ship, looking at the sunrise; and together, each with his or her own thoughts, they listened as old Teyo the Teacher chanted in the sun.

A SONG OF THE SUN

See, the sun rises! Sharp are her eyes,
She builds a bridge across the brine,
Lights leaping waves; the ocean lies
Ready for her rule, as red as wine.
   O see me, Sun! Give me your light,
   To me your strength, for in the night
   I have felt need of your warm might—
     O see me, Sun!
She climbs a cloud-ladder into clear skies,
With her warmth she soothes the world,
As far as the Sailing-Star she flies,
You blackest banners of Night, be furled!
   O hear me, Sun! I follow, you lead,
   For I have wandered in loss and need,
   And I will come after with all my speed—
     O hear me, Sun!
In evening she sinks, her steps slow,
Leaving, she lingers, her last look sad,
The stars she scatters, that seeing their glow
We may in mind remember, be glad.
   O save me, Sun! Make me like you,
   Keeping a steady course and true,
   Let my last setting bring honor to you—
     O save me, Sun!

Chapter 17

"Again?" Trennon Fane asked, dismayed.

"Again," Perion insisted.

Trennon sighed, looked up at the mast towering overhead, and started once more to climb the rope; and on the other side of the mast, Perion himself clambered up, hand over hand, through the rigging. They met at the watchtree, Perion as always a few moments ahead. "I don't see the good of this," Trennon grumbled.

"You will. When you have to have the stamina to cross a wilderness, you'll see the value. We call it 'training' where I come from."

"Sounds like my name."

But not your nature, Perion thought. Still, the young lord had gained muscle and endurance in the month they had been running. He could now, at Perion's command, fall to the deck and do fifty push-ups without resting; and, to Perion's credit, he was on the deck, too, matching Trennon effort for effort. The women aboard the ship still marveled at the spectacle of two lords voluntarily exerting themselves; but at least they were becoming used to the two men sharing the shipboard duties, and at times even grateful for the four extra hands.

Atina had very wisely sailed straight for Eastrock from Home. Eastrock was a boondock island, not volcanic, but hardly more than its name suggested, a long, narrow spit of land that seemed mostly jumbled ship-sized rocks. Out of the regular shipping lanes, Eastrock supported perhaps a thousand people on a number of poor estates. Its people were hungry for news of the wider world, and unsophisticated enough to believe that Atina was only now setting out on her hunt for Aslandian lords.

The two men stayed belowdecks while Atina went to pur-

chase provisions. She had brought with her a considerable
sum of money—her father's farewell present to her, she
explained, though Perion surmised that Atina had liquidated
her holdings in Shelda Bay—and, they discovered, Perion
himself had unsuspected treasure aboard. He had elected to
reoccupy his old cabin, and when, a day out from Home, he
was packing his few belongings into the chest, Atina noticed
there the aluminum case they had taken from the water.
"What is that?" she asked.

Perion took it out. "Survival kit. Look." He pressed a
catch and opened the case. "It's watertight, you see. Here are
some water-purification tablets. This thing here is a desalini-
zation kit—it'll produce about a liter of water a day, drink-
able water from seawater. These things are ration wafers,
food, very unpalatable. This is a water container—there's a
liter in there, water from Earth. Imagine that."

Atina opened and closed the case a couple of times. "You
must have been a wealthy man," she said. "This chest is
worth a fortune in itself."

"That?" Perion asked, surprised. "It's only a cheap aluminum alloy. It isn't even sturdy—you could bend it with
your bare hands."

"But it is metal!" Atina said. "Bright metal. A whole
estate could not buy such a case on Home."

And Perion got the idea then. They would use the case as
an item of barter. The plan worked, too; for Atina took it
ashore on Eastrock and returned jubilant from the estate of a
distant kinswoman, bearing with her provisions enough for a
long, long voyage. But some of the things Perion wanted,
chiefly fabric and waterskins, were just not available on
Eastrock, and so they faced at least one more landing.

The one more stretched into two; and the last was a hasty
one, because a traveler from Home had recently touched at
lonely Twopoints Island, and had brought the news of Atina's
flight with the trade goods she carried. Still, Atina was able
to buy, at greatly inflated prices, waterskins enough to satisfy
Perion; and then the ship turned her nose to the north, seeking
the west-trending winds closer to the equator.

The days grew hot. The work aboard the ship was not
particularly hard, but it was constant, and as the air seemed to
thicken to a barely breathable density, tempers frayed. Septimo,
the first month of waning, passed, and they were into Otimo.

Overhead, the sun shrank as Kalea swung around on her eccentric orbit, and each day its heat lessened an imperceptible fraction; but each day they drew nearer the line, too, and the net effect was a rise in temperature.

They suffered from nerves as well as from heat. The escape had been a time of high excitement, and the aftermath, dull days of sailing and avoiding other vessels, was a distinct let-down. Selridir in particular had been keyed up and ready to fight hand-to-hand if necessary; now, finding no real outlet for her anger, she grumbled and cursed at the rest of the crew, who were ready to give back as good as they received from her.

They had no proper cook. Zerba volunteered to fill the position, but her dishes were basic and without imagination, and the sameness was a constant irritation. Teyo strung fishing lines to the stern, and the days when she caught a fish were festival, for they brought fresh food—often just a morsel big enough to tease the taste buds only but not to satisfy the stomach—to vary the round of dried fruits and vegetables, dried meats, and crusty, tooth-dulling bread.

Under the deep blue sky, they kept a constant lookout for sails. Atina would hail no vessel, would turn and run if a sail were sighted, for she would not trust even a ship from Home. "My family has many rivals," she explained once to Perion. "They would be glad enough to gain favor with the Council by turning me in. I'm sure after our little escapade in the bay they must be furious with me. Still, by running, I bring all their wrath on my own head; the Council can legally do nothing against my family now."

Storms caught them, sweeping in low and dark, trailing streamers of rain. Perion had to take the tiller once when the ship seemed on the verge of breaking up. Choking from the water rained on him from the sky and dashed over the rail into his face, Perion squinted ahead, seeing a mountain of water, netted with white foam, rolling impossibly high toward him; then the ship buried its beak in the wave, a knee-high wash of water flowed down the deck, breaking at his ankles, and the ship was lifted up, up, up, only to shoot over the edge and in a long, belly-dropping plunge fly down the far side. With the sails furled, except for a jib, and a sea anchor dragging behind, they somehow managed to keep underway; but after the storm had blown itself out a day and a half later, they were all soaked, exhausted, miserable—and Trennon, the most inexperienced sailor of them all, was deathly seasick.

But somehow they endured. Perion spent long evening hours studying the maps and charts, showing Atina where they must go, and sometimes he questioned Trennon, trying to find out all that the other man knew about the geography of his section of the world. That proved to be precious little.

"North of the mountains is a waste," he said. "The plants that grow there are low and poisonous, and there are beasts as well. The few estates planted there make their way by mining— copper and tin, for the most part. But few would choose to live there. Even the water is said to be bad; they must bring it over the mountains with them, or pay a high price to have it shipped, for the rains are seldom and not dependable."

Of the beasts Trennon knew little, save that many were said to be venomous and carnivorous. The Aslandians, it appeared, had not pushed beyond the upper slope of the mountains, but had stayed in the relatively cool uplands. Beyond and below lay true desert, a barrenness of rock, as Trennon described it from his hearsay knowledge.

But Perion was more interested in another site, anyway, a quarter of the globe from the peninsula of Aslandia. Here, if the sketchy maps told the true story, there were serried, volcanic mountains, with passes between; and in one particular place, a puzzling, nearly straight stretch of cliffs that plunged straight down into the water. One deep inlet had been charted near this cliff, and that, Perion hoped, was the same inlet that appeared on the western edge of the map left by James Smith of the distribution of landing pods.

The datacard he studied with special care. The map really was a simulacrum, a near-photograph, created by the dataset on one of the lost command pods as it swept over land and sea. At maximum magnification, Perion could resolve objects as small as a few tens of meters at the point where the path fell over the coastline. If he was right—if the inlet on the charts matched the one in the data—he could plot a way in past the mountains. Then, the card indicated, the land gave way to true desert, to sand desert in this case, the face of the land marked chiefly by barchan dunes. But to the west, on the very fringe of the area marked on the card, the land seemed to be more suitable for a journey by foot, more level, with less sand.

Tantalizingly, in the very northernmost point, where the card indicated a stasis-shielded command pod had landed (what, Perion wondered, had become of its occupant?), the terrain seemed shaped by flowing water; but there resolution was on the order of a kilometer or more, and he could be sure of nothing.

He measured the distance again. It looked like at least five hundred and seventy-five kilometers, *if* they could keep to an almost straight northward line of march. That, Perion hoped, would lead them to more hospitable land. Then they would turn east, and in another long march of three hundred kilometers or so, they would set out for the command pod. They would complete two legs of an immense right triangle; the desert showing on his datacard would cover the hypotenuse. That indeed was the shortest means of travel—if one had air-conditioned skimmercars and an unlimited supply of water and food. But for a party on foot . . .

Perion began again to calculate weights, distances, and the imponderable strength of muscle and will.

The watchtree was a cool spot, high above the deck. Perion sat on one side of it, Trennon on the other, each with a hand braced in the rigging. "Your turn to keep watch," Perion said. "You feel up to it?"

"Fine, as long as the sea doesn't try to turn the bloody ship upside down," Trennon returned. "You think I am doing well?"

"Yes," Perion said, looking at his companion critically. "You are stronger than you have been. And thinner. And no longer as pale as beach sand."

"No," Trennon agreed, looking at his tanned arms. "But not as dark as you." He squinted into Perion's face. "Your hair and that barbaric beard have changed color, I think. They are much lighter than they used to be, nearly blond now instead of brown. And your face is almost the color of blackwood. I can't get over it. Except for your facial hair, you look like a tough woman, not like a lord at all."

Perion laughed. "Few of your old acquaintances would call you elegant, either."

Trennon's grin was a little rueful. "I suppose not. What if fat old Yannow Tully could see us now, eh? Imagine his look of horror."

"I hope he's doing well on his new estate."

"A hoat is always happy in his wallow," Trennon said, using a word roughly equivalent in meaning to "fat boar."

Perion stood, bracing himself against the roll of the ship. The horizon was wide and empty. "Anyway," he said, "we must have given Halindo the slip by now."

"I wouldn't count on it," Trennon said darkly. "We've come close enough to a vessel or two to be identified by any aboard with sharp enough eyes. And a hunter of Aslandia never gives up. Our track across the water may be invisible to our eyes, but they say a hunter can follow a trail through the air if she must."

"Well, I'll worry about Halindo when I see her sail," Perion said. "Until later, Trennon."

He won a smile from Varo as he clambered down to the deck. "You learn more every day, don't you?" she asked. "I still can't get used to a man actually doing that. It looks wrong, somehow, like a day when the sun dims."

Sundim, or eclipse, was rare on Kalea, and when it occurred it was never total, for Lun's angular size was only half that of the sun. Still, the occasions were long remembered and sometimes spoken of in deep superstition. Those days when the sky deepened, the sun blinked, were days marked in legend and song as particularly portentous ones, for good or ill.

But to Varo, Perion smiled. "Men do what they are driven to do by their own need," he said. "As countries sometimes are driven by forces they cannot control, sometimes to destructive ends, so individuals find in themselves things they never expected, some for good, some for evil."

Varo shrugged. "I am no master of lore," she said. "But what you say of countries is true. The Under Islands fight us and the Aslandians; the Aslandians fight us and the Under Islands. And all for what? For more land." Varo resumed her task, coiling a rope, and fell into a bleak mood, it seemed. "We have too many people. But a man wishes to leave many sons behind, to carry his memory and his seed. And a woman who has had a girl-child will try again and again, wishing each time for a boy. A woman blessed with a son will try again and again in hopes of having two. Families grow faster than the water scum on a still pond. And now all the good land is taken. There had been talk of doing what we now do—sailing to the north land. But my people think of trying to colonize the land, the narrow space between the mountains and the sea. To do that, they will have to fight the beasts there, and the strange barbarians. And Aslandia is much closer to these lands than we; they surely would battle us for our right to live there."

"Maybe our journey will solve that problem," Perion said.

"For how long? Still, if it takes away the cause of war, it is a worthwhile effort."

Perion nodded, not telling Varo that humans had always found excuses for war, that merely opening new lands to human settlement would not solve the basic problem. He mused on that problem as he went aft. They had to see themselves as a whole, that was it—each Aslandian, each Under Islander, each barbarian, each Homereacher had to see herself or himself as part of a group, the group of humanity. That spirit was hard to produce, to maintain. But—Perion allowed himself a strict inner feeling of duty—perhaps it could be imposed from above by a strong leader, one whose word could not be questioned.

Teyo was in the stern. She held a waterskin, which she offered to Perion. "Try it," she suggested.

Perion took a mouthful. It was hot, and it was flavored mildly by rack, a strong wine-based distilled spirit, very expensive; but the water was good. "How long?" he asked.

"The water has been in this skin for eighteen days now, and there is no change in taste or wholesomeness."

"Good." Perion hefted the waterskin, estimating its capacity. He was hoping to carry twenty days of water per person, at one liter per day—not enough in this climate, but perhaps sufficient to take them across the arid region. Perhaps. But the weight was a problem. He thought each of them would carry at least thirty kilos of water, food, and supplies—but thirty kilos was a staggering load. Of course, as they continued into the desert they would consume water and food and lighten their packs; but as the packs grew lighter, their strength would falter, so the advantage was canceled out.

Teyo had restoppered the waterskin and replaced it in a latticework box lashed to the deck. She said, "You have decided on the ones who will go?"

"I think so. Atina, Selridir, Trennon, and I. The rest of you will run the ship to the Lonely Island, the one Atina spoke of. It won't be too far away from the northern lands, and the Homereachers there will protect the ship from Aslandians, as long as Atina herself is not aboard.''

"You will need me," Teyo said.

Perion said, "I thank you for your wish to go. But it will be a hard journey, Teyo. You are old, and the way is dangerous. I would not have your pain on my conscience.''

"Trennon goes, and he is not as strong as I.''

"True; but if we succeed, we will bring back a whole new way of life, and one that would horrify your Council. I think it is right that men and women share the dangers, for in the end they will learn they must share much else. And Trennon grows stronger each day.''

"And he has youth," Teyo said.

"That is true.''

"My thoughts will go with you, Tom Perion.''

"Thank you for that. But cheer up, Teyo; if all goes well, I shall bring a flying vessel to Lonely Island, and I shall give you a ride to the new lands myself. Think of that, old Teacher! You and I, flying above the clouds.''

"May it happen.''

Just then, from above, Trennon called out, "A sail! A sail!''

From aft, near the tiller, Atina called back, "Where away?''

"To port and to stern!''

Perion and Teyo hurried to the tiller. Atina stood there, shading her eyes, staring away to the south and west. After a moment, Perion saw the sail, a little triangle against the horizon, very small indeed. "What is it?" he asked Atina, for he had come to have great respect for her eyesight and her judgment.

"Too distant to tell. Maybe an Aslandian trader, though they usually don't come this far to the east—there's only the Lonely Island and the barbarian Rim in this part of the world. Still, we'll bear away from it—if we can see him, he can see us. Let's trim sail and strike a new heading, more northerly. We'll see if this sail gives chase.''

It did not, or at least it seemed that it did not, for they soon left it behind, and it failed to come into view again before the sun set. Atina did not leave the deck the whole day, but stood there tense, straining; and in the watchtree first Trennon, then Illa stood looking out into nothing but empty seas. As the sun sank, Atina studied its glow, and then turned her eyes to the northern horizon. "I think we shall be in sight of land soon," she said. "We are drawing very close to the Rim of the World. See the clouds there?"

Perion, looking to the north, saw faraway piles of pink and dusty blue, faint with distance. "A storm?" he asked.

"Such as is common around the Rim at this time of year. The wet winds from the sea strike the mountains, take their moisture high; it turns into cloud, then rain. The waterside of the Rim is well washed by rain, some of it dense forest, other parts high bare cliffs cut with leaping waterfalls. We are close enough to see the storm, but not the land."

"Then a fair wind tomorrow, Captain Theslo."

"Thank you, Lord Perion."

Landfall was delayed. That night was a dark one, and morning came quickly. With it came the cry of Varo, now herself taking a turn in the watchtree. "A ship behind!" she cried.

Perion had come on deck merely to escape the stifling heat of his cabin; he lay on a pallet against the starboard rail. Now he leaped to his feet and went aft again, finding Atina already at her post.

"Damn," she said, "No need for guesses now. See it?"

Perion saw. It was still very distant, at least ten kilometers, but it was clear now. The triangular sails swooped high above a sleek black hull. Atina spoke for all of them: "Damn Halindo. They said she could follow a track across the waves of the water. I never believed it until now."

"What do we do?" Perion asked.

"Lengthen sail and run," Atina said grimly. "Few Aslandians can outrun the *Windbird* when he turns to. We'll see what stuff this Aslandian is made of."

All hands took a turn, and soon they were spanking straight down the wind, heading north and east. This would take them to the edge of the north continent some bit farther east than Perion had wanted, but at the moment that seemed of little consequence. What mattered was that they escape the hunter.

For all the morning it seemed a dead heat; and then Perion thought they began to gain. By midafternoon, it was clear that they were pulling ahead in the race. The other's sail had dwindled almost as small as it had been at Varo's first sighting. But it was still there, ominous, as the night came over them.

"Now," Atina said when the darkness was quite complete, "we see how smart the Aslandian is. All lights off, everywhere. Cookfire, too. Get ready; we're turning south by east."

They made the turn, then hove to, a bobbing ship on a calm sea. For all the light that showed, they might have been in the belly of a great sea beast, as Perion dimly remembered one person from Earth legend was said to have been. They drifted with a gentle current, pushed by the wind only to the extent that the wind could get a purchase on bare masts and wood. At the helm, Atina fought hard to keep his nose steady, to keep the ship from taking broadside any of the dripping waves that rolled underfoot. "We'll wait it out," she said.

Wait it out they did; for the next day, when the bloody sun rose above the surface of the ocean, there was no other sail visible. Many of the crew had been awake all night, and the others had had but scant rest; yet from all of them, a cheer arose at the sight of the empty horizon.

"We haven't won," Atina warned them. "But we've shaken pursuit for a time. They will assume we will hold our original course; we will instead turn more easterly, and hold off as long as we can. By the time we reach the area of our landing, they very likely will have turned to retrace their steps, realizing our trick." Atina glared around her at the jubilant sailors. "So why are you standing here? Raise sail! We have a place to go!"

They made the turn. Atina, taking only fitful rest, seemed always on deck the next few days. At last they headed north again, and that night Perion saw the faraway clouds in a new light, that of electricity, as huge lightning discharges illuminated them. They seemed pink and pallid this far away, and the thunder could not carry; but they were almost always flashing, and Perion imagined the tumult and the lash of the storm beneath.

Northward they pushed, almost due north now; and two days after the turn, early in the morning, Illa, up in the watchtree, made the landfall. Perion, standing at the bows, looking ahead, saw only a purple line, scarcely a pencil line, ruled along the horizon. It was difficult to realize, at first, that the smudge was land, rock, burning mountains and crumbling soil. But it grew as they continued, until Perion could see its sawtooth irregularity, and the clouds that already, in late afternoon, were building above it.

That night he had no reason to imagine the storm. He, and the ship, were in it. Atina dropped sail and rode it out, though it was not really a fierce gale. But the lightning put on a pyrotechnic display, great jagged rivers of light opening in the air, rushing down on them, dissolving in a chaos of sound. They could see quite well by the flashes at the height of the storm, for the lightning discharges were almost constant, turning the ship's world into a weird black-and-white hologram, shadows all sharp as knives, highlights drained of all color. The rain, when it came, was fitful, varying from pelting, stinging drops to sudden blinding deluges; and with the rain came hail, cracking into the deck and raising welts on flesh when it struck.

But after midnight the storm died down, passing farther to the north, leaving the crew tired, wet, and dispirited. Then Teyo called out, "Look! Candles!"

Perion turned his eyes skyward. Yes, there they were, the candles—an electric discharge at the tips of the masts, a soft glow, St. Elmo's fire they had called it once. But now it was—

"Kalea's Candles," said Atina.

"They bring good luck," Selridir said. "Or so they tell me."

"I hope it may be so," Atina said, but Perion knew she had as little faith in luck as in the Sailing Star.

Still, he found it hard to be entirely downhearted, and for some reason he knew that the candles, with all their load of superstition, were partly behind his mood.

They snatched a few hours' sleep, those who could, and the next morning they were up early. This time Perion looked due north as soon as he rose from his damp pallet. What he saw made him catch his breath.

It had come closer in the night, this Rim. There it was now, an easy day's sail, almost upon them. But how it towered! Here the Rim seemed literally that, an edge to the world, for black cliffs reared nearly vertically from the sea, up one, maybe two kilometers; here and there some blocks reached even higher, and behind them Perion caught glimpses of purple mountains, capped with white.

Snow.

They were within a hundred kilometers or so of the equator, and there ahead and above were fields of snow.

Teyo came up beside him. "There is the land," she said. "It seems a forbidding place."

"Only to those who lack the knowledge, Teyo. We will conquer it."

"Better to work with a person than make her your slave," Teyo said, and it sounded as though she were quoting. "For one who works with another gains double labor and friendship; one who makes a slave earns resentful work and enmity."

"Then we will work with the land," Perion said. "I don't intend to enslave Kalea, Teyo."

"Do you not?" she asked and moved away.

The question echoed in Perion's mind for many days thereafter.

Chapter 18

The ship danced with the sunbeams in a deep bay, an inlet created when the world had split. The *Windbird* was between cliffs, a hundred meters high on the seaward side, a hundred and fifty on the landward; and, as Perion knew, at the foot of the landward side there was a narrow beach, a series of washes and gullies, and, here and there, a way up.

Eight of them had made the climb this far. Now they were atop the first range of cliffs, and could stand and wave down at the toy-sized ship, and see the little figures of those left aboard wave in return. Even old Teyo had come, and despite Perion's misgivings, he found her true to her word: she climbed more rapidly and with more sureness than did Trennon Fane, and she carried with her a respectable burden of food.

For the time being, at least, they needed to carry no water; freshets sprang everywhere, and they had but to dip a hand to find cold, refreshing liquid. They climbed almost bare rock, but now and again some tough tree had taken hold and had grown, twisted and stubborn, hard against the stone. They used the exposed roots and trunks as handholds whenever they could, but for the most part the party moved sideways and up, for the cliffs were terraced and layered, and these paths were easiest.

They had climbed perhaps half a kilometer up steep slopes when they crossed the topmost bluff of the cliffs. Perion caught his breath. He looked, it seemed, into Eden: dense trees were everywhere, and they grew to immensity, towering fifty meters high, branching out into thick green crowns, throwing dappled shade on other, lower growth that seemed to aspire to overthrow the trees, to take the sun in their place. He heard the gabbles and cackles of the creatures he now thought of as birds, and in a moment he saw them, now wheeling high overhead in ragged clouds, now, with wings half folded, swooping in among the trees. Everything was alive, it seemed. This side of the bluff ran level, or nearly so, for a kilometer or more; then it dropped, and the trees filled a broad valley between the edge of the cliff and the taller mountains whose sides were visible here and there through the trees, and at least one of whose snow-topped peaks jutted still farther into the sky.

"Beautiful," Atina said.

"But don't let that fool you," Trennon Fane panted. "We aren't too far west to be sure that we are entirely away from barbarians; they're roving folk, anyway, and this valley certainly looks ripe for some of them to have settled in. And there may be animals."

"There are animals," Perion said. When Trennon turned a raised eyebrow to him, he nodded to his left. There, on the bare stone a few meters away, was a whitened pile of droppings. "Something left that here," he said. "Something large, from the look of it."

"I suggest we go carefully," Trennon said.

"Wise suggestion." Perion grinned. "Let's go."

The black volcanic rock sloped more gently on this side, dropping perhaps one meter in five, and here and there in its cracks, where a little soil had accumulated, plants sprouted, bristly low stalks a poisonous yellow-green, or occasional splashes of a darker, clovery foliage and tiny blue flowers. The ancient rock was pitted and chipped, and often they came across bowllike depressions anywhere from twenty centimeters to a meter across, the larger ones holding a little water cupped in them. Perion looked at them, then scanned the sky; overhead, the clouds were gathering already, the undersides looking ragged and gray. Atina noticed his concern. "Something is wrong?"

Perion gestured at the depressions. "Lightning scars. They could be very old—or very recent. I don't want to be on exposed rock when the lightning begins."

But they had passed the rock and were on turf, springy and spongelike, laced with tough, long grasses, when the first drops of rain began to fall. Atina looked at the sky, then surveyed their surroundings. "There," she said, pointing to an outcropping of boulders perhaps five meters high. "They'll provide some shelter from the wind. Let's go there."

The tents they pitched would have won no prizes for beauty—they were constructed of ship's canvas carefully oiled and sealed against moisture, strung over light poles and guyed heavily against the wind's pull—but they kept off the rain. Lying prone in the tent he shared with Atina, Perion watched through the triangular opening as day became overcast gloom, lashed with whips of gray rain, illuminated now and again by nerve-jarring, earth-shaking bolts of lightning. At times the discharges were so close that Perion could hear the electrical crackle microseconds before the shattering blast of thunder; he thought, too, that he could even smell the ozone. But the tent was snug enough, and before true night was far advanced, the storm had played itself out to a steady drizzle. The thunder had moved inland, and its echoes rumbled and rolled across the distance like the sound of a faraway rockfall.

Just as Perion hovered on the edge of sleep, Atina began to worm out of the tent. "Where you going?" he muttered.

"To stand watch. I'll call you in time for the next watch. If there are animals and perhaps barbarians around, I don't want to be caught off guard."

Perion dropped into sleep, and was awakened moments later, or so it seemed. "Quiet," Atina said. "A few small night creatures, but nothing large. Watch until the red star vanishes behind the trees to your right. Then call Selridir."

Perion emerged into damp night. The sky was still overcast in most places, but a break away to his right revealed the star Atina had spoken of, a glowing red giant about as bright as Betelgeuse at home. Grumpily, Perion wondered what he would do if it disappeared behind the clouds; but he had his datakit in a specially tailored pocket of his sleeveless jacket, and at a pinch he could always go by that. He consulted it. It told him that the time was not quite fifteen, a little before midnight. He decided he would watch until about eighteen before calling Selridir. The boulder behind the tent provided an opportune lookout point, and he climbed it, finally locating a position where he could stretch out his legs, lean partially against a rounded spur of the boulder, and see in all directions—as far as the thick night allowed. He listened for some minutes to the sounds of the night: the crisp ticks and drips of water soaking into the soil, the rustle of leaves caught in the fitful gusts of the wind, a few high twittering cries from overhead—bat analogues, he reasoned—interspersed with the intermittent buzzes of night insects going about their business. Once his arm itched, and reaching to scratch, he dislodged a cold, soft-bodied, many-legged something which popped gooseflesh over his arms; but it had not bitten him, and he could not locate it, so he settled back to watch and listen. Once something rustled not far from the tents, but he saw nothing. From the sound it was very small, rabbit-sized perhaps, and when he stirred to try to locate the sound more clearly, it ran away with a swish and a clatter.

Time passed slowly. He watched the red star come and go through scudding drifts of cloud, and he consulted his datakit once when he thought he must have been on watch for two hours. Only forty minutes had passed. He sighed, squirmed against the rock, trying unsuccessfully to find a softer, more comfortable portion, and tried to stay alert. His right hand, extended along a curve of the boulder, drummed unconsciously, a recurring rhythm—*dot-dot-dot-DOT-dot-dot-DOT-dot-dot-DOT*—for a long time before he realized that the beat originated externally, not from within his own head. The rhythm he tapped matched a sound he was only half aware of hearing.

Perion held his breath. Yes, there it was, right on the edge of sound, a vibration in the night air, coming from—where? Ahead, somewhere, from the sound of it. He searched his memory for some similar sound, found none. It could be a drum, he thought; but it could be the mating cry of some woodland animal, too. He listened intently, and at last, straining after the sound, he could no longer be sure whether the noise was really there or whether he imagined it. He checked the datakit. It was close enough to time for him to call Selridir. He squirmed down from the rock, located her tent by feel, and called her out. She came much more readily than he had, and was alert from the moment she stepped into the night air. "Cool here," she said.

"Because of the altitude and the rain," Perion acknowledged. "Selridir, listen carefully. You can hear something?"

Selridir was silent. Perion held his breath. At last she said, "I hear only the sound of the wind in the grass, and the small noises of night insects. What do you hear?"

"Nothing, I guess," Perion said. "I imagined I heard drums before. But I may have been mistaken." He stretched, feeling his cramped muscles ease their tension. "Back to sleep for me. Good watch, Selridir."

"Thank you, Tom."

He woke again to a bright morning, with only a few wisps

of cloud here and there. They gathered wood from a few lightning-blasted scrub trees that grew scattered about and with some difficulty finally got a fire going. Teyo cooked a sort of stew of dried fruits—looking at her, Perion found himself irresistibly reminded of the witches of ancient Earth folklore—and served them breakfast. After last night's meal, a joyless affair of chewed dried fruit they had munched after pitching the tent, the hot food seemed almost festive. Before the sun had risen very far, they had struck camp and resumed march. An hour or so brought them to the edges of the forest, and again Perion found himself awed. The trees were huge, many-branching, umbrellalike, strung with looped and trailing vines, some as thick as Perion's arm. The undergrowth, too, was thick, unlike that found in typical rain forests on Earth. From the riot of colors, mostly yellows and oranges, that he could glimpse, Perion guessed that a vigorous substrate of funguslike plants occupied the forest floor. The middle height was leafed with ferny plants, but on a gigantic scale, each one shooting five or six meters in the air before spreading its leaves to the scant sun passed through the taller trees. The smells were rich, from a loamy scent of decomposition and decay to the sweet aromas of flowering plants and the carrion reek of some of the fungi. High overhead the pseudobirds flapped and chirred, and more than once one of them clambered down a tree trunk upside down to take a look at the invaders. Twice, from far off to their right, a strange sound reached them—a low bawling, faintly like the bellow of a bull, Perion thought, but also somewhat reminiscent of the roar of a big cat, heard at great distance. He had no wish to investigate the source of the sound.

"There is a trail," Atina announced. Perion saw it too, now, an arched passage obviously well used. "We'll take it."

"It's an animal trail," Perion said nervously.

"Probably. It was not put here for our convenience," Atina said.

They pushed in. They entered a world of green gloom, with the soil beneath their feet springy, made up mostly of decomposing wood, and on either side of the path their way was lined with the knee-high fungi, fantastic domes and fans brightly colored, sometimes unpleasantly aromatic, their forms littered with dead leaves and bird droppings, and sometimes

half excavated by curious black insects, amazingly supple as
they bustled over the surfaces, but when touched, as Perion
found when he brushed a couple off his leg, hard-shelled at
the same time. He caught one and examined it. As long as he
held it, the bug was rigid, a two-centimeter-long black capsule with no visible legs or joints. But when he placed it in
his palm, the creature promptly squirmed and wriggled like
an earthworm, the covering no longer hard. He dumped it off
to the side of the trail and continued to follow Atina.

It was hot and humid, breathless, in the depths of the
forest. The trail trended northward generally, with occasional
side turns and more than one tributary trail. Once they rounded
the enormous bole of a tree, stumbling over unexpected roots,
and came face to face with a small group of creatures,
waist-high, yellow-and-orange, with absurd ducklike mouths
and long antelope legs; these sprang away, but not before
Atina had whipped out her sprinbo and fired once. One of the
beasts had reversed direction and had leaped into the air; it
died in midleap, its muscles visibly losing purpose, and when
it hit the ground in a heap, a last pink breath exploded
through its nostrils. Atina's bolt had pierced lungs and heart,
and the creature quivered away its last vestige of life as they
came up to it.

"You know this kind of animal?" Perion asked.

"It is like a chazel, a beast native to some of the islands to
the south of Home," Atina said. "Differently colored, though,
and smaller. But definitely the same type of creature. Good
eating."

Perion ran his hand over the skin. It was furred, in a way,
with a velvety nap. The duck mouth, he saw, was the typical
three-lobed affair, with the two bottom lobes truncated and
small. "A grazing animal," Atina told him. "The trail here
leads to the grassland. The herd must shelter in the forest and
feed in the open. At least the pathway was not made by
flesh-eaters."

Selridir and Teyo made quick work of butchering the animal. They left the offal behind—already it had begun to
attract clouds of a spidery, long-legged fly—and when they
reached a large enough clearing, they built a fire and cooked
the flesh they had taken. Perion admitted that it was good,
and Trennon Fane ate his share; but to Perion, Trennon
confessed revulsion. He was not used, he explained, to seeing
his food killed before he ate it.

They made a little more headway that afternoon, and when the storms came again, they found themselves better protected than formerly. The canopy overhead broke most of the rain, and the lightning was not as intense. Still, Perion, remembering the strictures of his training, insisted that they pitch tent in a clearing of a type, far away from the trunks of the taller, lightning-attracting trees. The others took watch that night, and Perion slept soundly. They rose and got underway early.

Two times in their passage through the forest they had crossed small streams. Now the land turned upward again, and they noticed that the trees overhead were thinning. They had crossed the lower part of the valley; now they headed upward, into the foothills of the true mountains. Before noon they had more or less left the forest behind, and now walked through parkland, with waist-high grasses and scattered trees. They caught sight, once, of a small herd of the chazels, grazing around one of the clumps of trees, but they were too far away to pursue. Once in a while they heard the darting rustles in the grass of small animals, and Selridir caught sight, once, of the source: a rapid, she explained, a small burrowing animal that was not much good for food. "Pests," she said. "They get into gardens and eat the young plants. Hard to catch, because they are so fast. I suppose that's where they get their name."

Perion thought to himself that a more likely explanation was that "rapid" was a corruption of "rabbit"—a homely Earth animal that sounded to be much like its facsimile here on Kalea. The speed of the creature would influence the change to "rapid," and by now the old word would have fallen out of the High Speech that the Teachers used for ritual purposes.

That night they camped on a rise. The stormclouds formed, but for once the storm did not break, and except for an isolated blare and roar of thunder, they were undisturbed.

The next morning dawned clear and fine, and emerging from the tent, Perion gasped. The haze of the previous evening had all blown away; now, to the north, he saw the range of mountains, seemingly near enough to touch. They were huge, crumpled, bare rock, purpled by distance, all sharp-peaked and crowned with snow. The size of them took Perion's breath. They were like the Andes, rising suddenly and close to the sea, but more massive, more recent. Looking at them, Perion understood how they daunted the Kaleans. They daunted *him*.

But he dared not let that show. Atina said, "You think one, two days' march?"

"About that before we reach the mountains," Perion said. "We'll send the others back as soon as we find a passage route through the range."

"Good. I do not like the idea of leaving the *Windbird* too long at anchor inside that inlet. He seems well protected there—but a bird at roost is never wholly safe."

They marched on in curious silence. It was as though the nearness of the mountains somehow overwhelmed them, reduced their thoughts to a level below speech. A human crawling in the shadow of those vast peaks could not help feeling insignificant and small.

The land turned to washboard, ridges and small valleys, and they slowed as they negotiated the difficult terrain. Toward sunset they headed up one last slope. "We will camp on top of the ridge," Atina panted.

"Sounds good to me," agreed Perion. Already the air felt wet, and the clouds overhead were darkening.

They emerged onto a narrow crest, grown heavy with the same wiry grass they had pushed through for days. This they trampled down. Selridir found a niche, hardly more than a ledge, that some past landslide had scooped from the face of the downslope. It provided shelter from the wind and adequate drainage, and there they began to pitch their tents. The sound stopped them.

"Listen!" Hetha hissed, unnecessarily.

This time there was no mistaking: the sound was the same Perion had heard that first night, during his watch, but now it was closer, more insistent. It was the sound of drums.

"Barbarians," grunted Trennon Fane. "And close."

"Do you know anything of them?" Atina asked.

Trennon shrugged. "No one knows much of the barbarians," he said. "Roving hunters, most of them, feeling no kinship with us. One of my sisters traded with them for a while. She says they are not truly dangerous if not attacked— much like any other wild animal, I should think. Their language is very different from ours."

"We'll have to keep careful watch tonight," Atina said.

Perion took the first watch; he was keyed up anyway, and not at all sleepy. He sat through the rain, uselessly trying to peer around him. The storm began to play out before midnight, and he wakened Selridir with the news that all was quiet.

In the tent, his wet clothing removed and a dry tunic pulled on, he sought sleep, but it eluded him. Finally, an hour or so after turning in, he got up again. Selridir recognized him even in the dark. "Unable to sleep?" she asked.

"I am. I have a feeling."

"So do I."

Irrationally, Perion felt like laughing. His mind had flashed back to his training on L-5, to How to Be a Good Pioneer. Nothing, then, was said about what to do when in barbarian territory!

To Selridir, he whispered, "You think that we—"

A last flash of lightning cut him off.

In its sudden light, he saw them: a circle of them, apparently surrounding the tents. Barbarians, he supposed; men and women together, clad in loincloths, armed with spears.

"I think we'd better wake the others," Selridir said.

Amazed at his own calmness, Perion did just that.

Trennon Fane was a wonder. He claimed to know perhaps a hundred words, all told, of one barbarian dialect; but he used those hundred to splendid effect. The eight from the ship squatted around a fire, companionably, with eight barbarians, two men and six women. The women were as dark as the men, their hair as long, their teeth as yellow; their breasts sagged and were dark-nippled, their faces deeply lined from exposure to sun and wind. The men were different mainly because of their beards. They seemed to take kindly to Perion, nodding at him in friendly fashion. He supposed that they took him for one of them, since he shared the same facial decoration. Beyond them, others, many others, squatted in the darkness.

Trennon said, "They are hunters. They are here to gather supplies of chazel meat and hides before their cool season. They want to know what we are doing."

The east already was red with impending dawn. Atina said, "Tell them we want no chazels. We are going to the mountains."

"I'll try," said Trennon, and he jabbered in what must have been strangely broken dialect. But with gestures and facial expressions to support it, the babble seemed to work. The barbarians consulted among themselves, broke into a monkey-chatter of dissent, and finally one of them, an old woman with three missing front teeth and a faint gray mustache, spoke forcefully and slowly to Trennon.

"She says there is great danger there. The sky-gods live there. They kill."

"Kill how?" Atina asked.

Trennon translated as best he could, and the old woman made a zigzag gesture and clapped her hands together.

"I can read that," Illa said. "Lightning."

The old woman continued, thumping the ground for emphasis.

"No one goes that way," Trennon said. "There is nothing in the mountains or beyond. The sun eats those who try to go north."

Perion edged closer to Atina. "You think they will try to keep us from the mountains?"

"They may, if that is a holy place of theirs. But I'm not sure. Trennon thinks the warnings may be friendly—they're more worried about our safety than about angering the gods."

Perion nodded. Looking around the campfire, he wondered. These, these *people,* ragged and illiterate, roving hunter-gatherers, were akin to him in the same way that Trennon was, or Atina: they had descended from those Earth colonists who had reached the surface of Kalea years and years ago. Yet the Aslandians, the Homereachers, and the Under Islanders had formed some sort of civilization, after all. They had language, writing, rules, complexities. These folks had gone backward, more than seventeen hundred years, back to the neolithic. What would Perion's mission mean to them? Perion felt inside himself a small pang of despair. The *Galileo,* large as she was, was still only one ship; and now she had an entire world to change.

He pushed the thought away. Trennon said, "I think it would be hospitable to offer them gifts. That might appease them."

Perion, who had been sitting cross-legged, rose to his feet. "A moment," he said, and went to his tent. He was back just as the sun rose, and he carried with him a canvas bag. To

Trennon, he said, "Tell these people that I have gifts for them. That we thank them for their warning. That *our* gods tell us we must go. That we bid them farewell."

Then he began to distribute the goodies: the foil-wrapped survival rations from his kit.

The barbarians were delighted, not with the wafers, which they sniffed, bit experimentally, and threw away, but with the wrappers. These they shredded and distributed, so that each one wound up with a postage-stamp-size piece of foil, to be hung from leather thongs around necks or tied to spears just behind their heads. The barbarians rose as one—Perion counted twenty-one of them, six men and fifteen women, a few of these only twelve or thirteen Earth years old—and with gestures of blessing, they faded away, being careful not to turn their backs until they were well out of spear-casting distance.

"Let's go," Atina said briskly.

"I think that would be best," Trennon said. "There must be a larger group somewhere not too far away. If they want presents too, they might return. I don't suppose you have much more of the metal-paper?"

"No more," Perion said.

"Then let's go. Those of you who will return this way, move quickly," Atina said. "Don't camp here. I think you'll be safer pushing into the forest, even if that means going without meals or marching at night. Understood?"

To a chorus of assent, they struck camp and began to move, not waiting for breakfast. They chewed dried fruit, leathery and acidic to the tongue, as they marched; and they kept up a pace that soon had them sweating.

Still the land rose, and now the trees grew even farther apart, and were stunted. The grass began to be interspersed with patches of bare rock, until finally there was more rock than grass. The mountains loomed higher and nearer, their tops lost in midday haze. Perion, studying them, suggested a course, and they turned a bit west of north, heading for a saddlelike pass between two high peaks. Still, by evening they had barely begun to climb the sides of the mountain, and they rested on a flat place exposed to the wind and the rain.

They woke stiff and sore the next morning, but began their climb again immediately. Once, at midmorning, they paused to look back into the valley. From this altitude they could see all the way across it, a slash of deep green pearled here and there with ground fog, and limited on the far side by a lip of black stone, the top of the bluff they had climbed so long ago. But that climb seemed simple in retrospect.

They did real rock-climbing now, linked by rope. Perion had had some experience at this sort of thing, and took the lead. For the most part he sought easier ascents, but twice they rappelled up the face of fissure-cut stone, using pitons of blackwood. Both times, from the vantage of the top of the climb, Perion pointed out easier ways of descent to those who would be returning; but, with the climbing knowledge of sailors deep in their bones, they assured him that the trip down would be no problem.

Perion worried about Teyo, but the old woman kept grimly up with the party, speaking but little as she matched them in every exertion. Where does she find the strength? Perion wondered; but he knew the answer to that, at least in part: she was devoted to the cause, and from that and her pride in family came at least some of her enduring vitality.

Luck was with them again on the second night of the ascent, for no storm came. But the weather was decidedly chilly—a mere twenty-four degrees, according to Perion's datakit—and that night he huddled close to Atina for warmth. Their nearness was curiously asexual, but from it, he felt, each of them took some small comfort.

They reached the pass on the next day. They stood higher than any of the Aslandians or Homereachers had ever stood, on a saddle of rock from which they could see almost the entire world. Perion peered away to the west and grunted. "Curious," he said. "I'd almost swear that—look, am I wrong, or is there a break in the mountains away over there?"

Atina shaded her eyes. "Hard to tell," she gasped—for her this air seemed thin—"but I think so. That would have been a better place to cross, you think?"

"I don't know. But after we cross the mountains, we may take a westward turn. Not much of one—just enough to have a look."

Then he turned his eyes northward. Impossibly, the land rose ahead, the mountains rearing still higher. But he had chosen well; a thousand meters above this pass was another, this one frosted with snow. But it was still a long march away.

They made the second pass late that day, and the Home-reachers were puzzled and a little afraid of the cold white stuff that disappeared under their touch, leaving only water; and the teeth in their heads chattered from the cold. But the snow was scant, only centimeters thick, and more important, the land beyond the second pass sloped downward.

"This is it," Perion said. "From here, the four of us will continue. The rest of you, back to the ship."

"Go carefully," Atina said. "Keep my ship safe for me until I return."

"No fear of that," Illa said with a smile that was half grimace.

That night was colder still, thin and bitter and crisp, and Perion felt exposed, perched on the very roof of the world. But somehow he got to sleep, and the next morning he stood with the others, looking both before and behind.

To the north, the rocky land gave downward, and here and there were patches of greenery; but the morning sun caught the red hues of desert beyond that, stretching far into the hazy distance. Behind, they saw the green valley, diminished by distance to a mere strip, and past it the silver rim of the sea. They ate a last meal together, and when time for movement came, they were reluctant to begin. Atina embraced the women who would return and had a last word for them all. But Teyo refused the embrace.

"You know I am coming with you," she said.

The argument was foredoomed. The old woman had come this far, and she would not be turned back; and so at last only three figures turned and began to descend toward the sea. Atina, Selridir, Teyo, Trennon, and Perion watched them go. Then the five of them turned their faces north and began to walk.

At midday they had reached the very summit of this pass, and were ready to descend. They paused for a long look back. "What is that?" Trennon asked. "Fog?"

Perion saw what he was pointing at, a thick plume, gray in the sunlight, at the edge of the forest. "Smoke, I think," Perion said.

"Perhaps lightning," Trennon suggested.

"Or perhaps not," Atina said. Her voice was solemn, yet she made no suggestion to turn back. "Let's go."

And, whatever it portended, they left the smoke behind.

Chapter 19

The valley looked like the anteroom of hell.

Perion stood on the lip of a cliff. Ahead of him, perhaps five kilometers away, a similar set of cliffs reared, vertical from the top down for the first five hundred meters or so, then buried in steeply sloped scree for five times that height. At last the sands leveled, forming a ruddy, flat floor, ashimmer already with heat, marked with upthrust, wind-weathered fingers of stone, a pool of copper-green water unstirred by any wind, and a few straggling growths of vegetation.

They had been long on the march here. By Teyo's reckoning, they were now in the first days of Dess, not long from the opening month of sunfall. The sun *was* less intense, Perion realized, and would grow more so; still, the temperatures at noon hit the low forties regularly, and the nights brought swift chill. The party had turned west after negotiating the last of the mountains, and had followed the shoulders of these to this point. Now they were on the edge of the deep valley, which meandered north and west, to join a still larger one in the distance.

The day before, Perion had dropped down into the valley itself, had spent some time there exploring, and had returned bearing chunks of rock. "My job," he explained that evening to Atina. "I'm trained to classify rock and soil, and I can't help doing it when I have the chance. Look at these." He passed a crumbly, soft rock to Atina, who turned it over without much interest.

"It is a rock," she said.

"No, a book," Perion told her. "Taste it."

"*Taste* it?"

"Just with the tip of your tongue."

With a dark look, Atina did. "Salt," she said.

"And look at this." He took the rock from her, turned it,

203

pointed out little whorled depressions in it. "Know what these are?"

"They look like clamshells," Atina said. "But they could not be. A clam surely could never have grown here."

"Not in the last fifty thousand years. But before that—yes. This was once a bay, an arm of the sea. Then the land rose—remember those black cliffs we passed?—and the water was dried away by the heat. That pond down there, the green one, is full of salt. Its edges are white with it. It exists now only because an occasional storm manages to toss a little rain over the mountains; otherwise, the valley would be dry as old bones." Perion rose, dusted his hands. "You know, this valley is close to sea level now. Perhaps even below sea level. I think there was once a large body of water here, going quite far north. If that ledge of black rock could be removed, the ocean would pour in again. Before long, in five hundred years or so, there would be an inland sea here again. Think of that!"

"It could never happen."

"I don't know. It happened once, on Earth, with a sea we called the Mediterranean. Like this, it was a vast depression, lower than the level of the world ocean. The ocean worked its way through an opening, just a narrow one, and filled the depression. That changed many things, the whole climate of the area." Perion had looked north, across the bluffs, in the dying light. "Think of sailing a ship across this desert," he said. "Think of an easy way to travel across it."

But they had no easy way now, and this morning Perion supervised their last preparations before they descended. They would not enter the valley, for it was likely to be a place even hotter than the high desert, but instead would skirt the depression, keeping to the tops of the bluffs, and strike out across the bare rock that bordered it. Here there was a lonely stream, a narrow leap of water down the weathered sides of the mountains, that found its way finally to the salty pond. But the water of the stream was fresh, distilled from snowcaps high above, and it might well prove to be their last reliable supply for many days. They had filled all the skins and had distributed the weight among themselves as well as they could. At Teyo's suggestion, Perion had fashioned a simple travois. They would take turns pulling this, and that would mean a little more water and food for each of them. Still,

Perion planned to hold rations to little more than a liter a day per person. That was not really sufficient, not in this heat; but it would keep them going, he hoped.

Teyo, too, had unexpectedly supplemented their food supply. In the cracks and fissures of the rockface grew tough, thick-stemmed scrub brush that bore a yellow-red fruit. This Teyo pronounced fit for consumption, and she had spent much time in gathering and sun-drying them. She had also, with infinite patience, contrived to capture with a noose about a dozen small animals, the size of cats. They were vegetarians, though, making their homes in burrows in the scanty soil or in rock dens. These animals, killed and skinned and sundried, yielded about a kilogram of meat each. It had a gamy flavor and the consistency of pine bark, but it was nourishment.

They had a waxing moon right now, and would have it for another six days or so. It would help, for they planned to travel at night as much as possible.

The sun was low now, sending long fingers of shadow eastward. "Ready?" Perion asked, shifting his pack. He carried, he estimated, thirty kilos, and only Trennon carried slightly less, perhaps twenty-five or so; still, even with the travois, they took a long chance.

"Ready," Selridir said. She shook her head. "Tom, I have never seen country like this. May you know well your way!"

"Thank you," Perion said. "But our way is simply as near to north as we can make it." He turned to Teyo, who with Trennon was first to pull the travois. "Teyo, does your religion say anything of a place of punishment for the dead? A place called hell?"

"No," the old woman said. "We believe that after death the spirits of people are taken to the Sailing Star, there to be purged of all their worldly sins. When at last they are pure, the sun takes them to a place of eternal delight. We know nothing of hell."

"A humane religion," Perion said. He looked north again. "Well, I fear that when you return, Teyo, you will be able to teach the other Teachers exactly what hell is like. Let's go."

They trudged across hammada, exposed bedrock, for much of that night. It was nearly level, with an occasional scatter of loose stone. They had to turn eastward to make their way around the tip of the valley, but before midnight they had turned north again and kept up a good pace. "Look at the sky," Trennon said to Atina. "I have never seen the stars so bright!"

"It's the dry air," Perion called back. "No dust, no water vapor. That's also why it gets cold so quickly at night."

But he himself was awed by the spangled face of the heavens, and now, with Atina's help, he began to learn the names of some of the brighter stars; but those in the north for the most part had no name, for few had seen them at all.

The constellations were unfamiliar, but now and again Perion recognized, or thought he did, a star he knew. Toward dawn, he found himself staring at a fuzzy orange thumbprint low on the northern horizon, scarcely visible when he looked directly at it, but more clear when he looked slightly to one side. Not a galaxy, surely. Even M31 was not that clear, and would not be from anywhere in the sun's galactic neighborhood. Perhaps a cloud of interstellar gas or—

"A nova," he grunted to himself.

"What?" Atina asked.

"A burned-out star," Perion said. "There ahead, low, you can see it. Not much now, but at one time it must have been a hell of a sight. It must have set the night afire in the northern regions."

"I could use a fire right now," Trennon grunted. "Will we have more snow, do you think?"

"No," Perion said. "You need moisture for that, as well as cold. And we're fresh out of moisture."

They encamped before sunup, digging into the sand that had gradually covered the rock and casting their tents low. Even so, the first touch of sun was like the breath of an oven, and before noon they sweltered. Perion's datakit registered a high of forty-three. Atina and he, and Trennon, who now shared their tent, by mutual agreement removed most of their clothing. They resembled barbarians now truly, Perion thought, half clothed and glistening with sweat, Trennon's beard coming in fair and sun-bleached already, as was his hair. His once midnight thatch was now almost red, as was Atina's. Perion could see from the fringe of his beard that he was well on the way to becoming a towhead himself.

He slept fitfully. In the afternoon, he crawled out of the tent, into a day dancing with heat. Mirages shimmered all around him, and looking back he saw the mountains floating in midair, like something from an *Arabian Nights* tale. The group had agreed on a spot behind a rock outcropping as a latrine, and he made his way there, shielding his eyes against the omnipresent glare.

When he got to his destination, he thought at first that he dreamed, for there was a little garden, green and lush, sprouting from the sand. But then he realized that the plants were rooted in the waste products of the party. He relieved his bladder and watched fascinated as the dampened sand seethed with activity, sending forth little blebs of green that quickly climbed to heights of a few centimeters before turning brown and bursting open, sending a thin black powder away on the desert wind. The spores must be everywhere, he realized, hidden in the sand, just waiting for moisture and nutrient to burst into their accelerated, hectic life. It was like watching a time-lapse motion picture of growth, the whole cycle from sprouting through sporulation over in a matter of minutes.

The five of them ate a supper, or breakfast, of dried fruit—out of curiosity, Perion dropped a fragment near the now-withered growth behind the rock, but nothing happened, and he concluded that the spores didn't like the acidity of the food—and then they struck camp and continued north.

Lun grew in intensity, and the sand deepened. Perion kept a careful estimate of their progress, aided by the datakit, and found that they were making anywhere between twenty and twenty-five kilometers per march. The waterskins began to deflate alarmingly; even at the bare survival ration Perion allowed them, the five consumed a great deal of water, and still their lips cracked and their sweat diminished from dehydration.

The heat grew worse. Before long Perion dreaded to check his datakit, but he did so nonetheless. The display climbed from forty-three to forty-seven, nearly half the temperature of boiling water, and ten degrees above normal body heat. In the nights they trudged to the north, watching the smudge of the exploded star climb just a bit higher each evening; in the day, they burrowed into the sand as well as they could, and for the most part futilely chased after sleep.

Four days onto the desert they came again to a change in terrain. As dawn came, they stared unbelieving at an unrelieved flat horizon, orange sand littered as far as they could see with stones, small, dark, and smooth-weathered by the winds. "It's like Mars," Perion croaked, surveying the desolation.

Though none of the others understood his allusion, they, too, felt the alienness of the surroundings, and they pitched the tents closer together that day than they had been doing. Before the sun rose high, Perion went out onto the rocky plain to explore a little. He picked up a rock, found it glazed with a thin layer of black oxide. He struck two stones together, and saw that the underlying rock was red, like the sand produced from it. Perion walked a little way into the scatter of stones, found none over a handbreadth in size.

The climbing sun was unmerciful, and he turned back to the tents. They were nowhere in sight.

Perion felt his heart thud within his chest. He had been sure that the tents were right over—no, not there. He turned in a complete circle, shading his eyes against the sun. He was, as far as he could tell, completely alone. And without water, with the sun as hot as it already was, his life would be measured in hours.

Panic rose within him. His first impulse was to run, fleeing the danger—but fleeing where, in what direction? He forced himself to think.

The sun had been casting the shadows of the stones to his left when he began, of that he was sure. He turned until his shadow stretched away to his right. Now he should be facing the camp.

But the concealing waves of dancing heat confused everything. And under them, the land looked so flat—where could the tents be concealed? Methodically, Perion stacked rocks into a rough little pyramid, knee-high. Keeping the sun on his left, he counted off a hundred paces, then stopped and looked back. The pile of stones was gone. Gritting his teeth, he tried to retrace his steps, counting mentally: sixteen, seventeen, eighteen, nineteen . . . on the twenty-fourth step, the little beacon materialized from the surrounding shimmer, and Perion yelped with joy. He was immediately ashamed of himself, but still he felt exultation at recovering sight of that miserable pile of stone. He scraped together another, then took fifty steps away from it. It was still in sight. He took ten more steps—and there, to his left, was a white glimmer.

He ran toward it, felt himself laughing and crying as he recognized the tents. Teyo sat outside one of them. "You return," she said matter-of-factly. "I was about to go in search."

"Thank you, Teyo," Perion said. "But forget that. The heat makes distances tricky here. From now on, we stay close together. We can't risk separation."

"You pick up no more rocks."

"No more rocks," Perion promised, and he crept into his tent. Despite the heat, he shivered himself into a semblance of sleep.

They crossed the plain of stones in three marches, and then the land turned on them again. Now they faced a low range of hills, more like the buried peaks of mountains than true mountains, and these slowed them as they crept and dragged themselves along. But in the heart of the jumbled and broken stone, they found a minor miracle: growing plants. The range of hills split into a Y, and in the delta of the Y grew the oasis, niggardly palmlike trees ten meters high, lower, thick-leaved spiky scrub, a few tussocks of grass. "There's water here," Perion said. They descended and searched for it.

Selridir found it, quite by accident. She had used her knife to cut into the trunk of one of the "palms," for similar plants to the south produced a thick, sweet sap that could be used as food. But this plant had no moisture to spare; the trickle of thin fluid that spilled from the wound was bitter to the taste, and there was too little of it to be of any use.

Walking away from the tree, Selridir cried out, and for a moment Perion thought she had vanished as the tents had, in an illusion of the desert; but no, there she was, sunk to her armpits in the sand. Perion cried for help and ran to her. He lay on his stomach and caught her arms and pulled, and in a moment Atina was there to help. They dragged her away, and then watched, fascinated, as the sand drained itself into a funnellike depression, and finally into a round hole a meter or so across. Perion cautiously crept on his stomach to the edge and looked over. Then he edged away. "It's a cavern," he said. "There's water at the bottom, an underground river. Let's see about getting down."

They used the ropes to fashion a means of descent. They dropped perhaps thirty meters to the cavern floor. Atina looked around. "This reminds me of the Council House," she said.

Perion nodded. The circle of light cast by the opening above was indeed reminiscent of the dim chamber and its skylight. But now they stood on a sand floor, in the cool darkness, and the walls of stone curved away and upward. The air had the scent of water.

It meandered in a tiny stream at the lower elevation of the cavern floor, a desert river of water half a meter across, a finger in depth at the center. But Perion tasted it and found it sweet.

They built a campfire that evening, and took a vote. They would rest here for a day and a night, replenish their water, and then set out again for the north. Perion urged this course and was glad to see that all consented. He knew his own strength had dwindled, and a look at the others told him that they suffered, too. Atina's eyes held a weariness he had never seen there before, and her already spare frame had wasted. Selridir, though uncomplaining, was a little lame. Trennon Fane was frankly all in, shambling on the marches like a man asleep.

But Teyo worried Perion the most.

She had not changed so much physically—though, Perion thought, she now looked like a mummy instead of a living woman—as spiritually. Her eyes were elsewhere these days, and not on the desert at all. She seemed off on a trek of her own, apart from theirs, and its ending was in shadow.

She went out that night to look at the stars, and Perion joined her. She nodded to him as he sat near. "You have come far with us," Perion said.

"The journey is indeed a great one."

"Your strength is much more than I thought at first," Perion said. "But now do you not grow weary?"

"As we all do. But I feel that all is well."

"Really?"

"Yes. You will reach your goal. You are the one foretold. You will bring the blessing of Kalea back to the world. Or the curse."

"The curse?"

"Yes. Every blessing is a curse, every curse a blessing. So much depends on how we receive it, you know. The sunlight, we see it now as a curse, for it weakens us. But without it there would be no life, and so it is a blessing, too. What you will bring will be for good or for ill—and you will have little control over which."

Perion gazed up into the wondrous sky. Something moved there. "The Sailing Star," he said, surprised.

"Yes," said Teyo. "I have not forgotten, even with the passage of time. It was due tonight. I think that bodes very well for your journey, Tom."

"Our journey."

"Ours, then. Know this—whether I go with you in body all the way or not, I surely go in spirit." The old woman sighed. "I have been wrong about so many things in my life. Like the others, when I read in the old writings that one day Kalea would send a leader to us, I saw the leader as a woman. And I thought, surely she will not come in my time. It was hard to accept you as that blessed one."

"I am not," protested Perion. "I am only a man."

"So you believe," Teyo said. "But I know. Kalea's will is not clear to us below, and we see things only darkly, as through a fog. But I have felt something new and alive in you. You yourself are not aware of it, or are aware only in a very remote way. But it is there, and it is real. I have seen you, and I have known your nature; and that makes me blessed, too."

Perion rubbed his arms. Teyo's primitive, simple expression of faith had moved him, and when he spoke his voice was thick. "I am blessed, if at all, for having known you, Teyo. You were the only one I could speak to at first; you could have counseled Atina to abandon me, or to break with me when the Council examined me. But you have stood by me, and you even came here." After a moment, he added, "Think of me as a man, and a man only, Teyo, for that is what I am. But think of me as a friend, too. We will reach our goal, I promise; and then you will see that all the wonders I have spoken of are true."

They sat companionably for several minutes. Finally, in a hesitant voice, Teyo said, "I would ask one thing. It is a silly favor, but one which means a great deal to me."

"What is that?"

"Teach me a song of the old ones, in the High Speech. For I truly believe you knew the old ones, and their songs have long been lost to us."

"I'm hardly a singer."

"Still. Teach me a song about the stars."

Perion thought a bit, then lifted his voice in song. Teyo was delighted; on the second chorus, she joined in. And the third time around, they formed a duet, singing to the night

sky in uncertain harmony, one voice old and high, one young
and low, an ancient tune of Earth.

> "Twinkle, twinkle little star,
> How I wonder what you are—
> Up above the world so high,
> Like a diamond in the sky. . . ."

Their voices grew louder and lustier as Teyo caught all the
words and the rhythm, and at last they bellowed their song
across the alien sands. Finally, from the cavern opening, an
irate voice—it was Selridir's—rasped out in the Common Speech,
"If you two don't shut up, I swear I'm going to come and tie
a knot in both your cursed necks!"

They fell silent. Then Perion shrugged. "A blessing—"

"—is also a curse," finished Teyo gravely.

Their laughter was even louder than their song.

The period of rest stretched longer than planned, for Selridir's
bad leg gave her some trouble; but nothing had been broken,
and with rest it mended. They all felt better after two days in
the cool depths of the cavern, and their spirits rose again
accordingly. They had hot meals for the first time in weeks;
they took careful account of the food on hand—enough at full
rations, Teyo said, for another twenty days at least, and more
than that if they kept themselves to a minimum consumption.
Perion calculated the distance they had come, and at noon he
went aboveground and looked at the sun and the shadows it
cast. He rechecked his findings twice.

When he dropped back into the cavern, he announced with
just a shade of triumph that the sun was directly overhead.
They now did the impossible, they all realized: for they had
stood beneath the sun.

"If the desert is not much larger than I think at this point,"
Perion told them, "we should be out of it in another twelve to
fifteen days, if we can keep our pace up. We still have to find
the command pod, but at least we'll be able to work our way
eastward through more hospitable country."

They consulted, and finally agreed to wait another day or
two, until Selridir's lameness had gone. In the meantime,
they would rest in the cavern during the day, refill their
waterskins, and carefully ration their food.

On the second day, while the others were sleeping, Perion found himself again restless. He decided to explore the cavern a little; but, recalling the episode on the plain of stones, he hesitated to go alone. Of the others, only Trennon was still awake. The Aslandian had bounced back rapidly from his strain and exhaustion, and now he, like Perion, seemed to have a surplus of energy. Perion approached him. "Want to go for a walk?"

"Where?" Trennon asked.

Perion nodded northward, in the direction of the little stream's flow. "See what's ahead. How far the cavern goes."

Trennon pushed up. "All right. We'll need torches."

They had discovered in building their campfire that one of the low shrubs had a high oil content and burned very readily. From several of these shrubs, Perion and Trennon fashioned a dozen torches each. These they kindled near their campsite; then they walked downstream, on the stone lining the bed of the little river.

The cavern—actually the bed of the underground stream, eroded over millennia—was straightforward, winding but with no side chambers. Still, Perion paused every hundred paces or so to smudge a mark on the stone walls. They went on for several hundred meters, their voices echoing eerily as the stone walls closed in or soared away. At last the ceiling dropped right down, and they found themselves at the head of a little cascade of water, trickling over the lip of a rock and down. The arched passage for the water was low, only waist-high, and the rocks slippery. But Perion, with a rope around his waist, made it to the edge of the drop, lowered his torch, and looked over. "It's a pool!" he exclaimed, the closed space distorting his voice. "A fairly large one, too. I don't think it's too deep. "Let's see—yes, there's a sort of beach around it, on the left at least. And there's another little stream feeding into it—I can hear it." He pushed away from the opening. "Want to chance it?"

Trennon shrugged. "It's madness. But to have come this far is even more mad, so let us try."

They secured a rope—that left them with only one—and Perion descended first, having some trouble with his torch. At the bottom, he stood ankle-deep in water and steadied the rope as Trennon clambered down. They waded to the little beach, a meter-wide stretch of damp sand, and kindled a second torch. "Look at that," Perion said in awe.

They stood in a vast rock chamber, the size of a cathedral, it seemed. The pool in front of them, dark-rippled surface throwing back the specter of their torches, was easily thirty meters across, and nearly circular. The beach they were on shelved into the water, and as Perion took a few steps into the pool, he saw that the center was deeper than he had thought, perhaps several meters. The walls were dark gray eroded stone, pitted and carved by eons of water, smooth to the touch, covered with a soft and yielding growth of fungi here and there. The other waterfall was twice the size of theirs in volume, but came through a much smaller opening. They had no hope of exploring that passageway. The pool drained at the far end through a low, broad arch. There was no going on from here.

A sound attracted Perion's attention. "You threw something?" he asked Trennon.

"No. Why?"

"I thought I heard—" Perion lifted his torch and peered out over the dark water. "Forget it. Probably nothing."

But Trennon was gazing intently into the edge of the water. "Something, I think," he said. "There."

Sure enough, Perion saw a scuttling movement and a little cloud of silt where Trennon had pointed. He went right to the edge of the water, and saw now tiny moving shadows on the sand. "Fish," he said. "Tiny little fish—there, see that one? Transparent. And look there." He scooped up a handful of sand, let it rinse away, and held at last in his hand a frantic, translucent, white little creature, segmented, many-legged, wriggling and struggling. He dropped it, and it disappeared in a moment into the sand. "Some kind of crustacean, or crustaceanlike animal. I wonder if you can eat them."

"There's a bigger fish," Trennon said.

Perion looked, and in a moment he saw it, a leaf-shaped creature as long as his palm. It flitted away. "The light attracts them," Perion said. "They're not blind, then. Wonder how they got here."

"I wonder if we could catch a few," Trennon said. "That would be a change from dried flesh and stewed fruits."

"Do you know how to go about catching fish?"

Trennon giggled. "We were not taught that skill in my lordship training."

Despite himself, Perion laughed, too. "Well, let's go tell

the others about the pool," he said. "Perhaps they—something is wrong?"

Trennon had stooped low to the ground and had lowered his torch; but it had burned low. He kindled a new one, and holding it close to the beach, he pointed. "No fish left this."

Perion saw a track, in low relief. Not the track of feet; the mark of a sinuous body dragged on its belly through the sand. Suddenly the cavern seemed very dark and huge indeed. "Let's go," he said, wading into the water. Trennon followed him, his torch high. It took a great deal of Perion's resolve to let Trennon climb the rope first; but he did, and then he made his way up into darkness, for Trennon could not climb with a torch, and his own had burned out.

They busied themselves with flint and iron and soon had another torch going at the top. Perion leaned through the opening for a last glance at the pool, and whistled his amazement. "Come look at this," he said.

Trennon joined him, braced hard against the rock. The torchlight glimmered on the water below—and now they saw a long, black body, half coiled, just a little farther along the beach than their steps had taken them. It was as thick as Perion's arm, and perhaps two meters long, a blunt-nosed, blunt-tailed *something*. "A serpent?" Trennon asked.

"I don't know. You think it's dead?"

"Can't tell."

Perion hunted for a piece of loose rock, found several, and chunked them in the creature's direction. One hit the water several meters from it, and it moved with surprising speed— *toward* the disturbance, not away from it.

Trennon cleared his throat. "Ah—I suppose that thing is too heavy to, uh, *climb?*"

"Certainly," Perion agreed.

But they returned to the campsite at a brisk march nevertheless.

Chapter 20

The serpent, from their description, was strange to the others, but they kept watch after that. On the third night, Selridir professed herself ready to travel; and so they pulled their laden waterskins to the surface, turned their faces to the north, and resumed their march.

After leaving the hills, they came to sand, shifting and treacherous underfoot. The winds were scorching in the day, chilling at night; and always they were peppered with abrasive, stinging sand. Earlier, Zerba had equipped the travelers with loose white robes and turbanlike headcoverings; these they broke out now, and seldom were they without them in the open, for the airborne sand stung the nostrils and irritated the eyes. Perion, like the rest, became accustomed to seeing the world through a narrow horizontal slit, and they pushed on.

The travois was of little use here, for its drag in the sand was more annoying than the extra weight it carried. The five agreed to dispense with it, and they redistributed its supplies in their own packs. These were lighter now than they had been when the travelers first left the mountains, for food and water alike had diminished, but they were still a burden, apt to make one slide awkwardly on a slope of sand, cutting into one's shoulders, pressing down relentlessly on one's spine.

Perion worried. They tired more rapidly on this leg of the journey, for in spite of the abundant water and the coolness of the cavern, the oasis had not really allowed them to renew their strength fully. Trennon, especially, often floundered in the sand, and more than once he took an alarming slide down the face of a transverse dune. Atina backed him up, took part of his load in her pack, and was always at his side. Perion approved, for he had other things to concern him now. He kept one eye on the distance they had covered as it stretched out, three hundred, three hundred and fifty kilometers, and another on the water supply. There was never enough water; the scant allowance seemed to vanish each day, disappearing in their thirsty bodies as it might drain into the quenchless sands of the desert.

After many nights of march, they came to another rocky area, reminiscent of the hills with the cavern; but though here, too, there was some life, chiefly sturdy plug–shaped plants like cacti, they found no water source.

"At least there are plants," panted Atina. "That is encouraging."

"Yes. I'd like them better, though, if they were edible," Perion muttered. "There are small animals, too. See the tracks?"

Whatever had left them was tiny, no bigger than a mouse, and they had nothing to fear from it. Indeed that night they saw some of them, in the light of a torch: skipping, pale creatures that darted in terror around the bases of the plants. And something else: for as Perion held the torch high, *something* swooped low, struck the flaming end of the torch a tremendous blow, and sent it tumbling, spraying sparks into the night. The five instinctively dropped, but the air was still. After a while, Perion pushed up again. "Bird," he grunted. "Or something like one."

"He won't come again," Selridir said. "I hope the bastard burned his feet off!"

Sand, sand, and more sand. Now at noon, if they stood facing north, their shadows pooled before them about their feet; but they took little cheer in that, for the sands were endless. Teyo spoke less and less, and more and more her gray eyes had a distance in them, a dream that was become real. They had gone for twelve nights beyond the oasis when, as they broke camp one sundown, Teyo simply sat down. "I will go no farther," she said.

Perion looked at her. "What?"

"My strength is ended, my son. This is my place of death."

Alarmed, Perion and the others clustered about her; and feeling her pulse, Perion found it erratic and thready. "What happened?" he asked.

"Age and weariness. Do not mourn, for I have seen the new world, its blessings and its curses. I have no quarrel with life. We part on the best of terms."

Perion gave her water, but she took a scant mouthful. "Go on," she urged.

"No," Perion said. "Not until you get your strength back."

But that was not to be. Toward midnight, Teyo, now wrapped against the night chill, called to Perion in a feeble voice. "I named you my son," she said simply.

"I am honored," Perion said. "I would gladly call you mother."

"Sing the old song once more with me."

And Perion sang the ridiculous nursery song there beneath the stars, his voice quavering. The old head nodded, and Atina stooped over the still figure. "You can stop now," she said.

Perion discovered he had water enough for tears, at any rate.

They buried her in sand, and Perion insisted that they mark the grave. They cast about for something to mark it with; at last Selridir discovered, not far off, a place where the wind had swept the sand from a scrabble of loose rocks. These they used to make a rough cairn. Before day was well underway, they had finished.

"I am sorry," Atina told her elder clan-sister. "We would burn you if we could."

"To send her soul to the Sailing Star," Trennon said. "I do not believe in it—but I hope she makes it, all the same."

"Look," Perion said, speaking for the first time that morning. Tendrils of green reached between the stones, yearning upward. "They grow because she is here," he explained. "She is being burned, in a way. The bones will be sucked clean by a green flame."

They camped there again that day, and when they made ready to leave the next morning, they discovered Teyo's terrible secret. Unlike their waterskins, hers were three-quarters full. The old woman had cut her own inadequate allowance of water by more than half, saving what she could for the others. Atina hefted the waterskins, then looked around hot-eyed. "Let's go," she said. "I'm *damned* if I let this water go to waste now."

Northward again, the stars high and cold over the group, they marched in the utter, eerie silence of full desert. They were like ants crawling along a bare rock mountain; they saw no sign of life, no beacon of hope, and even with Teyo's supply added to their own, their water dwindled. By unspoken consent, they extended their marches now, continuing until the sun had climbed well into the sky, beginning them as it sank toward its rest on their left. They cut back on the amount of water they allotted themselves, to less than a liter a day. When they thirsted, they chewed on dried fruit, sucking from it moisture more imaginary than real. The sand was terrible footing, and Selridir's limp reappeared, aggravated by the shifting, treacherous desert under them.

Small blessing: once they trudged into an overcast day, the sun a mere bright spot behind a flat layer of cloud, not hot enough to sap their strength. They staggered on until well into the day, then slept a few short hours before resuming their march.

But every blessing is a curse: they could not see the stars that night, and they navigated by means of Perion's dataset. But here, as on Earth, magnetic north and true north were two different directions, and Perion feared that they strayed too far to the west on that course. Atina supported Trennon now, with one arm around his shoulder, as they walked. The sky cleared the next day, and the night after that found them still floundering in the sands.

"We can't go on," Perion croaked to Atina. "Trennon can't take it much longer."

"No," Atina agreed. "He will, though. And so will we all. Because we must."

He studied her in the growing light of dawn. "You look awful," he said.

"We're all pretty ghastly," she agreed. "Blackened lips, blistered feet, hollowed cheeks, hair straggling and caked with sweat. By the Goddess, Tom Perion, I did not believe you had it in you."

"Maybe I don't."

"No. You've got us this far. You'll take us the rest of the way."

Perion looked back at the campsite. Trennon staggered around there, trying ineffectually to help Selridir pitch one of the tents. "I hope so," he said, feeling within him an ache deeper than muscle-weariness, edging on despair.

They marched again that night. Perion took the lead, Atina and Trennon came behind him, and Selridir followed. Life

became a series of simple, horrible stages: lift your right foot;
swing it forward; put it down; lift your left foot . . .

Perion found himself imagining Teyo walking beside him.
He made up dialogues in his head, hearing both his remarks
and the old Teacher's testy, querulous replies. I'm going to
lie down, he said. No, my son, she told him, you are not.

—But you did.

—I stopped only when my body could no longer go on.
Your body can go on.

—I don't believe it.

—Yes, you do. Look inside you. You'll find strength
there.

—Inside me I find hunger and thirst. Most of all thirst. I
could drink a lake of water. I could stuff myself with the
snows of the mountain. I could swallow an ocean.

—You are not looking deeply enough.

—I don't know where to look.

—Think of me. Look at what I did.

—But you died.

—But I kept going until I died. And on less water than you
have had.

—How?

—How do you think?

—You are the Teacher?

—Don't be impertinent.

—I thought, those last weeks, you were not with us.

—Ah.

—You seemed elsewhere. Distant.

—Ah.

—Is that it? I send my mind elsewhere?

—No. Your spirit.

—Your spirit was elsewhere?

—Yes.

—Where?

—You know.

—I don't know.

—Look inside, look inside.

—Oh. I see.

—Yes.

—But Teyo, it won't work for me.

—It will.

—You thought of the Sailing Star as a ship; I know it is

something different, something unlike anything you could know.

—Still.

—But I don't believe it is the work of the Goddess.

—We walk our own paths to faith, my son.

—All right. Dammit, all right.

The *Galileo* is very large. It takes a long time, for example, to walk along the spine that attaches the crew quarters and holds to the propulsion system. You start back at the ion-plasma drives, and you head forward. You walk through a tunnel—drag yourself through, rather, for here the spinning craft does not build up enough force really to give the illusion of gravity. But there are handholds and footholds. You drag yourself a meter at a time, and each time you are a little closer.

And after you do that for days and days, you get to the tertiary hold. Look at this one. The tertiary hold has a cycling device; here are the backup controls, in case of disaster, and the intricate webs of piping, pumps, and other equipment that make life in the stasis pods possible. Somewhere in here there is a tank, and that tank holds water. More water than you could ever drink in a lifetime; water to swim in, water to burn. Hydrogen and oxygen in luxurious combination. Why, it would take you a whole damned day just to walk through the tank, if it were empty.

And it is.

The ingenious devices recovered every molecule of water they could, but they were not in stasis; in real time, the water diminished a little every year. At some point in the *Galileo*'s long misadventure, the last drop of water was sent to the last sleeping traveler; and now the tank is dry, though it may be many decades before the sleepers perish.

So walk through it. Come to the secondary hull. Ah. This is a real beauty, the secondary hull. Now you can stand up, because the ship here is large enough to give you the feeling of one G as she rotates. And *look* at all this junk! What a glitzy collection of impressive technology! So what the hell does it do?

Well, for one thing, it distills time. Sure. Like water. *Forget* the water! Where were we? Ah, yes. This here sterling example of Earth technology, son, slows time up, that's what it does. It generates a stasis field. And if you're in a stasis field, you can't even *move*!

Wait a minute, be honest. It's all relative, as St. Albert is reputed to have remarked. If you are in the stasis field, you can move, subjectively, just as well as you can outside; but to an observer on the outside of the field, you, sir, are a stone statue.

Oh, you're moving. You can't *stop* time with a stasis field. But you can sure as hell slow the old sucker down. Listen to that pulse, now. A *lub* occupies days. You could grow a beard waiting for that *lub* to finish. It rolls on, ponderous. And then a deathly pause, for a week or so. Then the *dub*. A family of four could have a fun-filled vacation on Luna waiting for that *dub* to finish. You could walk pretty near the whole length of the ship while waiting for that *dub*. And then it starts all over again, a cosmic inanity, as meaningless and simple as putting one stupid foot ahead of the other, *lub-dub, lub-dub, lub-dub*, an idiot sound echoing in the empty corners of the universe, going on and on and on.

And you'd better sure as hell hope that old sound never stops, my boy. Because when it stops, you stop.

That's what it's saying. Listen to it: If-I stop-you stop-if I-stop you-stop, *lub-dub, lub-dub, lub-dub*.

Get with the beat, boy!

Now, look here. See this? Miles and miles of glistening stainless steel. Don't open 'em. See, these things are in stasis. That's right. And it's *cold* in there, too. Cold enough to freeze the—ah, sorry. But do you know what's clustered there in the cold, in the congealed drippings of time?

I'll tell you, boy. It's animals.

Yeah.

No, of course there's no cow in that little bitty compartment.

Well, wait a minute. There's *kind* of a cow in there.

Yeah. It's just a baby cow, you see, and it hasn't been born yet, and when it is born, its mama will be a stainless-steel-and-glass vat, and it will suck a rubber tit. But for all that, it will be a cow. A newborn calf, all spindle legs and nodding head and plaintive bleat. But right now it ain't much to look at, son. Just a little old microscopic speck, is all. But good blood, son, mighty good blood.

And horses here, and oxen there, big bruisers bred from the water buffalo of the old Far East, but with their genes tickled so they are the *gentlest* old critters you ever did see. And chickens—yep, we got chickens, though of course they're eggs, quick-frozen and ready to thaw. But when you thaw 'em, by God, son, those little old yellow fuzzy chicks are gonna be just as lively as their brothers and sisters were when they hatched out in Terrasystem five thousand years agone.

Say, you reckon they still have chickens in Terrasystem? Reckon they still have people?

Five thousand years is a long time, son, a *long* time. Hell, maybe the chickens done got a dose of advanced gene manipulation and is *runnin'* the show now, huh? Wouldn' that be sumpin' now?

But we got all sorts of things here. We got plants, we got bugs. No foolin'. Bugs. Got bees—they got no stings, though, 'cause our engineers are tender-hearted old bastards who didn't want the kiddies on New Terra to be stung when runnin' barefoot over the honest-to-God green grass we got in these other compartments. Got butterflies. Got to have bees and butterflies to pollinate the flowers. Oh, yeah, got flowers.

And all sorts of food crops, son. Corn and wheat and barley and rye and rice; nineteen kinds of beans; seven breeds of tomato; we got okra, for God's sake, *okra*; who the hell ever eats okra? But name any other vegetable, we got it. From asparagus to zucchini and back again. Same with fruits. Oranges and lemons, say the planners at Earth Deep Space Administration; and apples and peaches, lascivious plums and figs, and watermelons. Ever think how much water is *in* one of those suckers, son? Know why a watermelon's full of water? Because it's planted in the spring, dummy!

Oh. We're out of the ag section. Shh. Be real quiet now, boy, *real* quiet. You're in God's own nursery now. Yep, in each and every one of these little nooks, there's a genuine guaranteed genius baby-child just waiting to be born. Not like you, either. Nope, not with that ancient inbred genetic imbalance, not with that predisposition to sire eight little girls for every little boy; nope, these are the new, and improved, types of human beings, all set to be slipped into some mama's lovin' womb and come out nine months later into a bright new world.

Yep, your time sure is out of joint, son. But don't worry. The kiddies are here to be born to set it right.

Now, up forward, you don't really want to go up forward,

to the primary hull. That's packed in the middle, see, with all
this navigational junk and suchlike, and tell the truth, we
ain't too sure we got the best deal on that. Seems it got a few
little bugs in it, if you know what I mean.

And there ain't nobody much to home here, anyways. *Was*
a passel of folks, though. Surely was. But they long gone,
most of them. Those are pearls that were their eyes. . . .

Say, something just struck me. I've heard this ship com-
pared to a dumbbell, you know? With one great big spherical
weight, that's the hulls we just been through, and a long,
long bar, that's the connecting hull, and then a little bitty old
weight, that's the propulsion system. But you know what else
it looks like?

A sperm.

It surely, surely does. Sent out into the womb of night, to
engender life on a lonely world. Earth the father sends his
seed through the universe, there to join with the egg of New
Terra, to begin a whole new earth, a whole new cycle of
living—*lub-dub*.

Is it worth it? I don't know, son, I surely don't know, and
that's the truth. Is it worth it? Look inside, look inside. . . .

Someone shook him. Again. "Tom! What's *wrong* with
you?"

"Hmm?" He focused his eyes, with difficulty, on Atina's
face. "Whassamatta?" he mumbled.

"I said it's time to stop! The sun's up already."

"Oh. Yeah. Stop."

"I can't understand High Speech!"

Perion took a deep, deep breath. In Common, he said,
"I'm sorry."

"What was wrong with you? You looked as if you were
somewhere else."

"I was," he said dreamily. "Somewhere else."

The sand rolled, oh, cruel, higher and higher; but now they
faced the steep sides of the dunes. The winds were in their
faces, not at their backs. And the sun was dimmer than ever,
and farther away on its annual ferry mission. Perion staggered
without seeing where he was going, but somehow his feet
picked the best routes, and somehow he kept them heading
north. The sand began to be spiked, here and there, with little
tufts of plants, not thickly, but enough to promise moisture

somewhere. They shared one evening the last skin of water. Each of them got perhaps half a liter. There was no more. At Perion's order, they left the useless empty skins, except for one apiece, on the sand.

They heard thunder that night, from somewhere a long way off; but the saw no lightning. Dawn caught them still on that endless plain of sand, and near the end of their strength. By common consent, they traveled on in the heat. Then Selridir, who had come up to prop Perion as Atina propped Trennon, gave a hoarse, startled cry, and pointed ahead. Perion ground his fists into his eyesockets and stared without believing what he saw.

There, a hundred meters or less away, was a little round pool of water, nestled between two dunes, the dunes themselves sparsely furred with tufts of grass. The pool was almost a perfect circle, and reflected the blue of the sky. Reeds grew around its perimeter, scantily but quite surrounding the whole pond. He turned back and saw Trennon and Atina struggling far behind. "Come on!" he cried, his tongue thick. "Water!"

Selridir had started ahead. Perion caught up Trennon's other shoulder and helped him stagger along—though Perion was hardly in better shape. Selridir was ahead of them, nearly to the pool.

Perion frowned. Something was not quite right. There, to the side of the pool—a little white pile of—

"No!" he shouted, and dropping Trennon's arm he ran forward.

But Selridir had stepped into the reeds, and they came to life, folding on her. He heard her outraged, frightened cry, and then he was beside her. He took a stick, an unused torch, from his back and swung at the thing. The reeds—tentacles, really, crusted and jointed—clutched at her, tugged her down. He struck at their bases, broke some, got a hand on her shoulder, dragged her back.

She was shaking, her eyes wide, when the others joined them. "It bit me," she said in a voice full of little-girl wonder.

Blood oozed through her clothes in several places. They tried to stanch it. But in a few moments Selridir cried out, "I can't see!" They held her through one convulsion. She died in the next.

Perion got to his feet cursing. The "reeds" still stirred with a hungry motion that was not the wind's, and in the center of the pond, a round orifice opened and closed, like a ripple. Perion struck a fire, set his torch ablaze, and cast it onto the surface.

The thing writhed, buckled, bubbled, and blistered. A foul black smoke sprang up. From the mouth opening in the center came a thin ululating cry. Perion lit another torch, and another: all he had. The thing was burned in a half-dozen places before finally it gave a shudder and the tentacles folded in on themselves, lifeless. Perion kicked the whitened bones of some desert bird aside, kicked at the tentacles. They broke at the base. The creature was dead.

"It poisoned her," Atina said.

"It's a camouflaged predator," Perion said. "Damn the thing! But it shows we're getting close. There must be enough prey around here for it to live."

"Birds," Trennon said, nodding toward the scattered bones. "They fly over, think they see a place to get a drink, cool off—and they're eaten."

"Let's bury Selridir," Atina said in a flat voice.

"Not here," Perion said. "Not in sight of this goddam thing."

They found no rocks for a cairn here, and instead left Selridir's pack, filled and weighted with sand, as a lonely marker. They continued northward; nothing else to do.

Perion tried again to go away, to find that other place; but he was afraid. If he conjured Teyo to walk beside him, she might become too real. Or he might become as insubstantial as she, and walk with her too far into madness ever to return.

But somehow they kept going through that day. They covered little ground, a pitifully small distance, really, but they kept moving. Night found them at the foot of an enormous dune. They pitched their tent without speaking, chewed mouthfuls of the dried fruit, found no saliva to soften them, spat out the lumps on the sand.

"We've had it," Perion told Atina. .

"I know" she said, her voice a hoarse whisper. "We gave it a try, though, didn't we?"

"We sure as hell did."

"Sleep tonight?"

"If we can. Tomorrow—we'll see."

Perion could not sleep, though Trennon dropped into oblivion readily enough. He sat outside the tent, under the stars, and put as much as he could onto one of the datacards. The things had a long lifespan. Very little could alter one, outside of an atomic blast or a concentrated magnetic field on the order of that created in a cyclotron. It was something to record the attempt, anyway. Then, idly, he switched the dataset to search, fed in the information that would allow it to home on a stasis field. He was not even surprised when he got a positive reading. It was there, all right. To the north and to the east. Only three hundred and ninety-four kilometers away.

It might as well have been a million.

The sun came up, his enemy. In the tent, Atina and Trennon still slept. Let them. He looked up at the overwhelming mountain of sand before him. Then, with a groan, he started to climb.

He slid back three meters for every four he gained, but slowly he got to the top, peered over, knowing that he would see only wave on wave of sand.

He gasped, looked again. Then he slid down the dune in a flurry of loose sand, sprawled at full length at the bottom. He could not get up again. The tent was there, not far away, but he could not, could *not* find his legs. He tried to call. His swollen tongue choked off the sound, a mere hiss, not as loud as the desert wind.

He bit his arm, hard. The salt of his own blood was on his tongue, He crept forward, hand over hand. "Atina!" he rasped.

She crawled out of the tent, looked aghast at him, bloody-mouthed, wild-eyed, creeping toward her like a demented thing.

"Hills!" he said. "Hills!"

She pulled him into the tent. The rest of the day was passed, for Perion, in fever and delirium.

But that night it rained.

Chapter 21

How she got them there Perion could never later remember, but somehow he was resting on a pad of grasses covered with canvas, and over him was a rock ceiling—a projecting overhang of rock, he noted with detachment, consisting primarily of limestone, with some shale admixture—and Trennon Fane ladled broth into him day after day. Sometimes he was back on the ship, and Teyo was feeding him; and sometimes it was Mela beside the couch, taking a professional interest in his welfare. But gradually it was Trennon, more and more, and at last there came a day when he was able to speak.

"Where?" he grunted.

Trennon was not himself, but he was at least up and about. He had scraped the beard from his face, and he looked like his own grandfather, wizened and too sharp of eye. "We're in a sort of little cave that Atina found," he said. "It's on one side of a little river valley. Atina's out now, hunting. Strange animals in these parts. Strange fish."

Perion was full of questions, but lacked the will to ask them. Later he was aware that the two of them stooped over him, and he felt a palm on his forehead. He opened his eyes and looked into Atina's face, ravaged and sharpened by adversity, but full of life. "Hello," he said.

"Well. You speak Common again. That's a relief after all those days of the High Speech. How do you feel?"

"Like you dragged me by my feet for the last hundred kilometers."

"I came close, at that. But Trennon helped. We got you here just three days after you sighted the hills, and you've been here ever since."

"How long?"

"A long time," she said. "It's nearly Farsun Day, the beginning of the year."

Perion tried to sit up, but could not. "I hurt," he complained.

"I'm not surprised. You were very hot for days and days—I feared that we would lose you, or that you would recover in body but not in mind. And that would be a shame after we had come so far."

"My talismans?" he asked.

"Here." Trennon brought the communicator and the dataset over to him. The dataset was dead.

"Take it and leave it in the sun," Perion said. "That will—will give it life again. A day should do it."

"Very well." Trennon stood, and as he did, Atina touched his shoulder. A quick smile passed between them.

"We are glad you are with us again," Atina said as Trennon went away.

"And I am glad to be back. But it was a near thing, I think."

Then he was too tired to speak anymore, and he gratefully accepted Atina's aid in sipping some warm broth and nibbling a few mouthfuls of cooked meat. Chiefly, though, he craved water, and he drank time and time again. He woke in distress late that night, and tried to rise. Atina was there in a moment. He explained his need, and she helped him out of bed and outside. There, under the stars, he proved to himself that at any rate his kidneys and bladder still functioned. But he felt deep shame, and tried to apologize to Atina.

"Hush," she said. "Don't be so—so *manly!*"

He spent the next day mending. Late in the afternoon, Trennon brought the recharged communicator and datakit to him. Perion used one of the blank cards and entered a program on it. Then he called both Trennon and Atina to him. "Look at this thing," he said, showing them the screen. "It's in locator mode now. Watch." He pressed a key, and an arrow appeared, pointing away to his left. At the bottom of the screen, numbers glowed in soft green. "This shows you the way to the command pod," he said. "And this number here at the bottom is the distance. You can't read the number, but never mind. If you just follow the arrow, you'll find it sooner or later.

"Now, when you find it, it will look like a silvery bubble—I think. I've never seen an exposed stasis field before, but I've read descriptions. All right. When you find it, you must get very near it—but don't touch it; be sure you never touch it—and press these three buttons, in this fashion." He demonstrated. "Then go away for a whole day and a night. When you return, the field will be down. The hatch will also come off. Inside the capsule you will find a person. I think he will be dead. But whatever his condition, there will be a panel inside the capsule, in front of the man, with this label on it. Look at the screen."

The small screen displayed the legend "MASTER OVERRIDE." Perion said, "If you need to see it again, press the same three buttons I just showed you, but in reverse order. All right?

"Now, one of you has to go inside the capsule and hold the talisman in front of that panel. I know you can't read, but you can make sure that the marks on the panel match those on the screen. Then you press, in order, these three buttons"—he thumbed the row beneath the original one—"and that's all there is to it. The command pod will wait until the *Galileo* is in range, then send a signal. The signal will cause the ship to wake up anyone left aboard; and they will track the signal and get someone to you."

Perion drilled them time and again. Finally, worriedly, Atina said, "You sound as though you won't come with us, Tom."

"I will," he assured her, "if I can. But I realized, yesterday, that I came close to—to going to the Sailing Star on my own. I wanted both of you to be able to operate this thing should I—not be able to do it myself."

Trennon grinned, and looked something like his old devil-may-care self. "You're getting better now, fellow. From the way you ate today, I'd say it's only a matter of time before you're marching ahead again, and urging us to catch up with you."

Atina gave him a warm smile. Then Perion insisted that each of them go through the drill, repeating in stages what they must do with the datakit. At last he was satisfied enough to accept more broth, some small red fruit surprisingly reminiscent of oranges in taste, and more water. He had a shivering fit that night, despite their piling on him all the spare clothing, and when he fell asleep it was into gruesome dreams. It seemed to him that he was still on the desert, that he lay on his back in the sand, and that crawling and spreading over his body was the creeping green plant. He brushed himself frantically and finally woke himself up.

He lay panting in the dark. Then he heard something else—a low moaning, grunts of effort. They puzzled him for a few minutes.

Then he understood the significance of Atina's glances at Trennon, of her touching him. He felt something small, cold, and ugly deep inside him. Holding it to the light of his mind, he was surprised to see that it was pure jealousy.

After two weeks, Perion tottered out of the cavern into the sunlight on his own. He sat overlooking the river and the trees around it, small trees, not more than five meters high, with bushy tops and dark green, shiny leaves. It was dry vegetation, not luxuriant, but there were plenty of the trees. The stream, too, was a respectable one. He could wade it—or could have, if he'd been able to walk so far—but it stretched seven or eight meters broad, and leaped over tumbled gray rocks with a great deal of energy. Atina had worked for days on the problem of fishing and finally had solved it: she used a sharpened, barbed stick and rested on the bank motionless for an hour or so, until an unsuspecting victim swam too close. Then, with a single thrust, she had him, and lifted him wriggling and flopping to the shore. In a good afternoon's fishing, she could land three or four, and always of good size. The fish were built on the same model as all the rest of Kalea's indigenous vertebrates, with tricky triple-action jaws and three sexes, but when cooked over an open fire they tasted just as good as trout from Earth.

Perion gained and lost ground. He grew stronger, but never felt completely well, and at odd moments he was apt to have a relapse of chills and fever, which left him dispirited and weak each time. On the other hand, he *was* able to walk, to gather firewood, to help with the everyday routines of cooking and keeping the camp trim. Occasionally he even practiced his profession, for the shale underlying the river was fossiliferous, and from it he began to see a tiny corner of the panorama of Kalea's evolution. The fossils he found were small, the norm being round, primitive crustaceans, most incomplete, and none larger than his thumbnail. But they told him that a sea once rolled here, more than likely a warm and shallow one. It was, as knowledge goes, only a tiny particle of information, but Perion felt better for having gathered it.

On some nights they saw the Sailing Star, heading south in

the evenings. It was a constant reminder and challenge for Perion, but at the same time he knew that if he tried too soon to venture toward the fallen command capsule he would be throwing away his life.

The year turned. Finally Perion felt well enough to travel— still not really well, but at least well enough. Atina had gone fairly far afield with her hunting, and she had a reasonably clear grasp of the lay of the land, at least in the neighborhood of the river valley. The desert began in scrub and sand over the range of hills to the south, not yet deadly but not hospitable either; and in this region, Atina said, were many of the pool-mimics like the one that had killed Selridir. "Most of them are small," Atina said. "No bigger than a platter. The other, the one you killed, must have been very old. They aren't really much like a pool at all when you know how to look for them—their skin is a dark blue, to give you the idea they reflect the sky, but it has no true reflectiveness. You can't see the sun in one. They send down a kind of root into the sand, and I think they find their moisture that way. Then they stay in one position, trapping whatever stumbles into their grasp. The little ones move—those the size of your hand and smaller. They look like grebs"—these, Perion knew, were crablike creatures—"scuttling along. Then when they're ready, they flip over and dig in, and their legs become the 'reeds' at the edge of the pool."

"Specialized adaptation," Perion murmured in High Speech. "They could live nowhere but on the edge of a desert," he continued in Common. "You killed them?"

"At first, every one. But then I stopped. They are not really dangerous if you know what to look for. And they have no will. They did not intend to kill Selridir. It just happened."

Trennon came into the little cave just then, laden with a sack of the red fruit. He set it down, touched Atina, and smiled at her. Perion fought down a little wave of envy. "These keep pretty well," he said. "They go withered and leathery in the sun, but you can eat them. We gather more before we set out?"

"We gather more," Atina said.

Perion studied directions, weather, and topography. Direction was simple—they would follow the datakit's indicator to the north and to the east. Weather was more problematic.

They had had one good rain, the soaking downpour that
saved them on the edge of the desert, and six or eight days of
mizzle. The heat in the valley still was unpleasant, but it was
tolerable, with highs varying from thirty-six on the overcast
days to forty on the clear ones. Shade and above all water
made a great deal of difference.

Topography too was a problem. The river valley here
flowed almost from east to west, so in going upstream they
would be nearing the site of the command capsule; but the
valley was sure to end before they got anywhere close, and if
the hills grew loftier, they could face a demanding climb
before they could hope to reach their goal. Still, with no
information other than that his eyes could gather, Perion was
for following the river upstream for as far as looked practical,
and the others concurred.

They began to accumulate supplies and to make plans.
Atina was especially anxious to bring in some meat. "There
are borrits around," she said, "or their clan-cousins. They're
good to eat, and their flesh dries well. These things are wild,
though, and they sense me before I can get really close. But
I've found where they come to drink at the river, and I'd like
to try for one or two. Their meat is very nourishing, and we
could use the provision."

Among his other diversions as he recuperated, Perion had
been training with a sprinbo. They had two, Atina's and the
one Selridir had packed, and he took the latter. It was very
much like a crossbow, though of different design, and he got
rather good at potting a scrap of cloth tacked to a tree trunk.
"Why don't we both try?" he asked, "We might get two."

"You feel well enough?" Atina asked suspiciously.

"Fine," he said, lying only a little.

Atina at last agreed, more to humor him than anything, he
thought, and early one morning he followed her downstream.
The day was already a hot one, and it was pleasant to wade
down through the ankle-deep water. He kept his footing the
whole way, several kilometers, and never once, he thought,
justified the exaggerated caution with which Atina would
grasp his arm to lead him across a particularly slippery spot.

They waded the river's width at last, and climbed the
hillsides opposite the bank where they were encamped farther
upriver. Atina settled in under the shade of some bushy
large-leafed plants, and Perion sat beside her. "The wind is

with us today," she said. "The water will carry away most of
our scent, and they will come down the hillside there. They'll
be very timid. The best time to shoot is when they're drink-
ing. Several will be back behind on watch while the first ones
drink. Don't aim for them—they're fathers, and their flesh
has a bad taste. The ones closest to the water will be the
young ones or the body- or egg-mothers. We'll try for those.
Not a very big one, though; you could wound one and have it
carry your shaft away without dying. We want meat, not an
injured borrit."

"Will they come soon?"

Atina squinted up at the sun. "Not until the sun has gone
halfway down the sky. It will be a long time yet."

So they had time to converse. They spoke of small, unim-
portant things at first—of the fruit supply, of the good fortune
of having found the little cavern, of the types of fish in the
river. Then, after their chat had fallen away to silence, Perion
found the nerve to ask the question he had been storing up:
"Trennon has become—your lord?"

Atina gave him a level look. "It happened," she said.
"For days after we got you to the valley, we despaired of
your life. He recovered enough from his exhaustion to help
me. But you lay wandering in fever for days. We both grew
tired again trying to win you back to life. In our weariness,
we offered each other comfort. It was a way of—I don't
know, a way of choosing life, not death."

"I see."

Silence sat between them, heavy as the noon heat. Atina
said, "If you wish, we could—"

"No," Perion said.

"My kinswoman Mela had enjoyed many different lords,"
Atina said. "You had nothing to say about her."

"It's different."

Atina sighed. "Everything is different."

"Yes, it is."

After another long pause, Atina said, "The ship you speak
of, the Sailing Star. It has other women on it?"

"I suppose."

"They would understand you?"

Perion laughed, not a merry sound. "Atina, on whatever
planet humans occupy, no matter what their social customs
are like, no woman has ever completely understood any man,

or vice versa. We can explore the universe, we can grasp the stars, but we can't see clearly into these heads of ours."

"I hoped—"

"No, forget it. I have no right to feel angry with you or Trennon."

She looked pained. "Angry? You are correct. I cannot understand you. Trennon, the morning after we—we were close for the first time, would not look me in the face. He said he felt violated, as though I had taken unfair advantage of him."

Perion smiled. "You just take care of Trennon. Be good to him. But don't ever let him go back to being a lord, with serving women and lackeys to attend his every need."

"Could any of us go back? I wonder," mused Atina. "I think not. Not in the same way, anyhow. And when we do go back—"

"That we have to think about, too. But not right now."

"No."

The tension between them had become so much a part of their lives that they were hardly aware of it until it snapped there in the shade of the shrubs. Perion, at any rate, felt he could relax now with her for the first time in many days. They grew silent as time wore on, keeping their vigil over the river.

The borrits would come to a quiet little pool, a side eddy of the stream, where a combination of rocks and fallen tree trunks had partially dammed the river. The approach was level and sandy on this side, with the shore gradually sloping into the water. As the two humans sat and watched, they saw occasional signs of life—the leap of a fish, the dip of a river bird diving for minnows, the wake of a swimming serpent, its fringed head lifted barely above the surface. "Harmful?" Perion asked, nodding toward it.

"Not really. Some serpents are bigger and have nasty bites, but one that small would flee you unless you cornered it. Quiet, now."

They were looking upstream, eastward, and the westering sun began to stretch the shadows of the bushes out before them. At last Perion heard a commotion in some scrubby brush on the hillside several hundred meters away, and he felt Atina tense. She very slowly brought her sprinbo up, and Perion followed her action with his own, being careful to make no noise.

The creatures were ludicrous. Perion thought of a tapir whose snout had grown to a mockery of an elephant's trunk, with the forelimbs of a cat and the hind ones of a rabbit. The borrits were fat-rumped and small-headed beasts, a dull brown above, a dirty white on their bellies. Three of them lumbered out from the brush, raised themselves high on their forelegs, and snuffled the air with their quivering snouts. Then, apparently feeling safe, they hopped lugubriously down toward the river.

Others followed. Perion counted at least eleven adults— they were in constant motion, and counting them was like trying to count goldfish in a crowded bowl—and five or six small ones. The larger ones were about the size of a small sheep. Two of these, as Atina had predicted, stayed well up the slope from the river, starting at every insect buzz and keeping their noses busy in the air.

Perion had managed to home in on one animal, one that moved more slowly than the others. It buried its face in the water, guzzled, lifted dripping jowls, and waded a little deeper, and a little closer to Perion. It was a target impossible to miss at that distance, and Perion kept his sprinbo carefully trained on a spot just behind the front legs—where Atina said the heart beat. He felt Atina's sudden tension beside him as she fired, and almost at the same instant he let his bolt fly. Immediately, even before the bolts hit their targets, one of the males at the rear bellowed, a rusty, grating *whoorooooo*, and the rest of the herd broke into flight. Perion could hardly believe that the same lumbering, comical beasts were running away, so swiftly did they make the slope and disappear into the brush; but Atina had already loaded another bolt and sent it into the struggling form of the animal she had shot. It took the shot in the chest, heaved, scrabbled uselessly at the sand with its hind legs, and died.

Only then did Perion look back in the water. His own target was there, quite still, nose and mouth underwater.

Atina grinned at him. "Good shot, Tom! Not like mine—I had to shoot again."

"We got two of them, at any rate," Perion said. "Let's take a look."

Atina's animal was the larger. It was quite dead now, and she used her blackwood knife to slit its throat and bleed it. "Let's haul yours out of the water," she said. "Then we'll hang them up and dress them. We'll put one of your drags together to get them back upstream. Think you can handle that?''

"Sure," Perion said carelessly. He grasped the other borrit's hind legs and leaned backward, pulling it across the sandy river bottom. Atina helped him wrestle it up onto the sand. "A clean shot," Atina said, admiring the placement of the bolt. "Here, help me turn it over."

Perion did, and had just straightened up when Atina gave a low cry. "Something is wrong?" he asked.

"Here." Perion looked where Atina's hands held the flesh, and saw a broken stub of an arrow protruding from the animal's other side, in the muscle of its foreshoulder. He remembered how it had moved slowly, more stiffly than the others.

"You must have wounded it earlier," he said.

"No. At least I don't think so. I've shot at them three times, and recovered the bolt twice. Let me see. . . ." She worked the barb out of the flesh.

"Well?"

Atina shook her head. "Let's not worry about it right now. Here, we won't take the whole animal. We'll take the haunches, though. Do you feel up to carrying a load?"

"I can do it."

Atina's butchery was swift. At her insistence, they dragged the carcasses away from the river, over a low rise, and under some thick brush. Then, with each of them laden with fifteen kilos of meat, they waded the river again and swiftly made their way upstream.

Trennon was there at camp, nursing a low fire of embers in which he was roasting some tuberous roots they had discovered days before, and he rose to greet them with a smile on his face. "Looks as though the two of you had luck," he said.

"What type, I wonder," Atina returned. They hung the meat, and Perion and Atina washed in the river. Then they came back to the campsite and Atina handed the broken bolt to Trennon. "This is what?" she asked.

He turned it over in his hands, looked at the point, then at her. "I can't believe it."

"I thought so."

Perion looked from one to the other of them, and finally

said in exasperation. "The two of you may commune silently, but I'm not in on the secret. This is what?"

"An Aslandian arrow," Trennon said grimly.

"It can't be," Perion argued. "We didn't have any—" He
broke off and looked at Atina's stoic face. "Oh."

"Exactly," she said. "Halindo. She's here. Somehow,
she's here. The bitch followed us!"

ON THE GUILD OF HUNTERS
(Excerpted from a datacard
recorded by Tomas Perion)

The social organization of the Aslandian Empire is
different from that of Homereaches, in some cases radically so, in some cases only superficially. Politically,
the Aslandians have evolved a loose confederation of
semiautonomous city-states, each city-state ruled by a
powerful family. The elder women, usually, are the
unquestioned family leaders, though a ruthless younger
sister or wife not infrequently rises to strong position.
Males in Aslandia are quite frankly treated as second-
class citizens, pets almost, to be pampered but not to be
consulted on matters of serious business.

The marriage customs parallel those of Homereaches,
from which they have evolved over the course of about
five hundred years. The family makes an agreement
with a neighboring one, the male is shipped, and a new
lord takes up his coddled, meaningless residence on an
estate. As in Homereaches, the Aslandian male has no
real voice in his destination and no choice of mates.
The estate he is granted will be in proportion to his
birth-family's power and influence.

Unlike the Homereaches, the Aslandian Empire is
divided up into freeholds of land. The families actually
possess the land they make their home on, whereas in
Homereaches the Council theoretically own all land and
grant terms of lease only to their people. This points to
a difference in the economic structure of the two civili-
zations. Homereaches is a modified socialistic state,
with supportive elements of plutocracy. Aslandia seems,

by contrast, almost feudal. In Homereaches, those who occupy an estate are under an injunction to be caretakers of the land, and to protect it; but at the same time to use it to amass personal wealth. Estates there are generally valued for their productive potential, with some specializing in food crops, others in timber, and still others in mining or production of finished goods.

The situation in Aslandia is rather different. Each city-state there is largely independent of the others, producing perhaps ninety percent of all it consumes itself. There the estates, rather than specializing in production, specialize in vocation. Thus, a given estate might be in essence a school for sailing, turning out both able-bodied seamen (women) and officers. Another might produce Teachers (less of a religious function here than in Homereaches, more of an educational one), and so on.

Prime is a city-state located centrally on the eastern coast of Aslandia. It has, according to Trennon Fane, a teeming population and a number of specialties. The Delev estate there, a Spartan compound of many hundreds of hectares, has long specialized in producing hunters.

Again, a comparison is in order. Enforcement of the law in Homereaches is through the Council, or their designated agents. If the Council decides, say, that a particular person must be burned alive because of a criminal act or incurable madness, the Council will also designate certain members of that person's estate, or of a neighboring estate, to carry out the decision. Failure to do so means loss of place in the Council, and, potentially, loss of the right to occupy the estate as well. Thus there is no standing police force in Homereaches, merely temporary, appointed groups of deputies.

But in Aslandia, the families have stronger needs for enforcement. Less unified than Homereaches, Aslandia is also subject to many more interfamily feuds, disagreements, and misconducts. The hunters evolved to fill this niche.

Hunters owe allegiance to no one, not even to their own estate. They are free lances; they may attach themselves to one family for an agreed-upon term, serve that

term honorably and well, and then immediately agree to
serve a competing family and serve it just as faithfully.
Though Homereachers see such shifting loyalty as near-
treason, the actions of the hunters are thought praise-
worthy in Aslandia. There any sustained feeling of
loyalty or attachment, at least on the part of a hunter, is
an aberration.

But hunters, while under hire, are implacable. Atina
says, and I am forced to believe her, that a hunter will
allow nothing to come between her and her goal, that a
hunter might die trying to carry out an order of a
family, but that she would never dishonor the family by
abandoning the goal.

Their training is intense, sustained, and complete. I
think I referred to their holding as "Spartan" earlier.
This is true in a behavioral as well as physical sense.
The Delev family includes women of many different
"true" families; some actually have Delev blood in
their veins, others are captured or even bought as ba-
bies. At any rate, they are all Delevs. From their first
year onward they are raised communally, and for a
Delev woman to know her true mother is a mark of
deep shame and reproach for them. Each is taught to
regard the others less as sisters than as competitors; and
while they will cooperate when on the same side or
working toward the same objective, they will unemo-
tionally turn against each other should their situation
change.

The children are put through a strict physical regi-
men. Many, if rumors Trennon has heard are to be
believed, never survive to puberty; but those who do
survive are top physical specimens by that time, tough-
ened and hardened by endless training and practice.
One of the rites of passage for a hunter occurs at age
five (about eleven or twelve in standard years), when
she and her agemates are taken to a rugged, barren
island. They must survive there for one season, about a
hundred and seventy days, on their own.

They are put ashore naked.

The island affords scanty vegetation and little easily
gotten animal food; the Aslandians stock it with wild
hoats, which are fairly formidable animals, ruminants,

and with rock cats, which are predators roughly the size of an old Earth panther. The island is in a very low latitude, within the limited tropic region of this planet. It has one spring of water, and that is not always reliable in especially dry years. It offers little in the way of shelter: there are brushy, low shrubs, but no true trees, and very little in the way of sizable stones. It is essentially a sandspit with a little vegetation and some very ferocious imported animal life. The children are delivered to this island in batches of a hundred or so. The island can reasonably support perhaps a third that many.

No adult comes near the island for the specified time. There are no rules. A child may, if she wishes and is strong and cunning enough, kill as many of her rivals as she can. There will be no punishment. Or she can try to attract enough followers to create a band, and find some security in that; but there are no rewards for this behavior, except such as the children themselves win.

At any rate, after the season has passed, a ship comes to take away all the survivors. Surprisingly, a majority of the children usually do survive; Trennon says it's seven out of every ten. No one asks them about what happens on the island, and they are not encouraged to discuss their experiences. Their survival is evidence that they have successfully passed their entrance examination to hunter training.

That lasts for another five Kalean years. In that time, the hunter candidates learn skills with all sorts of weapons, from swords (and many of them as adults carry scarce bronze swords or daggers) to bows, from garroting nooses to clubs. They further sharpen their skills of endurance and survival, and compete against each other in annual games—games that often produce casualties.

At ten Kalean years of age, the candidate becomes an apprentice hunter. She will be "blooded" by an older girl, one with some experience. The two form a team for two years—and this is the only real lasting attachment a hunter ever makes. The one exception to the general rule of complete independence is that no hunter will knowingly take an assignment in which she must combat her master, and if this should happen by accident, both master and student are legally released from the terms of their contracts. At any rate, during the two-year term the student is expected to perform at least one assassination on her own. Assassination, for motives of revenge, advancement, or legal execution, is a frequently practiced art in Aslandia, it seems.

At age twelve the hunter, how fully trained, strikes out on her own. The Delevs furnish her with basic equipment and a living allowance until her first assignment; she then pays a tithe to the Delev estate for the remainder of her active career.

On the question of marriage, Trennon and Atina are divided. Trennon holds the opinion that a hunter may, if she wishes, interrupt her career long enough to be temporary harema to some lord of special distinction; any children she produces, though, will be sent to the Delev estates (if female) for training. Atina, on the other hand, sees the hunters as unsexed beings, incapable of any real emotion. She says that rumor in Homereaches has it that hunters never mate, that they all die virginal.

Whatever the reality, hunters do die. Their working life is surprisingly long; Trennon has seen still-active hunters at an Earth age of seventy or higher. It seems that what they lose to age in strength they make up for in cunning and wisdom. Still, some retire to the Delev estate and become the trainers of the younger generations of hunters, others go into "private" life—meaning they purchase or rent small holdings—and the bulk die before the problem arises.

Of the one hunter I have seen, Halindo Delev, I know little. She looks to be a formidable foe, a woman of great physical prowess and of a high, though controlled temper. Whether she is the killing machine of legend, I do not know. But I do know this: she is supremely dangerous.

Any woman who could survive that desert crossing is potentially an assassin whose peculiar gifts are to be respected and feared.

Chapter 22

They broke camp and were off within two days. In the meantime they had kept a nervous watch, but had seen no sign of any intruders. They followed the same plan Perion and Atina had used to ward off premature recognition by the borrits, wading upstream along the river. With water no problem and heat less than it had been, they made good time, despite having to make occasional portages around short stretches of especially rough water or past small cascades. By sundown they had covered more than thirty kilometers, and they selected a hidden shelter, a thick-growing clump of brush with an open space in the center, for the night. They lighted no fire.

"You think there are many?" Trennon asked Atina that evening.

"I do not know. But if any of them are here, Halindo is one; and if she is the only one, she is enough."

"This is madness," Perion said. "They could pay her enough to pursue you this far? Past any hope of her own return?"

"Hunters do not hunt for money," Trennon said. "Not really. They do it because it is what they are; it is how they define themselves. They know nothing else."

They spent some time talking over the nature of hunters, and then set watches for the night. Perion took the first, partly because he feared that he would not have the strength of will to remain awake if first he found sleep, and partly because he spent the time communing with his datakit, feeding it more information about the customs and ways of this strange world. He was undisturbed through his watch, and he woke Trennon. Lying on the earth, Perion felt the inner aches and pains awakened by the day's march, and he knew in his heart that the disease inside him had not yet finished with him. It lurked there, deep in his inward shadows, like a beast in a dark forest, waiting for the time to spring.

But as long as they stuck to the river valley his body served him without collapsing. They made less headway each day as the valley steepened and the river turned into a leaping, splashing mountain stream, and at last they paused before a deep, V-shaped valley through which the river, now hardly more than a creek, poured. The valley turned away to the southeast, and their way, according to the datakit, was north-easterly from here. "Well," Trennon sighed, adjusting his pack, "it looks as though the easy work's over. It's all up and down from here."

They climbed into the early afternoon of that day, before Atina noticed that Perion was shivering, even in the heat. She called a halt, and they encamped in an exposed position on the side of a hill; Perion could go no farther that day.

The fever was not as high as it had been, though, and he passed a fairly restful night. At his insistence, they traveled again the next day, really making only a few kilometers, but at least they gained the top of a long ridge and had easier footing for as long as it held out.

They were still on the ridge, though farther on their way, two mornings later. From here they had a good view of the valley behind them and of a slender ribbon of waterfall, still shaded in its nook of the valley at this hour. Perion was too low to look at the scenery, but the cooler air at this elevation seemed to exhilarate Trennon, and he surveyed their surroundings with evident pleasure. The hills here were really long parallel ridges, for the most part, green with vegetation and rounded by eons of weather. To the north, the hills marched in diminishing rows, and somewhere out there, Perion was sure, was alluvial and coastal plain. To the south and east, the hills were higher, and in the far distance to the east the sun climbed over purple, vague mountains. Soon they would have to descend and then renew their up-and-down progress, following the pointer of the dataset and diminishing its tantalizing number: 171 km.

"What is that?" Trennon asked suddenly as Perion eased into his pack with some help from Atina.

They looked. Far away and below, something, something white, moved on the flat rocks that the stream clashed around. It was on the far side of the river now, but its intent was to cross. Perion strained his eyes for all he was worth, but saw only a white dot. "An animal?" he guessed.

"I do not know the animals of this land," Atina returned doubtfully. "It may be. But it could be a human, too, in white clothing. Let's move."

They moved, into the toil of descent and ascent, fighting gravity both ways. They were still in arid country, but twice in the next few days they were hampered by rain, warm plopping rain that made footing unsure and that did nothing to cool overtaxed muscles. Another ten kilometers, another six, another eight . . . so they crept along.

But the hills were less steep now, more rounded, and they began to find pathways around them. They broke into a rolling plain thick with a grassy plant, and densely populated by stilt-legged grazers, lacking horns but having other attributes of antelope. Atina was delighted with their sudden springing grace and their speed, but they did not pause to hunt.

Several times Atina had cast worried glances at Perion. As they rested once on the march across the plain, she said to him, "You feel well?"

He shrugged. "I can keep going. I can't seem to shake this fever. If we can get to the command pod—"

"Goddess," Trennon swore. "This pod of yours works magic, too? It can cure you?"

"No magic," Perion said. "But there's a hospital facility aboard the ship. It could cure me, I think—if I can get to it in time. In the old days, it took years, sometimes, for a disease agent to be identified, for a serum or treatment to be devised. The hospital up there does all that in a week or so."

Atina shook her head. "We'll go easier if you wish. You just seem so—distant. As if you are not really with us as we walk. You remind me of—of someone else."

Perion smiled. He knew whom Atina was talking about. He had been speaking to her, in a corner of his mind, only a few minutes before. *Lub-dub,* he thought. If I stop, you stop.

They walked, stopped when he was sick, continued when he could put one foot in front of the other. Another twenty kilometers, another fifteen, another ten.

They came upon the pod unexpectedly. Perion's datakit told them it was nearby, somewhere, but the distance calculator could not be fully accurate in this land of rolling hills, and Perion thought they had at least ten more kilos to cover. But they came over a low rise, and there it was.

It looked, he thought, like a gigantic pearl nestled in a green-velvet case.

Both Atina and Trennon looked at it for a long, silent moment, and then both turned toward him. Perion gritted his teeth—they had chattered since morning—and grunted, "That's it. What we've been looking for. And the stasis generator is intact."

They walked down the hillside and circled it, in a group. "Don't touch," Perion warned again. "It's a high-energy field, with a negative polarity here. It will kill you if you touch."

"It seems to be buried in the ground," Trennon said.

True, the field looked like an enormous half-sphere of otherness, as large as a room in a house, four meters high at its apex. Its pearly luster, on close inspection, swirled lazily, lines of force forming, dissolving, re-forming, making shifting patterns like those in a soap bubble. Perion stopped when they had completely circumnavigated the field and unslung his pack. "It's been here a long time," he said. "When it first arrived, it would have rested on the ground. This is how much the soil's built up since that time."

Atina took a deep breath. "Well."

Perion fumbled the datakit. His hands shook, and sweat dripped from his face. "I have to check first," he told them. "I have to see if the occupant is still alive. If he is, I have to use a different release procedure." He coupled his communicator to the dataset and keyed in a code. The communicator beeped once, and he slumped to the ground. "That is all. It will take at least a day to get the answer—even electromagnetic energy moves slowly in stasis, and the simple connection that must be made to return the answer to us will creep like a snail."

"I don't understand any of that," Trennon objected.

"Pitch the tent," Atina said.

Perion shook his head. "No. Not here. Camp back over the rise. Too close here to be entirely safe." He tried to push back up to a standing position, but lacked the strength. He looked up at them with hot eyes, embarrassment and request for aid mingled in his gaze.

They half-carried Perion back to the tent site. That night he was feverish again, and in the morning only a little stronger. But at last the dataset came to life, and he consulted it. He grunted at the display. "As I thought. No life remaining inside the pod. We blow the field. Help me up."

They had descended the rise again and stood before the shimmering stasis bubble when a voice came from behind them. "Atina Theslo. I have come far for you."

Perion did not even feel surprise, just a dull resentment. They had come this close, and then . . .

He turned. Halindo was a shambling grotesque, an ill-sketched caricature of herself. She had hacked her hair short. She wore a white tunic, sleeves torn out, and white trousers—or more accurately, tunic and trousers that had once been white before soaking in stains of mud, sap, juice, and blood. Her keen face was hag-thin, eyes sunken deep in their sockets, cheeks hollowed by deprivation and strain. Her arms were mere skin pulled tight over bone. But she held a sword in her right hand, and she stood steady on her feet.

"You—came alone?" Atina asked, in frank wonderment.

"Not so. Ten others I brought with me. Ten when we started. They have all died." Halindo's eyes were unreadable. "I was only ten days behind you when I found your ship. I would have caught you, perhaps, in the Edge Lands, had my crew come with me willingly. I had to persuade them."

"You found my ship? You saw the members of my crew?" Atina asked, concern sharp in her voice.

"Your ship and crew I released. The only ones who died were barbarians who tried to keep us from the mountains. Them I fought with blade and blaze."

"The smoke," murmured Perion. "We saw the smoke."

"The grass burned faster and hotter than I thought it would," Halindo said. "Many of the Edge folk died. But the Homereach sailors I released, for you are my quarry. Your people are all safe and away now, for all I know. I have come to kill you, Atina Theslo. You challenge my right?"

"No," said Trennon Fane.

Halindo turned, a fierce frown distorting her features. "You are Aslandian?"

"I am."

"Your speech marks you." To Atina, Halindo said, "You

hide behind a man? I did not expect this of you. Have you no pride at all?"

"I did not ask him to speak."

Perion groaned. "Halindo, for God's sake—"

The hunter looked at him, cool and distant. "I remember you. The man from the hearing. The mad one."

"He brought us here alive," Atina said. "He told us we would find this wonderful thing at the end of the journey. You call him mad?"

"He brought you to your death, far from your clan and kin," Halindo said. "Come, we know how this must end, and you waste time. You challenge me?"

After a heavy silence, Atina said, "I challenge."

"No!" Perion's voice snapped the word out like a whipcrack. "You have no need to fight! Understand what I say, Halindo: this thing here, this thing of light, is from another world. It will take us away from here, all of us. No one need die. This madness, this killing, this senseless revenge—it must stop now. We go to the Sailing Star. You understand what I say? We go not in spirit, not in imagination, but in body. And all things will be changed. The Goddess will not allow you to come if you kill, for that is not her way."

Halindo spoke with a gentleness that staggered Perion. "I serve our Goddess in my fashion, man, as you do in yours. I am a hunter, and hunters voyage to the Sailing Star in only one fashion—by death. Away, now! Do not come between a hunter and her prey."

Atina turned away, drew her sword from its sheath, slid out of her pack. "Let the two of us fight," she whispered to the men. "Halindo is weak and half crazed. I may have the advantage. I'll try to overpower her."

"No," Trennon said. "Perion is right. This insanity must stop. We've come so far for this, and now we stand so close—"

"Come," said Halindo, up the slope. "Come now, Atina Theslo, or I shall kill the men first, you afterward."

"Get out of the way," Atina said, pushing past Trennon.

The two men exchanged a look, and Perion took a step forward. Trennon caught his arm. "No," he said. "We must give her the chance."

Atina stopped a few paces from Halindo, carefully lowered her sword, rested its tip on the ground. Halindo, eyes alert, came forward, placed her sword tip nearly touching Atina's. "Do you have a final request?" Halindo asked in a soft, almost solicitous voice.

"It is this," Atina said. "If I be killed, you will hold yourself satisfied, your vengeance complete. My companions will be free to go. And of them I ask that they not hinder you or seek counterrevenge in any way. But I do ask that you allow them to burn my body, as is our custom in Home-reaches."

Halindo nodded. "It is unusual for a hunter to make a request. But I know my weakness of eye and hand after the long journey, and my request is this: if I be killed, you must burn my body as you wish your own burned, and remember me in funeral rites, for I have none here to mourn me."

The tips of the swords came up, and the two circled each other. Perion could tell that Halindo was very weak, each step a visible effort. But she had the coiled threat of a poisonous snake in her every movement, and he could not help thinking that, exhausted as she was, Halindo was still more than a match for Atina. Halindo lunged, Atina parried, and they danced sideways, each seeking advantage. The men had to move back, and the two women broke from their posture on the spot where, a moment before, Trennon and Perion had stood, on level ground, near the half-sphere of the stasis field. The two men moved to their right.

The combatants moved with precision and a deadly grace, and Perion found it somehow eerie to watch the two women against the backdrop of the silvery, shining hemisphere of other-time, for it made them mere silhouettes, and the enmity that the men could read was written all in posture and atti-tude, not in expression.

The fight was a silent one. The blades rang oddly when they clashed, two artifacts of an alien wood almost as hard as iron, and certainly as lethal. Halindo's skill with the sword was clearly the greater, but Atina had more reserve strength. They came together, exchanged blows, and sprang apart, only to renew the attack, with no sure result on either side.

Then Atina got in one good blow, laying open Halindo's left upper arm. The woman flinched back, then sprang ahead again, furiously hacking, breaking Atina's advance, forcing her to move away, to forfeit the brief advantage. Halindo

gathered her strength, then came forward again, low, and
Atina moved to counter.

How it happened Perion could not be sure, but somehow
Atina lost her footing on the grass and stumbled, and immediately Halindo was there, her whistling sword twisting in
wickedly under Atina's guard, catching the other's blade just
at its join with the handle, snapping it short. The force of the
blow spun Atina, and she fell, landing on outthrust arms in
the grass.

Perion had been momentarily paralyzed by the fall; now,
with a cry, he started forward, but Halindo had already
stumbled back into position from her off-balance lunge, and
the sword was already in the air for the deathstroke—

It never came. Trennon was faster. The Aslandian lord
caught Halindo around the waist, head down, and bore her
back. She made one harsh caw of surprise before they collided with the stasis field.

Perion grabbed Atina's face, held it away from the field as
she tried to rise. "No!" he shouted. "Don't look! Don't
look at them!" He sprayed her face with flecks of saliva.

Behind Atina the couple hung frozen, Halindo's back arched,
her mouth wide, Trennon's knees quivering. They were stuck
in the stasis field like flies on flypaper, and already dead.
White-hot bolts of lightning played around them, and there
came a bubbling, hissing sound and the stench of burning
meat. Perion dragged Atina up the rise, using all his force to
prevent her tearing away from him. "No, it's all right," he
babbled. "It's all right, it's all right, no, don't look." He
knew the sound of his voice told her that nothing was all
right.

She stopped him at the crest of the hill and from there took
her one look at the charring thing that still twitched and
fluttered against the light of the sphere. Atina made a sick
sound deep in her throat and turned away.

Perion punched a three-digit code on his datakit. The screen
lit briefly, and a high beeping sound began. Then Perion
hustled and hurried Atina over the crest, until they were out
of sight of the field, back at the camp. "We have to stay
here," he panted. "Until it happens."

"I can't just leave Trennon there!" Atina cried. "And I
swore to burn Halindo, to give her funeral rites!"

"It's all right," he said inanely. "She will be burned.

We'll give her funeral rites. And Trennon. Believe me. Believe me."

And his voice was so odd that Atina did believe him.

The explosion came in the deep darkness of early morning: an actinic flash far brighter than any lightning stroke either of them had ever seen, and a bone-jarring concussion far beyond sound. Heat washed over them like a warm wave, and on the crest of the hill the grass wilted, browned, and burned.

They saw the results at sunrise. A tubular capsule lay canted in a perfectly hemispherical hole, and radiating from the hole in all directions were streaks of black carbonized grass, silvery streaks of fused soil, and, in one place, a tapering arm of fine gray ash. Here and there red sparks still winked where the uprooted grass smoldered.

"It releases all the energy at once," Perion said. He felt light-headed. "The energy explodes, outward, away from the field. You can drain it slowly away, over a week or more, but we didn't have the time. So—I'm sorry, Atina. They were burned."

"That is as I promised," she said flatly.

"I didn't want Trennon to do it. I would have done the same—I think I would have. But he was faster."

"Either way, I am dishonored."

"No. When a person is set on death, and when a bridge to life is given her, and she will not cross that bridge—that is dishonor, Atina. It was all Halindo's. Never yours."

"You seem sure of that."

"I had a good Teacher," Perion said.

They each said a few words, ones that seemed appropriate, and then they opened the capsule. The remains inside were one Gregory Daviss Maclendon, master engineer. He had been dead for many weeks, subjective time, and objectively he had died even before the *Galileo* had reached this planet, perhaps thousands of years ago. The body was intact, for there were no bacteria in the clean pods, and the controlling mechanism, sensing his death, had taken the moisture from Maclendon's body, effectively mummifying it and so protecting it from the microscopic life in the man's own intestines. The dry blood was light. Perion dragged it out, and over it he said, "Atina, this seems crazy, but could we burn him? It is as if he were one of my clan."

They gathered grass and shrubby wood and started the fire over the rise. Then Perion returned to the pod. He had no need of the datakit now. He used the intact pod controls to send the necessary message to the *Galileo*. He climbed back out. "Now it's just a question of when the ship comes into range," he told Atina. "We can move the tent here. It's safe now."

"Whatever you say."

Perion frowned at the emptiness in her voice. But she worked alongside him in a detached, calm way as they moved camp.

They sat that night beneath the stars. Perion shivered again, half from illness, half from reaction. He said, "Believe me, Atina, I did not intend this to happen. Trennon—Trennon must have loved you very deeply. He gave his life willingly, to save you. That is something you must remember."

"Don't talk. You don't need to talk."

"I do, though. I've been wrong about many things, but I am right about this one: Trennon Fane loved you. And you've got to remember that, and you must live your life so you will keep his memory in honor, as it should be kept. He came here not for riches or for power, but to find some meaning in his life. You must live your life now so that his sacrifice has meaning. To do otherwise—would be to do wrong."

"You are suddenly a wise man."

"Not wise. Wiser than I was, maybe. Wise enough to know that we are not going to conquer a world, after all. Oh, we'll change it, all right, but we won't rule it. You people have earned the right to have a voice in your own future. You've established a culture, you've created your own society— dammit, you've *survived*. And you haven't lost your dreams. Your civilization is different from anything we ever imagined or planned, but it's worked for you for nearly two thousand years.

"So we aren't going to sweep from the sky in flaming vessels to terrify and cow the rulers of the Under Islands, of Aslandia, of Homereaches. We will come humbly, offering whatever help we can; and we'll offer pathways your people can follow if they wish, not tunnels that they will be forced to follow.

"And things will change, because they must. Everything does—we change or we die. But Kaleans will help direct that change, and we will bring possibilities, not rules."

Atina laid a hand on his arm. "You are full of talk tonight."

"Yes. When I talk, my teeth don't chatter."

Atina sighed. "It is important to you. Now hear me: I do not blame you, not really, for anything that has happened. But it is difficult to face something like this. And the deaths. You are a lord, Tom Perion, in your own right, whether you realize that or not. And you are a good man."

In the darkness, Perion grinned. "I wonder—if you had known that all this was to come, would you have fished me out of the sea?"

"Beware the sea, for he lures you with beauty and then drowns you," Atina said, and her voice led Perion to believe she was quoting some proverb.

He looked away to the north. The red hazy thumbprint was bright tonight, the air clear and clean and dry. "But *would* you have saved me?"

"Yes, Tom. For the sake of Teyo, if nothing else. For the joy you brought to her."

"Thank you," said Perion. "I'm very cold." He shivered again, and Atina came to fold him in her arms and hold him safe from the night.

THE COMING OF
MORNING

The voice of the capsule woke them very early. In the brightening dawn sky the *Galileo* passed invisibly, high overhead. Perion clambered inside the capsule, and Atina waited outside, quiet and listening. When Perion came back out a few minutes later, Atina said, "Spirit voices?"

"No, human. On the communicator," he said. "I spoke to Desea Chung, an apprentice electronics specialist. They're awake up there—all the survivors. Seventy-seven people are alive on the *Galileo*. All except nine of them are women." He grinned at her. "That's the way it goes, eh?"

"What did she tell you, this woman?"

Perion sighed. "Their first concern is to move the *Galileo* to a higher orbit—make it go farther up in the sky, closer to the stars. Probably the low orbit itself triggered the jettisoning of my capsule to begin with. As the ship came lower into the air, it began to make heat. The heat activated certain—devices, things that made my capsule leave the ship."

"I do not understand."

"It is hard to speak of things for which you have no words," Perion said. "But you will see for yourself before long. Anyway, Desea says that the manual controls are still intact, but most of the automatic systems—the ones working without people—hit a massive overload somewhere along the way. Probably, she thinks, the ship came too close to a nova, a new star, an explosion out there, in the sky. That caused the ship to miss its target. It tried to heal its own damage and chose a second target. It did well, considering the damage—and here we are."

"They are coming for us?"

"Yes. They plan to launch a landing ship within the next day. It should arrive here at sunrise tomorrow, or a little after. I've set the capsule beacon, and I've asked them to

254

bring the ship there, south of the capsule, out on the open plain. But they won't stay, not on this trip. They will just pick us up and take us back.''

Atina shivered. ''To fly through the sky . . . it does not seem real.'' She touched his forehead with a cool hand. ''And your illness?''

''The hospital section is not damaged. But you and I will be isolated there for many days. We will have to ride up in a special section of the lander, and on the ship, you will have to remain with me in the hospital ward. You will not mind that?''

She smiled. ''If I have not minded being close to you so far, I am very unlikely to start now.''

They went about their breakfast in a kind of abstracted silence, and when they had finished, they sat looking at each other for some moments. Finally, Atina said, ''I am afraid.''

''Don't be. These people will be kind.''

''No, not of them. Of myself, I suppose. This is a world I have never known. Up until now I have kept going because even here things are familiar—the wind blows, the rains fall, the sun shines. I can find water to drink, or food to eat. But there, above the world, in the Sailing Star—that is what I fear. Being somewhere different.''

''I have been through it,'' Perion said slowly. ''Your world was, for me, as strange as the *Galileo* will be for you. I know the fear you mean. I cannot remove it—but you will allow me to help, to be with you?''

''Of course I will. You came through your own ordeal very well.''

''Did I?''

''Yes. See what you have accomplished.''

''But look at the deaths.''

Atina sadly smiled. ''What was it you said? We must give those deaths meaning, now, by the way we live. Let the dead have their honor, Tom. We cannot bring them back to life, but we can make sure their memories live.'' Atina rose. ''I will make the camp ready,'' she said.

Like an old married couple expecting callers, they tidied up. Perion would wear the silvery exosuit, Atina a carefully kept white tunic and trousers, the uniform of a Captain. They were awkward with each other; in donning the clothing, they seemed to have masked some part of themselves, to have hidden something vital away from each other. The rest of the day and the night were peculiar, for each of them had thoughts too deep and too private for easy expression. But in the night they drew close again, and there in the dark they took comfort in each other's presence. They slept a little, but only very fitfully, and long before dawn they had given up and sat awake with their backs toward the command pod, their faces upturned toward the northern sky.

Once the radio behind them crackled into sudden life, and Perion listened intently. To Atina he translated: "They will release the lander this time around. It will arrive here in a little more than one hour." He nodded toward the red smear in the sky, now low, sinking toward the horizon. "I mean it will be here before the red glow sets," he explained. Hours were not used as time divisions on Kalea, and though she knew of them from his talk, she had little concept of how long the unit was.

The two of them drew nearer each other and sat in silence. Atina leaned forward, hugging her knees; Perion leaned back on his elbows. Very far away to the east, the sun shone on the rim of the world. The wash of light it brought pushed the shades of night back, back, and back again, a bright tide implacably sinking all before it. The light fell on broad rivers and high mountains, on grassy plains and still bays and open, restless ocean, on gleaming white polar icecap and tawny sands of deserts, on thick, teeming jungles and quiet, motionless pools, and still it came forward, swallowing all the wonder, all the variety of Kalea, and still it washed toward the waiting command pod.

And there, just before the rushing tide of dawn took them, two figures small against the landscape scanned the sky and stood suddenly, crying out. From the north a brightening spark grew, coming lower and closer, taking on a shape and a purpose, a direction and a destination.

The two stood to wait for it, their shadows long in the first light of a new day.